Readers love Heidi S[tephens'] and feel-goo[d...]

'I write this with tears still i[n...] written, funny, moving, insp[iring and life-affirming]'
★ ★ ★ ★ ★

'Witty with a real sense of warmth . . . If you want a great escapist book, this is perfect'
★ ★ ★ ★ ★

'Heidi Stephens can do no wrong'
★ ★ ★ ★ ★

'This one blew me away'
★ ★ ★ ★ ★

'I ABSOLUTELY loved this book! It made me laugh and cry'
★ ★ ★ ★ ★

'What a beautiful, beautiful story . . . absolutely perfect'
★ ★ ★ ★ ★

'Warm and real and honest . . . Genuinely could not recommend this book more'
★ ★ ★ ★ ★

'A five-star read that will make you fall in love again'
★ ★ ★ ★ ★

'A delightful and addictive read that ventures beyond pure romance exploring the complexities of love, marriage, and self-discovery'
★ ★ ★ ★ ★

'Beautifully written, full of charm and a story that will capture your heart, this is the perfect read!'
★ ★ ★ ★ ★

Heidi Stephens has spent her career working in advertising and marketing; some of her early writing work includes instruction manuals for vacuum cleaners, saucepans and sex toys. Since 2008 she has also freelanced as a journalist, liveblogging *Strictly Come Dancing* for the *Guardian*. Now, in May, Heidi can be found somewhere around the world, liveblogging *Eurovision*. Her debut novel, *Two Metres From You*, won the 2022 Katie Fforde Debut Romantic Novel Award. She lives in Wiltshire with her partner and her Labrador, Mabel.

By Heidi Stephens

Two Metres From You
Never Gonna Happen
The Only Way Is Up
Game, Set, Match
Same Time Next Year
Snowed In With You

HEIDI STEPHENS

SNOWED IN WITH YOU

Copyright © 2024 Heidi Stephens

The right of Heidi Stephens to be identified as the Author of
the Work has been asserted by her in accordance with the
Copyright, Designs and Patents Act 1988.

First published in 2024 by Headline Accent
An imprint of HEADLINE PUBLISHING GROUP

1

Apart from any use permitted under UK copyright law, this publication may
only be reproduced, stored, or transmitted, in any form, or by any means,
with prior permission in writing of the publishers or, in the case of
reprographic production, in accordance with the terms of licences
issued by the Copyright Licensing Agency.

All characters in this publication are fictitious and any resemblance
to real persons, living or dead, is purely coincidental.

Cataloguing in Publication Data is available from the British Library

ISBN 978 1 0354 1355 3

Typeset in 11.6/15pt Bembo Std by Jouve (UK), Milton Keynes

Printed and bound in Great Britain by Clays Ltd, Elcograf S.p.A.

Headline's policy is to use papers that are natural, renewable and recyclable
products and made from wood grown in well-managed forests and other
controlled sources. The logging and manufacturing processes are expected
to conform to the environmental regulations of the country of origin.

HEADLINE PUBLISHING GROUP
An Hachette UK Company
Carmelite House
50 Victoria Embankment
London EC4Y 0DZ

www.headline.co.uk
www.hachette.co.uk

To Jon
My only brother, but that's all I'll ever need

PART ONE

CHAPTER ONE

'Is everyone here?' asked Sasha, impatiently scanning the meeting room for absentees. Lucy glanced around for the usual latecomers, namely Jonno, LUNA's Creative Director, who refused to be held back by something as inconveniently immovable as *time*. He sauntered in just ahead of Fran, the agency's Senior Account Director, who used performative lateness as a way of reminding everyone how busy and important she was.

'Good,' said Sasha, moving to the front of the room as the nervous chatter died down. In-person meetings for the entire account team were unusual, and usually indicated bad news. Since it was the first day back in the office after New Year, the rumour was that something big had gone down over the holidays. Lucy had money on 'the client has slashed their advertising budget, so half of you are being fired with immediate effect', whilst Jonno had punted for 'the client has slashed their deadlines, which means all of you are expected to work longer hours for no extra money, but we will provide budget pizza and warm beer if you're here past 9 p.m.' There was a drink at their favourite pub riding on the outcome.

'So, Team Titan,' said Sasha with a warm smile. *Uh oh*, thought Lucy. Definitely late-night sloppy pizza and warm Peroni. Titan was the UK's number two condom brand – the designer choice of social media influencers and aspirational Gen Zs – and their market share was growing faster than the barrage of weak penis jokes that inevitably followed publication of the latest sales data. The LUNA team in Bristol had won the pitch to do all their advertising three years ago, when Titan was barely more than a fledgling start-up. Now it was one of LUNA's most prestigious accounts and it was a daily battle not to have the business stolen by the team in London.

'I've had an email from Kristoff,' continued Sasha, raising her voice just enough to bring the room to order. 'He's asked us to join them for a planning weekend. In two weeks' time.'

The room went deathly quiet as everyone weighed up the likelihood of this being any fun. Titan was a good client with decent budgets, but they were also a bunch of beige, clean-living Americans fashioned from designer athleisure, expensive dentistry and protein shakes. The company had been founded four years ago by Kristoff Berg, a dazzlingly handsome Swedish-American entrepreneur who'd made his first million before he could legally drink in the US. He was now in his thirties and, with him at the helm, Titan was carving a lubed-up path through the European market and making their gold-packaged condoms a must-have lifestyle choice.

'What IS a planning weekend, exactly?' asked Steve, one of the Design team. A few people raised their eyebrows in his direction, silently acknowledging his willingness to put his head above the parapet. Until a year ago, Sasha had been Managing Director of the Bristol agency and strategic lead on the Titan account, but now she was a member of the Group Board based out of London, and topping every patronising industry list of women over forty who were smashing it in advertising. She may once have been 'one of them', but now she wielded untold power and everyone in the room knew it.

'It's an opportunity to get together for a few days and review the account,' said Sasha mildly, as half the team hunkered down in their chairs so they were less visible. The last time Kristoff had visited the Bristol office, Lucy had heard that he'd declared the deli lunch incompatible with his dietary regime and sent his assistant out to find some Huel, although nobody seemed to have witnessed this incident first hand. Luckily Lucy never had to spend time with them in person – Senior Copywriter was a backroom job and Kristoff and his team mostly worked out of Geneva for spurious tax reasons.

'And why can't that be done during working hours?' asked Steve. Jonno glared at him, silently entreating him to pipe down before Sasha swept Titan into her designer handbag and took it back to the grown-ups in London.

Sasha sighed heavily and pressed her lips together. 'Well, the good news is that there are only six spaces. So if you'd rather not go, you can absolutely opt out.'

Steve nodded firmly and crossed his arms. 'Brilliant, I'm out. No offence, but my weekends are sacred.' Lucy knew for a fact that Steve spent his weekends doing CrossFit with no shirt on, because the first rule of CrossFit is that you have to tell everyone you do CrossFit. Jonno called him the Severn Bore, but never to his face because the veins on Steve's neck popped out when he was annoyed.

'None taken,' said Sasha dryly. 'And the sacred nature of your weekends is duly noted.'

'What kind of planning are they thinking?' asked Kim, loudly flicking to a fresh page in her notebook and writing PLANNING WEEKEND in large letters at the top. Kim was another keen bean on Jonno's team, who wrote her entire life in one of those bullet journals. Once she'd left it open on her desk and Lucy had spotted *Can you teach yourself to like spinach?* in the Thoughts for the Day section. If Kim had hidden depths, they were unlikely to pose a risk of drowning.

'Yeah,' chipped in Lou, who was the more junior of the two art directors. 'Where is it?'

Sasha smiled at Lou. 'It's in Zermatt. In the Swiss Alps.' She paused dramatically as the room collectively sat up like a mob of meerkats, then started to chatter excitedly.

'Wait, what?' exclaimed Steve, looking around at the group. 'It's a ski trip?'

'I believe skiing is an option. Amongst other winter pastimes,' said Sasha smoothly. Lucy could tell how much she was enjoying herself, and wondered for the umpteenth time exactly how old she was. The glossy dark curls and glowing skin suggested early-to-mid forties, but Lucy also knew that she'd been working in the industry for well over twenty-five years. Either she'd started very young, or more likely was the human equivalent of her dad's car. The chassis was original, but several parts had been replaced.

'Fucking hell,' grinned Steve. 'I'm back in, then.'

Sasha shook her head and picked at a bit of fluff on the shoulder of her cashmere sweater. Her fingernails were dark red and immaculate, which prompted Lucy to tuck her flaking festive manicure under her armpits. 'No, I don't think so,' she said smoothly. 'I'm afraid you opted out, and that's very much a one-way ticket. Any other questions?'

'So what's it all for?' asked Kim, as Steve slumped in his chair, looking mutinous.

'A prize,' said Sasha. 'For all the awards we've helped Titan win over the last year. They've offered to pay for six members of the Titan team to go. There'll be a working session or two, but primarily it's a reward for all our hard work.'

'What if you don't ski?' asked Matty, who was in his mid-twenties and had recently taken over responsibility for Titan's TikTok output. Lucy knew he'd grown up on a council estate in south Bristol and joined the agency as part of a social mobility initiative. Half the agency disappeared off to the Alps every winter, not that Lucy was one of them. Her mother was an orthopaedic nurse who'd seen too many horror-movie fractures, and her dad had arthritis in his lower back from thirty years of bending over lab specimens. So skiing hadn't been part of her childhood, and adulthood hadn't exactly been a big adventure so far. But that was a whole other story.

'Skiing isn't mandatory, obviously,' said Sasha, giving Matty a reassuring smile. 'But you can have a day of lessons, if you fancy it. According to the email I've had from Kristoff, there'll also be spa treatments and snowshoe walks, that sort of thing. All equipment provided. And, of course, some actual work.'

Everyone chattered excitedly again, the work aspect now entirely forgotten and irrelevant.

'So who's it going to be?' asked Sasha, looking around the room. 'We need to agree on six.' Lucy did a quick headcount – there were fourteen people in the room, including Sasha, so this was about to get messy. She grinned at Jonno, who was clearly thinking the same thing, and sat back to enjoy the show.

'Can't the agency pay for ALL of us to go?' asked Rachel, who'd recently been promoted onto the account and liked to give the impression she was a warm and inclusive human being. But Lucy knew that Rachel would happily trample every one of them to get a place on this trip, then throw her grandmother under a speeding bus for good measure.

'No,' said Sasha. 'The Titan team have hired a chalet. Four of them, six of us.'

'We have to share?' asked Rachel, looking aghast. Lucy said nothing, but silently agreed. She'd rather shit a Swiss army knife than share a bedroom with Rachel – there was a good chance she'd wake up with a pillow over her face.

Sasha shook her head, pressing her lips together in a silent gesture of suppressed annoyance that Lucy had seen a thousand times. 'No, it has ten bedrooms.'

'Fuck me, they've hired a chalet with ten bedrooms?' It was the first time Jonno had spoken, and his voice boomed out in the small room. Jonno only had one volume, and it was 'East End fruit and veg trader'.

'Yes. Well, it's more of a small hotel, apparently. Titan have exclusive use. So everyone has their own en-suite room.'

'So how do we choose?' asked Rachel hopefully. 'Pick names out of a hat?'

You wish, thought Lucy. Rachel had only joined the account six months ago, long after the award-winning campaign was finished. A lucky dip was the only way she was going.

'No,' said Sasha emphatically. 'We discuss it as a team, like sensible adults, and agree who deserves to go.' She put on her glasses and checked the notes on her phone. 'We'll be heading out on Thursday the nineteenth of January and flying back late on the Sunday. Can anybody *not* make that?'

A jolt of pain pierced through Lucy's chest, forcing her to suppress a gasp. The twentieth of January was Leo's anniversary, which she'd booked off to spend with her parents. It was never an occasion she looked forward to, so maybe being out of the country wasn't such a bad idea. She could feel Jonno looking at her curiously, and flicked through the notebook in her lap like she was looking for something important.

'Anyone?' repeated Sasha impatiently.

Video Derek put his hand in the air. 'I, umm, have a thing.'

'What kind of thing?' asked Sasha.

'Just a thing. Um, the usual, you know. Volunteering.'

Lucy gave Derek a smile that she hoped communicated her utmost admiration and respect. Derek was an absolute saint who spent most of his free time volunteering at a Bristol drop-in centre for troubled teenagers. And unlike Steve, he only ever talked about it if asked directly.

'Fine, no problem,' said Sasha. 'No Derek, but the rest of you are welcome to share your opinions on who should go.'

Lucy said nothing and waited, knowing that there was no chance on earth she wasn't going to be on this list. She'd written every word of the winning campaign across every platform, so obviously somebody was going to put her name forward. The question was, how did she make sure Jonno went too? If she wasn't going to be remembering Leo in the usual way, she needed Jonno there for emotional support.

'I'll start,' said Jonno. 'Lucy should be on the list. Without her, none of this would have happened.'

'Other copywriters do exist,' muttered Rachel.

'Yes, but this campaign was written by Lucy,' said Jonno, giving Rachel a withering look. 'Can any of you really imagine a scenario where she'd be left behind?'

Everyone shook their heads, apart from Rachel, who hated it when other people were given nice things, or experienced feelings of happiness.

'Right, that's Lucy,' said Sasha. 'Assuming you do actually want to go?'

'Yeah, course,' shrugged Lucy, nudging painful thoughts of Leo aside in favour of a winter-wonderland fantasy involving accidentally falling over in the snow and being rescued by a hot ski instructor with very warm hands.

'Good, one down. Anyone want to recommend anyone else, before you all start pitching for yourselves and this turns into *The Hunger Games*?' Lucy kept quiet, mentally crossing her fingers that someone would say Jonno's name. It couldn't be her; everyone knew they were best mates.

'Jonno,' said Steve, who had missed out himself but clearly wasn't going to sacrifice the whole Creative team. 'He did most of the design work, and the client loves him.'

'Agreed,' said Sasha. 'Anyone object to Jonno?'

'Not an objection, per se,' said Kim, clearing her throat. Jonno had recently turned her down for promotion, and apparently she was about to get her revenge. 'I'm just wondering if it's appropriate for directors to go?'

'On what basis would that not be appropriate?' asked Sasha, raising her eyebrows and giving Kim a look that would melt an ice cap from outer space.

'Well,' said Kim, looking mildly panicked. 'It's just, you know, you guys already get to do a lot of cool stuff that we don't.'

Sasha's eyebrows were now glued to the light fittings. 'Such as?'

'I don't know,' muttered Kim, casting around the room for help. 'Like, awards dinners and events and fancy hotels abroad.'

'Fancy hotels abroad?' asked Sasha, blinking furiously.

'Yeah, like when you and Jonno went to Cannes.'

Sasha laughed. 'For the Lions festival. It's the biggest creative event in our industry, and it was all work. Where would you have preferred we stay? In a hostel? A caravan?'

Kim hung her head. 'No, obviously.' Lucy smiled to

herself, remembering all the stories Jonno had told her about debauched nights out and passing out on a sunlounger at 5 a.m. Whatever Cannes was, it definitely wasn't work.

'Jonno obviously deserves to be on this trip,' continued Sasha. 'He and Lucy devised this whole campaign, based on MY strategy.' She glared at Kim, waiting for her to object.

'Well, you should definitely be going,' said Fran, Titan's Account Director and the cheerleader for anyone who had influence over her bonus. Jonno glanced at Lucy and pulled a face, as if he'd just tasted Fran's arse-kissing and the flavour wasn't to his liking.

'Thank you, Fran, you're absolutely right,' said Sasha triumphantly. Fran beamed, entirely oblivious to the laser glares being fired her way as one more place was claimed by management. 'So that's me, Jonno and Lucy. Three spaces left. Who are we thinking?'

Lucy glanced in the direction of Nate, who was tucked into the corner of the room like he was trying to blend into the paintwork. So far he'd said nothing, instead scribbling feverish notes on a sheaf of paper that Lucy recognised as the client brief for Titan's latest campaign. He'd been working for Fran on the Titan team for over a year, having moved to Bristol from the Pukka Paws pet food team based in Paris. Lucy found him surly and uncommunicative, and not just because he was half French. He wasn't actively an arsehole, exactly; he just gave off an air of being a bit superior, like team socials were all a bit beneath him. Jonno called him 'French Exit', because he always left the party early without saying goodbye.

She watched him for a moment, entirely lost in the Titan brief like nobody else was in the room. Dark, floppy hair that curled at his neck, long eyelashes and full lips, like a picture she'd once seen of a young Mick Jagger. Cold and impenetrable, but inarguably good-looking.

'So that's Maya and Olly,' said Sasha, as Lucy snapped back into the room and tuned back in to what was happening. She was happy with both those choices; Maya was Titan's Senior Art Director and smart and funny, and Olly was invariably the first person in the agency who'd down a bottle of wine and climb onto a table to lip-sync to Beyoncé. He was Sasha's PA, but at the time of the winning Titan campaign he'd stepped up to Project Manager, organising people and photo shoots and making sure the whole project stayed on track.

'One place left,' said Sasha. 'Who's it going to be?'

'I'd like to put my name back into the ring,' said Steve. 'Because—'

'Denied,' interrupted Sasha, as Maya and Olly started whispering excitedly. 'Can we just focus, please? These are hot tickets, and I'm not spending the next month listening to you all whinge on about how it should have been you. State your case, or pipe down.'

'Oh my GOD, guys,' exclaimed Fran. 'I can't believe none of you have nominated me. Like, really?'

'Buckle in, kids. Fran's about to blow,' muttered Jonno.

'It's MY account,' wailed Fran. 'I've been the Account Director for Titan for THREE YEARS.'

Nobody said anything, as any joy Lucy had been feeling about being on the list farted into the room like a deflating balloon.

'Right, but doesn't Nate actually do most of the work?' asked Rachel smugly. Several people took a sharp intake of breath as Nate looked up, and Fran narrowed her eyes as the temperature in the room dropped by ten degrees.

'That's outrageous,' spat Fran. 'Yes, of COURSE Nate helped, it's too big an account just for me. But I'm the Account Director, and they're my client. I've, like, *nurtured the relationship.*'

'They hate her,' whispered Jonno. 'They call her Funsponge Fran, because she sucks all the joy out of the room.'

Lucy covered her mouth with her hand, her shoulders shaking with laughter.

'Well,' said Sasha, her voice slightly strained. 'Does anyone have an issue with Fran taking the last space?'

Lucy didn't dare look up, instead focusing intently on her trainers.

'Fran it is,' said Sasha bleakly. 'Along with me, Lucy, Jonno, Maya and Olly. Well done, everyone.'

Lucy smiled gamely, thinking that even though Funsponge Fran was the fly in the ointment, the list could definitely have been worse. And at least she'd been saved from a weekend with Psycho Rachel or Moody Nate.

CHAPTER TWO

'So, we're off to the Alps for fun times in the snow,' said Jonno, grinning as Lucy placed his pint, her white wine and two bags of crisps on their usual table in the Brunel Arms. Their post-work Friday drink was a long-standing tradition, and nobody else from the agency was invited. It was their time to dissect the week and offload all their grievances. But since they'd only returned to the office a few days ago, there was really only one thing to talk about.

'You are OK with going that weekend?' added Jonno, ducking his head to catch her eye. 'I know you've usually got a family thing around then.'

'It's fine,' said Lucy, wafting him away as if it really didn't matter. 'Thanks for nominating me. I would have returned the favour, but everyone already thinks we're sleeping together.'

Jonno laughed and necked a quarter of his pint in one go. It was a new ale in the Brunel's ever-revolving door of IPAs with stupid names – this one was called Fainting Lizard. 'You're way out of my league, babe. Did I tell you that Sasha asked me about that at the Christmas party?'

Lucy's eyes widened as she sat on the bench opposite him. 'Really?'

'Mmm,' said Jonno, wiping the foam off his lip. 'She'd heard it from Fran, and wanted to know if it was true.'

Lucy shook her head and rolled her eyes. 'That sounds like peak Fran.'

'NO bitching about Fran,' interrupted Jonno. 'You'll get me started. But you're right – literally everyone in the agency thinks we're doing the dirty.'

'Why?' said Lucy, tipping half the crisps into her mouth at once, then washing them down with a swig of wine. It was a source of much irritation amongst her female colleagues that Lucy appeared to have some kind of superhuman metabolism that magically cancelled out her workaholic single woman junk food diet, meaning she could live on crisps and wine and coffee and seemingly never put on any weight. 'Because men and women can't possibly just be mates?'

Jonno shrugged. 'Probably because you're beautiful, I'm charismatic, and we have at least one date a week in this pub.'

'It's not a date, and we've done some of our best work in this pub,' replied Lucy, folding her arms and looking wistfully at the decor. Mostly old black-and-white photos from back in the day when this part of the city was a little more genteel and home to fewer students puking up spicy margaritas.

'I don't dispute that. And anyway, whilst I am happy to acknowledge that you are an unattainably hot woman, I don't fancy you.'

'That's helpful,' said Lucy, acknowledging the compliment with a soft smile. 'Because I don't fancy you either.'

Jonno's eyes widened in fake outrage. 'Why not?'

'You're too old, for a start.' This kind of conversation was familiar Friday pub territory for Lucy and Jonno, who had started at LUNA on the same day over ten years previously and bonded over a week-long induction in the London office. They'd formed a powerhouse creative team that had delivered some of the agency's most successful and award-winning work. For different reasons, they'd both turned down offers to spread their wings elsewhere, and stuck together.

'Shit, Luce. I'm forty-four.'

'I know. Twelve years older than me. When you were twenty-one, I was nine.'

'OK, that sounds really wrong.'

'It IS wrong. But it's the undeniable truth. Also, you are the most happily married person I know.'

'That's also true,' said Jonno, nodding furiously. 'Can we drink these outside? I need to smoke.'

'No,' replied Lucy. 'It's January. And anyway, I thought you'd given up?'

'I tried, but vaping is awful,' said Jonno helplessly. 'I need all that glorious tar in my blood to function. My creativity is fuelled by poison.'

'Talking of poison,' muttered Lucy. 'We need to talk about how we're going to manage Fran on this trip.'

Jonno shook his head and gave Lucy a stern look. 'No, I can't.'

'Come on. You're a strong man, you can do it.'

'I can't. It's easy for you, you're a nice person. But I've only managed . . .' he checked his watch, '. . . six whole days into 2023, and I'm struggling.'

'Maybe you need to accept that hating Fran is the other poison that fuels your creativity.'

Jonno frowned. 'No. We made a vow we would make it to the end of the month without being mean about Fran, and I need you to help me get through it. It's our Dry January, remember?'

'What about when we're stuck in the mountains with her?'

Jonno pulled a face. 'I reckon it's OK if we're on foreign soil. I was really hoping she'd do the magnanimous thing and let French Exit come.'

Lucy snorted with laughter. 'Have you met Fran? She's a fu—'

'NO,' said Jonno, holding up his hand. 'We must resist.'

'Anyway, why would we want Nate there? He barely ever speaks.'

'Exactly. He's human wallpaper, and unlikely to create distraction. Which reminds me, does he pronounce his surname Lam-butt, or the French way? Like *Lom-berrr*?' He rolled the *r* from the corner of his mouth, like a bad impression of a Frenchman.

'I have no idea. I've always gone for bog standard Lam-butt.'

'Me too, because he's too beige for anything more exotic than the arse of a sheep. But on the upside, he'll blend into the background of our weekend adventure.'

'Unlike Olly and Maya.'

'Mmm. They'll do their own pissed-up party-animal thing, and poor Sasha will get lumbered with Fran because they'll have to suck up to the client. We both know that Fran is a total arse-kissing b—'

'Oh my God,' gasped Lucy, pressing her hands over her mouth. 'You failed!'

'Shit,' muttered Jonno. 'Pretend I never said that. I'm getting another pint. You want more wine?'

Lucy shook her head and picked up her phone while Jonno was at the bar, wondering whether she was in the mood to see Anthony. She scrolled back to his last message – a close-up of his hand wrapped around his erect penis, accompanied by *Happy new year, babe. Got you a present.* She tapped out a quick reply. *Impressive. Can I unwrap it later?*

'Who's your booty call tonight?' asked Jonno. She slammed her phone face down on the table. 'Iron Manuel, or Tentpole Tony?'

Lucy rolled her eyes. Jonno called Marco 'Iron Manuel' because he was a competitive triathlete, and also Spanish. 'Tentpole Tony' spoke for itself.

'Marco's in London. He's just been promoted to Head of Insurance Risk Assessment for heritage buildings.'

Jonno licked his lips and winked. 'Wow, I love it when you talk dirty.'

'Stop it. It's a very interesting job.'

'Is it, though? Does he tell you about fire safety measures in the Royal Albert Hall while he's sucking your toes?'

'I would actually kill him if he ever went anywhere near my toes.'

'So Tentpole Tony, then?'

Lucy sighed. 'He prefers Anthony.'

'Hmm, sure. Any new dick pics?'

'Yes, actually. Do you want to see it?'

'No,' said Jonno emphatically. 'I still haven't got over the feelings of inadequacy from the last time. That man has a cock the size of a baseball bat.'

'No, he doesn't. It's a perfectly normal size.'

'For a horse, yes. For a human, no.'

Lucy laughed and finished her wine. Marco and Anthony were what she called 'a mutually beneficial sexual arrangement' that had been going on for the best part of eighteen months.

'You know this fascinates me, right?' said Jonno. 'Are you sure you don't want another wine?' She shook her head, knowing that two could easily become four and then she'd have a foggy head all weekend.

'I'm well aware,' smirked Lucy. 'Mostly because you never stop asking about it.'

'They know about each other, right?'

Lucy nodded and rolled her eyes. Jonno had definitely asked this question at least twice before.

'And you've never banged them both at once?' *OK, that's definitely a new question.*

'No. Anthony floated the idea once. He's officially bisexual, but Marco is totally straight. So I said no, on the basis that might be a weird dynamic.'

Jonno grinned and stuffed a handful of crisps into his mouth. 'I should have guessed that Iron Manuel would assess the risk of a threesome and decide it didn't meet his health and safety requirements.'

'I didn't say that. He and I have had a threesome, just with another girl.'

'Ah yes,' said Jonno gleefully. 'I forgot you were also a casual muff-tourist.'

'You have such a lovely way with words.'

'Is Marco's cock the same size as Tony's? Like, could they have a lightsaber battle?'

Lucy snorted with laughter. 'No, not that it's ANY of your business. Marco has many other talents.'

'Shit, why is your life so much more fun than mine?' Jonno pouted and drained the dregs of his empty pint glass.

'You've got a beautiful, successful wife and two gorgeous daughters, J,' said Lucy. 'Which begs the eternal question – what the hell are you doing in the pub with me on a Friday night?'

'Marcia's away,' he said. 'She's taken the kids to Morzine with her sister. They've got a massive chalet with a chef and a chalet girl and nannies and all that shit.' Whilst Jonno was the agency's Creative Director and earned good money, his wife Marcia was some kind of breakfast cereal heiress. They'd met on an ad campaign shoot in New York almost twenty years previously, where Marcia had been one of the models and Jonno was a cockney wideboy Art Director, handsome but very much the downtown boy to her uptown girl. She'd agreed to a date primarily to upset her father, who wanted her to marry the preppy lawyer son of a family friend. Things had got a little out of hand, and Marcia and Jonno had gone on to have an unexpectedly successful and devoted marriage.

Lucy frowned. 'Why aren't you there?'

'I managed three days over New Year with five teenagers in total, then used work as an excuse to leave before I lost my mind. She's back on Sunday, anyway. Do you want to get dinner? I'm flying solo.'

Lucy's phone buzzed, and she glanced at the reply from Anthony.

'Brilliant,' muttered Jonno, frowning into his pint. 'The look on your face suggests that's a much better offer.' At that moment the door to the pub opened, admitting a blast of wintry air along with Fran and Kim.

'Not better, just different,' said Lucy with a wink, standing up and pulling on her coat. If Anthony was coming over, she needed to shower. 'Have a lovely evening with these two banter legends.'

'I hate you,' said Jonno.

Lucy blew him a kiss and hurried outside, almost colliding with Nate as he leaned against the bin in the street outside, tapping on his phone under a street light.

'I'm sorry,' he said, stepping to one side. 'You should maybe slow down.' He gave her a sardonic half-smile, his fringe falling into his eyes in a way that she found irrationally annoying. She'd heard somewhere that he'd grown up in the UK, hence the lack of French accent, but she'd also heard him speaking French on the phone to clients on a number of occasions. Usually there was something oddly sexy about men who were bilingual – it gave them an air of competency, and eliminated the risk of going abroad with someone whose idea of speaking a foreign language was just shouting really slowly in English. But on Nate, it just came across as sullen mumbling, like he'd actually rather not be talking at all.

'Places to be,' she said, conscious that this was probably the longest one-to-one encounter they'd ever had outside of a LUNA meeting room.

'That's a shame for both of us,' he said, his words

creating vapour clouds in the glow of the street light. Lucy narrowed her eyes, not sure if he was taking the piss or not. He looked away awkwardly, his body twitching with restless energy.

'Have a good weekend, Nate.' Lucy shrugged her bag onto her shoulder. This conversation clearly wasn't going anywhere, and she had other plans.

'You too, Lucy,' said Nate, but she was already on her way to the bus stop and didn't look back.

'I need a favour,' said Anthony, making Lucy shiver as he stroked his long, elegant fingers down her bare thigh. She used an app to control her central heating, but had forgotten to turn it on in a fluster of delayed buses and her hurry to get home. So, the whole place had been frigid, prompting her to drag Anthony into the bedroom before he'd barely got his coat off, figuring it was the human equivalent of rubbing two sticks together to start a fire. At least the flat had been tidy, but clutter and chaos were not how Lucy operated. Living spaces, like relationships and everything else in her life, were kept clean and simple.

'Mmm,' said Lucy, still riding the post-orgasmic wave of tingling limbs and a sweaty flush from her neck to her knees. She'd never considered Anthony as a long-term prospect – for a start he was an amateur boxer and rode a high-performance motorbike, both of which felt quite stressful qualities in a life partner – but he knew exactly how to get Lucy's blood flowing. In fact, she'd never really considered anyone as a long-term prospect. The reasons were complicated, and even Jonno hadn't probed that particular wound with any real enthusiasm.

'It's my cousin's wedding in a few weeks, it's gonna be, like, a massive family thing. I need a date.'

Lucy twisted round to look at him. 'Why wouldn't you ask someone else? Or go on your own and find a date when you get there?' Anthony was, by any measure, a ten out of ten, so it wasn't like he'd have any trouble finding female company.

'Because the family will rip the shit out of me all night if I don't turn up with a super-hot woman. It'll be fun; my auntie Jade is doing the food and she's amazing.'

'Oh well, if Auntie Jade is cooking, I'm there.' Lucy grinned, ignoring the reference to her being 'super-hot' and trying to keep her tone light and playful. In reality this conversation was well beyond the boundaries of their agreed relationship, and she wasn't quite sure what to make of it.

'My cousin Lee is marrying a posh girl. So you won't be the only one there.'

'I'm from Croydon, Anthony,' said Lucy. 'I don't think that makes me a posh girl.'

'Yeah, but you SOUND posh,' laughed Anthony. It was hard to deny – Lucy had ditched the South London accent the minute she'd headed north to university in Liverpool, and reinvented herself as generic, well-spoken home counties. She hadn't known what she wanted to do with her life at that point, but it seemed like she might have more choices if she talked like someone who worked at the BBC. Her twin brother Leo had laughed at her, accusing her of turning her back on her roots. Lucy had pointed out that their parents were pretty middle class by anybody's standards, and they'd both spent years at school pretending to be more South London than they actually were to avoid being relentlessly beaten up.

'So you'll come?' said Anthony hopefully.

'When is it?' Lucy was partly playing for time, but she'd also remembered the work trip. She wasn't sure if a clash would be a disappointment or a relief.

'The twenty-eighth of January. It's a Saturday.'

'I'm away the weekend before. A work thing in Switzerland.' She turned her head away, immediately hoping she didn't sound like she was showing off. Anthony had several jobs – bricklayer, underwear model, Deliveroo rider – but none of them ever took him to Switzerland.

'Get you, Miss Jet Set.' She could hear the teasing in his voice, and feel his erection nudging insistently at her hip. Fifteen minutes was all Anthony needed to recover before he was good to go again, like an overheated laptop. 'Is that a yes, then?'

Lucy shrugged, feeling slightly cornered but not wanting to make a big deal out of it. In the eighteen months they'd been sleeping together, Anthony had never asked her for anything that wasn't incredibly sexually specific. 'Sure,' she said. 'If you don't get a better offer between now and then.'

'That would be a shame for both of us,' whispered Anthony, the tip of his finger brushing her cold nipple and making her gasp. Nate's face instantly popped into her head – hadn't he said something similar earlier, outside the pub? She closed her eyes and tried to concentrate as Anthony's head disappeared under the covers and her body caught fire again, but Nate's dark eyes and shaggy

Mick Jagger hair kept sliding into her thoughts. *French Exit*, she thought. *Not nearly as fun as Anthony's face in my grand entrance.* She smiled to herself and closed her eyes as Anthony slowly and expertly took her to a place where she couldn't think about anything at all.

CHAPTER THREE

Nine days later, on Sunday morning, Lucy stood in front of the bathroom mirror, trying to rearrange her hair into something that looked vaguely woke-up-like-this sexy. She had, in fact, been up for a while, but liked to look like she hadn't. Artfully constructing a messy bun, showering thoroughly, cleaning her teeth, adding a subtle touch of lip balm and mascara.

Not that looking good took a HUGE amount of effort, to be fair. Her mother Shirley had been a model in the 1980s before she'd gone into nursing, and her father Richard was a tall, square-jawed lab technician she'd met at Croydon University Hospital. Lucy had inherited her mother's willowy frame and her father's thick, strawberry blond hair and green eyes. She'd been a pretty child who'd grown into a beautiful woman, and she was grounded enough to acknowledge this reality and admit that it made life easier, for the most part. Not enough to earn friends without needing to be a decent human being, obviously. Looks only got you so far.

Her phone buzzed with a message from Marco. *Puncture c u one hour.*

Marco was a man of few words, but he worked in insurance so she could hardly expect him to be one of life's romantic poets. She padded through to the kitchen and made herself a coffee, then put the door to her flat on the latch so he could let himself in. She'd hear him lugging his bike up four flights of stairs long before he made it through the door and unleashed those stupid clicky shoes on her wooden floors, but at least this way she'd be in bed looking come-hither and sexy when he arrived. In the early days Marco had asked her not to shower before they hooked up, because he liked her to be what he called 'naturally womanly'. But that was a hard no for Lucy – the idea of not being clean, or Marco stripping off after a couple of hours of sweaty cycling and rubbing his muddy ankles on her Egyptian cotton sheets, gave her the ick.

Lucy took her mug back to bed and propped herself up on a mountain of pillows, trying to revel in the blissful luxury of being single and childless and having absolutely nothing to do. The alternative was contemplating WHY she was single and childless and had absolutely nothing to do, but nobody needed to go there.

She scrolled through her phone and completed her daily Wordle – she was currently on a winning streak of 482 days, which she was keen not to break. Today's word was SPLAT, which she solved in three attempts after a lucky first guess. There was a simple pleasure in a three-go win that was also an onomatopoeia, but maybe that was just being a writer and a self-confessed language nerd. She didn't know any others, so she couldn't ask.

Lucy closed Wordle and skipped to TikTok, deciding to see if Kristoff had an account so she could prepare herself for small talk in Zermatt on Thursday. She'd been on several video calls with him as part of the wider Titan team, but they'd never had a one-to-one conversation or met in person. As expected, he had an account – called KristoffTheTitan, which was all kinds of embarrassing for him – mostly featuring him being drop-dead gorgeous and important in glamorous locations. If he wasn't boarding a jet to some world forum on sexual health or a celebrity gala, he was working out with his shirt off in one of his home gyms in Geneva, New York, London or Stockholm, showcasing an incredibly honed physique. There was also a video from his thirty-fifth birthday a few months before, featuring thirty-five cakes stacked on top of each other to create a giant erect penis that was hidden under a Titan-branded condom made of parachute silk. *Stay classy, Kristoff*, thought Lucy, rolling her eyes.

Sasha and Fran didn't have TikTok, but Sasha was very active on LinkedIn (too boring to read on a Sunday) and Fran was on Instagram. Lucy scrolled through her grid, but there was nothing remotely interesting, just pictures of hilly landscapes, a yappy-looking white dog, a Christmas tree, a glass of wine on a cafe table next to pair of sunglasses. A distinct lack of creative effort on Fran's part, but that was par for the course. *Maybe she should get Nate to do that for her too.*

On a whim, Lucy searched for Nate Lambert, and was surprised to find he had an Instagram account. His grid was mostly arty shots of Bristol or Paris and the occasional selfie looking a little shy and awkward, usually in sunglasses. More intriguing was the black-and-white shot of him surfing, windblown and focused and incredibly fit, which made Lucy wonder who had taken it and whether they'd been as aroused as she was by the sight of his strong thighs in a wetsuit. Another picture from a year ago featured an acoustic guitar on a chair, which was intriguing because he'd never struck her as the musical type. But then Lucy realised she knew pretty much nothing about him – Nate could have three kids, a vegetable allotment and a houseful of foster kittens, for all she knew. No sign of cats on his Instagram, but there were a few pictures of him hugging a black Labrador that reminded Lucy a little of Sasha's dog Walter, which she'd often brought into the Bristol office before she spent most of her time in London. Sasha had a house near Bath, but Lucy had heard from Jonno that her promotion to head office had come with a huge bonus that had allowed her to buy a flat in Chiswick too.

Lucy looked at her watch and realised she'd been browsing Nate's Instagram for nearly half an hour. She had no idea why, since he wasn't even coming to Zermatt and she wouldn't have to pretend to find him interesting. But there was something about him that made her want to find out more; and it hadn't escaped her notice that he was incredibly photogenic.

She clicked on her own Instagram profile and looked at her empty grid, wondering if she'd ever feel comfortable enough to post something of her own. She'd thought about it lots of times – maybe a video about how her skincare routine had changed since she was in her thirties, or a photo montage of her favourite parts of Bristol, complete with funny captions. But it had always felt dishonest and wrong to showcase her life in that way; to post photos or videos that plastered over the cracks of days when she did nothing more than two lots of laundry and an online word game. So her social media accounts existed just for viewing other people's content, in moments where she needed to detach from her own life and live vicariously through someone else's.

Lucy shook her head and switched back to Nate's Instagram, feeling restless and jittery. She was just zooming in on a shot of him laughing at a wedding, the dark hair of a woman just visible at the edge of the frame but her face tantalisingly out of shot, when a knock on the door made her jump. Marco's face appeared, his legs caked in mud and his face red from the effort of carrying a three-grand bike up from street level.

'Hey, cariña,' he said with a smile that made Lucy forget all about Nate's wedding plus-one. 'I'll just have a shower and then I will be there.'

Lucy grinned and relaxed into the pillows, putting her phone down and sipping her coffee as Marco took off his shoes and padded through to her pristine bathroom. She'd matched with him on Tinder a couple of summers ago, at a point where she'd realised that she didn't want a romantic relationship of any kind, but absolutely wasn't prepared to forgo great sex. Anthony had come first (literally and figuratively), but he was a busy man, juggling several jobs and not always available when Lucy wanted company. So she'd added Marco into the mix, and one or either of them was usually free when Lucy found herself at a loose end. They came, they left. No strings, no pressure, nobody snoring in her bed or wanting anything more than she was willing to give.

'Sorry I'm late,' said Marco, appearing in the bedroom

with a white towel wrapped around his slim hips. When he wasn't assessing insurance risk on the UK's most treasured landmarks, Marco was a competitive triathlete – he'd taken part in the UK Ironman four times, and had the red M logo tattooed on his shoulder with four black lines next to it. He was due to compete in his fifth later this year, so he could add the diagonal line to the tally and presumably move on to a new challenge before he started to look like the wall of a prison cell.

'It's fine,' said Lucy, carefully putting her mug and phone on the bedside table as the familiar hum of arousal started to pulse through her veins. 'I don't have any plans this morning.'

Marco smiled seductively and sat on the edge of the bed, simultaneously leaning in to gently kiss Lucy's neck and loosening the towel around his waist.

'I have so many plans for you, cariña,' he said huskily, taking her hand and putting it somewhere that left her in absolutely no doubt about the nature and origin of his plans. Lucy closed her eyes and arched her back, wondering whether Spanish women found the British accent as sexy as she found Marco's. Italian was just as hot, but what about French? Her mind momentarily drifted to Nate talking on the phone in the office, which somehow merged into him peeling off that wetsuit and pressing his hard, wet body against hers.

'My God, you are SO ready for me,' whispered Marco, making Lucy gasp as his lips trailed down her neck and his fingers began their steady rhythm. Lucy's bed on a Sunday morning was Marco's church, and the only thing she needed to do was lie back and receive his devoted worship.

'What are you doing for the rest of the day?' asked Marco, pulling some clean cycling leggings over his sturdy thighs. Months ago, Lucy had suggested he leave a spare set at her flat so he didn't have to put sweaty kit back on, then she'd wash the dirty stuff for next time. The irony didn't escape her that Marco had never spent the night with her and she was only vaguely aware of when his birthday was, but she happily did his filthy laundry.

'Life admin,' said Lucy, who needed to clean out the fridge and wash her sheets, but that was about it. 'Nothing very exciting.'

'I'm going to a conference in Paris in a couple of weeks.'

'That sounds nice,' said Lucy, reminded of the video Nate had posted on Instagram of him cycling around the Bois de Boulogne in Paris. It had been taken by somebody riding the bike behind, but frustratingly there had been no indication of who that might be. Did he have a girlfriend? Or a boyfriend? And why on earth was she thinking about THAT when there was a half-naked Spanish athlete in her bedroom?

'Yeah,' said Marco, pulling on a fresh pair of white socks. 'I thought I might stay for the weekend. Do you want to come?'

'I'm sorry?' Lucy snapped out of her Nate-based reverie and furrowed her brow at Marco. 'Did you just invite me to Paris?'

'Yes,' said Marco, giving her a challenging look. 'Why?'

He smiled awkwardly and pulled a red Lycra top over his head. 'Because it's Paris, and my work is paying for everything, and we will have a nice time.'

'It sounds romantic,' said Lucy warily, imagining the pair of them walking hand in hand through the Tuileries, Marco kissing snowflakes off her nose. She hadn't been to Paris in years, not since a school trip when she was eleven. In fact, now she thought about it, she hadn't really been *anywhere* in years. Her parents' place in Croydon, a reunion trip to Liverpool Uni that she'd bailed on after an hour, lots of pub walks in Somerset or Gloucester or Devon with Jonno and his family to climb some hills and get some country air. But that was pretty much it.

'What's wrong with romantic?' Marco threw his dirty clothes into her laundry hamper, Lucy trying not to scowl as he didn't put the lid back on properly, then came to sit on the end of the bed.

Lucy sighed. 'I don't do romantic. That's not what this relationship is.'

'I know that,' said Marco patiently, reaching out to take her hand. 'But I also enjoy your company and thought it might be fun. Have you ever been to Paris?'

'Yes,' said Lucy. She remembered the school coach trip to Euro Disney – Leo had been sick on the coach and Lucy had been nominated to mop it up with paper towels, like being Leo's twin sister made his vomit her responsibility. 'But it was a long time ago.'

'It's a beautiful city in the winter,' said Marco. 'I'd

like to enjoy the food and the culture, and you seemed like the kind of person who might appreciate that too.'

Lucy didn't disagree, but it felt like she and Marco would be crossing a line. Going to a wedding with Anthony already felt like wobbly ground, but a Parisian mini-break was a whole other level.

'I'm inviting you to Paris for a weekend of wine and food and culture, Lucy,' said Marco, clearly sensing her discomfort. 'I'm not asking you to marry me.'

'And I appreciate the offer,' said Lucy. 'But I don't think it's a good idea.'

'Fine,' said Marco, shuffling up the bed and leaning over to kiss her. 'What is it British people say? I'm not angry, just disappointed.'

'Maybe I could make it up to you,' said Lucy, lifting his Lycra top and stroking her hand across his hairless stomach. Touching his abs felt like running her hands over a marble statue. Like Michelangelo's *David*, but with tattoos and a padded crotch.

'It drives me crazy when you do this,' said Marco, his breath catching as Lucy's hand trailed lower. 'You are a master of distraction and misdirection. You are like Derren Brown, but SO much hotter.'

'That's the nicest thing you've ever said to me,' whispered Lucy.

'I've just invited you to Paris,' laughed Marco.

'I know, but I'm pretending that never happened,' said Lucy. 'Maybe you could take your clothes off again?'

Marco made a noise that was somewhere between a groan and a sigh, the conversation about Paris already forgotten as they fell back into the pillows and their familiar, exquisite routine.

Lucy lay in the bath, the hot, foamy water soaking away the aches and pains of two hours in Marco's very strong and capable hands. She'd relax here for half an hour, then get her act together. Maybe she'd go for a walk, or do a YouTube workout. She smiled to herself, knowing that neither of those things had the smallest chance of happening. Cleaning was the only thing she did religiously, because keeping her personal space immaculate made her feel calm and in control of things. Her therapist had asked all kinds of questions about that, back in the day.

Her phone buzzed on the edge of the bath, and she glanced at the screen to see a message from her mother. *Are you free to talk about plans for next weekend?*

Shit, thought Lucy, all her bathtub zen instantly draining down the plughole. It was Leo's eleventh anniversary next weekend, and whilst she obviously hadn't forgotten, she'd hoped the tenth anniversary last year might mark the end of the annual trek to Croydon cemetery, followed by a lacklustre roast lunch at the same soulless pub in some godforsaken Surrey village, firmly in the Gatwick flight path. At least this year the anniversary was a Friday, and there would likely be other people in the pub. She vividly remembered the year it had fallen on a Tuesday – they'd been the only ones there, apart from a small group of pensioners silently sipping sherry, clearly dressed for a funeral.

She ignored the message, slowly counting the seconds

until her phone rang and *MUM* lit up the screen. *One, two, three . . .* she made it to twelve before the phone started to vibrate. Her mother would let it ring out, then leave a passive-aggressive voicemail, which Lucy would avoid listening to until the tiny tape recorder symbol started to haunt her. Most of the time her mother called back before she made it that far.

Lucy sank further down until her chin was immersed in the warm water, irrationally annoyed at her mother for calling during her bath. This was her meditative time, when her blood was flowing and her body was still tingling from Marco's attention, and she could empty her head of everything else for an hour. Now she was thinking about Leo again, and feeling guilty about going away next weekend, even though she hadn't missed a single one of the ten anniversaries that had passed so far. Every year the same routine, as if the Red Lion was in some way special to Leo rather than conveniently close to the ring road with a good-sized car park and a decent selection of vegetarian mains.

Lucy played out the inevitable conversation in her head. Her mother would gasp in horror at the news that Lucy wasn't coming, and Lucy would try to explain that it was a team-building thing with work, but Shirley would feign confusion. She had refused all attempts to understand her daughter's job – anyone would think Lucy was a computational fluid dynamics engineer rather than a copywriter in an ad agency – so Lucy had given up trying years ago. Then Shirley would get breathless and insist that Lucy speak to her father, who would listen patiently and attempt to understand Lucy's need to do something different this year, to be somewhere else. He'd promise to smooth things over, while Shirley squeaked and huffed in outrage in the background.

I'll go and see them the following weekend, thought Lucy, then remembered that she'd promised to go to a wedding with Anthony. That had been a mistake, but he'd caught her in a moment when her knees were weak and her guard was down. *The weekend after that, then*, she decided. She'd have to be careful not to mention Anthony or the wedding, or they'd think she'd got a boyfriend. One of the many benefits of not having a social media presence was that her parents couldn't pass judgement on her life – not that there was much to judge right now.

I miss you, Leo, she thought, her eyes swimming with tears. She let them flow into the rapidly cooling water, too tired and heavy to move her arms. *You don't mind if I go to Switzerland, do you? You'll forgive me, just this once?*

Leo didn't answer, but then he didn't need to. He would have forgiven Lucy anything, and she knew he would have hated the idea of her missing a mountain adventure in favour of another frigid lunch with their parents. She'd always known what he was thinking, it came with being a twin. *Apart from that one time*, thought Lucy, giving in to the surge of memories that pinned her helplessly in the bath, like her body was a block of metal engraved with words of pain and loss and loneliness.

CHAPTER FOUR

'Are you ready for this?' said Jonno. 'I have big news. Huge.'

'Where are you?' asked Lucy, grabbing the handrail of the seat in front as the double-decker bus took a bend at high speed. 'Are you already at the airport?'

'I haven't even left home yet. Olly's organised a cab, it's due any minute. I'm picking up Sasha on the way. He and Maya are getting a different one.'

Lucy watched the suburbs of south Bristol fly by, glad that she hadn't accepted Olly's offer of a taxi, which came with the risk of having to make small talk with a chatty driver. The Airport Flyer stopped just down the road from her house, and only took fifteen minutes. 'What about Fran?'

'That's why I'm ringing. She's not coming.'

'*Whaaaaat?*' screeched Lucy, prompting everyone else on the bus to turn and look at her in alarm.

'I shit you not. She's torn her Achilles tendon.'

'Ouch,' winced Lucy. 'How did she do that?'

'Not sure, some kind of incident at spin class, apparently. Got her foot caught in the pedal, fell off the bike, ping.'

'Holy shit,' gasped Lucy, swallowing down a dry

heave at the thought of how much that must have hurt. 'Is she OK?'

'Apparently she's been to hospital and she's got crutches and one of those plastic boot things for now. They might need to operate.'

'Wow, that's bad.'

'It's the gym I feel sorry for. Imagine the chaos Fran's going to unleash once she's off the painkillers and fully lawyered up. Still, great news for the rest of us.'

'What's happening to her space on the trip?'

'No idea. Sasha was sorting it out last night.'

'Maybe it'll be Derek. He deserves it.'

'Nope. He's got a thing, remember? With a bunch of delinquent teenagers. Anyway, I need to chase up this cab, it should be here by now. See you in a bit.'

Lucy suppressed a squeak of excitement. 'Can't wait!' She ended the call and sat back in her seat, her mind racing as she tried to process this unexpected turn of events. Fran not coming was definitely good news, unless of course you were Fran. Then again, if Fran's space wasn't taken by somebody else, Sasha would almost certainly latch on to her and Jonno, given that Maya and Olly were their own special kind of mayhem. So maybe it wasn't such good news, after all.

Her phone vibrated in her hand with a message from her mum, checking if she'd left the country yet. She took a deep breath and tapped out a reply.

I'm on a bus to the airport. I'll message when I get there.

The reply came through instantly. *Please don't forget. And give me your flight number, so I can get your dad to check when it's landed.*

Lucy took a screengrab of her boarding pass and sent it to her. Sometimes it was hard not to feel suffocated by her mum's need to be in control, but given everything they'd been through as a family, it was understandable. It came from a place of worry and fear, which Lucy supposed was a kind of love, in its own way.

She put her phone in her pocket and relaxed into her seat, already anticipating swapping the grey, drizzly skies of Bristol for the fresh, crisp chill of the mountains. It would be good for her to get out of this city for a few days, even if the idea of it made her feel nervous and jittery. She'd moved here to be closer to Leo, but she could take him with her to Switzerland. Like emotional carry-on baggage, but since she was only taking a cabin bag, she was limiting her memories to the good ones.

Lucy was lost in her thoughts when the bus pulled up outside the terminal, the air brakes hissing as they came to a stop. She grabbed her wheely bag and hurried through the revolving doors into the warmth, heading straight to the spot where she'd agreed to meet the others. But the only person there was . . . Nate.

She came to a halt by a pillar ten metres away and watched him for a moment, not yet ready to get caught up in the awkwardness of stilted conversation. He had one hand buried deep in the pocket of his dark grey ski jacket, the other scrolling through his phone. A set of headphones were pulled down around his neck, half-covered by his curly hair. He had the same twitching, nervous energy she'd seen outside the pub, like he'd downed one too many espressos and couldn't keep his hands or feet still. Presumably being dragged into this had been pretty last minute, so perhaps he'd had a sleepless night hunting down appropriate clothing while Fran tried to make her accident all his fault. It seemed obvious now that he would be her replacement, but somehow she hadn't expected him to make the cut. Without the pressure of having to pick someone who actually deserved it, Lucy had expected Sasha to choose someone a little more client-friendly.

You can't stand here staring at him all day, thought Lucy. *Go and say hello.* The idea of being alone in his company made her inexplicably nervous, but what did she have to fear from Nate Lambert? And anyway, Jonno would be here soon.

'Hey,' she said, giving him a warm smile as he looked up curiously. 'I take it you're standing in for Fran this weekend?'

Nate nodded, his blank expression suggesting he'd rather be anywhere else. Lucy felt a surge of annoyance that he was taking up a space when everyone on the team apart from Derek would have happily taken Fran's place. 'Did you hear what happened to her?' he asked.

'Yeah,' said Lucy. 'Jonno called me earlier. I hope she's OK.' Nate's eyebrow-raise was almost imperceptible, but clearly communicated 'I know you're lying', so Lucy quickly changed the subject. 'Are the others here yet?'

'No,' said Nate. 'I had a call from Sasha ten minutes ago. Apparently there was a problem with the taxis.'

Lucy blinked, wondering why Sasha had called Nate and not her. Perhaps she'd tried, but Lucy's bus was hurtling through a signal blackspot. She quickly glanced at her phone for missed calls, but there was nothing. 'What kind of problem?'

Nate shrugged. 'I think Olly was supposed to book them, but it seems like he got over-excited about the trip and forgot to send a confirmation.'

'Oops,' said Lucy with a grin. 'Are they all sorted now?' Jonno and Sasha both lived in tiny villages over towards Bath, and getting a taxi during peak school-run time had probably caused a few headaches. Likewise Olly lived somewhere up near Filton, but presumably he could get a train or a bus. Lucy had no idea where Maya lived.

'I don't know, Sasha said something about bad traffic and an accident.' He looked wrung out, and Lucy felt a moment of sympathy that he'd clearly been on the receiving end of Sasha losing her shit in fifteen different ways. They'd all been there at one time or another.

'How come you made it? Do you live nearby?'

Nate nodded. 'Bedminster. I got the bus.'

'Same, I'm in Southville.'

Nate checked his watch and nodded vaguely, like he couldn't be less interested that they lived so close to each other. 'We should probably go through,' he said, gesturing towards the escalator. 'I guess they'll find us when they get here.'

Lucy nodded and glanced at her phone, hoping for a reassuring message from Jonno. 'Have you checked in?' she asked, wondering if he'd had time to do it online. Nate nodded, so they rode the escalator and joined the queue for Security, Lucy standing behind Nate and wondering whether the curls on his neck were thick and wiry, or soft and fluffy, like baby hair. She resisted the entirely insane urge to touch them, instead surreptitiously inspecting the contents of his incredibly organised plastic bag of toiletries. Mostly grey Clinique Men bottles and tubes, and some generic Colgate toothpaste. They said nothing to each other for twenty minutes while they waited in the queue, and by the time Lucy emerged from putting her shoes back on after Security he was at the entrance to Duty Free, already on his phone. He pulled a face as she approached, then turned the handset to face her. It was Sasha on a video call, prompting Lucy to feel a flurry of annoyance that she was calling Nate again, rather than her. Presumably she was seeing him as a Fran substitute, which didn't bode well for him this weekend. Sasha loved a video call, and the consensus in the office was that she used it to check nobody was working at home in their pyjamas.

'We're not going to make the flight,' she said, stony-faced.

'What, none of you?' asked Lucy, glancing at Nate. He was leaning in so close she could smell the woody scent of his shampoo, or maybe it was his aftershave. She forced herself to focus and not get distracted.

'No,' said Sasha. 'Olly and Maya are on the train; there's some kind of signalling issue and they're not even in Temple Meads yet. We're in Jonno's car, but we're stuck on a country lane, going nowhere. There's been an accident. It's clearly bad, an air ambulance has just flown over.'

'I'm really sorry,' said Lucy. Sasha turned the camera towards Jonno, who shook his head. She could see his jaw twitching with stress and frustration.

'So what's the plan?' asked Lucy.

'We'll have to get another flight in a couple of hours. Olly's trying to sort it out now.'

Lucy breathed, wondering if Sasha had unleashed the full extent of her fury on Olly yet, the poor bastard. 'Do you want us to wait?'

'Absolutely not,' said Sasha. 'Get out there and work your charm on Kristoff; he's spent a fortune on this trip and we already look like fucking idiots. It's down to you two to save the day.'

Lucy smiled gamely, although her nerves were already jangling. 'When are they arriving?'

'They got there yesterday; I spoke to Kristoff last night. They were planning a team-building day today, something to do with building igloos.'

'Right. Sounds horrific.'

'I'm serious, Lucy,' said Sasha, giving Lucy her best glacier-forming stare. 'You and Nate both need to step up. Do whatever they want this evening – go skiing by torchlight, drink Jägermeister through a pair of Kristoff's boxer shorts, whatever it takes to keep him entertained. We'll be there as soon as we can.'

'OK, we will.' She looked up at Nate, who pointed to the departures board and held up six fingers to indicate their gate number. 'We need to go, our flight's boarding.'

'No pressure, mate,' said Jonno, and Sasha turned the phone in his direction so Lucy could see his pained smile and his white knuckles gripping the steering wheel. 'But just so you know, the future of the Titan account is currently resting entirely on your shoulders. Try not fuck it up, yeah?'

'Can you ski?' asked Lucy, turning to Nate who was now settled into the aisle seat next to her, apparently somewhat reluctantly. Lucy had suggested he take what would have been Jonno's seat, but she was beginning to wonder why he'd accepted. He'd said almost nothing while they waited at the departure gate, choosing a seat in the furthest corner, before losing himself in whatever was playing through his headphones.

'Yes, of course,' he said, in a tone that seemed unnecessarily snippy to Lucy. 'But I prefer not to.'

Lucy pulled the in-flight magazine out of the pocket and flicked through it aggressively. 'Sorry I asked.'

'Can YOU?'

'No,' said Lucy. 'It's not included in the UK comprehensive school curriculum, and unlike France, Croydon isn't great for après-ski.'

'I grew up in Clevedon,' he said witheringly. 'That's not great for après-ski, either. And I'm only half French.'

'Which half?' she asked, figuring that they were stuck together for the next few hours, and she might as well make friends, or at least try to find out something about him. God knows today wasn't shaping up to be much fun otherwise.

'The French half,' deadpanned Nate, putting on his headphones. Lucy sighed and went back to ignoring the articles in the easyJet magazine and looking at the ads instead, hoping to spot anything that looked remotely original or interesting. It was all perfume and skincare, which invariably featured the same airbrushed movie stars looking deathly bored in wispy clothing. Apparently there was no need to have any kind of personality as long as you smelled nice.

'How do you want to manage this evening?' asked Nate, taking his headphones off again.

Lucy turned to look at him. 'Manage what?' He looked fidgety and unsettled, like he'd been overthinking this question for a while.

'The clients. It's just that . . . I've never met them.'

'Really? Haven't you worked on this account for over a year?'

Nate shrugged. 'Yeah. But Fran does all the client meetings; I just do all the work.'

Lucy smirked, delighted that Nate could, at the very least, muster a bit of snark about Fran. 'Well, that's awkward,' she said. 'Because I've never met them either. In person, anyway.'

Nate's eyes widened in surprise, and Lucy realised for the first time exactly how long his eyelashes were.

'Copywriters hardly ever go to the client meetings,' she continued. 'We're usually not very client-friendly; we either talk too much or not at all. I mostly work backstage and let Jonno manage front of house.'

'Hmm,' said Nate thoughtfully. 'I'd assumed you were out front, doing your Lucy thing.'

'What's my Lucy thing?' she asked, furrowing her brow and already suspecting she might not like the answer.

'I don't know,' said Nate, squirming uncomfortably. 'You're just . . . the kind of person people notice, I guess.'

Lucy looked away, feeling slightly blindsided by the whiplash segue from Nate seeming bored and unengaged, to throwing out comments that felt both personal and critical, somehow. She decided to change the subject to more comfortable territory. 'Why do you put up with Fran, out of interest? Let her take credit for all your work?'

Nate held her gaze for a moment, like he was trying to work out her motivation for asking. 'I don't know. I guess I'm not very client-friendly either.'

She blinked twice, not sure if he'd answered her question or not, and slightly dazzled by how good-looking he was up close. Did he know? Perhaps the whole closed-off, taciturn thing was an act to make him seem more mysterious?

'Well, that's not going to work this evening,' said Lucy. 'I've heard Kristoff likes smart conversation, so if you've got any suggestions on deep and meaningful podcasts we can namedrop, I'm all ears.'

'Let's see how they are when we get there,' said Nate. 'If they want to talk work, I can take the lead – I know their annual plan inside and out. But . . .' He hesitated, and Lucy smiled.

'But what?'

'If they want to party, it's up to you.'

'What makes you think I like to party?' Lucy squirmed, conscious that to other members of the team she and Jonno probably looked like an exclusive little clique who spent half their life in the pub. She'd never been the type to have a big circle of friends, and she didn't naturally open up to people. Alcohol loosened her corset a little, but she only ever drank at the weekends. Not that Nate would know that; she could see how she probably came across as a wine-fuelled chaos party girl, when in reality she was anything but.

Nate smiled softly. 'Lucy, I've seen you stand on a table in a bar and sing.'

'What song?' asked Lucy, pretending to be shocked but now starting to enjoying this more talkative, playful Nate. There had been more than one occasion over the years when she had stood on a table in a karaoke bar and belted out a song – usually after too much wine, and as an opportunity to lose herself in a moment of vocal self-sabotage.

'I can't remember. Kelly Clarkson, maybe?'

Lucy felt her cheeks flushing as she remembered her rendition of 'Since U Been Gone' at the agency summer party the previous year. 'Was I any good?' she asked tentatively, hoping he might throw her a tiny compliment. She'd been pretty pissed, but it had definitely sounded great in her head.

'No,' said Nate. 'You were shit, and the whole thing was actually kind of embarrassing for all of us.'

'Right, and I suppose you're Elton John?' snapped Lucy. She realised that this was what annoyed her about Nate – he wasn't rude, exactly, just able to vocalise what she secretly already knew but had chosen not to face up to. He did it in the office sometimes too – in just a handful of words, he could make her feel exposed and vulnerable, like he could read her mind and see deep into her soul. Lucy was pretty sure it was done unconsciously and entirely without agenda, but she still found it unsettling.

'No,' said Nate, looking at his fingernails. 'I play guitar, not piano.'

So the guitar was his, then. She briefly considered mentioning it, in a casual *Oh, I saw your guitar on Instagram* kind of way, but that definitely sounded like she'd been stalking him on social media, which she absolutely had. *Just out of interest, who was the person videoing you on a Parisian bicycle three years ago?* There was no way to have this conversation without sounding a bit mad.

'I thought I sounded OK,' she said feebly.

'Drunk people always think that,' said Nate. The plane started to back away from the stand, so he put his headphones back on again and closed his eyes.

Lucy pressed her lips together and turned back to her magazine, silently fuming that Nate would bring up something like that, just for the opportunity to humiliate her. *Turns out he was way hotter when he said nothing*, thought Lucy. *He can feel free to French Exit through the emergency doors any time he likes.*

CHAPTER FIVE

Lucy climbed into the back of the people carrier, originally booked for six people, but now only carrying two. She'd hoped the seating would be configured so she and Nate could sit comfortably apart, but no such luck – it was set up like a London cab with two rows of three seats facing each other. Lucy chose the row that would be travelling forwards, on the basis that facing backwards made her feel sick, and it was no surprise that Nate chose a seat on the same side – he was still looking a bit pale and stressed after their turbulent descent in high winds, and a landing that had made Lucy's teeth rattle. His silence had continued as they made their way off the plane and through passport control, only breaking it to acknowledge Lucy's updates from Jonno that they were on a flight three hours behind Lucy and Nate. It meant that they'd miss dinner but would be there for late drinks.

'I'm sorry if I was weird on the plane,' said Nate as the car navigated its way out of the airport. 'I really struggle with flying.'

'Right,' said Lucy, finally realising why he'd been so uncommunicative in the airport, then spent most of the flight wearing headphones with his eyes closed. 'Why didn't you just say so?'

'Because it's easier just to grit my teeth and get through

it.' He looked out of the window and wiped his hands on his jeans, as if they were clammy. Lucy wondered what it must be like to put yourself through something that actively made you scared. She'd stayed in her comfort zone for so long it was difficult to imagine, but on the rare occasions she flew somewhere, it was no big deal.

'What's the issue, specifically? The people? The weird noises and bouncing about? Or the unlikely physics of aviation?'

Nate half-smiled, colour slowly returning to his cheeks. 'All of the above. Given the choice, I'd rather get the train.'

'Me too,' said Lucy. 'Not ideal for a long weekend, though. Why did you say yes to coming, if you don't like flying? You didn't have to be here.'

'No, I guess not. But Sasha called and—'

'Hang on, let me guess,' laughed Lucy, holding up her hand. 'She told you it was time to step up, and that this was a fantastic opportunity to raise your profile with the client without Fran stealing your thunder.'

Nate gave a hollow laugh. 'Almost word for word. Did you write that speech for her?'

Lucy shook her head. 'No, I've just worked with her for a very long time.'

'Well, that was pretty much it,' said Nate, pulling a face. 'And she's right, obviously. I'm just . . . it's . . .'

'Look, it's fine,' said Lucy, not wanting to get into sharing mode with someone she worked with and currently didn't like very much. 'You speak fluent French, right?'

Nate nodded. 'Yeah.'

'The Titan Marketing Director is a French woman

called Thérèse. I've done a few calls with her and she's lovely. Just chat to her about their strategy or something, tell her about all your trips to Paris.'

Nate turned to look at her, his brow furrowed in confusion. 'How do you know I've been on trips to Paris?'

Lucy froze, wondering if he could hear the squealing brakes in her head. 'Oh, I just assumed. You used to live there, right?'

'Yeah,' said Nate. He gave her a knowing smile, and she knew she was busted.

'And I looked at your Instagram,' she added casually.

Nate laughed and shook his head. 'Why would you look at my Instagram?'

'I was looking at the socials of everyone on this trip. Getting to know everyone, finding conversation starters, that kind of thing. I'm not a stalker, honest.'

'But you didn't know I was coming until you got to the airport.'

Fuuuuck, thought Lucy, the panic-cogs now spinning at a hundred miles an hour. 'Yeah, that's where I looked. While we were waiting to get on the plane.'

'Right,' laughed Nate, and Lucy dared to breathe for a second. 'Fair enough. With those kind of research skills, you should work on Rachel's strategy team.'

'I'd rather boil my head,' said Lucy, gratified that she'd apparently got away with her stalker behaviour AND made Nate laugh. 'Have you seen Kristoff's TikTok?' *If in doubt, deflect.*

'I try not to look at TikTok too much,' said Nate, waving his phone feebly. 'It sucks away too much of my day. Will it make this road trip go faster?'

'Probably not,' said Lucy quickly, relieved she didn't have a social media presence so Nate could stalk her the way she'd stalked him. 'But worth looking for some common ground in case he corners you later. He's Kristoff the Titan.'

'Of course he is,' said Nate, putting his headphones on and losing himself in his phone as Lucy watched the landscape fly by. She'd looked at Google Maps a couple of weeks ago and knew that the journey from Geneva to Zermatt followed the north side of the lake, but they were sat on a busy highway, surrounded by traffic, so she couldn't enjoy the view. Instead she thought about the pictures she'd received from Anthony last night; she occasionally sent him a reply, but there weren't many angles on a woman that didn't look like a nurse was about to approach with a giant speculum.

'I'm all up to speed on Kristoff's TikTok,' said Nate twenty minutes later, pulling off his headphones. 'You don't seem to post at all, though. Or on Instagram.'

'No,' said Lucy, a little taken aback that he'd looked. 'I'm a consumer, rather than a creator.'

'Shame,' said Nate airily, peering out of the window at the blurry grey vista.

Lucy said nothing, feeling slightly blindsided by his change of tone. There was nothing for Nate to find, other than an ancient private Facebook account from her teens that she never used, but didn't want to delete because of all the photos of Leo.

Why do I even care? she thought. She was considerably more senior than Nate in the LUNA hierarchy, so there was no professional benefit from earning his approval.

And even though she was willing to acknowledge he was undeniably hot, she definitely wasn't interested in having sex with him. She barely knew him and wasn't really sure she liked him, for a start, so why shit on your own doorstep? And if she wasn't trying to impress Nate or get him into bed, what did it matter what he thought of her?

There's something about him, thought Lucy, leaning her head against the curved headrest and sinking into the heated seats. *He doesn't say much, and what he does say is kind of rude, but it feels like he can see through me.* Right now that definitely didn't feel like a good thing, but they were only stuck with each other for a few more hours, until the fun people arrived.

When Lucy woke up a while later, two things immediately occurred to her. Firstly, that her head was no longer on the headrest, but was now on a strong, ski-jacketed shoulder that presumably belonged to Nate. And secondly, she'd been having a mildly erotic dream about Marco's strong legs that somehow morphed into Anthony's penis, and her left hand was now very evidently on Nate's leg. *Oh God, have I been stroking him?* she wondered in horror. There had definitely been some robust stroking in the dream.

Lucy kept her eyes screwed tight shut, trying to work out how to extract herself from this situation with her dignity intact. Maybe she could gently remove the hand, then flip her head back to her side of the car without appearing to have woken up. Or maybe Nate was asleep too, and he'd be none the wiser.

'Hi,' whispered Nate, so close that she could feel his breath in her hair. 'You OK?'

'Mmm,' said Lucy sleepily, snatching her hand away and trying to rub the creases from her face as she sat up. 'Apparently I've been using you as a pillow. I'm really sorry.'

'It's fine,' said Nate mildly. 'Your head was flopping about a bit, so I moved over to provide support before you snapped your neck.'

Oh God, thought Lucy. *This is mortifying.* She yawned and wiped a bit of crusted saliva from the corner of her mouth and hoped she hadn't been actively drooling on him, like a hungry Labrador. 'Thanks,' she muttered.

'What were you dreaming about, out of interest?' asked Nate. 'At one point you were gripping my leg so hard I thought you were going to crush it.'

Giving a handjob to one of my not-boyfriends, thought Lucy, wondering if she could just open the car door and throw herself into the evening traffic.

'Sorry about that,' she said vaguely, checking her watch. 'I was trying to hold on to something, but I can't remember what. Wow, I was asleep for nearly two hours.'

'Yeah, we're not far away now,' said Nate. 'You can't see much out there, but we're definitely gaining some altitude.'

Lucy peered out of the window, but it was pitch black beyond the lights of other cars and roadside homes. She checked her phone – a message from Jonno saying their flight was more or less on time, so hopefully they'd be there by nine. Nate had shuffled back to the other side of the car so she stretched out her arms, wishing she could get out of the car and walk around a bit. A trip to the bathroom wouldn't go amiss, either.

Nate leaned forward and spoke to the driver in French, which Lucy understood enough to know that he'd asked how long before they were in Zermatt, and could they take a break. She smiled to herself, thinking about how good Leo had been at tuning in to what she needed without her having to say anything. Maybe Nate had the same talent, or maybe he just needed a wee and she was overestimating the power of her womanly energy.

'*Dix minutes*,' said the driver. Lucy checked her watch again, calculating what time they'd arrive in Zermatt. Cars weren't allowed in the village, so they'd go as far as Täsch, about five kilometres away, then get an electric shuttle bus from there. She was hungry and needed a drink, but also felt like she'd been travelling for days and definitely wouldn't say no to an early night. Hopefully the Titan team would turn out to be as clean-living as she'd heard, and would be in bed by 10 p.m. with some whale music and an eye mask.

'HEYYYYY,' shouted Kristoff as Lucy ducked into the bar a few doors down from their hotel. 'The LUNA advance party are here, get another round in!' Lucy smiled weakly, already slightly overwhelmed by the textbook Alpine decor of wood panelling, furry throws and various heads of dead animals lined up on the walls. Under a particularly outraged-looking stag was a table set for ten, which was clearly for the Titan team because each placemat already had a gold pack of condoms on it.

How was Kristoff hoping the evening was going to pan out? The mind boggled.

'Hi,' said Lucy. 'Thanks for waiting, and sorry everyone else is running late.'

'It's no problem,' said Kristoff heartily, reaching out to shake both their hands. 'You're Lucy and Nate, right? Sasha gave me an update on all the travel drama.'

Lucy nodded, slightly dazzled by his puppy-like enthusiasm. Kristoff was aggressively handsome in a Disney villain kind of way – tall and fit with dirty-blond hair, startling blue eyes and perfect teeth, and a sing-song American accent that still held on to the tiniest hint of Swedish, like that made him more interesting. The whole effect was like somebody had made a Ken doll out of Alexander Skarsgård, which wasn't exactly repellent, but definitely wasn't Lucy's type. Aside from anything else, she wouldn't *ever* consider screwing the client – she might not do relationships the way most people did, but she did have some kind of moral compass.

The rest of the team introduced themselves – Thérèse, Nick and Paul. Thérèse was familiar but the two other men were new to Lucy, so she committed their names and job titles to memory in case she needed to make intelligent conversation later. If this whole weekend tanked their relationship with Titan, it wouldn't be her fault.

'Let's get you a drink,' said Kristoff, making a space so Lucy could get to the bar. She surreptitiously checked out his outfit – designer jeans, white T-shirt, grey blazer and white leather trainers. There were no overt logos or blingy details – it was a top-to-toe masterclass in wearing a thousand-dollar outfit whilst looking like you'd made no effort whatsoever. Lucy couldn't help but admire him for it, and he undeniably smelled incredible.

'So, Lucy,' he said with a boylike grin, and she braced herself for an onslaught of over-confident flirting. 'I just want to say that I'm a huge fan of your writing. We wouldn't have made it so far without your incredible work.'

'Oh,' said Lucy, feeling wildly wrong-footed. His blue eyes were dazzling, but his expression was one of utmost respect and admiration. 'Thank you.'

'I'm surprised we've never met before.' He lifted his hand to attract the barman. 'Jonno has clearly been hiding you away.'

'It's my choice,' said Lucy quickly. Jonno had repeatedly invited her to client workshops or awards events, but she'd always said no. 'I prefer to keep my head down.' She blushed, because that sounded a bit like a sex reference, but Kristoff either didn't get it or didn't care. Lucy ordered an Aperol Spritz and smiled helplessly, frantically raking through her library of interesting Kristoff topics and coming up with precisely nothing.

'Well, we're really glad to have you here,' he said. Lucy had been determined not to like him, having assumed he was a typical rich entrepreneur playboy with an excess of confidence and a dearth of time and respect for the little people, but apparently Kristoff Berg wasn't like that at all. She glanced over at Nate, who was standing with the rest of the Titan team looking a little lost, and wondered fleetingly if Kristoff was the only person she'd misjudged today.

'One Aperol Spritz,' said Kristoff, taking the giant

wine glass from the barman and handing it to Lucy. 'Welcome to Zermatt.'

'Thank you,' said Lucy, taking a sip and wondering why she hadn't ordered something she actually liked. It was Leo, of course – she and her brother had discovered Aperol on a family camping holiday to Italy when they were sixteen, long before it had made it to any of Croydon's sticky cocktail bars. Their parents had allowed them to join in with a pre-dinner aperitivo, so the two teenagers had both drunk an Aperol Spritz every day and decided it was the only thing they would drink when they were sophisticated adults. It had tasted like paint stripper then and it tasted like paint stripper now, but she still knocked back one or two in Leo's honour whenever the occasion presented itself. And in the Alps, it felt like a must.

'So, how was your journey?' asked Kristoff, clearly keen to keep their conversation going. Paul appeared at his shoulder to show him a message he'd just received on his phone, so Lucy took the opportunity to glance over at Nate again, who was now chatting to Thérèse the Marketing Director. By the nature of Thérèse's expressive hand gestures and the fact that her lips were moving at a million miles an hour, Lucy assumed the conversation was in French. There was a momentary break while Thérèse reached over to pass Nate his drink, and he looked up and caught Lucy's eye, glancing between her and Kristoff. His expression was . . . what? Confused? Jealous? Lost? He definitely looked like he wanted to be somewhere else, but Lucy couldn't tell if that was by her side with her head on his shoulder, or a very long way from this bar.

CHAPTER SIX

'I'm so glad you're here,' sighed Lucy as Jonno hugged her tightly, looking tired and harassed. Behind him, Sasha, Maya and Olly immediately fell into the group of clients in a flurry of greetings, handshakes and apologies, but Jonno had ignored everyone else and made a beeline straight for Lucy.

'Been a tricky evening?' he asked, swiping the glass of wine from her hand and draining half of it in one go. He waved his arms at the barman and pointed to Lucy's glass, then held up two fingers.

'No, it's been fine,' said Lucy. 'Dinner went on forever and I've eaten my bodyweight in cheese. The kitchen is still open for you guys, Kristoff is going to get them to bring out some more food.'

'Thank God, I'm starving,' said Jonno, glancing over at Kristoff, who was on the phone at the head of the dinner table. 'What's he doing?'

'A conference call with New York,' said Lucy with a shrug. 'The wheels of commerce never stop turning.'

'Condommerce,' said Jonno, turning to the barman and accepting two glasses of wine. 'Can you just give us the bottle?'

'Cheers,' said Lucy, clinking Jonno's glass.

'Cheers,' replied Jonno. 'How's Kristoff been?'

'He's actually really good company,' said Lucy. 'Not what I expected at all.'

'He's a good guy,' said Jonno. 'But very much a ladies' man, by all accounts. I did wonder if he'd take a fancy to you.'

'It wouldn't matter to me if he did,' said Lucy dismissively. 'But for what it's worth, he's been entirely professional. Apart from trying to persuade me to go to some bar up the mountain.'

'See, that's how it begins,' laughed Jonno. 'Men like Kristoff tempt you up a mountain, and before you know it you're having sex on a sheepskin rug in front of a roaring log fire. Where's French Exit?'

'He sat next to Thérèse for dinner; they've been prattling away in French about Titan strategy, so I think she's in love. Then we got the message you guys had arrived and he disappeared. I thought he'd gone to the bathroom, but he never came back.'

'Christ, he could give Funsponge Fran a run for her money. Here, have a top-up.' He slopped another inch of wine into Lucy's glass, just as Kristoff finished his phone call and stood up. 'Good, looks like he's done, so we can get some food. I could eat that dead stag.'

'Jonno!' exclaimed Kristoff, sidling over and wedging himself between the two of them so he could wrap his arms around both their shoulders.

'Hey, K-Dog!' boomed Jonno. 'How's the world of designer cock-jackets?'

'Always on the up, J-Dog,' said Kristoff with a grin, as Lucy did a tiny sick in her mouth. *K-Dog and J-Dog?* She could practically feel her vagina healing over.

'You need a drink?' asked Jonno, looking appalled at Kristoff's lack of beverage.

'I'm all good right now,' replied Kristoff. 'We've got a big day planned tomorrow. Maybe you can help me persuade Lucy to come with us to a bar in the mountains. She's being very non-committal.'

'Non-committal is Lucy's middle name,' said Jonno, chugging down more wine. 'In fact, she's—'

'What's the bar like?' interrupted Lucy, before Jonno told Kristoff about her lack of meaningful commitments.

'It's great,' said Kristoff. 'Run by this guy called Gunther and his family. Very cute, good pizza, live music sometimes, gets a little rowdy once the Jägermeister starts flowing. We all went up there last night, had a great time.'

Jonno turned to Lucy, his brow furrowed in fake confusion. 'Why wouldn't you want to go to a place like that?' he asked, his mouth twitching with laughter. 'You've never said no to a bar before.' She gave him a tight-lipped grin, imagining all the ways she was going to punish him for this.

'I can't really ski,' said Lucy, plastering on her most charming smile. In reality she'd never skied in her life, even on a dry ski slope, but Kristoff didn't need to know that.

'It's fine, there's a piste bus,' said Kristoff. 'It's got those caterpillar tracks, so it can take non-skiers up the mountain so they don't miss out on the party. You can meet us there.'

'Sounds great,' said Lucy, not very convincingly. Taking a tank up a mountain sounded terrifying.

'Excellent,' said Kristoff, flashing his most charming smile. 'I'm actually thinking about buying the place, I've always wanted my own mountain bar. It's got a two-bedroom apartment too, so I could work from there during the ski season, get some cool people to run it. Make it the best bar in the Alps.'

'Is it for sale?' asked Lucy.

'Everything is for sale,' replied Kristoff with a shrug. 'You just have to name the right price.'

What must it be like to have that much money and confidence? wondered Lucy. Not that she'd ever been short of money, exactly. When Leo had died, the company he worked for had paid out an employee life insurance policy of four times his annual salary, and it turned out he'd put Lucy's name on the beneficiary form on his first day. Her mother had taken this as some kind of personal attack, but her dad had smoothed things over as usual, then suggested that Lucy put the money towards her two-bed flat in Bedminster. She'd had various lodgers over the years, allowing her to overpay on her mortgage until it was gone. For the past two years she'd lived alone, putting her disposable income into savings for some unspecified future adventure that felt too terrifying to think about right now. But buying a mountain bar, just like that? Clearly she and Kristoff inhabited very different worlds. She realised he was still talking, and tuned back in.

'So on Saturday we work, but tomorrow we ski and drink and party,' he said.

'Surely it makes more sense the other way round?' said Sasha, joining them at the bar and kissing Kristoff on both cheeks. 'Hello, Kristoff.'

'Sasha! So good to see you,' said Kristoff. 'There's a crazy amount of snow forecast for tomorrow night; they may close some of the pistes. So we thought we'd have fun first and work later.'

'Fair enough,' said Sasha. She nodded at Jonno's refilled glass of wine, which was halfway to his mouth. 'Is that mine?'

Jonno sighed and silently handed it over, then turned to the barman and waved his hands for another bottle.

'Plans for tomorrow, everyone,' said Kristoff, clapping his hands to get their attention. The chatter died down, and Olly and Maya moved closer, accompanied by the three other members of the Titan team. 'Now all our guests have *finally* joined us.' Sasha glared at Olly, who looked like a man who'd been systematically disembowelled over many hours. Lucy glanced around to see if Nate had returned from wherever he disappeared to, but there was no sign of him.

'Actually, plans for tonight first – more food is on its way, so you guys can eat and relax. Tomorrow, we ski.'

'What's the weather forecast?' asked Thérèse.

'Some snow forecast tonight, so plenty of fresh powder tomorrow,' said Kristoff. 'We can explore all the best runs and make sure everyone has a great day.' He looked at each of them hopefully, and in that moment Lucy could see why women found him charming and irresistible. Here was a man who could afford to outsource every minute of this trip to various minions, but instead had decided to personally ensure everyone had a good time. His eyes settled briefly on Lucy, and she realised that she could probably capture the heart of a man like

Kristoff, if she wanted to. At least for the weekend, anyway. Luckily, she didn't want to, which made things considerably less complicated.

'I still can't ski,' she laughed.

'Neither can we,' said Olly quickly, gesturing to him and Maya. 'We're going to the spa, you can come with us.' Lucy pretended to nod enthusiastically, even though the thought of it gave her a headache. Olly and Maya were both fabulous fun individually, but putting them together was like adding a shot of prosecco to a Pornstar Martini. Overly sweet, unnecessarily extra. Also, if there was one thing she never did on the anniversary of Leo's death, it was go anywhere near water.

'Ooh, I would love a spa day,' said Thérèse. 'Count me in.'

'Sasha and I are definitely up for skiing,' said Jonno, grinning at Lucy like he was some kind of superhero who'd swooped in to save her. *Better late than never.*

'Paul, Nick and me too,' said Kristoff. Nick was Titan's lead product manager; an expert in innovative condom marketing that Titan had headhunted from the market leader. It was a source of great distress to Jonno that nobody called him Titanick, but maybe it was only the British who loved puns.

'What about your other guy?' asked Kristoff. 'The one with all the hair. Nate. Where's he gone?'

'He had to go back to the hotel,' said Lucy quickly. 'He had a headache.' She glanced at Sasha, who raised her eyebrows in question. Lucy had no idea why she was covering for Nate; it wasn't like she owed him anything. But he'd been thrown into this circus at the last minute, and it didn't seem right that he was in trouble before their first day had even ended, even if leaving without saying goodbye to your hosts was kind of rude.

'Hope he's OK,' said Kristoff dismissively. 'Can he ski?'

'Yeah,' said Lucy, at exactly the same time as Sasha. Lucy looked at her with interest, wondering how Sasha knew about Nate's on-piste proficiency. She'd never seen the two of them have so much as a conversation, although Nate had definitely worked in the agency's Paris office for a while. So maybe he and Sasha had been on another client trip together.

'Are you sure you don't want to try skiing, Lucy?' said Kristoff. 'I'm happy to organise a private instructor.'

'I'm fine,' said Lucy cheerfully. 'I might join these guys at the spa, or just go for a walk or something. Really happy just to be here.'

'We're all happy you're here,' said Kristoff, wafting his hand to take in the whole group. 'Who wants another drink?'

Lucy had barely been asleep a couple of hours before she woke up with a raging thirst, too much wine and Aperol having left her throat feeling like the lining of a budgie cage. There'd been a bottle of water in the room when she arrived earlier, but that was long gone. Lucy had no idea if the tap water was OK to drink – logic suggested that Swiss mountain water was probably cleaner and fresher than whatever came out of her taps in Bristol, but equally she wasn't willing to risk spending the weekend welded to her bathroom toilet.

She pulled on a hoodie and joggers, thinking there

might be some bottles in the breakfast room downstairs. The Alpina was more of a boutique B&B than a hotel, run by a local Swiss family. Thérèse had said they set out a fabulous continental breakfast in the morning and freshly baked cake in the afternoon, but otherwise expected the guests to go elsewhere for beer and food and entertainment. The corridor leading to the wooden staircase was dark and empty, heat blasting from the radiators as snow battered the windows. Kristoff had been right about fresh powder for tomorrow, but if this was 'a little snow' then she couldn't help wondering what bad weather might look like. Hopefully it would stop long enough for her to go for a walk, spend some time with her memories of Leo, and take some nice photos to show Jonno later.

There was a small light on in the breakfast room, guiding Lucy towards the dozen or so bottles of Evian on a counter by the wall. She took one and quickly unscrewed the lid, taking a minute to watch the snow through the terrace doors as she drank it. The fierce wind whipped it in all directions, and it was already banked a little way up the glass. She shivered, her bare feet cold on the tiled floor, then grabbed a second bottle before poking her head into the guest lounge next door. There was still a fire burning low in the hearth, with three whisky glasses and a poker set abandoned on the coffee table, so clearly some of the group had stayed up late. Not Sasha – she'd gone to bed at the same time as Lucy. And not Nate – he'd never reappeared after dinner. Probably Jonno and Kristoff, plus one of the others. Hopefully it was Thérèse and she'd hustled all their money.

Leo would have liked it here, thought Lucy. It was eleven years to the day since he'd died, but maybe if he'd been here they'd have been part of the group playing poker and drinking whisky until dawn. Or would they have drifted further and further apart, and been strangers by now? The first option was easier to stomach, but the last-woman-standing version of Lucy felt like a distant memory. *I miss you, Leo*, she said silently to the flickering flames, hoping her words would be carried on the wind to wherever Leo was now. *And I miss the version of your twin sister you took with you.*

She heard a noise on the landing and hastily wiped away her tears, then hurried back up the stairs. She was about to turn the corner onto the landing when she heard a click of a door, followed by a whispered male voice and a female laugh. Since nobody on this trip was supposed to be sharing a room, her instinctive reaction was to slam on the brakes, lean flat against the wall as close to the corner as possible without being visible, and listen hard.

'Try to get some sleep,' whispered the male voice. It sounded unmistakeably like Nate, which made her head spin a little. Whose room would he be in at one in the morning? And what if he came this way and saw her eavesdropping like a little sneak?

'See you tomorrow,' said the female voice. *Wait, what the fuck?* Was that . . . Sasha? Lucy couldn't resist easing her head away from the wall so she could glance around the corner, just in time to see Nate extract himself from Sasha's lingering embrace. Lucy watched in amazement as Sasha blew Nate a kiss and leaned against the doorframe with a sleepy smile as he hurried off down the corridor, still in his clothes from earlier. Lucy leaned back against the wall, her mind racing and her heart pounding. *What the hell have I just seen?*

She waited for the click of Sasha's door, then peeked around the corner again to check the coast was clear. Further away another door closed softly, presumably Nate going back into the room two doors down from hers. She tiptoed back down the corridor, processing the words she'd heard and the embrace and the blowing of a kiss and that over-familiar smile on Sasha's face. Nate had been fully dressed, but what had Sasha been wearing? In the shock of seeing her face, Lucy hadn't thought to register anything from the neck down. Something black, definitely. A dress? Or skimpy mountain-sex lingerie?

Lucy silently eased her door shut, then grabbed her phone and hurried into the bathroom to have a wee and message Jonno. She opened WhatsApp, then immediately closed it and put her phone on the edge of the bathtub. Sasha was on the agency Group Board, and if she was having a fling with one of the account managers, they'd almost certainly both lose their job. Also Sasha was probably a good ten or fifteen years older than Nate, although obviously that was nobody's business but theirs. But it wouldn't go down well, because women in leadership were supposed to be unimpeachably virtuous and never rock the boat.

Does Jonno know? Lucy considered the question for a moment, and decided that he almost certainly didn't. He'd NEVER have been able to keep it to himself; gossip that huge would send him into meltdown. Two pints on a Friday ensured Jonno spilled his guts on all kinds of things that Lucy shouldn't know – the artworker on the Pukka Paws account getting fired for watching Pornhub in his lunchbreak, the data analyst who was in treatment for a gambling habit, the big row over exec bonuses that Jonno had heard about from a mate in Head Office.

They told each other everything, but in the years they'd worked together, there'd never been anything this big and potentially explosive. She sighed heavily and silently apologised to him, because on this occasion, in the spirit of the sisterhood, she was going to pretend she'd seen nothing.

Lucy hurried back to bed and hunkered down under the duvet, rubbing her feet on the sheet to warm them up as she mentally reconstructed her view of Nate. She'd thought he was surly and dull – human wallpaper, Jonno had called him. But now he was reborn as Sasha's hot toyboy, leaving the party early so nobody would catch a whiff of the sexual tension and guess that he and Sasha were planning a late-night liaison. Lucy smiled to herself, ashamed to admit that it made Nate considerably more interesting. *It's always the quiet ones you have to watch.*

CHAPTER SEVEN

On Friday Lucy didn't come down to breakfast until after ten, hoping to avoid another entreaty to go skiing, or accompany Olly and Maya to the spa. She'd had a fitful sleep full of confusing dreams about Sasha and Nate and Leo, and neither option seemed any more appealing in daylight than it had the night before.

The first thing she noticed was the breathtaking view through the doors to the terrace. The window in her room looked out onto the back of another property, but here she could see the whole picture postcard, with the valley perfectly framing the distant Matterhorn. The sky was a dazzling blue, the village groaning under a heavy blanket of pristine snow. Lucy pulled out her phone and took some photos, briefly considering sending them to her mum, but knowing it would cause offence if she looked like she was having a nice time when Leo was still dead.

'Hey,' said a voice. Lucy turned away from the window, expecting to see some other stragglers, but there was only Nate.

'Hi,' she said, her heart sinking. She'd fallen asleep last night with a small feeling of admiration for Sasha and Nate for managing to work in the same company whilst having a secret affair, but she'd woken up with a whole bunch of questions. Lucy was certain that Sasha had been leading the account when he started work in the Bristol office, so is that how Nate got the job on Titan? If Sasha had smoothed the path for him, it was a huge betrayal, and presumably he was party to all kinds of pillow talk that gave him an advantage. In the cold light of day, it all seemed a lot more like Sasha and Nate were mugging off the whole team, and she'd planned to avoid him today so she didn't inadvertently let slip that she knew.

'Everyone else has gone,' he said.

Lucy nodded and pressed the cappuccino button on the coffee machine. It creaked and gurgled for a moment, then started spouting frothy milk. 'Why are you still here?'

'There's an avalanche warning,' said Nate with a shrug. 'I decided not to go.'

Lucy laughed, shielding her eyes from the dazzling sunshine through the window.

'Don't laugh,' snapped Nate. 'Half a metre of snow fell last night, and there's more coming later. The risk is level three, they've already closed all the off-piste.'

'Right,' said Lucy, resisting the urge to roll her eyes. 'But wouldn't they close the rest of the slopes if the risk was actually high?'

'They did some blasting this morning.' Lucy noticed that he was nervous and fidgety, like he'd already had too much coffee. *Or not enough sleep.*

'Blasting what?' she asked, draining half her mug in one go. She wasn't really very interested, but it felt polite to ask.

'The slopes. They use explosives to set off controlled avalanches, you could hear them earlier.' He rubbed at his face with one hand, his eyes repeatedly glancing at the window like they might be buried alive at any moment.

'OK . . . So what's the problem?'

Nate looked down, colour rushing to his cheeks as he hugged his arms around himself. 'It's nothing,' he said, standing up and shaking his head in frustration. 'Maybe I'm coming down with something. Probably picked it up on the plane.' He glared at Lucy, like she'd stuffed a mystery virus in her hand luggage and everything that was shit in his world was her fault. She bit back a snappy retort about how he wasn't the only one having a difficult day, because that implied she wanted to talk about it. But the last person she wanted to discuss Leo with right now was Nate Lambert. He might still be good-looking, but any intrigue he'd held for Lucy before last night was now well and truly gone. She'd been open to discovering a different side to Nate – hoping for it, even – but nothing she'd seen in the last twenty-four hours had convinced her he was anything other than dismissive and rude, not to mention that he was boosting his career off the back of a secret relationship. Sasha was welcome to him, frankly.

'I'll see you later,' he mumbled, grabbing his mug and leaving the room. Lucy let him go without comment, and turned her attention to the table of breakfast options.

By eleven Lucy was in need of some fresh air, so she zipped up a grey, knee-length duvet coat, pulled on a white bobble hat and added a pair of giant sunglasses for good measure. The whole look wasn't exactly Victoria Beckham does Chanel, but it would do for a walk around Zermatt in the sunshine. Everyone else was up the mountain and Nate was nowhere to be seen, so it wasn't like she was going to bump into anyone she knew.

The first thing Lucy discovered was that packed snow was deceptively slippery to walk on, even in the fur-lined boots she'd specifically bought for the trip. The fresh powder banked up on the footpath was impossible to navigate, so she picked her way along the edge of the ploughed road through the village like a child learning to ice skate.

'Hey, British woman, you need ice grips,' said an amused male voice. Lucy turned to see a man on the wooden decking of a coffee shop, leaning against a pillar as he smoked furiously. He was about forty, wearing a black ski jacket with silver trousers that hugged his muscular thighs like foil-wrapped hams. Dark hair, with a well-trimmed beard and white marks around his eyes from ski goggles. A local, then. Or maybe an instructor. The accent sounded like he spoke German, either way.

'How did you know I was British?' asked Lucy, pulling off her sunglasses and contemplating whether her hair was clean enough to shake it free in a sexy fashion. She'd sprayed half a can of dry shampoo on it this morning, so there was a reasonable chance it might freeze into whatever shape it was in when she removed the hat.

'Because you're wearing all the wrong clothes,' said the man with a wry smile. 'Jeans retain moisture, you need ice grips for your boots, and you will boil to death in that coat as soon as the sun touches you.'

'Well, thank you, that's super-helpful,' said Lucy snarkily. 'But I'm sure I'll be fine.'

'Don't be like that,' said the man, his smile broadening in a way that made Lucy's thighs tingle. Lovely teeth, despite the smoking habit. Why were hot European men so committed to tobacco? The rest of the world had given up years ago. 'Come and have lunch.'

'You've just insulted my outfit, and now you want to buy me lunch?' asked Lucy incredulously.

'No,' said the man. 'I want to *give* you lunch. This is my cafe. What's your name?'

'Lucy.' She put her sunglasses back on, hating herself for wishing she'd bothered with a bit of make-up.

'I'm Leo,' he said, holding open the door to what looked like a very cosy and welcoming cafe. 'Come in.'

Lucy's blood ran cold and a wave of guilt and pain washed over her. 'No . . . I won't, thank you,' she stuttered. 'I have to . . . I need to be . . .' She turned and hurried away as best she could on the slippery road, ignoring the man's calls of 'Hey! What did I say?' echoing behind her. She kept moving through a breathless blur of tears until the road met a small patch of pristine snow. She could hear a river running nearby, but couldn't see it beyond the dazzling blanket of white. Someone had cleared a narrow path to a wooden bench against a low wall, so she followed it and sat down, wishing she'd grabbed a coffee somewhere along the way.

You would have liked it here, Leo, thought Lucy, huddled into her coat and looking up at the awe-inspiring view of the Matterhorn. She'd briefly worked on a Toblerone pitch a few years back, and it felt strange to be looking at the real-life image from the packaging. The sun was now bathing the village in late-morning warmth, but she could see heavy clouds starting to roll over the tops of the mountains.

If I believed in heaven, I'd feel closer to my brother right now. But Lucy didn't believe, and if there WAS a heaven there was a decent chance that Leo wouldn't meet the entry criteria. He'd been a problematic teenager, self-managing his mental health issues with various substances over the years, which earned him some druggie friends that Lucy hadn't approved of. They'd been inseparable as children, but steadily grew apart as they got older – Lucy had stayed on at school for A levels, but Leo had gone to the local tech college to study graphic design, then moved to Bristol for a job. They texted a lot, and it seemed like maybe he'd got his life back on track with a really good career and no drugs. Until the day she'd been pulled out of a nineteeth-century poetry lecture at Liverpool University to learn that her brother had taken his own life. *A fall*, they'd called it, but nobody *fell* from Clifton Suspension Bridge in January. To this day she associated Elizabeth Barrett Browning with the most profound, bone-aching feeling of grief. *How do I love thee? Let me count the ways.*

Of course Lucy blamed herself, for not being there for him when Leo had needed her. They were *twins*, and protecting Leo had always felt like part of the job. She'd spent hours and hours re-reading their text exchanges from the weeks before, trying to spot signs she'd missed, but there was nothing. She was angry with him for ages, for not trusting her and hiding his feelings, something he'd never done when they were children. It took months of therapy to break down her absolute conviction that she could have saved him. Her parents had been through a whole other world of pain, of course, but they were a generation who didn't like to talk about things, particularly to strangers.

The sound of laughter brought her back to reality and she twisted round to glare at a group of skiers walking along the road behind her, trudging in heavy boots and helmets, skis over their shoulders. Skiing looked sexy, but also a lot of hard work, and she wasn't sure she could be bothered with all that equipment. Across to the left, at the bottom of the piste, a vehicle pulled to a stop. It looked like a minibus, but with tank tracks instead of wheels – this must be the piste bus that Kristoff had mentioned last night. The driver climbed out, then slid back a side door for three passengers. He nodded to them all as they disembarked, then lit a cigarette, his first exhalation creating a huge cloud in the cold, still air.

What would Leo do, right now? thought Lucy. *Today, I need to be more Leo.* She stood up decisively and tottered across the road, almost tanking it on a patch of black ice, until the man noticed her and watched her approach with amused interest.

'Are you the bus that goes up to the mountain bar?' she asked, hoping he spoke English, then remembered she was in Switzerland and everyone spoke English.

The man nodded. 'Half past eleven,' he said, checking his watch. 'I go in ten minutes.'

'Is it a decent place for lunch?'

The man nodded. 'Of course. I am Ulrich, my brother Gunther owns it. There will be live music later, lots of dancing.'

'Right,' said Lucy. 'And if I can't ski, how do I get back?'

'Is no problem,' shrugged Ulrich. 'Six euros to go up, ten euros if you also want to come back. Cash only. Last bus back is ten o'clock. After that you will probably have to sleep with Gunther.' He grinned, like this was a joke. Or maybe it wasn't.

'Hmm,' said Lucy, nodding thoughtfully. 'Look, I need to go back to the hotel first, grab some cash. Can you wait for me?'

Ulrich shrugged. 'You have ten minutes, then I have to go. But I will be here again in an hour.'

'Don't leave. I'll be back,' said Lucy, hurrying across the road. In her haste she'd forgotten about the patch of black ice and skated across it, her legs veering off in different directions and prompting a comedy whirling of limbs and squealing until she regained her balance.

'You need ice grips,' shouted Ulrich. Lucy muttered a torrent of swear words under her breath and made her way tentatively back to the hotel. She ran up to her room and grabbed twenty euros, then hurtled back downstairs to find Nate waiting at the bottom of the stairs.

'Are you OK?' he asked, taking in her pink cheeks and mad hair. She quickly pulled the bobble hat back on and took some calming breaths.

'I'm fine,' she said, wondering how she could get past him without sounding rude, then wondering why she cared when rudeness didn't seem to bother Nate one bit.

'I was thinking of finding somewhere for lunch later,' he said. 'Do you want to come with me?'

'Oh,' said Lucy, wishing he would stop blindsiding her like this. Either be a decent human being, or be consistently shitty – at least she'd know where she stood. 'I was actually just about to go up the mountain,' she said, patting her pockets to make sure she had everything. A phone, some euros, her Metro bank card and a Charlotte Tilbury lip balm. That would have to do.

'What's up the mountain?' asked Nate.

'A bar that Kristoff told me about,' said Lucy. 'There's a piste bus.'

Nate was silent, and the unasked question loomed between them. Lucy sighed inwardly and forced a smile. 'Would you like to come?'

Nate looked up at her from under those ridiculous eyelashes, and forcing herself into Sasha's Louboutins for a moment, Lucy could definitely see the appeal. If you could get past the rudeness, there was a quiet intensity to him. A certain charisma, like he'd perfected the art of separating himself from all the noise. Lucy had thought she'd have lunch alone, but actually maybe some company would be nice, even though Nate wasn't exactly her first choice. It was possible to spend too much time with your own thoughts, especially today.

'A bus?' he asked, looking unsure.

Lucy nodded. 'Yeah, it's perfectly safe.' She wasn't entirely sure of that, but they needed to get moving. 'I've just been talking to Ulrich the driver and it leaves in –' she checked her watch, '– four minutes.'

Nate pressed his lips together and briefly closed his

eyes, like he was trying to make some kind of life-changing decision. 'OK,' he said decisively, standing up and dropping his book onto the table. 'I'll grab my coat and boots.'

'Do you have ice grips?' said Lucy. 'It's like Bambi on ice out there.'

'Of course,' said Nate, his brows furrowed in confusion. 'It's January in the Alps. You'd be crazy not to have ice grips.'

'*Fucksake*,' muttered Lucy as Nate disappeared up the stairs. She hovered in the doorway, glancing at the clock on her phone and hoping Ulrich's timekeeping wasn't up to Swiss watch standards. Nate was back in less than a minute, and quickly followed her out into the snow.

'We need to hurry,' said Lucy, picking her way along the edge of the road.

'Where's the bus?' asked Nate.

'At the end of this road,' said Lucy, squealing as she lost her footing and skittered backwards, her arms windmilling. 'Christ, these boots are rubbish.'

'Come on, get on my back,' laughed Nate.

'Your back?'

'I'll piggyback you, or we'll never make it,' he said, turning away from her and holding out his arms. She hesitated for a second, then yanked her coat up around her waist and jumped onto his back, wrapping her arms around his neck as he hooked his hands under her thighs.

'Let's go,' said Nate, starting to run along the edge of the road through the village, the metal studs on his boots digging hard into the packed snow. Lucy let out a nervous shriek as he jogged faster, dodging around piles of snow and bollards and lamp posts and tourists. People grinned at them as they bobbed past, and Nate's breath created plumes in the air as he kept going, holding her legs firmly around his waist so she didn't jiggle up and down too much. She gripped tighter around his neck, trying not to strangle him as she started to giggle at the juvenile stupidity of it. It was the kind of thing Leo would have done, and today was all about being more Leo.

'There's the bus!' shouted Lucy, as they reached the end of the road and crossed over to the bottom of the piste. Several people were still boarding, so Nate slowed down and gently lowered Lucy to the ground.

He turned to look at her, his cheeks pink and his expression triumphant. 'We made it.'

'Yes, we did,' said Lucy, her feeling of childlike euphoria now battling her need for a wee after all that jigging about. Who *was* this complex, unfathomable man, who was afraid of the mountains and yet had the balls to risk a relationship with senior management? Who was moody and rude and left the party early, but clearly still had a playful side? If there was one thing Lucy was determined to get out of this unexpected lunch, it was to find out more about what made Nate Lambert tick.

CHAPTER EIGHT

Wouldn't it be ironic if today was the day my parents lost their other child, thought Lucy as the piste bus tracked along the edge of a precipitous drop into the valley below. *Awful for them, but at least they'd be able to do all their grieving on one day.*

She'd thought that taking the window seat would be a generous gesture towards Nate, who looked entirely unsure about the whole business the minute he saw Ulrich and climbed aboard his rickety tank/bus hybrid, particularly as the blue skies and sunshine were quickly disappearing behind the heavy cloud cover that was moving in on a brisk wind. But within minutes of setting off, Lucy was vowing never to be the Good Person again – Ulrich drove like he'd previously only ever driven a bumper car at the fairground, with a complete disregard for skiers, pedestrians, trees and the possibility of plunging into the snowy abyss. Hanging off the edge of the mountain seemed to be the norm, as was turning corners on the banked-up edge of the piste so the bus listed sideways like it was on a rollercoaster.

As Ulrich responded to the rapidly diminishing visibility by putting on a pair of *Top Gun* aviator shades and lighting a cigarette with no hands on the wheel, Lucy started thinking about who might read the eulogy at her funeral. Jonno, ideally, but her mum would almost certainly pull rank and use it as an opportunity to talk about Leo instead. Would Anthony and Marco sit together? How would they even know she was dead? Maybe such a dramatic mountain crash ending would make the local news, so they'd find out that way.

Meanwhile, Nate kept his eyes closed throughout, sitting bolt upright with his hands gripping the seat in front, a visible sheen of sweat on his forehead. Eventually all the windows steamed up with the warmth of their combined bodies, obscuring the view and making the whole experience marginally less petrifying. She took deep, slow breaths, rubbed her sweaty palms on her non-absorbent coat, and prayed for it all to be over.

By the time they pulled up outside the bar fifteen minutes later, Lucy was actively trying to stop herself being sick and Nate was now wide-eyed, pale and clammy. It was also snowing heavily, but not in a delightful, winter-wonderland way where you stick your tongue out to catch snowflakes and shoot cute videos. At this altitude it was sideways shards of ice in a biting wind, leaving no time to fully appreciate the stone building and wooden terrace nestled in the trees at the side of the piste. The sign over the door said *Die Guntherhütte*, but Lucy wasn't hanging about to admire it.

'You can breathe now,' said Lucy, as they bustled through the jumble of skis and poles on the racks outside into the steamy warmth of the bar and started to shed layers of clothing.

'That was horrible,' said Nate, his voice hollow with fear. 'We're not leaving for a long time, right?'

'No,' said Lucy with a smile. 'I thought we could have

some lunch, stay here for the afternoon, and get pissed enough that the trip back down won't seem so bad.'

'I am totally on board with this idea,' said Nate, his mouth twitching into a feeble smile. The bar was already busy with an early lunchtime crowd eating pizzas and drinking tall glasses of beer, but the other passengers from the bus grabbed the last tables, leaving only the high stools at the bar. They bagged two, and Lucy left Nate in charge of swooping on the next available table whilst she went to the bathroom. The combined jiggling of the piggyback and the bus ride had left her bladder ready to burst, and it was hard not to let out an audible sigh of relief when she finally sat down on the loo. Even the freezing cold seat couldn't spoil her moment of bliss, although her reflection in the mirror afterwards came close. She looked, by any standards, like she'd just rolled out of bed, which was fine earlier when she was out for a walk, but now she wished she'd made more effort.

'What do you drink?' asked Nate when she returned to the bar stools.

'Right now I'd drink lighter fluid, just to forget,' said Lucy, holding out her hands to see if the colour had returned to her knuckles. 'But white wine is fine.'

Nate flagged down the man behind the bar, who came over with two lunch menus. 'You came on the bus?' he asked, and Lucy realised this was probably the eponymous Gunther, brother of psychotic Ulrich and potential future millionaire once he'd done a deal with Kristoff for this bar.

'How can you tell?' asked Nate.

'It is the only way to get here if you are not on skis,' said Gunther. 'Which you are not dressed for. And also you look like you have both visited the gates of hell.' He finished on a booming, manic laugh, and Lucy wondered if the whole family was, in fact, insane.

'Two glasses of white wine,' said Nate, giving Gunther a deadpan stare. 'Large ones.'

'No problem,' said Gunther, leaving the menus and grabbing two wine glasses from the rack above his head. Lucy looked around the cosy bar, not much bigger than the average semi-detached house, clad in yellow pine with red curtains over the tiny windows. It was blissfully warm, with a huge wood-burning stove in one corner, draped in steaming hats and gloves. Packed out, you could maybe squeeze fifty people in here, and the atmosphere would be intimate and fun. She could totally see Kristoff buying it, filling it with mood lighting, stuffed animal heads and designer vodkas, and turning it into an exclusive Alpine hotspot for the rich and beautiful.

'Here,' said Nate, handing Lucy a huge glass of wine. She smiled her thank you and took a gulp, watching the sideways snow through the window for a moment and wondering if there was any chance the sun would come back out later so they could sit on the terrace. At the moment that looked unlikely, but maybe steamy warmth and good wine was better. A red-headed woman in her thirties sat at the end of the bar, giving directions to an older man setting up a keyboard on a stand in the opposite corner to the fire. He propped a guitar against the wall and unpacked a microphone. The sticker on the keyboard read *Night Fever*.

'This is a cool place,' said Nate, holding up his glass. '*Salut.*'

'I'm sorry about the nightmare journey,' said Lucy, clinking his glass. It felt unfair to remind him, but they had to talk about something. The idea of sitting here in awkward silence for the next couple of hours felt far worse, and Lucy could already feel the regret kicking in.

'It's fine.' Nate shrugged. 'We're here now. Do you think we'll actually have to do any work tomorrow?'

'Hmm,' said Lucy, taking another slug of wine, glad of a new subject. 'Depends on how pissed Kristoff gets later.'

'When are the rest of them coming?' asked Nate. Lucy felt a wave of annoyance as she realised that Nate had probably only come up here in the hope of seeing Sasha, and for him this lunch was just about killing time before the others arrived. But if that was the case, why agree to come so early? It was barely twelve, the others might not arrive for hours. And last night he'd left the bar early, presumably to *avoid* seeing Sasha. Maybe he was already planning their getaway for alone time back at the hotel, leaving everyone else safely up the mountain.

'No idea,' she muttered grumpily, spotting a group at a booth in the far corner standing up to put on their coats. 'Quick, grab that.' Nate jumped off his stool like it had just caught fire, and positioned himself next to the table before the couple waiting by the door had even noticed the ripple of movement. They glared malevolently as Lucy and Nate exchanged pleasantries with the outgoing group and slid into the empty booth, then plodded over in their ski boots to take the now-vacant stools at the bar.

'Nice work,' said Lucy, piling up the dirty plates and beer glasses so the waitress could clear them. 'This is a great table.'

'We could ask those people to join us,' said Nate, cowering under the ongoing stares from the bar that Lucy was ignoring. 'There's room for all of us.'

'Absolutely not,' said Lucy, trying not to take offence at his apparent unwillingness to be alone with her, and considering for the first time that her aversion to Nate Lambert might be entirely mutual. The idea made her uncomfortable, not to mention mortified that it hadn't previously occurred to her. Was she really that arrogant, to assume that she was instantly, delightfully likeable? It wasn't like she had a huge crowd of friends hanging off her every word. She spread her arms along the top of the curved bench, feeling suddenly cold, and grateful for the heat pumping out of the vents under the windows. 'Look, another table is leaving. It's fine.'

Nate anxiously watched the new table dance as Lucy picked up the menu. The food options were carb and grease heavy, which suited her just fine. Whatever she ate and drank this afternoon would be burned off through terror-fuelled bus adrenaline later.

'I wonder if they're having fun skiing,' said Nate, looking worriedly out of the window at the driving snow. 'The weather looks awful, I hope they're OK.'

'They'll be in another bar, I expect,' said Lucy. 'The Titan guys won't take stupid risks; Kristoff is worth too much money, and Jonno's wife would kill him. He's got two kids.'

'I bet Kristoff is a good skier,' said Nate.

'Jonno is too,' said Lucy. 'I'm not sure about Sasha.' She looked up at Nate to see if there was any reaction, but he didn't blink. Presumably their relationship had been going on for a while, so he'd had plenty of practice at playing dumb.

'I wonder how Olly and Maya are getting on with Thérèse at the spa,' he mused.

'Hello,' said the waitress, beaming at them both as she shovelled all the dirty plates and glasses onto a tray and swiftly wiped down the table with a damp cloth. 'My name is Chantal, what can I get you?' She was in her twenties and heartbreakingly pretty in a wholesome, mountain-girl way, with huge brown eyes and similar colouring to Gunther and Ulrich, which made Lucy wonder if she was Gunther's daughter. Kristoff had said something last night about this place being run by a family, so that would make sense.

They ordered pizzas, then Chantal gestured to their empty wine glasses. 'Another glass?' she asked, her gaze fixed on Nate like Lucy wasn't even there. Lucy ignored her, instead watching a small child clomp across the room in ski boots and open a cupboard full of board games.

'Maybe a bottle?' replied Nate with a shrug.

Lucy smiled, and decided that this afternoon might actually be OK.

'Do you have any family?' asked Nate, clearly trying to make small talk and picking the worst possible question. Lucy had navigated it many times before, but today it felt like an extra kick in the guts. Maybe this was why she'd always spent Leo's anniversary with her parents – to avoid conversations like this.

'My parents live in Croydon,' she said, trying to sound upbeat and normal. 'I have a brother, but I don't see much of him.' Time had taught Lucy not to deny having a sibling, because being an only child prompted a whole other conversation that quickly descended into outright lies and fabrication. An estranged brother was pretty common, and not very interesting.

'You're not close to your brother?' asked Nate, his eyes widening.

No, thought Lucy, her head spinning as she took another slug of wine. *This absolutely cannot be the thing we talk about.*

'It's no big deal,' she said dismissively, not wanting to raise a red flag that would prompt further questions. 'We don't have much in common.'

'He's not like you?' asked Nate.

'What do you mean?' demanded Lucy, looking up at him sharply. Did Nate *know* about Leo? That she'd had a twin? She felt cornered, and a hot feeling of panic rushed to her cheeks.

'Oh,' said Nate, clearly taken aback by the forcefulness of her response. 'I . . . just wondered if you and he were alike.'

'What do you mean?' asked Lucy. 'What am I like?'

He glanced at her for a moment, clearly trying to work out how to answer when the conversation had taken a weird turn. 'Interesting,' he said, lowering his eyes to his glass and blushing a little. 'Talented. Beautiful.'

Lucy laughed in surprise, not sure if Nate was taking the piss. He barely looked at or spoke to her from one day to the next, and *now* she was talented and beautiful?

'I'm serious,' said Nate. 'You're a really interesting woman.' Lucy noted that he'd dialled back on beautiful and talented, which made her wonder if he'd actually ever said those words out loud in the first place. Maybe her inner narcissist had subconsciously added them in?

'And yet you've never shown the smallest amount of interest up to now,' she said, giving him a challenging look. 'That's more interesting, don't you think?'

'Maybe,' said Nate. 'I guess we've never had the chance to get to know each other. You know what the office is like. You spend more than five minutes a day talking to a colleague, and everyone assumes you're sleeping together.'

That's rich, coming from you, thought Lucy, wondering if he'd used this guileless, just-making-conversation charm offensive on Sasha. It didn't *feel* like he was feeding her lines, but that was all the more reason to be on her guard. She'd always had a friendly and mutually respectful relationship with Sasha, but you definitely wouldn't want to get on her bad side.

'Like you and Jonno, for instance,' added Nate.

'We're definitely not sleeping together,' replied Lucy quickly, rolling her eyes.

'I know that,' said Nate patiently. 'But people gossip about it anyway. It's something to talk about.'

'Well, it's absolutely not true.'

'I'm just saying that you're not easy to get to know. If I tried, everyone would assume I had an ulterior motive.'

'And you don't?' Lucy raised her eyebrows in question.

'No,' said Nate, draining his glass and reaching for the bottle. 'I definitely don't.'

'Do you play board games?' said Lucy, conscious this was a whiplash change of subject but needing a way out of this conversation. 'We could play one while we're waiting for our food.' *And avoid talking*, she thought.

'Sure.' Nate slid out of the booth and opened the door to the games cupboard. It was well stocked and orderly, with lots of games that Lucy had heard of, plus a few she hadn't. 'No word games though,' he said emphatically. 'I am not playing Scrabble with someone who writes for a living.'

'Can you play Rummikub?' said Lucy, leaning over to peer into the cupboard. 'I haven't played for ages.'

'Sure,' said Nate. He carefully extracted the box from the stack and sat back at the table. 'This is numbers. I can do numbers.'

It was Leo's favourite, thought Lucy, as Nate opened the box and started to lay out the tiles. They'd played a lot as kids, but Lucy had more focus and patience than her brother, and she usually won. Leo would make up extra rules in the hope of beating her by stealth, but that rarely worked. She looked out of the window at the swirling snow, wondering if it was a more respectful honouring of Leo's memory to let Nate beat her, or to kick his arse six times in a row.

'Lucy?' asked Nate.

She turned to look at him, realising she was smiling. 'Sorry, miles away.'

'You ready?' He handed her the stand to put her tiles on.

Lucy took a deep breath. 'Yeah,' she said. 'I'm ready.'

CHAPTER NINE

'A decider?' said Nate hours later, when they were three games all. Nate had a quick mind and was a good strategist, so they'd been closely matched. There'd been a break for pizza and another bottle of wine had been drunk in the process, which had definitely impacted their ability to spot opportunities for using up their tiles. But it had meant they hadn't had to make difficult conversation and, all things considered, it had been a good afternoon. Most importantly, Lucy felt like her brother would have approved of her choices on Leo Memorial Day. Better than eating grey beef and watery gravy in a bleak pub in Croydon, anyway.

Lucy's phone vibrated on the table, and she fumbled as she tried to pick it up. She was, by any standards, really quite drunk.

'It's Jonno,' she said. 'I'll find out where they all are.' She stood up and tottered unsteadily towards the toilets, answering the phone on her way. 'Hey,' she said, 'hang on a second.' For the first time she noticed that the bar was nearly empty – the only people left were two men who'd been sat in front of them on the death bus, along with Gunther, Chantal the waitress, an older woman who'd just emerged from the kitchen, who Lucy assumed was Gunther's wife, and the couple who'd been setting up

Night Fever's instruments earlier. There'd been no music yet, but right now there was hardly anyone to play for.

'Hey,' said Lucy, closing the toilet door behind her and locking it. 'I'm back. Where are you?'

'We're at the hotel,' said Jonno. 'The others are back from the spa and we've just wiped out an entire chocolate cake. Where are you?'

'I'm in a mountain bar with Nate, the one Kristoff was talking about last night. The bus up here made me shit my pants. Why aren't you here?'

'They closed all the pistes an hour ago. It's a total whiteout, didn't you notice? You should head back.'

'Shit, OK,' said Lucy. 'We'll get the next bus.' The idea of getting in Ulrich's puke-wagon in this weather filled her with terror, but it wasn't like they had other options.

'How are you and French Exit getting on?' asked Jonno, and Lucy could hear the amusement in his voice. 'Are you having a steamy Alpine romance?'

'No,' said Lucy, clamping the phone between her ear and her shoulder as she unbuttoned her jeans and sat down. The seat was still freezing cold, and her thighs instantly came out in goosebumps.

'Not even a snowy blowy?'

'You're such a poet,' laughed Lucy. 'And people wonder why I'm the copywriter.' She rattled a length of toilet paper off the roll and held the phone with one hand as she twisted round to wipe.

'Wait, are you having a piss?'

'Yes,' said Lucy. 'Don't pretend you've never called me whilst holding your dick.'

'No, but that was very different,' laughed Jonno. 'I thought we'd promised never to mention it.'

'We'll be back down in a bit,' said Lucy with a grin. 'Save me some cake.' She ended the call and pulled up her jeans, then washed her hands and hurried back to the bar. Nate was turning all the Rummikub tiles face down, ready for another game.

'Jonno just told me that all the pistes are closed,' she said, not sure if this was normal for a ski resort in January.

'Really?' said Nate, looking alarmed. 'Since when?'

'An hour ago, due to bad weather, apparently. They're all back at the hotel. We should probably head back.' She walked over to the bar, where Gunther was loading glasses into the dishwasher. 'We've just heard that all the pistes are closed.'

'Yes,' he said. 'Visibility is poor, it's not safe for skiing.'

'Why didn't you tell us? We need to get the bus back.'

'It's fine,' he shrugged. 'You looked like you were having a nice time, so there was no rush. The kitchen staff have all gone already, and Ulrich will be here in half an hour to take the rest of you back to the village.' He nodded towards the corner where the band had set up earlier. 'There's no point in these guys being here if we have no customers this evening.'

Lucy glanced over and saw the man packing away his keyboard while the woman collapsed the microphone stand. Neither seemed particularly fussed about the dramatic weather outside or the prospect of Ulrich's death bus, so maybe this kind of thing was normal after all. Lucy's only experience of snow was in the UK, where three inches brought the entire country to a standstill.

She looked at the fuzz of flakes on the window, and was suddenly reminded of a day when she and Leon were eight or nine, when school had been closed and their dad had unearthed an old wooden sledge from the garage. He'd dusted off the cobwebs and polished up the rails, then loaded the whole family into the car and carefully driven half an hour to Colley Hill near Reigate, on the basis that if you were going to go sledging, you should pick the best possible spot.

All the other kids were using cheap plastic sledges or makeshift tea trays and bin bags, but Lucy and Leo had a proper sledge that could seat both of them at once and rocketed down the hill in a perfect trajectory. After hours of breathless, adrenaline-fuelled fun, their mum had pulled homemade flapjacks and a flask of hot chocolate out of her bag, and they'd passed the cup between them in the steamy warmth of the car. Lucy couldn't remember a more perfect adventure – it was a story that was often told on this day, and for a tiny, fleeting moment she wished she was with her mum and dad.

'So will you and Chantal stay here?' she asked, snapping herself back into the room.

'Of course,' said Gunther with a beaming smile. 'And my wife, Monica.' He gestured to the older woman who Lucy had seen coming out of the kitchen earlier. 'We are a family, and this is where we live. This kind of thing happens all the time.'

Lucy nodded, feeling vaguely reassured, and sat back

down with Nate, who was now packing the game away into the box. 'You OK?' she asked.

'Yeah,' said Nate, although he looked a bit clammy, the sheen on his forehead she'd noticed on the bus having reappeared. 'Not really looking forward to the trip back down, if I'm honest.'

'Me neither,' said Lucy, wondering how she'd ever imagined that a carb-heavy lunch and a bottle of wine would help. Now she just felt drunk, nervous AND sick, which didn't feel like an ideal combination for an out-of-control tank heading downhill in a snowstorm.

There was a sudden boom that rose up through the floor into the back of Lucy's teeth, followed by a resounding crack like a thunderclap that made her jump out of her skin. It morphed into a deep, slow rumble that shook the building from its very foundations. Lucy and Nate both froze and stared wide-eyed at each other, clutching the shaking table in fear and confusion. It continued for a few seconds, then stopped.

'What the fuck was that?' gasped Nate, swaying sideways like he might faint.

'Avalanche,' said Gunther, as six pairs of eyes all fixed on him, Monica and Chantal. 'A big one.'

'Seriously?' Nate pressed his hands to his cheeks, his eyes wide with fear. 'What should we do? Do we need to leave?'

'Please, it's OK,' said Gunther, holding up his hands. 'We are safe here; there is nothing above us but sky. There is no danger.'

'Do you think anyone could still be out there?' asked one of the men from the bus. He spoke English, but his accent was German, or maybe Dutch. He peered out of the window, now an iron-grey wall as the light faded into the late afternoon.

'No,' said Monica calmly. 'They closed all the pistes over an hour ago, so everyone will be safely back in the village by now.'

'Apart from us,' said Nate, looking pale and haunted.

'There are other huts on the mountain, people who live up here through the winter,' said Monica, her voice soothing and relaxed. 'Avalanches are not unusual in January. We plan for these things. Please don't worry.'

'So what happens now?' asked Lucy, sick with worry. Her stomach was sloshing with wine and pizza, and she could already feel a queasy hangover setting in. The prospect of being featured in a Channel 5 disaster-documentary about dramatic mountain rescues definitely wasn't helping.

Gunther smiled and rubbed his straggly beard. 'We wait to hear from the mountain safety people. They know we are here and will call us.' He picked up his phone from the bar and waved it. 'Look, we still have Wi-Fi. It's fine.'

Lucy instinctively picked up her phone to check – she was still connected to the bar Wi-Fi. 'Will Ulrich definitely be able to take us back down, do you think?' she asked. Much as she'd had an unexpectedly nice afternoon, she'd feel a lot less exposed once she was back down in the village.

'There will be no buses until they have said it is safe,' said Monica, picking up her phone. 'Ulrich is down in the village, I can see his location on here. He will wait to hear from the safety people, then let us know.'

'Have another drink,' said Gunther, holding out his arms like they were all congregants at his church of wine and pizza. 'Relax, enjoy the adventure, make some new friends. We will let you know when we have news.'

Lucy slumped back into her seat, her heart rate slowly returning to normal and the tension easing from her body. This whole situation felt so surreal, and she had no idea what to do. She looked at Nate, who was staring at his hands, his eyes wide and his lips silently moving. She watched him carefully for a minute, realising that in this moment he reminded her of her brother. The same folding inwards of his body, and the twitching, restless hands. It also explained the strange mood swings out of nowhere, like he didn't trust the world to keep him safe.

'Shit, I've just realised,' she said softly. 'You have an anxiety disorder.'

Nate gave her a fierce look, like he thought she might be mocking him. She smiled softly and held his gaze, hoping he'd see that she understood.

'Yes,' he said. His voice was barely more than a whisper.

'Why didn't you tell me?' she asked.

Nate shrugged and swallowed hard. 'It's low level, mostly, and circumstantial – day to day I'm usually fine, but it's hardly a conversation starter.' He half-smiled, and Lucy could see that talking was helping.

'What circumstances make it worse?' asked Lucy. It felt important to know, considering their situation, and it definitely wasn't her first time at this particular rodeo.

'Airports and flying are hard,' said Nate. 'I've got

some calming stuff I can listen to when I travel. Social situations are a whole other thing.'

Hence the headphones in the airport and him leaving the party early, thought Lucy, kicking herself for not spotting it sooner.

'This morning the mountains were too big, the sun was too bright and the snow was too deep. I definitely should have read the signs and stayed at the hotel.' Nate forced a laugh, like he was trying to brush it off as nothing, but Lucy knew it wasn't nothing.

'I'm sorry,' she said, feeling inexplicably guilty. She'd been so caught up in her own dramas that she'd entirely failed to notice that Nate was struggling. And even worse, she'd dismissed his strange behaviour as rudeness, when it was clear he was only trying to hold it together.

'Just keep breathing, OK?' she said gently. The bar felt quiet after the bustle of lunch – Gunther was speaking in a low voice to the man and woman from the band, and the two tall men at the next table were hunched over their phones. Right on cue, Lucy's phone vibrated and she snatched it up. It was Jonno, on a WhatsApp video call.

'Hey,' he said as she answered it. He looked pale and worried. 'I'm with Sasha and Kristoff. You guys OK? There's been an avalanche.'

'I know, we heard it,' said Lucy. 'The building was actually shaking. But we're fine, we're still in the bar.'

'Thank fuck for that,' said Jonno, rubbing his hand over his face. 'We were worried you might already be on the bus coming back down.'

'No, we're still here. We may have to wait a while, though.'

'I've just spoken to the owner of our hotel; they're pretty sure nobody was in the path. They closed the mountain an hour ago.'

'Yeah, the landlord here said the same.' Lucy breathed, relieved that they weren't going to be a sidebar in a Swiss mountain tragedy. Survivor's guilt and PTSD were both familiar territory, but she could do without another two years of therapy.

'Is Nate with you?' It was Sasha's voice.

'I'm here,' said Nate, as Lucy turned her phone so he was on camera. He kept his voice steady, and Lucy wondered if Sasha knew about his anxiety. She must do; it wasn't the kind of thing you could hide for very long, and Lucy had worked it out within hours. 'We're both fine,' he added. 'Everything's cool.'

'Keep us posted, yeah?' That was Kristoff's voice, before he appeared on camera looking like a chiselled god in black ski gear. 'The bar will be open when you get back.'

'They're literally IN a bar,' said Jonno, and Lucy could hear his eyes rolling even though the camera was still on Kristoff.

'We'll let you know as soon as we're on our way,' said Lucy. 'Don't have any fun without us.' She ended the call and looked at Nate, wondering what was going on inside his head right now.

'Can we keep talking?' he asked.

'Sure,' said Lucy with a soft smile. Clearly nothing was going to happen for a while, and she owed him this. 'What would you like to talk about?'

'Tell me how you know about anxiety disorders,' said Nate.

Lucy looked away, wondering how much to tell him about Leo. A few hours ago she'd successfully deflected the conversation, but an entire mountain had shifted between them since then. They'd gone from being colleagues who barely knew each other, to two people who were sharing an avalanche experience. By any standards, they were definitely no longer strangers.

'What do you mean?'

'You don't seem like a very anxious person,' said Nate with a shrug. 'Apart from earlier on the bus, when you looked like you were making plans for your own funeral.'

'I was,' said Lucy, smiling weakly. 'I was wondering who might say nice things about me during the service.'

'Lots of people, I should think. But if you're not sure, you could write your own eulogy in advance. I'm sure you'd do an amazing job.'

Lucy said nothing, registering the compliment. She realised with surprise that in some ways she wanted to talk about it, because Nate of all people would probably understand. But equally this was something she *never* talked about, even to Jonno. It was hard to know where to start.

'Hey,' said Nate, his warm hands suddenly on hers.

Lucy looked up, suddenly aware that her cheeks were wet with tears. So much for maintaining composure. She searched for a deflection, but all the potential lies felt bitter on her tongue. 'I don't have anxiety,' she said, taking a deep breath as she gently extracted her hand. 'But I know someone who did. My brother Leo . . . my twin brother, actually.'

Nate's eyes widened, the way people's always did when they found out. 'Wow, your brother is your twin?'

'Mmm,' said Lucy, dabbing at the pizza crumbs on the table so she didn't have to look at him. Was she really going to talk about this? With Nate Lambert, of all people. Apparently so. 'He died eleven years ago. Today, actually.' The words rushed out so fast, she wondered for a moment if Nate had heard them.

'Shit,' he gasped, visibly shocked. 'Lucy. I'm so sorry.'

'It's OK,' said Lucy, even though it was very, very far from being OK. 'He'd have thoroughly approved of this.'

Nate smiled, visibly relieved that he hadn't put his foot in it. 'Which bit?'

'All of it, probably,' she said, feeling the warmth return to her fingers. 'The wine, the food, the board games, the drama.'

'How old was he?' asked Nate.

'Twenty-one,' said Lucy. 'He'd have seen all this as a big adventure.' *And so would I, once upon a time*, she thought to herself.

'Fuck, that's so young,' said Nate. 'How did he . . . if you don't mind me asking?'

Lucy took a deep breath. 'Can we not talk about that? I'm not being rude, but it's a long story and today is . . . a difficult one for me.'

'Of course.' Nate held up his hands. 'I'm really sorry.' He looked at her and smiled, and it communicated warmth and solidarity and understanding. Nate wasn't dumb; he'd probably filled in the gaps in this story already. But she appreciated him backing off nonetheless.

'Don't be,' said Lucy. 'But what I will say is that Leo suffered from anxiety since we were kids, and I learned to recognise the signs. Sometimes it was low level, other times full-blown panic attacks.'

'And you were the one who could talk him down.'

'Yes.' There was an awkward silence as pain knifed through Lucy's chest. *Apart from that one time when it really mattered.*

They were quiet for a moment, and Lucy wasn't sure where to take the conversation next. Telling him about Leo had crossed a line into a strange kind of intimacy – Jonno was the only other person at the agency who knew she'd lost a brother, but any questions had been shut down very early in their friendship. She glanced at Nate, wondering what was going through his head after the avalanche. If Leo had been anything to go by, it could be anything from racing thoughts of impending doom to flashing lights and sirens.

They both looked up as the woman with the guitar propped herself on a bar stool and strummed a few chords to tune up, then launched into a song. Lucy listened to the first verse, then started to laugh, hoping she could distract Nate from the motorway pile-up happening in his brain. 'Jesus, really?'

'What it is?' asked Nate, looking around for whatever new disaster the mountain was throwing in their direction.

'She's singing "Tragedy". By the Bee Gees. Or Steps, if you're our generation.'

'Christ,' said Nate, rubbing his pale face with his hands. 'Is this appropriate right now?'

'I would say . . . definitely not,' smirked Lucy, picking up the wine bottle and shaking the last few drops into her glass. Right now, sobering up felt like the worst idea ever. The woman delivered the chorus in a breathy voice at funereal pace, like the acoustic John Lewis advert version of a Bee Gees classic literally nobody asked for.

'This situation is too much,' said Nate to nobody in particular, his voice wavering and his fists clenching into white knuckles. He closed his eyes as his breathing came faster. 'I don't . . . I can't.'

'Hey, it's OK,' said Lucy quickly, resting her hand on his arm in the hope that she could provide some kind of anchor before he spiralled. 'Just breathe, OK?'

Nate nodded, letting Lucy hold his other hand tightly in hers. He was freezing.

'Tell me what's real right now,' she said softly. She'd done this many times with Leo as a teenager, grounding him in what he could see and hear and smell and touch, and not the terrifying potential outcomes that fought for space in his head.

Nate opened his eyes and looked at her. 'I can't—'

'Yes, you can,' said Lucy gently. 'Come on. Tell me what's real.'

'OK,' said Nate with a deep breath, and Lucy knew it wasn't the first time he'd done this exercise either. 'This bar. This . . . cushion I'm sitting on, and the wooden bench underneath, and the table, and the box for the board game. And two empty wine glasses.'

'Good,' said Lucy. 'What else?'

'This sweatshirt I'm wearing, and my hands, which are cold.' He held out his other shaking hand, and Lucy pressed them both between hers, gently massaging them to get the blood flowing. Nate said nothing for a moment, his gaze fixed on her fingers. Lucy tried to tune in to what was happening in his head, and hoped this was helping.

'Keep going,' she said.

Nate took another deep breath. 'It smells of pizza and woodsmoke and pine in here. And you're definitely real.' He smiled softly, and Lucy felt herself blush from the intensity of his gaze. 'You haven't brushed your hair today, and you don't have any make-up on. You have very green eyes, though.'

'No time for hair and make-up this morning,' laughed Lucy, loosening her grip on his hands but not letting go. 'Does that feel any better? We can carry on?'

'Stay there for a minute,' said Nate, closing his eyes and taking a few slow and deep breaths. Lucy said nothing for a while, just watched him breathe as the blood started to flow back into his fingers and the colour returned to his cheeks. 'Thank you,' he said weakly. 'That helped a lot.'

'Andrea, sing a different one,' said Gunther, as the singer dragged out the final notes in a tortured, angsty fashion. Her partner joined her at the keyboard and leaned over to mutter something, which prompted a look of grim acceptance from Andrea. She wore a long, floaty green dress and biker boots, a look that was more Tori Amos or Joni Mitchell than the Bee Gees.

The keyboard struck up a jaunty tune and Andrea started to sing again.

'"Stayin' Alive"? In an avalanche situation? Really?' whispered Lucy.

'Are you some kind of Bee Gees expert?' asked Nate, his mouth twitching into a smile.

'NO,' laughed Lucy, folding her arms defensively. 'Well, not deliberately. My dad was a big fan when I was a kid.' She pulled a *what the fuck is this?* face at one of the tall men at the next table, who was watching the impromptu gig with wide eyes and an open mouth. He nudged his friend and they both came over to Lucy and Nate's booth, joining in with the surreptitious giggling. They were a little younger than Lucy and Nate, maybe in their late twenties, and wholesomely good-looking.

'We should introduce ourselves,' said the shorter of the two men. 'Since we're stuck here together with the Alpine Bee Gees. I am Willem, and this is Alexander. We're both from Amsterdam.'

'Ahh, you're like royalty,' said Nate, shaking their hands. 'I'm Nate.'

'We like to think so,' said Willem, clearly delighted. 'In fact, Alex is actually a baron.'

'I'm sorry, what?' asked Lucy, looking at all three of them.

'Oh,' said Nate, blinking at Lucy. 'Um, Willem-Alexander is the name of the Dutch king.'

'Really?' said Lucy, who had never heard of Willem-Alexander, mostly because she was only now discovering that the Netherlands HAD a king. 'How would you know that?'

Another booming, teeth-rattling crack, another rumble, and the whole building started shaking again. Nate grabbed Lucy's hand as Andrea stopped singing and they all froze once again, and for a moment Lucy imagined the whole mountain collapsing in on itself like a house of cards and sweeping them away on a tumbling tide of snow. She looked at Nate, who was watching Gunther give Monica a worried glance as the glasses rattled against each other on the rack above their heads. *If Gunther's not happy*, thought Lucy, *this is very bad news.*

After what seemed like an age but was probably less than ten seconds, the rumbling stopped and everything was silent again, apart from the merry crackling of the wood burner. Nobody said anything for a moment, until the silence was interrupted by Lucy's phone buzzing.

'Who's that?' said Nate. 'Is it Sasha?' He grabbed her phone and glanced at the notification, then quickly handed it back with a mumble of 'Right. Not Sasha. Sorry.'

Lucy shook her head in confusion, then looked at her phone. It was a message from Marco, that read *At a very dull insurance seminar, would much rather have my face between your incredible legs. ¿Cómo estás, preciosa?*

Oh crap, thought Lucy, squirming with embarrassment as Nate fiddled with his beer mat, his cheeks scarlet. *Nate definitely didn't need to see that.*

CHAPTER TEN

'Everybody please be calm,' said Gunther, holding up his hands. 'We are all fine, and there is no need to panic.'

Lucy looked around at the room of distinctly un-panicked people. Everyone was either in shock, or not daring to move or make noise in case it triggered another avalanche. Either way, they were all frozen in their seats, waiting to see what might happen next. Lucy's phone buzzed again, prompting a narrow-eyed glare from Nate. Probably Marco again, with more specific and anatomical suggestions about how Lucy might relieve the boredom of his insurance seminar. The only saving grace was that it hadn't been one of Anthony's dick pics; she'd never be able to look Nate in the eye again. She ignored the phone and focused on Gunther, wondering if the burning heat in her face would ever subside.

Gunther's phone blared out a ringtone that sounded a lot like 'Enter Sandman' by Metallica, providing both welcome distraction and a frisson of worry about what the news from the village might be. They all sat in silence and listened hard as Gunther spoke intently to the person on the other end. The conversation was in German and Lucy couldn't understand much, but Gunther was mostly listening with a grave expression, which definitely didn't bode well.

'OK, everybody, let's talk together,' he said, after he'd ended the call. Lucy and Nate shoved up so that Andrea and the keyboard player could squeeze into their booth, and Gunther, Monica and Chantal pulled up three extra chairs.

'Can we do this in German?' asked Gunther in English, looking first at the two Dutch men, who nodded happily, then more pointedly at Lucy and Nate. Lucy shook her head apologetically, having done Spanish at school. The basics she'd learned had been much enhanced by all the dirty words Marco had taught her.

'*Ja, kein problem,*' whispered Nate.

'You speak German too?' hissed Lucy.

Nate nodded. 'Yeah. And Dutch and Spanish. *¿Cómo estás*, Lucy?' He gave her a deadpan stare, and Lucy blushed, wondering if now was a good time to mention that she had a shelf of awards for really impressive words written in English. Possibly the wrong audience, to be fair.

'OK, then for the benefit of the English *Fräulein*, we will do this in English. Can everyone here speak good English?'

Everyone nodded, and Lucy caught a withering glare from both Chantal and the keyboard player from the band. She shrank further into the bench and quietly died all over again.

'OK, I have spoken to the mountain safety people,' said Gunther. 'It is not safe for them to check the pistes tonight – it's dark, the weather is still very bad, and there may be more avalanches. Nobody is hurt, and they know we are OK, so they will meet again in the morning.'

'We're staying here tonight?' said Alex the Dutchman, his hand pressed against his chest in horror, clutching imaginary pearls.

'Yes,' said Gunther. 'There is no other option.'

'Just for one night?' asked Willem. Before the avalanche, Lucy was pretty sure they were having a conversation about one of the two men being something to do with the Dutch royal family. A baron, maybe? She couldn't remember the details now.

'That, I cannot tell you,' said Gunther, turning his palms upwards. 'It will depend on the situation tomorrow. If the piste is clear and safe, Ulrich will come up with the bus, probably with some other big machines to help clear his way. But if the piste is blocked or there is still avalanche risk, it may take a little more time. A few more hours, maybe one more night.'

'Can't they send a helicopter to rescue us?' asked Alex. *Oh, hark at Baron von Princess*, thought Lucy, rolling her eyes at Nate.

'In this weather, most definitely not,' said Gunther, shaking his head, then grinning broadly. 'And also, my friend, you don't need to be rescued. We are all safe here – we have firewood and food and water, and the Guntherhütte is not in the path of danger.'

'Does anyone need anything?' asked Monica. 'For example, does anyone need to take urgent medication?'

Lucy briefly considered making up a chronic illness, so they'd scramble a rescue party led by hot Swiss mountain men and a pack of fluffy St Bernards. The look on Alex's face suggested he was thinking the same thing, and Lucy wondered if he'd go with type 1 diabetes or something more obscure. But in the end everyone shook their heads regretfully.

'Where do we sleep?' asked Lucy, deciding it was time to address the elephant in the very small and uncomfortable room. All the surfaces in here were hard, apart from the upholstered booth seating, which were narrow semi-circles with very thin cushions. Any sudden movements, and you'd either fall off or smack your head on the table.

'We will squeeze in,' said Gunther with a dismissive wave of his hand.

'Squeeze in where? With who?' replied Lucy.

'It's all fine, we will manage,' shrugged Gunther breezily. 'Tonight we have music and good food and drink, and by bedtime you will not mind whose bed you sleep in.'

'I fucking will,' hissed Lucy, catching the death stare Monica was throwing Gunther.

'I will give you more information as soon as I can,' said Gunther. 'Please relax and enjoy our hospitality. The bar is open, and there is nothing to pay, obviously.'

The group dispersed to different corners of the pub to make phone calls and send messages, everyone moving tentatively and keeping their voices low in case loud noises set the mountain off again. Lucy looked at Nate, who was pale and sweaty again. 'Are you OK?'

'Yeah,' he mumbled. 'Trying to remember to breathe.'

'Gunther says we're safe,' she whispered.

Nate gave her a bleak look. 'Well, with all due respect, Gunther would say that.'

'Do you need to make any calls?' *To Sasha, for example?*

'Yeah,' said Nate. 'I guess I should.'

'I'll call Jonno, let him know what's going on.' She

slid out of the booth after Nate and checked her phone – there were several missed calls and three unread messages from Jonno alongside the one from Marco, and her battery was down to twenty-six per cent. Presumably one of the other eight people still on this mountain had an iPhone charger, but she'd worry about that later. It was only just gone five o'clock – what the hell were they going to do for the rest of the evening? She couldn't even get drunk, because she was already drunk.

'Hey,' she said to Jonno, who answered before she'd even heard it ring. 'There's been another avalanche, just wanted to let you know I'm still alive.'

'Fucksake, Luce,' he said with a huff of exasperation and relief. 'Why didn't you answer or reply to my messages?'

'I haven't even read them yet. We've been having a meeting about the fact we all have to stay in this bar for the night.'

'We wondered if that might happen. There's drama down here too – we've been told to leave the village as soon as possible. There's insane amounts of snow coming, total freak weather apparently, and they're going to close the road up the mountain.'

'Shit,' said Lucy, her mind racing. Everything felt like it was going at a hundred miles an hour, and she definitely wasn't feeling entirely in control of things right now.

'Yeah. Everyone's packing up, we'll be out of here within the hour.'

'Where are you going?'

'Geneva. Kristoff's booking us a house on the lake. So we can still do all the work stuff tomorrow.'

Lucy gasped. 'Wait, you're fucking off to Geneva and leaving us here?'

'I don't have any choice,' pleaded Jonno. 'We're being kicked out of Zermatt, all the hotel staff are being evacuated too. They're expecting the worst snowstorms in decades, apparently. Avalanche warnings keep going off. We need to get out.'

'And what about me?' Lucy was aware her volume was rising and people were looking, even though she'd moved over to the space next to the wood burner.

'I know, I'm sorry. Apparently you're safe, because you're so high up.'

Lucy took a deep breath, trying to put a lid on her growing panic. 'I'd just got my head around staying here tonight, but nobody's mentioned there's worse weather coming. What if I'm trapped here for weeks?'

'Oh God, don't be such a drama queen. Look, I've checked with loads of people and those huts are built to be totally stormproof. You're definitely not in the path of anything that could avalanche.'

Lucy smiled for what felt like the first time since she and Nate were playing board games. It was less than an hour ago, but it already felt like another century. 'Wait, is avalanche a verb?'

'Fuck off, Dictionary Corner. Drink the bar dry and take loads of videos; stick it on TikTok or Instagram or something. People live for this kind of thing.'

'I don't do social, you know that,' said Lucy, grudgingly accepting that real-life, high-pressure situations where strangers were thrown together made the kind of content she would definitely watch. Maybe Nate would take a video, or one of the Dutch guys.

'It's going to be fine, Luce,' said Jonno. 'The storm should all be over by tomorrow, then hopefully you'll be able to join us in Geneva.'

'Yeah, OK.' She tried to bring her stress levels under control, rationalising that Jonno didn't have any choice but to leave. And even if he was allowed to stay in Zermatt, there would be nothing for him to do.

'How's Nate?' asked Jonno.

'He's fine, I think.' Lucy didn't mention Nate's anxiety challenges, because it wasn't anyone else's business. Presumably Sasha knew already that her boyfriend was prone to meltdown, and was probably pretty worried right now. 'He's on the phone. How are Kristoff and Sasha and the others?'

'Revelling in organising manoeuvres – Sasha's glued to her phone as we speak. It's a good excuse for them to take charge and rally the troops. Spirit of Dunkirk and all that.'

'About twenty thousand troops died in Dunkirk, J.' She glanced at Nate, wondering if he was talking to Sasha. He was walking back and forth by their table, his left hand raking through his hair.

'OK, bad example. Do you want me to call your parents or anything? Let them know you're OK?'

'No, I'll do it,' said Lucy, wondering if there was any way she could avoid it. Would an avalanche in Switzerland make the news, if nobody had died? She had no idea, but she'd definitely told her dad the name of the place she was travelling to, so they might get wind of something. It felt wrong to add to their emotional burden, today of all days, but it also didn't feel right to say nothing at all.

'I'll message you when I'm in Geneva,' said Jonno. 'Let me know if you need anything.'

'Well, right now I'd like a helicopter and a hot bath,' said Lucy.

'I can provide neither of those things,' said Jonno. 'I am, as ever, totally useless.'

'Mmm, but I love you anyway.'

'Yeah, all right, bugger off,' said Jonno. 'I'll talk to you later.'

Lucy ended the call and took a deep breath, looking around at the eight other people in the room. Gunther, Monica and Chantal were all deep in conversation behind the bar, no doubt playing Tetris with floor space and spare pillows. The two band members were whispering quietly in their corner, and everyone else was on their phone, presumably sending messages like these might be their final words to their loved ones. The weather outside suggested that was infinitely possible, so Lucy scrolled to her parents' home number. *Might as well get this over with.*

'Lucy, darling,' said her mother's voice after a few rings. 'We wondered if you'd call today. I know you said you were going away, but I told your father you wouldn't forget.'

'Hi, Mum. I just wanted to—'

'We thought of you earlier, when we were with Leo.' Shirley and Richard Glover weren't religious people, but any conversation about Leo brought out a kind of breathless piety, like they were whispering in church.

'Have you spent time with him today?' continued Shirley. She meant spiritually, of course – Leo's ashes were scattered amongst some rosebushes in Croydon cemetery. Lucy had sat on the memorial bench nearby on many occasions, but she'd never felt as close to Leo there as she did in Bristol. She'd moved to the city five months after he died, as soon as she'd finished her uni finals. Even after all these years the city felt like it was full of him; the pubs he'd loved, the hills he'd climbed, the places he'd hung out. For Lucy, Bristol preserved some of Leo's spirit – creative, uncompromising, a little unpredictable and occasionally hectic. A city that was sometimes charming, but still had sharp edges, just like her brother.

'Yes, of course,' said Lucy. 'I'm actually calling because I'm stuck in Switzerland, Mum. I'm in a bar in the mountains above Zermatt, and there's been an avalanche.' She closed her eyes and pressed her lips together, knowing that unless she was gasping her final breaths right now, any Lucy news would be taken as an unwelcome intrusion into a day that was all about Leo. But her phone was running out of battery, so there was no time for platitudes.

'You're in a bar?' said her mother, with the same aghast tone she might use for 'You've run away to join the circus?' Lucy shook her head, kicking herself for not seeing that one coming. She loved her parents, obviously, but they'd never made any real effort to hide that Leo had been their favourite child. He was her father's clever, creative son, and her mother's emotionally fragile, precious boy. His death had immortalised him as forever twenty-one – a little troubled and lost, but with so much potential – whereas the subsequent eleven years had rubbed away any residual shine from Lucy. Single, childless, living far from home, a job that they didn't understand and didn't score them any points with the neighbours. And most damning of all, the audacity to still be walking and breathing despite Leo being gone.

'I came here for lunch with a work colleague, but that's not the point. There's been an avalanche.'

'Goodness,' said her mother, clearly still snippy about the bar thing. 'Is anyone hurt? You *sound* fine.'

'I AM fine. Everyone's safe. But we're stuck up a mountain, at least until tomorrow, and my phone is running out of battery. I didn't want you to see it on the news and be worried.'

'We don't watch the news,' said her mother. 'You can't trust the mainstream media. We stopped watching after those awful stories about your father's work.' Richard Glover worked as a research scientist for a pharmaceutical company who had been involved in some questionable opiate-pushing scandal in the US. Richard led a team developing drugs to treat various forms of depression and anxiety, a decade's work driven by the tragic and untimely death of his son. So he'd never come close to the scandal, but Lucy's mother had taken it personally anyway.

'Jesus,' muttered Lucy, feeling suddenly exhausted. 'Fine, Facebook then. I just wanted to let you know I was safe.'

'You should have been *here*,' said her mother, the emphasis clearly on the final word. 'With your father and me.'

'I'll come and see you when I get back, Mum. I

promise. I need to go, battery's—' She ended the call, relieved that it was done and she'd only been made to feel mildly like shit. One of the reasons she'd never felt in any hurry to have children was because it would inevitably mean spending more time with her parents, although that definitely wasn't the only reason. As it was, she saw them three or four times a year at most, and only ever if she made the trip to their mock-Tudor detached house in Purley, south of Croydon. They refused to come to Bristol, which considering the suspension bridge loomed large over the city, was probably fair enough.

How have I ended up here? thought Lucy, deciding that, all things considered, and even in the midst of an avalanche, it was still better than the alternative.

CHAPTER ELEVEN

Lucy checked her battery again, which was now down to twenty per cent. She looked over at the two Dutchmen – Alexander had stood up, so she walked over. 'You guys OK?' she asked.

'I'm going to do a video for TikTok,' said Alexander. 'I have over a million followers.'

'Really?' asked Lucy, glancing at Willem for clarification. He rolled his eyes and nodded.

'They will be worried,' said Alex. 'But also it's fabulous content. Are you happy to be in it?'

Lucy shrugged, not really sure but also not wanting to be pegged as the uptight British woman. She fished out her lip balm and applied it liberally, conscious that she looked a bit of a mess and quite a lot drunk, but maybe that would help with adding some real-life authenticity. She'd experienced an avalanche, not a hot stone massage and a glycolic facial.

Will Nate want to be part of this? she thought, looking up at him. He was still on the phone, pacing in circles and raking his hand through his hair. *Who is he?* she wondered again, trying to reconcile the moody, closed-down Nate she'd known before this trip with the confident, sexy version who she'd seen emerging from Sasha's room in the early hours. And now she'd peeled back another layer to find a third Nate – a man with an anxiety disorder that clearly consumed him when things felt out of his control. Like Leo, he was complex and unfathomable, and Lucy found herself both wary of that connection and eager to find out more.

'Hey guys, I'm in Zermatt in Switzerland for the weekend,' announced Alex, snapping Lucy back into the bar. Willem was holding a phone up so Alex could smile into the camera, and Lucy marvelled that he hadn't stuffed a ring light and tripod in his rucksack.

'So,' continued Alex breathlessly. 'I came up to this bar on the mountain for lunch, but just before we were about to leave we had two avalanches, and now there are nine of us stuck here in a mountain bar for the night.' He paused and widened his eyes for drama, and Lucy wondered how many thousands of followers were already hanging off his every word. Everyone in the bar had stopped talking to watch, including Nate, who had finished his call and sidled back to the table to sit next to her.

'It's called the Guntherhütte,' continued Alex, pronouncing it far better than Lucy could have. His English was also immaculate, but with a slight American twang that suggested he'd watched a lot of US TV. Willem walked around Alex in a slow, steady circle so anyone watching could get a three-sixty view of the bar and the awkwardly waving guests, then stopped so Alex could continue narrating. 'It's a really cool place. But anyway, I'm just checking in to say that we're all safe, and hopefully we'll be heading back down to Zermatt tomorrow. There's a HUGE storm outside, but since, incredibly, there is still Wi-Fi in this bar, I thought I'd introduce you to my fellow mountain refugees.'

Alex took the phone and turned it to face Willem, who was clearly used to being both a cameraman and an extra in one of Alex's videos. 'So, first up in the Gunter-hütte, lots of you already know him – it's Willem.'

'Hello,' said Willem, waving at the camera. 'I also come from Amsterdam, and I'm WillemMulder84 on TikTok and Instagram.' He spelled out his name, clearly not wanting to miss the opportunity to milk this ludicrous situation for followers. 'I just want to tell my family and friends that we are very safe here right now, and as far as we know nobody was hurt in the avalanche. So there is no need to worry – we have beer and food and good company, and hopefully we'll be home tomorrow!'

Alex gave him a thumbs up and handed back the phone, taking the opportunity to reset his stance with a tilt of the chin and a pout that accentuated his cheekbones. 'I can see from the comments just now that some of you are new here,' he said, which made Lucy wonder how quickly the news of Alex's avalanche drama was spreading. 'You can find me on TikTok, Instagram and YouTube, so don't forget to follow me. I'm BaronAlexJansen across all social media channels.' Lucy rolled her eyes at Nate, whose mouth twitched into the tiniest of smiles. She noted the 'Baron' in Alex's handle, wondering if that meant he was genuine Dutch aristocracy, or if this was one of those titles you could buy online for a couple of hundred euros. Regardless, he was undeniably good at this.

'Tell us what the avalanche was like,' said Willem.

'Oh wow, it was scary,' said Alex. 'We were literally, like—' He stopped suddenly as the keyboard guy from the band appeared from nowhere and thrust his beaming face in front of the camera, dragging the singer along behind him.

'I'm Felix,' he said, earning an outraged glare from Alex. 'This is Andrea, and together we are Night Fever. We keep the wonderful sound of the Bee Gees alive.' Willem raised his eyebrows in question at Andrea, as if to say *Do you actually want to be part of this?* and got a tiny headshake in return.

'Are you on TikTok?' asked Willem, keeping his focus on Felix rather than Alex's sulky face.

'We're on Facebook and YouTube,' said Felix. 'Just search Night Fever Bee Gees Tribute Switzerland. We are from Zurich, and we—'

'We will definitely do that,' interrupted Alex, who was clearly getting cold out of the spotlight. 'Now let's meet our hosts,' he continued, heading over to the bar and wafting his hands at Gunther to indicate that he should get involved.

'Hello, I am Gunther,' he sang, waving at the camera with a beaming smile. 'I own the beautiful Guntherhütte here in Zermatt, and we will be making sure everyone is safe and looked after tonight. There is a lot of snow and it's pretty wild out there, but we are all fine. Tonight we will sing and dance and party!'

He picked up an empty beer glass and mimed drinking from it just as Monica elbowed her way in front of him. Lucy tried not to laugh, not sure if it was because she wanted to be on camera, or was keen to shut Gunther up before he made an idiot of himself. 'Hello, I am Monica, I am Gunther's wife and also run the Guntherhütte. This is my daughter Chantal, who is twenty-six and does not have a boyfriend.'

Chantal stared wide-eyed at her mother, looking mortified, then smiled as Willem turned the camera in her direction. 'Hi,' she said with a feeble wave. 'How many followers do you have, Willem?'

'About five thousand,' laughed Willem. 'But Alex has over a million.' He turned the camera back to Alex, who was smiling modestly, as if Willem shouldn't have mentioned it.

'And finally, our new friends... what were your names again?' said Alex, walking over to Lucy and Nate's table.

'I'm Lucy, and this is Nate,' said Lucy with an awkward, two-handed wave. 'We're work colleagues from Bristol.'

'Sure you are,' smirked Alex, prompting a blush from Nate. 'Are you on TikTok or Instagram, Lucy?'

'No,' said Lucy, feeling undeniably lame. 'But Nate is.'

Alex turned the camera to Nate, who raked through his hair with one hand and held up the other. 'Hi,' he said, his voice sounding weak and husky. Lucy couldn't help thinking that even with dark circles under his eyes and a slightly dishevelled air, he probably looked great on camera. 'I'm not on TikTok, but I'm NateLambert89 on Instagram.'

'And how's your day been so far?' asked Alex, a definite air of flirtatiousness in his voice. Clearly he'd noticed how great Nate looked on camera too.

'Um, bit weird,' laughed Nate. 'I only came up here for pizza and wine.'

'And now you're spending the night on a Swiss mountain,' laughed Alex. 'You OK with that?'

'Ha,' said Nate, looking a little flustered. 'I'm not sure. We haven't worked out the sleeping arrangements yet.' He smiled shyly, and Lucy wondered how Sasha would feel if she somehow saw this video. Somebody would tag a LUNA person in it eventually, or more likely Jonno would be searching for anything tagged #ZermattAvalanche right now. Conversations about sleeping arrangements were unlikely to go down well.

'And how are you feeling right now?' It was a big question, for Nate in particular, and Lucy prepared herself to rescue him if things started to spiral.

'I'm OK,' said Nate, his brow furrowed thoughtfully. 'The avalanches were pretty scary, obviously. But we've been well looked after, and nobody is hurt, so I'm trying to pretend this is all a big adventure. And I couldn't ask for better company.' He gestured vaguely with his hand at the rest of the group, but his eyes were fixed firmly on Lucy. The dark intensity of his gaze made her shiver, and for a moment it felt like they were the only people in this bar. *He means me*, she thought, which made her feel both breathless and confused at the same time. The shifting sands between her and Nate were all mixed up in wine and Sasha and Leo and this insane situation. She'd attempt to unravel it later, no doubt whilst getting zero sleep on the floor of this bar.

Willem held the camera on Nate for a second, until Alex cleared his throat and it deftly swung back for him to wrap up. 'So that's the situation in the Guntherhütte,' he announced. 'I'll shoot some more video later, so keep checking back. We're all fine here, and hopefully we'll be safely back down the mountain tomorrow. Thanks for watching!' Willem ended the video as Alex struck a final, preening pose in the spotlight of a Guntherhütte ceiling lamp. It had a brown floral shade with a lacy edge and gave Alex's face a sickly glow, but apparently it would do.

'Some things we need to organise,' said Monica, clapping her hands like a teacher trying to get a class to quieten down. She was in her late fifties, with a short, cropped haircut that looked usefully low maintenance for a woman who probably didn't get to the salon much. She reminded Lucy a little of her own mother; the same all-seeing, all-knowing look, like she had eyes in the back of her head. And a similar lean physique too, bordering on too thin; for Shirley that was the result of decades of nervous energy and an unwillingness to sit down in case stillness let the darkness in.

The group gathered around in a loose semicircle – Alex and Willem perching on one of the pine tables, Alex's phone primed for content opportunities, and Felix and Andrea from the band on stools over by the bar. Gunther was next to Monica, his arms folded, and Lucy and Nate stayed in the booth where they'd been sitting all afternoon, followed swiftly by Chantal. Lucy nervously wondered if Sasha had seen Alex's TikTok yet, and if she was already planning Lucy's slow and painful death.

'Gunther and I have talked about sleeping plans for tonight,' said Monica. 'Andrea and Felix, you are OK to share Chantal's room? It has a double bed, and she can sleep on the sofa in our room.'

'Yes,' said Andrea, looking relieved. 'We are married,' she clarified for the rest of the group, like there might be some puritans in the building. Since Felix was at least twenty years Andrea's senior, and at least six inches shorter with four strands of hair and a straggly beard, Lucy had to assume that he was either a) very rich, or b) hung like a chandelier. Her thoughts briefly drifted to Anthony's message, and she wondered if she should use any of her precious remaining battery to reassure him and Marco that she was OK. What was the protocol there? In the year and a half she'd known both of them, situations of mild peril had never been explored.

'You two? You are a couple?' said Gunther loudly, interrupting Lucy's disconnected train of thought. It occurred to her that she was currently a bit hot and sweaty, which she could attribute to getting lunchtime pissed. Probably not ideal for sitting this close to Nate, but hopefully she'd be able to have a shower at some point before she started to smell like Swiss cheese.

'No,' said Nate quickly, and Lucy was gratified to see that, up close, he didn't look entirely sober either. 'We work together, but we're definitely not a couple.' *You can calm down*, thought Lucy, mildly offended by how fervently he was making this point. *Your secret girlfriend isn't about to storm the Guntherhütte.*

'But you are OK to share a room, yes? We have a storage room in the attic that we can put airbeds in. It is nice and warm.'

'Absolutely not,' said Lucy, conscious that Sasha's level

of understanding of their situation might be tested if they were sharing a bedroom. 'We hardly know each other.' After everything that had happened today – the bus ride, the conversation about Leo and Nate's anxiety, the avalanche – that didn't feel strictly true any more. But if Nate had remembered he had a hostile girlfriend and was trying to create some space between them, Lucy wasn't going to let anyone think she cared.

'Ah,' said Gunther. 'Well, this is maybe a problem.'

'It's fine, I'll sleep on the floor down here or something,' said Nate mildly. 'Lucy can have the room.'

Lucy felt several pairs of judgemental eyes glaring at the demanding British woman who seemed to be insisting on having a room of her own. The only exception was Chantal, who was looking at Nate like she'd happily vacate her sofa in favour of his hard floor. 'No,' said Lucy quickly, feeling her neck get hot. 'Nate and I can share. Are there two beds?'

'Of course,' said Gunther. 'They are the kind you inflate, we use them for our grandchildren. If these two gentlemen don't mind sharing the sofa bed in our family room?'

'We are actually a couple,' said Alex, tilting his chin defiantly. 'I hope nobody has a problem with this.'

Gunther gave them a beaming smile and held his hands wide. 'You are in Switzerland, my friend. We have sex with anyone who is respectful enough to take a shower first.' He glanced at Lucy while he said this, and gave her the tiniest wink. Maybe it was better to share her room after all, even if it was with Nate.

'Hopefully it is only for one night,' added Monica,

shooting another laser glare at Gunther. 'And they will clear the piste tomorrow.'

Lucy nodded and tried to look amenable, deciding not to mention the update from Jonno about the incoming weather and closing the road out of the village. They all had phones and would find out soon enough.

'There are some things we need to do,' said Monica. 'Ladies, maybe you could join me in the kitchen to prepare some cold food for everyone? We should save the gas for hot water. Then the men can help Gunther bring in some firewood.'

Lucy started to voice a complaint about gendered division of labour, then realised it would mean she didn't have to go outside in a snowstorm and decided not to die on that frozen hill.

'When we are done, we can relax,' said Gunther happily. 'We have plenty of food and drink and music. We are all safe, and nobody is hurt or missing in the avalanche, so we should celebrate.'

Lucy sighed heavily, wondering whether anyone would mind if she went up to her frozen attic and read a book. It had been a long and stressful day, and the idea of partying with a bunch of strangers suddenly felt exhausting. Apparently her hangover was definitely kicking in.

'My grandmother is Dutch,' said Nate as the group started talking and moving around again.

Lucy shook her head, wondering if this was some kind of spy code. 'I'm sorry?'

'You asked earlier how I knew that Willem-Alexander is the king of the Netherlands. It's because my grandmother is Dutch and a huge fan of the royal family.'

'Really? Ours? Or theirs?'

'Both, actually. She came to the UK and joined that big queue when the Queen died.'

Lucy raised her eyebrows. 'Did you queue with her?'

'Yes,' said Nate, the set of his mouth daring Lucy to take the piss. 'For ten hours. I'm a good grandson.'

'I'm sure you are, Nate,' said Lucy with a wry smile, wondering how on earth she'd ended up trapped on a mountain in Switzerland with Nate Lambert and this random bunch of strangers. She picked up her phone and checked for messages, but there was nothing new. *Who would message?* she thought sadly. Jonno and her parents knew where she was, Anthony and Marco only tapped her up for sex, and there wasn't anyone else. There hadn't been anyone else for a really long time.

Lucy shook her head and put her phone in her pocket, noting that Alex had unearthed a charger from his bag and already plugged his in at the next table. She'd ask to borrow that as soon as he was finished, thinking that she might even make her own video later. She wouldn't post it anywhere, obviously, but it might be nice to have a memory of this adventure before everything went back to normal.

She glanced at Nate, who was pulling on his coat ready to help Gunther and the others bring in wood for the fire, and wondered what normal would be like for them when they were back in Bristol on Sunday. Would he be keen for things to revert to how they were before, with them barely acknowledging each other? Or would they have a new connection, forged over wine and confidences in the Swiss mountains, that would lay the foundations for some kind of friendship? Something had definitely shifted between her and Nate today, and even though Lucy didn't know what that meant, it wasn't something she could un-shift. *And,* she realised with a jolt of surprise, *I don't think I'd want to, even if I could.*

CHAPTER TWELVE

'What's the longest you've ever been cut off up here?' asked Lucy as she sliced tomatoes for a salad. It felt strange to be behind the scenes in the kitchen; she hadn't ventured into the murky area behind a bar since she'd worked in various pubs and bars as a student in Liverpool. All of those had been absolute hovels that ran the gauntlet of the Food Standards Agency daily, so she was gratified to see that this one was spotlessly clean and there were no signs of mouse droppings or rusty meat cleavers.

'A week,' said Monica, peeling the lid off a tub of what looked like chopped sausages. The buffet menu this evening seemed to be heavily based around processed meat, cheese, mayonnaise and cold potatoes; on top of the pizza she'd eaten at lunchtime, it was reasonable to assume that Lucy's natural tendency to stay slim was about to be tested. Although maybe at some point they'd be able to roll her down the mountain, like a human snowball.

'But that was just very bad weather,' continued Monica. 'Rather than an avalanche. We have enough supplies for a long time, we are prepared for things like this. But we would prefer customers.' Chantal sighed dramatically behind them as she unloaded the industrial dishwasher, and Lucy wondered what it must be like for a woman in her twenties to live up here with her parents. Presumably she had time off to ski, and spent her free time hanging out with friends in the village. Lucy watched her tuck a curly tendril of hair behind her ear as she chewed the corner of her lip, and wondered whether Nate had noticed her. He'd have to be blind not to, she was gorgeous.

'We had a week of gigs booked for hotels in the village from tomorrow,' said Andrea gravely, as she whisked some kind of creamy vinaigrette dressing. 'This is very bad for us.'

Lucy looked up at Andrea and Monica, feeling guilty that she hadn't considered the impact of their lost income. She'd been so caught up in her own drama, it hadn't even crossed her mind that it might cause all kinds of problems for everyone else.

'Does it happen a lot? Closing the village and asking everyone to leave?' That news had filtered through via various phone calls after their meeting, and caused a further frisson of worry in the Guntherhütte.

Monica shook her head. 'I've been here for fifteen years,' she said. 'Only twice before.'

'Do you ever have times when there isn't any snow?' asked Lucy.

Monica shrugged and began layering slices of cheese into a fan shape on a plate. 'Sometimes it isn't so snowy in the village this early in the season, but there is always snow on the glacier. We are open all year round; it is always busy here.'

'Your friend is very handsome,' said Andrea, apparently opting to change the subject before they got into a heavy discussion about the impact of climate change in the Alps. They were a similar age, Lucy guessed, but

Andrea's delicate features and long hair piled up into a knot so it didn't shed into the food made her look younger, like a fragile doll. Lucy noticed that Chantal stopped what she was doing and listened, even though she kept her back to them.

'He's a work colleague,' said Lucy quickly. 'He's not really a friend.'

'You have been playing games and drinking wine all afternoon,' said Monica with a knowing smile. 'This is a good beginning for something more than a friendship, I think.'

'It's not like that,' muttered Lucy, ignoring her muddled thoughts about how, exactly, she would like things to be between her and Nate in the future. 'I think he has a girlfriend, so us being stuck here together is a bit complicated.'

'And what about you?' asked Monica. 'Do you have a husband? Or a boyfriend?'

'Or a girlfriend,' added Andrea quickly, throwing Lucy an apologetic glance that clearly communicated *different generation, sorry*.

'I don't have a boyfriend,' said Lucy. 'Well, technically I have two, but I'm not sure either qualifies as a boyfriend.' *Oops*, she thought. *Apparently I'm oversharing. Definitely still drunk.*

Monica raised her eyebrows and smiled, as Chantal's curiosity got the better of her and she abandoned the dishwasher to join the group at the counter. 'OK, this sounds cool. Tell us more,' she said.

Lucy looked at them, wondering how candid to be now she'd done some *in vino veritas* blabbing. It wasn't like she ran a sex dungeon, but still. She could do without being stuck on a mountain with three women who thought she was an STD-riddled whore.

'I guess I have two guys that are . . . a sexual arrangement. Separately, not together,' she clarified quickly. 'But I'm not in a proper relationship with either.'

'How interesting,' said Andrea, and Lucy was relieved to see that she looked genuinely intrigued rather than scandalised. 'So, how does the saying go? No strings attached?'

'Exactly,' said Lucy. 'It's a deal that works for all of us.'

'Do they have other women too?' asked Chantal, her eyes wide.

'I don't know,' said Lucy. 'It's none of my business.' *Why am I telling them this?* thought Lucy. She'd never been one for sharing girly confidences; Jonno was the only person she told her secrets to. Nobody else at LUNA knew about Anthony or Marco, and she made a conscious effort to give off a vibe that discouraged people from asking about her personal life. But this felt like exceptional circumstances, somehow, and it wasn't like she was ever going to see these women again. What did it matter?

'That sounds very . . . what's the word?' said Monica, her brow furrowed with concern. 'Sterile? Is that the right word in English?'

'Mmm,' said Lucy, relieved that Monica's reservations seemed motherly, rather than horrified.

'Don't you ever want to fall in love?' asked Andrea, tilting her head at Lucy with a sad pout.

Lucy laughed and shook her head. 'No. I prefer it this

way. Van Gogh once said "the more you love, the more you suffer".'

'Wasn't Van Gogh totally mad?' asked Chantal.

'He cut off his ear,' said Andrea. 'Which is definitely crazy. I think he was a tortured artist.'

'I'm definitely not mad,' said Lucy. 'I just . . . like to keep things simple, I guess.'

Monica shook her head as she washed her hands at the sink. 'That's a little sad, I think. You are very beautiful and seem like a kind person. But it is none of my business, of course.'

'Look, I'm not dead inside or anything,' said Lucy, still slightly confused as to why she was baring her soul to three complete strangers over cheese slices and Van Gogh quotes. Then she remembered all the times strange women had told her their deepest secrets over the sinks in pub toilets, and realised the culprit was always booze. 'I have a great life, good friends, I love my job. It works better for me this way.' She shoved aside the sardonic voice in her head pointing out that she had a life that rarely ventured beyond Bristol, and a social life that was mostly spent alone, in the pub with Jonno, or in bed with Anthony or Marco. Hardly a rollercoaster of adventures.

'Then that is all that matters,' said Andrea, leaning towards Lucy and dropping her voice to a stage whisper. 'Do you prefer one of them more than the other?'

'They have different qualities,' said Lucy, laughing. 'That's all you need to know.'

'For now,' said Monica, giving Andrea a wink.

'How long have you and Gunther been married?' asked Lucy, keen to shift the spotlight elsewhere.

'Thirty-five years,' said Monica. 'Gunther was the brother of my best friend, I have known him since I was a child. We got married when I was nineteen, and worked together on a farm thirty kilometres from here. We bought this place when Chantal was eleven. She has two older brothers who have families of their own, but they both live in Zurich.'

'I'm not married,' said Chantal. 'I don't even have a boyfriend.' Her tone was slightly accusatory, like working for the family business was akin to joining the local convent.

'Do you ever meet nice men here?' asked Lucy, imagining the parade of Swiss bankers who must stomp through the Guntherhütte on winter weekends, waving their gold credit cards. Or men like Kristoff, with perfect teeth and casual ambitions to evict the incumbent family and build an executive gin palace. Probably best not to mention that.

'No,' said Chantal bleakly. 'Sometimes a man comes in and I wonder if he will be the one who will take me away, but it never happens.' Lucy wondered if she'd had that thought about Nate, and whether he was prepared to be the object of her Cinderella fantasies for the next twenty-four hours.

'This is not such a terrible life,' said Monica. 'You have grown up in these mountains with your family.'

'And now I would like to have someone in my life who is not my family,' said Chantal grumpily. 'That does not seem so unreasonable.'

'We always wanted you to carry on the family business,' said Monica.

'Not on my own,' huffed Chantal.

'Felix and I have been married for ten years,' said Andrea, a little louder than strictly necessary. 'He was a friend of my father's.'

'Was?' asked Lucy.

'He married my papa's only daughter and took me away from our home town to sing music in bars,' said Andrea, and Lucy could feel the pain even though she was smiling. 'They are not friends any more.'

'Do *you* enjoy singing in bars?' asked Lucy.

'Yes,' said Andrea. 'I always wanted to be a singer. But I would like to sing other things, sometimes. Felix only likes the Bee Gees.'

'Wait, what?' said Lucy, momentarily horrified. 'You *only* sing the Bee Gees?'

'Yes. Felix has been a fan all his life.'

'He takes the idea of being a tribute band very literally,' added Monica, her mouth pursed in disapproval.

'He would think of it as disrespectful to sing anything else,' said Andrea. 'He once waited many hours for Robin Gibb after a concert and told him that he only ever sang the Bee Gees, and Robin said that was a wonderful thing. So now he says it is a matter of honour.'

'Can't he ask Robin for permission to diversify?' asked Lucy.

'Robin died in 2012,' said Andrea. 'Please don't mention it to Felix, he gets very upset. He tried to go to the funeral in England, but they wouldn't let him into the church. So now we go every year in May to lay flowers on his grave.'

'Right,' said Lucy, as Monica raised her eyebrows to communicate how entirely unhinged she thought Felix was. 'What if I made a request? Asked you to sing something else?'

Andrea shook her head, looking alarmed. 'Felix does not take requests. Unless it's a Bee Gees song. But when I'm alone, I sing Adele songs. She is a beautiful singer.'

'Isn't a Bee Gees-only set quite short?' Lucy could only think of three or four Bee Gees hits, but she was hardly a superfan.

'You would be surprised,' said Andrea wearily, like this wasn't the first time she'd had this conversation. 'They had many hits, and also wrote some very famous songs for other artists. For example, they wrote "Islands in the Stream" for Dolly Parton and Kenny Rogers.'

'Oh, I love that song,' said Lucy.

'So do I,' said Andrea, looking slightly haunted. 'Thankfully.'

Lucy pressed her lips together, suppressing the urge to laugh. The realisation dawned on her that she was trapped in a mountain bar with a Swiss ladies' man, his long-suffering wife, their lonely daughter, two Dutch gays, one of whom was possibly a minor royal, an anxious work colleague who was secretly sleeping with their boss, and a Bee Gees tribute act that didn't take requests. Even in her wildest dreams, she couldn't make this shit up.

'Shall we carry this through?' asked Monica, picking up a tray of plates of artfully placed meat and cheese. They gathered up as much as they could carry and transferred it to one of the tables in the bar, where the rest of the group were knocking back shots of Jägermeister, their cheeks pink from the cold.

'The weather is pretty scary,' said Nate, his face crumpling into a grimace as he swallowed down the shot. 'But Gunther says the best way not to think about it is to stay drunk. This stuff is disgusting.'

'Can I get some of that?' asked Lucy, holding out Nate's shot glass so Gunther could fill it up with the dark, syrupy liquid. The snow was still battering the windows, but there was now a stack of logs next to the blazing wood burner, and the room felt warm and steamy after the cool of the kitchen. The prospect of not sobering up suddenly felt extremely appealing.

'Be my guest,' said Nate with a shudder. Lucy tipped up the glass and swallowed it down, a foul mixture of cough medicine and aniseed. She pulled a face at Alex, who was shooting a video of everyone knocking back shots and chatting animatedly in various languages, most of which she didn't understand. Monica started handing round plates for the buffet, and the whole scene felt like the most bizarre party Lucy had ever been to.

'I need a caption,' said Alex. 'Something funny.'

'Jäger party in the snowbound Guntherhütte,' said Lucy. *'If you can't get home, you might as well get drunk.'*

'That's perfect,' said Alex, looking at Lucy with a new-found admiration.

'Lucy's a writer,' said Nate. 'A very good one, actually.'

Alex had already gone back to tapping frantically on his screen and wasn't listening, but Lucy appreciated the compliment all the same. She and Nate edged back into their booth where they could watch the unfolding party.

'How's your day going so far?' asked Nate, nibbling at the corner of a slice of cheese.

Lucy thought about it, processing what felt like thousands of tiny events since she'd woken up barely ten hours ago. The bus ride, lunch, wine, playing board games with Nate, the avalanche, the phone call to her mother. And that was before she even scratched the surface of the hundred different ways today had been about Leo.

'Today was always going to be a weird day,' she said, her eyes fixed firmly on her plate. 'And usually I spend it with my parents, which is . . . difficult in a different way.'

'Yeah,' said Nate. 'I bet that's pretty tough.'

'But I figure if Leo was here he'd be loving the drama and drinking Gunther's bar dry. He'd also be telling me to write everything down, so I don't forget.'

'Isn't that what phones are for?' asked Nate.

'Yeah, I guess.' Lucy saw that Alex was videoing again from over by the door, but this time she turned away a little and ignored him. 'We should talk about you. You haven't told me anything about your family.' She glanced sideways at him, taking in the strong profile and his hair falling in loose curls over his ears, still wet from the snow.

'Nothing much to tell,' said Nate. 'I have family in France, but I've lived in and around Bristol since I was a baby. A couple of years in Paris when I first joined LUNA, then back home.'

'Can I join you?' said Chantal, sliding into their booth with her plate of food before they could answer.

'Sure.' Lucy tried not to feel annoyed that an opportunity to find out more about Nate had been interrupted. She rationalised that they were in a small bar with seven other people, so any private conversations would have to wait until they retired to their attic later. In Lucy's head it was a dark, cobwebby space accessed via a ceiling hatch and lined with itchy insulation, like the attic at her parents' house. But maybe in Switzerland they did things differently.

'*Du sprichst Deutsch, ja?*' said Chantal to Nate, gazing at him in wonder. Lucy's German didn't extend much beyond ordering two beers, but she knew enough to understand that Chantal was trying to cut her out of the conversation.

'Yes, but Lucy doesn't,' said Nate firmly. 'So I think English would be more polite.' Chantal looked crestfallen, and Lucy resisted the childish urge to stick her tongue out.

'Of course,' said Chantal. 'We learn English at school from very young here in Switzerland. What kind of work do you do?' She addressed the question to both of them, but it was clear that Chantal was really only interested in Nate. Lucy was too tired to compete for Nate's affections, so she said nothing.

'We both work for an advertising agency,' Nate replied. 'But Lucy is the talented one. She's an amazing writer.'

'Oh,' said Chantal, looking a bit sick. 'That's nice.'

'I write ads for condoms,' said Lucy. 'It's hardly Dostoyevsky.'

'Condoms?' Chantal's expression was a picture of innocence. 'That's very useful, after what you were telling us in the kitchen. I hope they give you lots of free samples.'

'I really need to charge my phone,' said Lucy quickly,

giving Chantal a hard stare and turning around to see if Alex's charger was still in use. He'd unplugged it and the cable was hanging loose, but before she could ask the question the lights went out and the room was plunged into darkness.

CHAPTER THIRTEEN

'Please, be calm,' said Gunther. Lucy blinked as her eyes slowly adjusted to the darkness, which was punctuated only by the flickering glow of the wood burner.

'Will the power come back?' asked Alex, his voice seeming louder in the sudden silence of the bar. Lucy hadn't been aware of all the ambient sounds until they were gone – the gentle sloshing of a dishwasher, the hum of the lights, the background burbling of a radio in the kitchen – but now there was just dark, heavy silence.

'Not tonight,' said Gunther. 'Our power comes from a generator, and clearly there is a problem but we cannot go out and fix it in this weather. To be honest I am surprised it has lasted this long.' He sounded cheerfully upbeat, and Lucy wondered how many other parts of this building he expected to break down in the coming hours. *Oh, the roof? I'm amazed that didn't collapse hours ago, with the weight of all that snow.*

'What do we do?' asked Nate, his face shadowy in the flickering firelight.

'Stay here,' said Monica, turning on the torch on her phone. 'Gunther and I will fetch some lights. Sit down, please, so you don't fall over anything.'

'I have a phone torch too,' Felix declared, like this was revolutionary new technology that only he had discovered. Lucy could hear him scrabbling around, then a dull thud as his phone hit the floor.

'Please, save your battery,' said Monica firmly. 'We do not know what is wrong with the generator, so it is good to keep as many phones charged as we can.'

'Fuck,' muttered Lucy, wishing she'd bagged Alex's charger earlier. Although without Wi-Fi she had no way to keep in touch with Jonno and the others anyway, so it wasn't like a charged phone would be any use.

'I've got about twenty per cent,' said Nate, the blue glow of his phone screen lighting up his face. 'I'll turn it off for now.'

'Mine is fully charged,' said Alex breezily. 'And I have a power pack. So I'll keep mine on in case we need to take a video or something.' Lucy shook her head and smiled in the darkness, marvelling that Alex's priority phone use in an emergency was shooting videos, rather than lighting the way or calling mountain rescue. If they had to leave this hut and trek to safety, she wasn't sure this random bunch of people was the support crew she'd pick, but at least the footage of their final hours would be social media gold.

'You OK?' she asked Nate, reaching over to touch his arm.

'Yeah,' he whispered, putting his hand over hers and squeezing it for the briefest second. It felt like a strange moment of togetherness in the darkness, like they were anchoring each other in the storm. Lucy had spent so much of this afternoon trying to keep Nate calm, she hadn't really thought about how comforting it would be to take reassurance and strength from someone else.

They all waited quietly until Gunther and Monica returned with various battery lanterns, torches and candles in jam jars, carefully placing them along the bar and on each of the tables. The return of light made the room feel less spooky and forbidding, and Lucy breathed a little easier. She huddled into the corner of the booth with her arms wrapped around her knees, wondering what they would do now.

'We still have bottled gas,' said Monica reassuringly. 'So there is hot water. Maybe some of us can shower tonight, and the rest of us tomorrow morning.'

'I don't have any clean clothes,' said Lucy feebly. In the scheme of things it probably didn't matter, but being in such close proximity to so many strangers, it suddenly felt very important that she didn't smell bad.

'I will lend you some pyjamas,' said Monica, giving her a warm smile. 'And if you like, I will show you where you can hand wash your clothes and hang them in front of the fire to dry while you are sleeping.'

Lucy felt tears brimming – a combination of tiredness, stress, booze and Monica being more motherly and kind than her own mother had been in years. 'Thank you,' she said. 'That would be lovely.'

'Have some more food,' said Chantal, pushing a plate of cold meat in Nate's direction. 'The fridge won't work now, so we need to eat everything.' Despite his brush-off earlier, Lucy could still see her surreptitiously checking him out from under her eyelashes as he took the plate and thanked her.

'Top up everyone's wine, please,' said Gunther,

thrusting a couple of bottles at Chantal. She grudgingly heaved herself out of the booth and started to circulate.

'What did you call a meal like this, when you were a kid?' asked Lucy, keen to keep Nate talking. Aside from it stopping her falling prey to negative thoughts, it was an excuse to look at him.

Nate looked over at the table of plates, his expression thoughtful. 'A carpet picnic,' he said with a smile. 'Apart from when we were with family in France. Then it was a selection of hors d'oeuvres.'

'Ooh, that's fancy,' laughed Lucy. 'In my house it was just picky bits.'

'I was always confused by the word buffet,' mused Nate. 'In English it describes the food, in French it's the piece of furniture you put the food on.'

'We have a rich history of bastardising other languages,' said Lucy. 'I did a linguistics module as part of my degree, I could bore you to death.'

'I doubt that,' said Nate, putting his empty plate on the table. 'Maybe we should sort out our beds, so we don't have to do that later.' He gave Lucy a searching look, and she wondered if he could tell she was feeling a bit wobbly about losing power and their connection to the outside world, or if he just wanted to be alone with her. Or maybe she was overthinking it, and he was just being practical.

'We will play some music soon,' announced Felix, taking a huge bite out of a sausage. 'I have no keyboard without the power, but Andrea has her guitar. Maybe "How Deep is Your Love".'

'Beds are a great idea,' said Lucy quickly, keen to avoid what was inevitably going to be an eternal, sausage-fuelled Bee Gees medley. She and Nate left their food for later, then took a head torch and followed Monica through a door marked *Private* behind the bar, which led to a separate part of the building that was clearly Gunther and Monica's home. What little Lucy could see in the gloom was uncluttered and cosy, with a homely smell of woodsmoke and pine. Monica pulled a pump and a bag containing two inflatable beds from a frighteningly well-organised cupboard under the stairs, and handed them to Nate.

'I will find you some sheets and blankets upstairs,' she said. 'And some towels. And maybe I also have a spare toothbrush.' Lucy wondered if she and Nate would be expected to share it, which somehow felt worse than having to share a bedroom, but decided to say nothing. Maybe it would be OK, as long as she got to use it first.

'Do you want me to do the other one?' asked Lucy, having done very little other than watch Nate pump up a bed in a room that was part attic, part storeroom. One half of the windowless space was taken up with stacked deckchairs and cardboard boxes marked *Sommer*, whilst the other half was a bare wooden floor with a steeply pitched roof and a stone chimney breast that funnelled all the heat from the wood burner below.

'No, I can manage,' said Nate breathlessly, switching the pump to his other foot. They were more robust than a camping mat or a pool inflatable, but very definitely not something you would reasonably describe as a bed.

Lucy fully expected to be lying on the floor by morning, and there was no possible way to arrange the two beds within the remaining space without them being dangerously close together.

'OK, what should I do instead?' asked Lucy. 'I feel useless just standing here.'

'Ask me a question,' said Nate. 'And then I get to ask one in return.'

Lucy was immediately suspicious, wondering if this was a trap. 'Why?'

'Because we're about to sleep together for the first time,' said Nate. 'We should probably get to know each other first.'

'You're very funny,' said Lucy, pulling a face. 'Fine. Are you in a relationship?' She hadn't intended for the question to sound so challenging, and now she was worried that Nate was about to offload about Sasha. It was bad enough that she knew, without him *knowing* that she knew. Or even worse, inviting her into his circle of trust and telling her all the sordid details.

Nate hesitated, then carried on pumping. 'There's somebody I like, but it's a little complicated.'

Lucy had a thousand follow-ups, but decided not to dig herself in any deeper. 'OK, fair enough. What's your question?'

'Are *you* in a relationship?'

'No,' said Lucy, deciding not to get into the details of Anthony and Marco the way she had with the women in the kitchen earlier. 'I'm very much single.'

'OK,' he said, his brow furrowing briefly, which Lucy put down to confusion about the filthy text message he'd seen on her phone earlier. 'Why are you still in Bristol?'

Lucy felt breathless for a second, wondering if Nate suspected how deep that question went. 'That's two questions,' she replied, playing for time.

'I know, but the first one provided very limited information.'

'Why would you want information?'

'Because I'm trying to work you out, that's all. And I was wondering why you're not in a bigger agency. Like in London or New York, or whatever.'

Lucy shook her head. 'Why would I be?'

Nate stopped pumping and looked up at her. 'Because you're the most talented copywriter I've ever worked with, and I think you're totally wasted on overpriced designer condoms.'

'Wow,' said Lucy, her eyes widening. 'Is this how you get women into your inflatable bed?'

Nate threw back his head and gave a full-bodied laugh that made his dark eyes sparkle. 'No, Lucy, I'm definitely making you a bed of your own. But I find you interesting, and you don't give much away about yourself.'

'Don't I?' Being the focus of Nate's attention in this way was making Lucy feel a little uncomfortable, like he could see into her soul.

Nate started pumping again, but slower this time. 'No. You and Jonno, you're a tight unit, you know? You don't really let other people in.'

'He's a good friend,' said Lucy. 'I've known him a long time.'

'I know,' said Nate. 'I'm not suggesting it's anything else. Is that why you don't leave? Because of Jonno?'

Lucy thought for a moment, wondering how open to be. Talking about Leo made her heart hurt, but she'd already told Nate most of it and, all things considered, she had nothing much to lose at this point. 'OK – honesty time?'

Nate stopped pumping and nodded.

'I like it in Bristol. It's where my brother lived before he . . . died.' Lucy faltered, then took a deep breath and carried on. 'After I graduated I bought a place there, to feel closer to him. LUNA is the best agency in Bristol, and Jonno and I are a really good creative partnership. So that's why I stay.'

'Wow,' said Nate, blinking at her.

'Well, you did ask.'

'No, really,' said Nate. 'I appreciate you being so honest.'

Lucy shrugged, surprised at how easy he was to talk to. Before today they'd barely given each other the time of day, and yet here she was, telling him her secrets. 'I'm blaming wine and altitude.'

'And Jägermeister.'

'God, the Jäger. Whose idea was that?' Her stomach still felt a bit queasy.

'Gunther's, I think.' Nate knelt down to remove the pump from the second bed and quickly put the plug in as the air started to hiss out. 'OK, you can do the bedding now.'

'Are you going back down to the bar?'

'Yeah, I need some more food. Monica mentioned a

load of ice cream that needs eating. Are you coming back down?'

'No,' said Lucy, feeling drunk and exhausted and a bit discombobulated by all this soul-baring and heavy conversation. 'I'm going to put on some of Monica's ugly pyjamas and try to get some sleep.'

Nate looked at his watch. 'Really? It's not even eight.'

'I know,' said Lucy, torn between needing to be alone for a little while, and a strange and powerful desire for Nate to stay so they could be alone together. 'But it's been quite a day, and I'm shattered.'

Nate looked guilty, clearly thinking he'd been talking too much when Lucy's head was full of Leo, probably.

'I'll be fine,' smiled Lucy. 'Just don't trip over me when you come back up.'

'I'll do my best,' said Nate with a weak smile. He paused for a second, then tilted his head. 'I definitely can't tempt you?'

Oh God, you definitely could, thought Lucy. Nate's face was half in shadow with his hair flopping over one eye, making his cheekbones look like razors. His hands were on his hips, highlighting the definition in his arms. He was unquestionably hot and she was starting to understand him better, but the thing he had going on with Sasha loomed large. Lucy had worked hard to get her life under control and keep things simple and uncomplicated, so why blow it all on a one-night stand with Nate Lambert?

'I'm OK here, thanks.'

Nate took the hint and headed down the creaky stairs, leaving Lucy to organise the bedding, then lie on her back in the milky torchlight. It was warm and peaceful up here, the chatter and laughter from the bar distant and reassuring, and she took a moment to take some deep breaths and enjoy being alone for the first time since she'd woken up that morning. She wondered fleetingly if Chantal was cosied up next to Nate in what she already thought of as *their booth*, and then asked herself why she cared. Maybe if she slept, things would feel clearer in the morning.

When Lucy woke, three things immediately occurred to her.

Firstly, that Nate wasn't on the airbed next to her – it was still neatly made with a smooth duvet and pillow. She glanced at her phone to see the time, but the remaining battery was long gone. So instead she looked at her smart watch, which was also entirely dead and useless. Apparently nobody in the 'what's the bare minimum acceptable battery life?' team at Apple had considered the impact of being stranded on a mountain during a power cut.

Secondly, that in her keenness to shut everything out she'd forgotten to clean her teeth or wash her clothes, so her mouth felt like the inside of a charity shop handbag and she was facing the unappealing prospect of putting dirty underwear back on in the morning.

And thirdly, that somebody downstairs was, for some inexplicable reason, listening to Ed Sheeran.

She lay in bed for a few minutes, processing all these new facts. Without knowing the time, it was impossible to know if she'd been asleep for twenty minutes or three hours, although it definitely felt like more than a nap. The clothes situation made her feel itchy; she hated not feeling clean, or wearing unwashed clothes. But clearly Ed Sheeran meant that some people downstairs were still awake.

Her thoughts drifted to Chantal, and an imagined scenario where she and Nate were the only ones left in the bar, having a nightcap in the glow of the dying fire embers, Ed Sheeran singing a smushy love song as they edged closer together . . .

Time to do some laundry, thought Lucy, hurriedly rearranging Monica's pyjamas where they'd twisted and bunched up in various places. She stretched a head torch over her bed hair and gathered up her clothes, then tiptoed down the stairs to the bathroom, which also contained the washing machine. She pressed the power button, hoping the generator might have magically repaired itself, but nothing happened. So instead she ran some hot water into the bath and threw her clothes in with some detergent.

Once everything was clean, she drained the bath and rinsed each item out under the tap, then wrung everything out over the empty bath until it was no longer dripping. By the time she'd finished, Ed Sheeran was singing the mawkishly sentimental 'Thinking Out Loud'. The idea of Chantal taking Nate into her loving arms made Lucy feel even more itchy, so she gathered up her wet clothes and padded through the corridor to the door that connected Gunther and Monica's house to the bar.

Lucy turned off her head torch and silently opened

the door, praying she wasn't about to get a prime view of Nate orally servicing Chantal by candlelight, then froze in stunned silence as she took in the scene. Gunther and Monica were to her left behind the bar, smiling and swaying gently. Chantal was next to them, her fingers pressed together in prayer in front of her lips, and her expression nothing short of enraptured. Andrea and Felix were in one of the booths, Andrea's head resting on Felix's shoulder. Alex and Willem were next to them, Alex holding up his phone and apparently filming a video. Lucy looked around the corner to see where his phone was pointed – Nate was sitting on a bar stool, playing Andrea's guitar and . . . singing.

Fuck, thought Lucy, as realisation dawned. *It's not an Ed Sheeran track, it's Nate.* She could only see his shadowy profile, but his eyes were closed and he was singing with such intensity that she actually gasped. His voice was uncannily like Ed Sheeran's, but somehow it was so much more than *Stars In Their Eyes*-style karaoke – there was a raw authenticity to it, a heartfelt, gut-punching realness.

Lucy watched in awe, entirely breathless and lost for words. Moving wasn't an option, because then Nate would notice her and the spell would be broken. Maybe it was Jäger, exhaustion and the uniquely stressful circumstances of this particular gig, but a song that had historically made Lucy want to puke was now making her want to cry.

Nate stretched out the final notes, then hung his head as applause broke out from every corner of the room. He held his hand up in thanks, then turned to look at Lucy like he'd known she was there all along. The smile he gave her set off a cage of butterflies in her stomach, and she couldn't help but smile back, no longer caring that she was standing in a doorway in floral pyjamas and a head torch, clutching a bundle of wet clothes.

Shit, thought Lucy. *The moody guy from my office is doing a candlelit Ed Sheeran tribute act, and apparently I now fancy the pants off him. This is very, very bad.*

CHAPTER FOURTEEN

'Lucy!' yelled Chantal, a little too enthusiastically for it to seem genuine. 'Are you OK? You look a little . . .'

'A little what?' asked Lucy, quickly pulling off the head torch and attempting to flatten her hair. Marco had once told her that she was one of those people who never looked truly bad – even when she was hung-over, her hair needed a wash, and she had period spots. But right now Lucy suspected she was testing that theory to the limit.

'Come and have a drink,' said Monica, extracting the bundle of wet clothes from her arms and ushering her to the empty booth she and Nate had made their own earlier. 'I'll hang these up for you.'

'Thank you,' mumbled Lucy, sliding into the corner. She felt a tiny buzz of pleasure when Nate shuffled in to join her, immediately pouring her a glass of wine. Her head felt fuzzy and hung-over and she definitely didn't need any more booze, but right now she was a little caught off guard by the whole Ed Sheeran thing and it seemed like the only way forward. The others all bustled over, filling up the remaining seats around the table, clearly keen to hear more from Nate and not let the moment end.

'You OK?' he asked.

Lucy drained half the glass, nodding vaguely in his direction. 'You never told me you were a singer.' She didn't mean for it to sound quite so accusatory, but after he'd made such an effort to big up her writing skills earlier, he might at least have mentioned this pretty interesting talent.

'I'm not,' said Nate quickly, and even in the dim light Lucy could see he looked mortified. 'I mean, I've always wanted to be, obviously, and I sing in the car and the shower. But that's it.' Lucy could see Felix leaning forward, getting ready to share his professional wisdom, until Andrea gently placed a hand on his arm and he changed his mind.

'Have you ever sung for an audience before?' asked Alex, and Lucy couldn't help but notice that he looked a little sour that Nate was hogging the Guntherhütte spotlight. Or maybe being the kind of person who engineered moments like this specifically for social media engagement, he was cynical about Nate's genuine surprise and sincerity.

'No,' said Nate. 'That was definitely a one-off.'

'You mean I almost missed your one and only gig?' asked Lucy, giving him a playful prod. 'Wow.'

'Don't,' said Nate. He looked nauseous, like he'd already boarded the regret bus and it was only going one way.

'I think your vocals could—' started Felix, holding up a finger.

'You can play guitar,' interrupted Andrea, leaning forward to block Felix's view of Nate. 'You are very good.'

'I taught myself from YouTube,' mumbled Nate. 'I've never done that in front of anyone either.'

'Being very drunk in a room full of strangers is extremely liberating,' said Willem. 'You should go on one of the TV talent shows. Like *The X Factor*, or *The Voice*. We watch the British versions on Dutch TV.'

Nate laughed and shook his head. 'Definitely not. I've thought about it loads of times, but I'm never going to have the guts to do that in front of an audience.'

'We are an audience,' said Monica kindly. 'A very lucky one.'

'Well, thanks,' said Nate. He stared at his hands, which were still shaking a little. 'Who else is going to have a go?'

'I definitely can't sing,' said Alex, looking slightly resentful about it. 'But I'm happy to take the videos. Willem has a nice voice.'

'Do you want to sing something together, Lucy?' asked Willem. 'I know the words to every Britney Spears song ever. Even the album tracks.'

'I need to drink more wine first,' said Lucy, draining her glass and reaching for the bottle. This whole situation with Nate, the rush of *feelings* she'd had when she'd seen him singing, had left her feeling agitated and confused.

'I think Andrea and I should sing some more,' said Felix, clearly annoyed that Nate had stolen Night Fever's thunder. 'Maybe "More Than A Woman".'

Andrea headed over to the stool and picked up the guitar, throwing Lucy a glance that she decided to interpret as a cry for help.

'Can Andrea sing something else?' asked Lucy lightly.

'What do you mean?' replied Felix, glaring at her.

'Oh,' said Lucy, as Andrea shook her head frantically. 'We love the Bee Gees, obviously. But I wondered if Andrea could sing something like . . . I don't know. Maybe Adele?'

'Only Adele can sing Adele,' said Felix gruffly. 'We sing the Bee Gees.'

'Tragedy,' muttered Alex, prompting Lucy to turn away, pressing her lips together to stop herself laughing.

'Oh,' said Nate, suddenly sitting upright and checking his old-school, functioning wristwatch. 'It's just past midnight, which means it's actually Lucy's birthday.'

Lucy looked at him and raised her eyebrows. Her birthday wasn't until June.

'Oh Lucy, happy birthday!' cried Monica, as everyone else joined in.

'Maybe just one Adele song, since it's Lucy's birthday?' said Andrea, looking hopefully at Felix. He pouted for a few long seconds, which gave Lucy time to give Nate a *what the fuck have you done?* look. He shrugged and pulled a *too late now* face in return.

Felix sighed, rubbing his hand over his stubbly jaw. 'Just one song,' he said to Andrea. 'I made a promise to Robin Gibb, remember?'

'I know,' said Andrea gravely. 'But these are special circumstances. It's just for Lucy, for her birthday.'

Felix nodded reluctantly and pressed the palms of his hands together against his lips, no doubt asking the Gibb brothers, alive and dead, for forgiveness. Andrea cleared her throat and strummed out the first few bars of 'Make

You Feel My Love'. Her voice was rich and pure, her eyes closed; she was entirely absorbed in the song. Lucy hugged her knees, a stupid grin on her face. She turned and looked at Nate, who spread his left arm along the back of the seat. It felt like an invitation, somehow, and for a moment Lucy was tempted to slide along and rest her head on his shoulder. Shoving her weird feelings aside, it still felt like some kind of . . . *something* might come out of this crazy shared experience. A friendship, maybe. Or an understanding. That obviously didn't justify intimate physical contact of any kind, but it was a nice thought all the same. Especially as Chantal was looking at her like she wanted to poke her eyes out, which was a bonus.

The whole room sat in silence for the duration of the song, swaying along and listening to Andrea pour her heart into every line. She had a soulful, husky voice that was, by any standards, wasted on the Bee Gees.

'That was beautiful,' cheered Monica as Andrea's voice faded out through the final line. She smiled, her face lighting up.

'It's actually a Bob Dylan song,' huffed Felix dismissively, as Monica disappeared into the kitchen, dragging Chantal with her.

'Then maybe Andrea should sing an Adele original,' said Lucy quickly.

'I would love to,' said Andrea, before Felix could interrupt. 'And since it's your birthday, you should choose. What's your favourite?'

Lucy thought for a moment, weighing up whether to ask Andrea for a crowd-pleasing belter, or the song she really wanted to hear.

'"When We Were Young",' she said quietly. 'Do you know the words?'

'Of course,' said Andrea. 'It's a beautiful song.' She began to sing, and Lucy wrapped one arm around her knees again and pressed the other one over her mouth. She thought about the last time she'd seen Leo, when they'd both spent Christmas at home with their parents. He'd been a little quiet, but Lucy had put that down to being stressed and anxious about a promotion he'd just had at work. He was only twenty-one, but already being noticed by management and earmarked for big things. He mentioned a relationship that hadn't panned out, but didn't go into details. They'd made vague plans to maybe go away together in June, to celebrate their twenty-second birthday and Lucy finishing her finals, but never talked about exactly where they might go.

Whilst at times during that week they'd regressed to childhood silliness and private jokes, Lucy had felt the loss of connection between them, the loosening of the stitches in their sibling fabric. It felt like an occasional glitch, or a record scratch when one of them would say something and they'd look at each other as if to say *who is this person?* But Lucy had rationalised that they were both adults now, living away from the baggage of home and school. Over time they would start to value each other in a different way, and find time to make new memories together. They were twins, and that was an unbreakable, everlasting bond. They'd hugged goodbye just before New Year, and the next time she'd seen her brother he was in a wooden box in Croydon crematorium.

The tears flowed freely down her cheeks; eleven years

of pain and loss and regret and unanswered questions. It was only when the song came to a close and the room exploded into rapturous applause that she noticed Nate's arm around her, his hand gently stroking her shoulder. One of them had moved closer during the song, and right now Lucy couldn't say if it was her or Nate.

'Was that for Leo?' asked Nate quietly, handing Lucy a napkin so she could blow her nose. All the attention was on Andrea for the moment, which felt like a relief.

'Mmm,' said Lucy, dabbing her face and trying to catch her breath. 'The song came out after he died, so it wasn't a favourite of his or anything. But it always makes me think of him.'

'What kind of music did he love?'

Lucy forced a weak smile. 'Dance music, drum 'n' bass, UK garage. He was a huge fan of Craig David, actually. We both were.'

'Me too,' said Nate. He turned to look at her, his eyes huge from wine and emotion, then reached out to give her hand a squeeze, before quickly letting go. 'I'm sorry, Lucy.'

A flickering ball of light appeared in the doorway of the kitchen, and it took a moment for Lucy to realise that it was . . . sparklers. Gunther started to sing 'Zum Geburtstag viel Glück', then Andrea struck up the music to the birthday song and everyone sang it in a combination of German and English.

'Ice cream,' sang Monica, placing a giant bowl of vanilla ice cream in front of Lucy as the sparklers fizzled out to burned sticks. 'I emptied the freezer earlier and most of it is buried outside in the snow, but we might as well eat the ice cream.' Chantal followed with a stack of small bowls and spoons, which she dumped in front of Lucy with a look that screamed *I'm going to have to wash these up by hand later, and I've decided it's your fault.*

Lucy felt her heart fill with affection for this eclectic collection of people, rubbing her puffy eyes with the heel of her hands and smiling at Nate as he handed her a spoon. They all piled into the ice cream, an end-of-holiday vibe in the room. Alex started taking more photos and videos, presumably for a bumper content spree as soon as the Wi-Fi came back. She grinned for a photo with her fake birthday ice cream cake, feeling infinitely better for drowning her hangover in more wine and food. Crying out some of the heaviness of the past twenty-four hours had felt good too.

'Tell me about Alex's royal connections,' said Lucy, as Willem slid into the booth next to her, shuffling her closer to Nate.

'He's sixteenth in line to the Dutch throne,' he said mildly, as though he was simply telling Lucy he worked in financial services.

'So if there was a really big plane crash, technically he could be king.'

'Technically, yes,' said Willem, his brow furrowed. 'But those fifteen people would never get on a plane together. It would need to be several co-ordinated plane crashes.'

'Who is sixteenth in line to the British throne?' Lucy asked Nate.

'You'd have to ask my Dutch grandma,' he replied with a wry smile. 'I think she's got them all written down.'

'Are you going to sing again?' asked Willem.

'No,' said Nate. 'That was very much a one-off. We've drunk all the wine, eaten all the ice cream, sung all the songs, and now it's time to go to bed.'

'Yeah, I think you're right,' said Lucy, stretching her arms above her head as she yawned lavishly. Somehow she felt less weird about sharing the attic with Nate than she had earlier – maybe because they'd both opened up a little this evening, or maybe because she was drunk again. His situation with Sasha still felt like the senior management elephant in the room, but Nate didn't seem bothered about how his girlfriend might react to the Guntherhütte sleeping arrangements, so why should Lucy care? Maybe Nate and Sasha had a casual arrangement, like she had with Anthony and Marco.

'You should get the cake video from Alex,' Chantal announced, slithering into the booth across from Lucy. 'When the power comes back on, you can send it to your two boyfriends, so they know you're having a good birthday.'

There was a beat of silence as Nate turned to Lucy. 'Two boyfriends?'

'It's really cool,' Chantal continued animatedly, waving her hands to get Willem's attention too. 'Didn't Lucy tell you? She's in a relationship with two different guys.'

'Oh, hello,' said Alex smoothly, pulling up a chair and resting his chin on his hands, clearly enraptured. 'This sounds like a conversation I don't want to miss.'

'That wasn't public information,' said Lucy through gritted teeth, fixing Chantal with her best laser death stare. 'That was a kitchen secret, between us women.'

'Don't let that stop you now,' chipped in Alex.

'Oh, I'm sorry,' said Chantal, not looking sorry at all. 'I just thought Nate would know.'

'No,' said Nate with a forced smile. 'And on that bombshell, I think it's probably time for bed.' He wriggled out of the booth and hurried off, saying goodnight to the rest of the crowd on the way.

'That was completely out of order,' hissed Lucy after he'd gone.

'How could I know you hadn't told him?' said Chantal, her face the picture of wide-eyed innocence. 'You told us in the kitchen, and we're complete strangers. And you said you weren't his girlfriend.' They spoke in strained whispers, so the rest of the group couldn't hear.

'I'm not his girlfriend,' said Lucy. 'We work together. Which makes my private life none of his business.' Willem and Alex glanced back and forth between the two of them, like they were watching a very intense tennis match.

'Oh,' said Chantal with a look of wide-eyed surprise. 'I'm sorry.' She tilted her head to one side, and Lucy realised she had totally underestimated Chantal. 'Are you angry because you actually like him?'

'Whoa, girl,' hissed Alex, recoiling dramatically. 'Shit got real.'

Lucy gave her a hard look, weighing up how much of her fury was because she was drunk and Chantal was a devious cow, and how much was because Chantal was one hundred per cent correct. 'Good night, Chantal,' she said, opting not to spoil what had actually been quite a fun evening. Alex was hovering with his phone, poised to start videoing their catfight, and some things were probably best left unsaid.

'Are you asleep?' whispered Lucy, stepping over Nate and plonking herself down on her airbed. It was already significantly less inflated than earlier, which didn't bode well for a good night's sleep. She stood her torch on the floor so it reflected off the ceiling, casting a warm glow around the room.

'Not any more,' said Nate, turning over and sitting up, being careful not to bash his head on the roof beams. 'What's happening downstairs?' He looked adorably ruffled in a white T-shirt that showed off nice arms. Nothing like Anthony's, obviously, but Nate was clearly no stranger to the gym.

'Nothing much,' said Lucy. 'I helped Monica, Gunther and Willem clear up. Washing up in a head torch felt like when you go camping as a kid.'

'Sorry, I should have stayed to help with that.' He fiddled with the duvet, not able to look her in the eye.

'It's fine, although you could have translated the argument Andrea and Felix were having. The only words I understood were "Adele" and "Bee Gees".'

'Well, I think we can fill in the gaps for ourselves there,' yawned Nate, ruffling his hair. 'Where did Alex and Chantal go?'

'They both made themselves scarce,' said Lucy. 'I think Chantal thought I might punch her, and I don't think Baron Alexander Jansen does washing-up.'

'He probably has minions for that kind of thing,' said Nate with a sleepy smile.

'Or possibly Willem, who is lovely. He's already invited us to visit him in Amsterdam, so I think we've made a friend for life.'

They were both quiet for a minute, and the silence felt deafening.

'Why did you lie?' asked Nate.

'About what?' said Lucy, even though she knew.

'I asked you earlier if you had a boyfriend, and you said no.'

'I didn't *lie*,' replied Lucy, having prepared her defence on the way up the stairs. 'I do have a couple of . . . arrangements, but neither of them are my boyfriend.'

'Why not?'

Lucy shrugged. 'Because that isn't the arrangement.'

'OK, but it's not "I'm single", either.'

'I can see how it might not seem that way, but I definitely still think of myself as single. It's just quite a big thing to tell somebody you don't know very well. I didn't want you to judge.'

Nate gave a barking laugh. 'You told Monica and Andrea and Chantal. You don't know them at all.'

'OK, but I'm never going to see them again, which is totally different from telling somebody I work with.'

'Mmm,' said Nate, clearly still not convinced.

'Look, it was kitchen girl-chat, I was a bit drunk. The regret has now kicked in.'

Nate smiled and shook his head, and Lucy hoped she might be forgiven. It surely couldn't have escaped him that he wasn't exactly being transparent about his love life either, so presumably he wasn't going to push it.

'These beds are really shit, by the way,' he said.

'I know. I tried sleeping earlier. That pile of deck-chairs is probably more comfortable.'

'Hopefully we're only here for one night, though,' said Nate, yawning again. 'With any luck we'll be with the others in Geneva tomorrow.' He glanced at his watch and pulled a face. 'Well, today now.'

'Mmm,' said Lucy. Nate would probably be shacked up in Sasha's hotel room this time tomorrow, and she'd be in bed alone. She hadn't messaged Anthony and Marco yet, although presumably neither knew about her Swiss drama and so had no reason to be concerned. She'd spent years cultivating a life where she was emotionally beholden to no one, but right now the idea that absolutely nobody was worrying about her left her feeling strangely empty.

'You OK?' asked Nate, looking at her doubtfully.

'Yeah.' Lucy smiled sadly. 'I need some sleep, I think.' She turned off the torch and snuggled down under the duvet, rubbing her cold feet on the mattress and hoping the friction of skin against polyester didn't start a fire.

'Goodnight, Lucy,' said Nate quietly.

'Night,' said Lucy, wishing for the first time in forever that she could snuggle into the warmth of someone else's body and just sleep.

CHAPTER FIFTEEN

'Lucy, wake up,' said a man's voice. She dragged herself out of a dream where she'd been waiting on the side of the road for a bus that Leo was on, but somehow he never arrived. She'd had variations on the same dream for years – sometimes the bus drove straight past and she'd catch a tantalising glimpse of Leo through the window, and sometimes the bus stopped, but when she climbed aboard to sit with her brother, he'd disappeared. Night after night of waiting for buses, so that she could talk to Leo about the morning that had tipped him over the edge. To ask him why he hadn't called her, or texted, or left a note, or done anything that might give Lucy some answers rather than this gaping, unfathomable void. But Leo was always just out of reach, and the conversation never happened. So she'd wait for the next bus, and maybe that would be the one.

She peeled open her crusty eyes to find Nate looming over her. 'You need to come and look at this.'

'What is it?' she said sleepily, turning her head and clamping her lips together so he wouldn't be subjected to her fetid wine breath. The loft had no windows so it was still dark, with the only light coming from the open door to the stairs and the floor below.

'Come and see,' he said, with the excitement of a little

boy at Christmas. She huffed and hauled herself out of a bed that was now nothing more than a synthetic membrane on the floor, scraping away the bits of hair that had stuck to her face. She followed him stiffly down the stairs, noting that Gunther's grey pyjamas paired with a white T-shirt really didn't look entirely bad on him, even through a rancid hangover.

'Look,' he said, pulling open the curtains covering the window on the landing.

'Jesus Christ,' said Lucy, recoiling from the dazzling glare and shielding her eyes. It took her a moment to process what she was looking at. She'd never seen so much snow in her life – it had entirely submerged the edge of the terrace, and the trees were groaning under the weight of it, with barely a branch visible. It felt like some kind of extreme Narnia.

'It's stopped snowing,' said Nate. 'Hopefully that means we can get out of here today.'

'Hope so,' said Lucy, turning away from the sunlight scorching her eyeballs. 'What time is it?'

'Nearly half eight,' said Nate. 'I went looking for coffee, but then I saw the view and thought you'd want to see it.'

'It's amazing,' said Lucy, not wanting to rain on his puppy-like enthusiasm. 'I might go back to bed for a bit, though. My head hurts and I feel like shit.'

'Me too,' said Nate. 'My tongue feels like an old blanket.' He pulled a face, and Lucy decided she could probably trudge back up the stairs without causing offence. Mostly she was keen not to spend too much time in daylight until she'd found a mirror and assessed how terrible she looked.

'If you find coffee, I'd definitely be interested,' she called back. 'Just black is fine. And also my clothes. Monica hung them in the bar to dry.'

'OK,' said Nate. 'I'll see what I can find.'

Lucy picked her way through the boxes and climbed back into bed, wishing she'd used the bathroom while she was downstairs, but not feeling desperate enough to go back down again. She lay in the murky twilight of the loft and waited, trying to remember how she'd started the day before the advent of smartphones. She'd been at school then, so presumably she'd slept until the very last minute. But now she set her alarm for twenty minutes before she needed to get up, so she could ease herself into the day with her phone. No actual news, obviously – nobody needed war and famine and politics at that time of the day.

She comfortably dozed off for a few minutes, until Nate reappeared carrying two mugs of coffee with a stack of Lucy's dry clothes under his arm. The loft was less murky now that the curtains downstairs were open and flooding light into the stairwell, so she was able to watch him navigate the tiny space. He was barefoot and handsome even through crusty eyes, and she thanked the heavens that it was still dim enough up here to shadow her crumpled face.

'You're a legend,' said Lucy, sitting up so she could take the mug. 'What's going on downstairs?'

'Not much,' said Nate. 'Monica and Gunther are both up and showed me how to use the gas stove. No sign of anyone else.'

'What's the plan for today?' She sipped the coffee, which was hot and strong and glorious.

'Monica said we should all meet in the bar for

breakfast at half nine, and they'll give us a briefing. Gunther has a plan, apparently.'

'Is it a plan for us both to be sipping wine by Lake Geneva by dinnertime, celebrating my fake birthday?'

'I'm not sure,' laughed Nate. He was sitting cross-legged on his bed, which looked like it had survived the night and was marginally less airless than Lucy's.

'Other than a hangover, how are you feeling today?' she asked, conscious that this time yesterday he'd been worrying (prophetically, as it turned out) about getting caught in an avalanche.

'I'm OK,' he said with a shrug. 'It feels safe here, I guess. I've decided to look at it all as a big adventure. Something to tell the grandkids one day.'

'Good decision,' said Lucy, trying to imagine Sasha in the LUNA boardroom, feeding Nate's baby in a mulberry silk Armani blazer. 'They'll probably make us do a presentation when we get back to Bristol, tell the team all about it.'

'Yeah, might leave that to you,' said Nate, pulling a face.

'So there's no breakfast until half nine?' Lucy couldn't tell if her stomach was rumbling from hunger, or still churning its way through a heady brew of Jägermeister, red wine, cheese and ice cream.

Nate checked his watch. 'Yeah. Forty-five minutes. I don't think you'll get a full English, but there's definitely a continental option.'

'I'm not sure I can wait that long,' said Lucy, draining her coffee mug. 'Do you think it would be rude to raid the kitchen for leftover cheese?'

Nate leaned over and plucked a paper bag out from under Lucy's pile of clothes. 'You could. Or alternatively, you may be interested in one of the pains au chocolat Monica gave me.'

'Gimme,' said Lucy, holding out her hand and hoping he couldn't see how willingly she'd marry him right now.

'Do you think we should take them downstairs?' he teased, pulling the bag away. 'I'm not sure eating breakfast in bed is very Swiss.'

'Give it to me.' Lucy flapped her hand at him. 'It's not like we're sparking up a fondue.'

'Yeah, but I'd hate to leave Gunther and Monica with mice in their attic.'

Lucy rolled her eyes. 'Fine. I'll put my T-shirt over my lap and sweep up the crumbs, then throw them outside later. Give it. It's my birthday.'

'Fine,' laughed Nate, handing her the bag. 'I'll be sharing your tablecloth, if that's OK.'

Lucy scooched up so Nate could sit halfway down her bed, unfolding her clean T-shirt and spreading it out between them like a picnic blanket.

'Oh my God, this is heaven,' said Lucy. It was a bit dry and clearly yesterday's stock, but she could feel the layers of pastry soaking up her hangover, and the sweetness of the chocolate washing away the bitter taste in her mouth.

'Mmm,' said Nate, leaning over so all the flaky bits landed on the T-shirt. He was close enough that she could smell the sleep on him; a warm, biscuity, comfortable smell that she'd never really encountered before. She'd welcomed plenty of men into her bed over the years, but once the sex was over and everyone had spent an acceptable amount of time in recovery, she always slept alone. This situation felt oddly intimate, somehow – the last man she'd sat on a bed and chatted to in a non-sexual capacity was Leo.

'That was perfect,' said Lucy, dabbing at the paper bag with a wet finger to get the final flakes of pastry. 'Thank you.' Nate brushed his hands together over the T-shirt, so Lucy could carefully gather the corners into a bundle and secure it with the hairband around her wrist. It would probably be better deployed taming her nest of hair right now, but needs must.

'You're welcome,' said Nate happily. She waited for him to move, but he stayed where he was, both of them cross-legged and facing each other like they were six-year-old girls playing a hand-clapping game. Lucy idly wondered what Sasha would think if she could see her boyfriend sitting on a bed with one of her team. She wasn't sure 'we were trying not to get flaky pastry on the bedding' would quite cut it.

'While you were downstairs, I was wondering what people did in bed before smartphones,' said Lucy, keen to keep the friendly conversation going before it drifted into some kind of sexual tension.

Nate raised his eyebrows and looked at her from under his floppy fringe. 'Oh wow, Lucy – do you really not know? Do you need me to draw you a picture?'

OK, thought Lucy, *that's definitely flirting. I'm not imagining this*. 'You're very funny,' she said throwing him a snarky look.

'So what's your morning phone routine? What do you look at first?'

'WhatsApp,' said Lucy. 'Usually early morning messages from my mother telling me things I mustn't forget.'

'Ha,' said Nate. 'What kind of things?'

'The usual. Birthdays of cousins or neighbours I never see, reminders not to become a victim of the latest phishing scam.' There was also often a late-night penis status update from Anthony, but Lucy obviously wasn't going to mention that.

'What else?'

'My daily game of Wordle.'

'Of course,' said Nate. 'You're a writer. Every day?'

'Yep. I've got a streak of nearly five hundred days.' Lucy gasped and clutched her hand to her chest. 'Shit, if we don't get Wi-Fi back today, I'm going to lose my streak.'

Nate laughed and pulled up one knee, wrapping his arms around it. There was still a shyness and hesitation about him, but it felt like he'd softened a little and was relaxing into her company. Presumably over the last twenty-four hours he'd decided she was someone he could trust, which was an undeniably nice feeling.

'Saving your Wordle streak surely qualifies for a rescue helicopter,' he said thoughtfully. 'We should get Alex on to it.'

'Do you think him being here is big news in the Netherlands?' asked Lucy. 'Like, does him being stuck on a Swiss mountain create some kind of constitutional crisis?'

'I imagine his fandom are going out of their mind at the lack of content,' said Nate. 'Weird to think this whole situation might be news, and we have no idea. The local paper could be interviewing your family right now.'

'That would be awkward,' said Lucy with a grimace,

wondering how long it would take for one of her parents to mention Leo, then feeling bad about having bitter thoughts when Leo would have given *anything* to be having this adventure right now. 'Where are your family?'

'Oh, here and there,' said Nate vaguely. 'Most of them in France, obviously. I don't see much of them.'

'But your dad's British, right?'

'Mmm,' said Nate vaguely. 'But we're not close. It's complicated.'

'Like your love life, right?'

He looked up at her, his brow furrowed. 'What does that mean?'

'Oh,' said Lucy. 'I asked you yesterday if you were in a relationship, and you said it was complicated.'

'Right,' said Nate. 'We should probably get up. Gunther has plans for us.'

Lucy nodded, adding the deflection to her file on Nate marked *Sasha*. 'But before we get up, we need to talk about your singing last night.'

Even in the gloom of the loft, Lucy could see Nate blush. 'No,' he said, shaking his head vehemently. 'I'm still cringing.'

'Why are you cringing? It was amazing.'

'You would say that,' he said, laughing awkwardly. 'We have to share a bedroom.'

'No, really, Nate,' said Lucy, her hand twitching to reach over and touch his arm, then deciding against it. 'It was extraordinary. You have an incredible talent.'

'Well, it's nice of you to say so,' he mumbled, picking at the fabric of the duvet. 'I write songs too.'

'Really?'

'Yeah. I've got notebooks full of them. They're probably not very good. I should get you to edit them for me.'

'I doubt I could do them justice. Which one is your favourite?'

Nate thought about it for a moment. 'There's this one I've been playing around with for ages, called "Vois Grand". It's a thing my grandma used to say a lot.'

'Big voice?'

'No,' laughed Nate. '*Vois* with an S. It's like *dream big*, that kind of thing. The song is in English, but I gave it a French title in her honour.'

'That's lovely,' said Lucy. The only grandparents she'd known had died in their seventies, when she and Leo had still been quite small, but an inspirational granny sounded nice.

'But there's not much I can do with it if I have to be fifty levels of pissed to get on stage and sing it.'

'Never bothered Liam Gallagher,' said Lucy with a shrug.

'Also it was an audience of seven people. And I was still terrified.'

'I was the eighth, and you didn't look terrified to me.'

'You turned up during my last song. I spent the first few shitting my pants.'

Lucy laughed, knowing that at some point they would have to go and join the others, but not wanting to break this spell. 'You need to put those pants back on today, just FYI.'

'I'm still wearing them,' said Nate with a grin. 'Never took them off.'

'Fucking hell, at some point they'll walk down the mountain by themselves.'

Nate stretched his arms above his head and yawned. 'I might ask Gunther if I can borrow some clothes today, so I can wash mine. In case we're a Dutch media sensation when we get rescued.'

'Good idea,' said Lucy. 'Nobody needs to be a Dutch media sensation in dirty pants. What did it feel like?'

Nate looked confused, and dropped his arms back to his sides. 'What did what feel like?'

'Once you were over the terror, and just singing?'

'Oh, are we still talking about that?'

'Yes,' said Lucy, rolling her eyes.

'OK. Um. Amazing, I guess.' Nate was quiet for a moment, his eyes darting around like he was trying to find the words. 'I've always dreamed about it. Being a singer, performing in front of an audience, getting a record deal. Like, there are moments in the middle of the night when I can't sleep when I've actually thought it might be possible, promised myself that I'll put some stuff on social. But then the cold light of day kicks in.'

'And then it doesn't seem possible?'

Nate gave a hollow laugh. 'Day to day I'm fine, but under pressure the anxiety can be pretty crippling. Booze helps, clearly. Listening to Chantal's horrible singing was the final push I needed.'

Lucy laughed. 'Just out of interest, what is it you're scared of?'

'That's not how anxiety works,' said Nate, shaking his head. 'It's not rational, it doesn't behave in a logical, consistent way. Last night my brain gave me a break, but another day it might bring me to my knees.'

'But if you were a recording artist you'd have people looking after you,' said Lucy. 'Lots of singers have mental health issues.'

'Maybe,' said Nate. 'But to get that far, I have to put myself out there. Right now I can't imagine ever being able to do that.'

'Well, maybe an audience of eight in the Guntherhütte is the first step,' said Lucy. 'I'm really proud of you, you know.'

Nate looked up at her, his eyes narrowed like he was wondering if she was taking the piss.

'No, really,' she continued. 'I know how hard that must have been for you. I saw the struggles Leo went through to do anything in front of people. Even standing up in class to answer a question. It used to turn him inside out.'

'Yeah,' said Nate, looking back at his feet. 'I know that feeling.'

'What was Chantal singing?' asked Lucy, keen to keep Nate talking.

'"Ne Partez Pas Sans Moi" – it's a Celine Dion song from the eighties. Monica said it won Eurovision, but I don't know if that's true. Apparently it was Gunther and Monica's wedding song, so they were happy.'

'Ah, that's sweet.'

'Although the song actually translates as "Don't Leave Without Me", which feels like an odd choice for a wedding.'

Lucy snorted with laughter. 'Maybe Chantal was aiming it at you. That woman is crushing hard.'

'What do you mean?' said Nate, frowning at her.

'Chantal. Don't bother with a candle in this power cut, because Chantal is carrying a HUGE torch.'

'That's ridiculous,' said Nate in disbelief.

'It's not. Why do you think she told you about my personal sexual arrangements? It was a tactical move to ensure you don't leave Zermatt without her. See? It all makes sense now.'

'No, it doesn't,' laughed Nate, his eyes wide. 'You're still drunk.'

'She wants you to take her away from all this,' continued Lucy, gasping dramatically. 'The song was a secret cry for help, because Gunther and Monica are keeping her hostage to the pizza oven.'

'Well, that's definitely not going to happen,' said Nate. 'Not my type at all.'

'And what is your type exactly?' said Lucy playfully. *Mature women with executive powers and designer handbags?*

'Not Chantal,' said Nate firmly, standing up and holding out his hand. 'Come on, time for Gunther's breakfast briefing.'

Lucy took his hand and hauled herself up, clamping her lips together and turning her head so he didn't get a waft of coffee and hangover wine breath.

'Another day in the mountains,' she said brightly, feeling oddly excited about what the day might bring. 'I wonder if we'll get the power back? I could charge my phone.'

'Hopefully our last day in the mountains,' said Nate cheerfully. 'Let's make it count, shall we?'

CHAPTER SIXTEEN

'We have a very important job to do today,' said Gunther, standing in the middle of the room as everyone picked at the breakfast bits on the table. Monica had knocked together a Swiss smorgasbord of bread, cheese, cold meat and various jams, and once everyone had wished Lucy happy birthday again, they'd piled in like it was their last meal on earth. By ten, Lucy was three coffees in and melting under Chantal's laser glares. Even with a couple of windows cracked to let some fresh air in, the bar smelled of last night's party and nine unwashed bodies, and the walls were closing in.

'Have you fixed the generator?' asked Alex, his phone glued to his hand as usual. Lucy's mouth twitched in Nate's direction, both of them recognising the social media equivalent of a crack addict who needed his next fix.

'No,' said Gunther. 'I have tried, but I think it needs a new part.' He gave Monica a shamefaced look, and got a steely glare in return. Lucy could only imagine the months of conversations about a replacement part for the generator that Gunther had ignored.

'Why don't you have solar panels?' asked Lucy, gesturing at the blue skies outside the window. 'You wouldn't get much power in January, but it would be enough to charge some phones and power your Wi-Fi.'

'This is also on my list,' said Gunther awkwardly, Monica's eyes now resembling tiny slits. Chantal rolled her eyes and sipped her coffee, having clearly been a spectator to this parental beef for some time.

'Anyway, today we are going to dig a path,' continued Gunther, pointing at the front door. 'From the entrance door to the piste. So if the rescue vehicle comes today, they will be able to reach us. The space between the piste and the door is too narrow for a snowplough, so we need to do this by hand.'

Everyone nodded, clearly keen to get active and expedite their rescue as quickly as possible. 'Are they coming today?' asked Alex, who evidently kept a full make-up bag in his backpack because he looked immaculate, whilst everyone else looked like they'd slept in a bus shelter. 'Have you heard anything?'

'There is no way for anyone to contact us,' shrugged Gunther, avoiding Monica's gaze. 'But the weather is clear, so there will be a team looking at the avalanche risk and deciding if it is safe to clear the path. So maybe they will be here this afternoon. If not, they will try again tomorrow.'

Alex paled, clearly appalled at the prospect of another night on this mountain without social media validation.

'If we clear some space now,' added Monica, 'there will be some time when the sun is above us and we can be outside. Maybe we can light the outdoor pizza oven.' She smiled as everyone in the room visibly perked up at the prospect of sunshine and pizza.

'Count me in,' said Lucy, desperate to get outside in the fresh air after a whole twenty-four hours indoors.

'It is your birthday,' Gunther protested. 'You do not have to work.'

'I definitely want to,' said Lucy firmly, as Nate looked away and covered his mouth to hide his smile. 'Really, I'd like to join in.'

'Then we will work hard, and work together.' Gunther clapped his hands like he was convincing his troops to fight for their country. 'We will each dig for a few minutes, then swap with the next person. It is hard work, so this is the best way.'

'I will not be digging,' said Monica. 'I will keep you supplied with drinks and snacks and encouragement.'

'Maybe you could dig and I could film?' asked Alex hopefully. 'I feel like it's very important to capture all of this for when they make a dramatic movie of our adventure. And also in case there is ever a time I need to make a claim on my travel insurance for post-traumatic stress counselling.'

'You can give me your phone,' said Monica firmly. 'I know how to make a video.'

Alex handed it over, looking mutinous. 'Use the preset filters,' he said grumpily. 'And make sure you get plenty of shots of me working hard.'

The group started to move around, draining coffee cups and stretching, anxious to get going with their task for the morning. Gunther pulled on waterproofs and gathered them all around the doorway so he could demonstrate the correct digging technique, the blast of icy air and the blinding wall of snow taking Lucy's breath away. Monica bustled around, finding ski trousers and jackets for those not appropriately dressed.

'I'll go first,' said Nate, after Gunther had shown them how to dig a V-shaped path with a secure bank of snow on each side. Lucy pulled a pair of waterproof trousers over her jeans and watched Nate from inside the door, not entirely unaroused by the sight of him digging furiously, his hair flopping over his eyes.

'I'm sorry,' said Chantal, leaning on the other side of the doorframe in a full ski suit and snow boots that made her look more mountain-Heidi-wholesome than ever. 'What I said last night was bad. I was drunk, but it wasn't cool.'

'No,' said Lucy. 'It wasn't. But forget it, it doesn't matter.'

'He is a very good singer,' said Chantal, hungrily watching Nate dig. 'Did you know?'

'No.' Lucy's tone was curt. 'As I said yesterday, we don't know each other very well.'

'Does he definitely have a girlfriend?'

Lucy thought about her answer – technically she didn't know what the arrangement was with Sasha because Nate hadn't talked about it, but that aside, she suspected that Nate would appreciate being taken out of the game at this point.

'Yes,' she said. 'I've never met her, but I know there is somebody.'

'Right, fine,' said Chantal sulkily.

Lucy glanced at her out of the corner of her eye, deciding to be magnanimous. 'I guess you don't get much chance to meet cute guys up here.'

'No,' said Chantal, folding her arms. 'Papa and Mutti want to retire soon, and the only way I'm going to take over this place is if I have someone here with me. I don't want to do it on my own.' She looked like she might cry, and Lucy actually felt a little sorry for her.

'I'm not sure Nate is the one, in that case,' said Lucy kindly. 'He's a very talented account manager, but I'm not sure he's cut out for mountain hospitality.' *Maybe one day Chantal will meet Kristoff,* she thought. *He'll buy this place, they'll fall in love, and she'll get her handsome millionaire prince.*

'It would just be nice to be noticed,' muttered Chantal, her lip wobbling. 'Everybody notices women like you. You have two boyfriends. I can't even find one.'

'They're not my boyfriends,' said Lucy. 'Neither is a proper relationship. I'm no more loved up than you are. It's just sex.'

'That would be OK too,' said Chantal. Lucy caught her eye, and they both started to laugh. Maybe she wasn't such a devious cow, just a bit lonely. Although perhaps to Chantal, Lucy's life seemed a bit lonely too. The thought made her squirm a little – how had things become so... *emotionless*? And when had she consciously made that choice?

Woomph. The snowball appeared from nowhere, hitting Lucy on the side of her face. She gasped, spitting snow out of her mouth as she turned to see where it had come from. Even through one eye, she could see Nate grinning at the other end of the freshly dug path.

'Right,' said Lucy, brushing her eye with a gloved hand and heading for the nearest snowbank, 'now you've done it.'

'We must keep digging,' said Gunther, looking mildly panicked that anarchy was about to be unleashed.

'In a minute,' said Lucy, throwing a snowball at Nate. It thumped into his shoulder, then another came back and hit her arm as she twisted away. She threw two in quick succession, one of which he dodged, but the other hit him on the side of his head and exploded into his hair. *Bullseye.*

'OK, OK,' laughed Nate, gasping for breath and approaching Lucy with his palms held up. 'I totally deserved that.'

'Yes, you did,' said Lucy, reaching over to brush a lump of snow from his shoulder. For a second he held her gaze and she forgot to breathe, noticing the snow caked into his long eyelashes. In that moment all she wanted to do was gently kiss away every flake, with nobody around to steal the moment from them.

'It's your turn, Lucy,' said Gunther, clearing his throat and breaking the spell. 'Five minutes of digging, and then it is time for Alex.'

'I'm totally not down with this idea,' muttered Alex, appearing in the doorway.

'Sunshine and pizza,' said Nate, passing Lucy the shovel, his cheeks bright pink from the cold. 'Think of all that incredible content.'

'I guess,' said Alex, perking up a little. 'Shame I have to do hard labour first.'

Lucy rolled her eyes and walked to the end of the few metres of path that Gunther and Nate had already dug, her heart still pounding in her chest from the snowball fight. The first few shovelfuls of powdery snow were easy, but it got harder and more packed the further down she dug. Within a few minutes she was panting hard and sweating inside Monica's ski gear, but determined not to give up before Gunther called time. The sun was already sparkling on the snow just a few metres away, and the prospect of an Aperol Spritz in a deckchair was enough incentive to spur her on.

When Gunther finally told her to stop, Lucy had added another couple of metres to the path that was slowly forming, and her shoulders and arms were now throbbing. Lucy handed the shovel to a mutinous Alex and listened to Gunther briefing the other five about how they could start to dig wider now, with two people at a time to create a big space where they could be outside. He produced another shovel, but Lucy's work was done for the time being. She headed back into the steamy warmth of the bar, where Nate was throwing more logs into the wood burner.

'Monica is making glühwein,' said Nate. 'I've just seen her upending bottles of Merlot into a giant saucepan. Apparently it will keep us warm.'

You could keep me warm, thought Lucy, wondering if Gunther and Monica ever actually fully sobered up until spring. Maybe that's how you coped with living on top of the world.

'Chantal, Andrea – come and join us,' said Lucy, waving them over. She and Nate had pulled two deckchairs over to join Alex and Willem in the patch of early afternoon sun.

Lucy noticed Felix appear from inside the Guntherhütte and make a move to follow Andrea, but Monica put her hand on his arm and held him back. Lucy couldn't understand the whispered conversation between them, but the sentiment was clearly 'leave her be, and let her hang out with the young people'. Felix nodded grudgingly, and filled his glass.

'More pizza,' said Gunther, appearing with a plate of steaming slices from the wood-fired pizza oven at the edge of the terrace. The toppings were a slightly eclectic mix of leftovers, but the dough and tomato sauce had been retrieved from Monica's makeshift outdoor freezer, so it tasted fresh and delicious. Monica herself followed with a jug of steaming glühwein and topped up everyone's glasses, and Lucy tucked into both in a state of bliss. She had sunshine and fresh air, she'd done some exercise, and now she had delicious hot food and wine in a stunning winter wonderland. She'd put on her sunglasses so the glare didn't hurt her eyes, which also meant she could check out Nate without him knowing. The only thing that would make today better was the news that rescue was on its way and there was a soft bed waiting for her in Geneva, rather than a hard floor in the attic.

'Everybody, listen,' said Gunther. 'It is now two o'clock, I don't think we will be rescued today.'

'Why not?' gasped Alex, looking aghast.

'Because it will be dark in a couple of hours,' he said. 'If the rescue vehicle was coming, they would be here by now. A sunny day after a snowstorm is very dangerous for avalanches, but I'm sure they will try again tomorrow.'

Lucy took another sip of wine, trying not to feel too disappointed. It wasn't like they were suffering, and today had actually been a lot of fun so far. She looked around at the others, who were clearly suppressing the same urge to complain.

'Let's play a game,' said Alex with a resigned shrug as

Gunther headed back to Monica and Felix. 'I ask somebody a question, and you have to tell the truth. But then you get to ask another question to someone else.'

Lucy looked around the group, assessing how drunk everyone was. Monica had been continually topping up their glasses for some time, and nobody was abstaining, so it was reasonable to assume everyone felt as plastered as she did.

'I would rather not be on your TikTok,' said Chantal.

'I promise not to video,' said Alex. 'This is just for us. Lucy, I'll ask you a question first.'

Lucy looked at Alex doubtfully. 'This feels like the kind of game you play at a sleepover when you're thirteen.'

'It is,' said Alex with a grin. 'That's why it's fun.' He looked around the group, clearly picking up on everyone's reluctance. 'Fine, you can refuse to answer if you like.'

'Whatever,' said Lucy, still not remotely sure about this.

'Good,' said Alex, rubbing his hands together. 'Which of your two boyfriends is better in bed?'

Lucy shot a look at Chantal, who had the decency to look mortified. 'I'm obviously not answering that,' said Lucy. 'Ask me something else.'

'Ugh, fine,' said Alex, rolling his eyes. 'How old were you when you lost your virginity?'

'Jesus,' laughed Lucy. 'What is your obsession with my sex life?'

'It's a fascinating question, it tells you a lot about someone.'

'I was sixteen,' said Lucy with a sigh. 'A friend of my brother's. It was messy and unpleasant.'

'The first time is always messy and unpleasant,' muttered Willem.

'You have a brother?' asked Chantal, visibly perking up.

'Yes,' said Lucy, glancing at Nate. 'But he's unavailable. Do I get to ask the next question?'

Alex nodded.

'Chantal,' said Lucy, making her jump. 'If you could swap this mountain for living anywhere else on the planet, where would it be?'

'London,' said Chantal, without hesitation. 'It looks very beautiful and historic, and I think in London people know how to have fun.'

'I've lived in London,' said Willem. 'It's a very dirty city. Amsterdam is nicer.'

'Hmm . . .' Chantal didn't look entirely convinced. 'OK, my question is for Andrea.' She paused for dramatic effect, then leaned in to whisper, 'What do you actually think of the Bee Gees?'

Andrea snorted with laughter, glancing round to check Felix wasn't listening. 'I do not love the Bee Gees,' she said. 'But I love Felix, and that is all that matters.'

'What a lovely answer,' said Lucy, feeling suddenly a little tearful. She had no idea what that kind of love felt like, where you would compromise on your own passions to make someone else happy.

'My question is for Nate,' said Andrea, after thinking about it for a minute. 'If you had all the confidence in the world to stand on stage and sing the songs of any artist, who would it be?'

'That's easy,' said Nate. 'I'd sing Elton John. No, George Michael.'

'Ooh,' said Chantal. 'I would like to hear both.'

'So would I,' Lucy agreed. 'Maybe later?'

'Absolutely not,' said Nate. 'I'm not nearly drunk enough.'

'Well, that's easily fixed.' Lucy grabbed Nate's glass and tipped half the glühwein from her glass into it. The pan was still steaming on the gas stove, so there was plenty more where that came from.

'It's your turn to ask a question, Nate,' said Chantal.

'So it is,' said Nate. 'Who's left?'

'Willem and Alex,' said Andrea, who was clearly the most sober one amongst them.

'OK, I'll ask Willem. When you leave here, who do you hope you will see again one day?'

'Hmm,' said Willem, thinking about it for a moment. 'All of you, obviously, we are mountain friends for life now. I'm expecting us to meet every year, right here in the Guntherhütte.' He looked at Nate and smiled shyly. 'But I think maybe you and I would be friends if we'd met in different circumstances, so I'm going to say you.'

'I think so too,' said Nate, returning Willem's smile.

'So, that means my question is for Alex,' said Willem, looking suddenly nervous. 'I had a big exciting plan for today, we were going to . . . well, it doesn't matter now. But since I have this opportunity, maybe I will ask the question anyway.'

'What question?' asked Alex, looking confused.

Willem levered himself out of his deckchair, colour rushing to his cheeks and his hands visibly shaking as he took a few deep breaths. He rummaged in his coat pocket for a small black box, then dropped to one knee on the snowy terrace. 'Alex Jansen,' he croaked, the words catching in his throat and his eyes brimming with tears.

'Oh my God, wait,' gasped Alex, flapping his hands and thrusting his phone at Lucy. 'Video this.'

Lucy swiped the screen and started a video as quickly as she could, her hands shaking more than Willem's. 'OK, go.'

'Alex Jansen,' repeated Willem, prising open the box and turning it slightly so Lucy could zoom in on a platinum ring with two bands of inlaid diamonds. 'I love you so much, and there is nobody on this planet I would rather be on this mountain with. Will you be my husband?'

Alex held one hand to his chest and carefully wiped away a tear with the other, pressing his lips together while he got a hold on his emotions. 'Yes,' he said. 'Yes, I will be your husband.' Lucy held the phone steady as everyone on the terrace whooped and cheered, conscious that Alex would never forgive her if she messed up this momentous video. She zoomed in on them both as they kissed, a stunning vista of snow-laden trees, mountains and blue sky behind them. It was, by any standards, one of those perfect and beautiful moments in life that Lucy knew she would never forget.

CHAPTER SEVENTEEN

'I don't want to do it,' said Nate, folding his arms.

'Yes, you do,' said Lucy firmly. They were back in what Lucy now firmly thought of as *their booth* in the corner of the bar, the remnants of another buffet supper scattered across the table. Chantal was busy in the kitchen with Monica, Gunther was behind the bar with Felix, experimenting with cocktails that could be made without ice, or poured over a glass full of snow. Alex and Willem were holding hands and dancing in front of the fireplace, as Andrea sang all her favourite love songs that weren't by the Bee Gees. Currently it was an acoustic version of 'Let's Stay Together' by Al Green.

'No, I don't,' insisted Nate. 'I'm not drunk enough.'

'You can barely stand up. If you were any more drunk we could lay you in front of the wood burner and call you a rug.'

Nate laughed. 'You can talk. Your eyes are crossed.'

'I'm drunk in solidarity with you. My fake birthday has been usurped by Alex and Willem's engagement party. They've asked you to sing. You can't say no.'

'What if I can't remember the words?'

'What does it matter? It's an audience of eight pissed people. It's good practice.'

'For what?'

Lucy glanced at him and grinned. 'For when you're ready for an audience of twelve pissed people. What did your grandma used to say? *Dream big*, right?'

Nate pressed his lips together, and Lucy could see him gathering his resolve. 'Fine. But can you ask Alex not to video me?'

'That would be like asking him not to breathe. Come on, it's his and Willem's night.'

'How is his phone still going, anyway?'

'He's got one of those power packs that holds about five charges. He's the poster boy for always-on influencers.'

Nate was silent for a moment, clearly looking for a way out. 'I can't sing one of my songs, not yet. I don't know, maybe George Michael. Which song should I sing?'

'Which is your favourite?'

'"I Can't Make You Love Me". It's beautiful, but probably not appropriate for an engagement party.'

'Maybe start with Elton. "Your Song"?'

'Yeah, I could do that. Better with a piano, though.'

'Can you play piano?'

'No.' He took a deep breath and stood up, as Andrea sang the final few bars. Alex and Willem whooped and cheered and shouted *'Nate Nate Nate,'* as Monica and Chantal drifted back from the kitchen, both of them drying their hands. 'If this is awful, I'm blaming you.'

'Fine,' said Lucy happily, topping up her wine and pulling her knees up to her chest as Andrea handed him the guitar with a nod of encouragement. 'I'll shoulder that burden.'

Lucy watched him make a meal out of putting his head through the guitar strap; he almost keeled sideways as he tried to mount the stool by the bar, and for a moment Lucy wondered if he was actually too drunk and nervous to do this. He'd been fielding requests all evening with good grace, and Lucy had watched his internal battle play out. He so badly wanted to do it, but was also afraid of it. She'd said little, stayed close and let him work it through for himself.

She watched him look around the group, seeming awkward and terrified to start. He locked eyes with Lucy and she smiled, giving him the tiniest nod, which seemed to give him the impetus to play the first notes. Lucy breathed more easily, marvelling at his transformation from shy, anxious Nate to someone who looked like they'd been doing this all their life. After a soaring and beautiful rendition of Elton he sang George Michael's 'Amazing', which got Alex and Willem back on their makeshift dance floor again.

'This one is for Lucy,' said Nate softly, after the applause had died down. 'And Leo.' Lucy gasped as he played the unmistakeable opening bars of Craig David's 'Rendez-vous', which nobody else in the room seemed to know, but Lucy sang along with every line. Chantal was watching from behind the bar, looking like she might swoon, and Alex was filming again. Lucy hoped Nate would realise what massive potential he had. *Either way*, thought Lucy, as Nate segued into another Craig David ballad, *he's wasted in advertising.*

'This has been the best day ever,' slurred Alex, giving Lucy a hug once the party had wound down. 'But now I need to take this man to bed.'

'I'm really happy for you both,' said Lucy.

Alex put his hands on Nate's shoulders and gave him an intense look. 'You're an incredible talent,' he said. 'You should . . . do something about it. I know people and can help you, if you like.'

'Thanks,' said Nate, colour rushing to his cheeks. 'It's nice of you to say, but that isn't going to happen.'

'Never say never,' slurred Alex.

'Well, maybe I'll get off this mountain first.'

'Hopefully tomorrow,' said Willem, grabbing Alex's hand and dragging him towards the door. 'We're going to have a shower. It's been thirty-six hours.'

'I need a shower too,' said Lucy, looking at Monica for a status update on the gas for hot water.

'We have enough,' confirmed Monica. 'If everyone sticks to less than three minutes. Gunther and Chantal and I will wash at the sink, we are used to it.' Chantal looked mutinous, like she'd actually prefer to languish in a giant foamy bathtub but never had any say in the matter.

'OK, we'll go and use it now,' said Willem. 'Lucy, it's all yours next.'

'I can wait until tomorrow,' said Felix, earning a wrinkle-nosed grimace from Andrea, who clearly disagreed. They all said their goodnights and drifted off towards their beds, leaving Lucy and Nate alone in the bar. There would be plenty of clearing up to do in the morning, but nobody had the energy for it right now.

'Nightcap?' said Nate, picking up a bottle from one of the tables and peering at the label. 'It's bourbon.'

'Better without ice than whisky,' said Lucy, who had

almost certainly had enough to drink for one day. But she was in no hurry for this day to end, and she definitely didn't object to sharing a moment that was just her and Nate. He poured a generous measure into two glasses and brought them over to their booth, sliding in next to her.

'Cheers,' said Nate. 'Here's to us.'

Lucy clinked his glass, wondering if 'us' meant the two of them, or the whole Guntherhütte crew. She sipped her drink and tried not to pull a face as it burned all the way down, leaving a pool of warmth in her stomach that was intensified by how close Nate was. His thigh was barely millimetres from hers, and it took all of Lucy's self-control not to reach out and stroke his leg.

'It's been a crazy day,' she said, not knowing what else to talk about.

'Hopefully we'll get out of here tomorrow.'

'Mmm.'

'Lucy—' said Nate, giving her a searching look. 'I just . . . there's something I want to say.'

They stared at each other for a long moment, Lucy's heart thumping as she wondered if Nate was going to kiss her. Obviously that was a terrible idea – they worked together and he was sleeping with Sasha. It could *only* end badly. And yet in that moment there was absolutely nothing she wanted more.

'What is it?' she asked, wondering if *please kiss me* was written all over her drunk, grubby face.

'I just wanted to say . . . thank you, I guess,' stuttered Nate. 'For making me get up there and sing tonight.'

'Oh,' said Lucy, feeling mildly gutted and also guilty

for making this moment all about her. 'I didn't make you. You made yourself. I just gave you a nudge.'

'Well, yeah,' said Nate. 'But . . . well, it felt good. And I appreciate your nudging.'

Lucy smiled softly, and poked him with her elbow. 'You're welcome. I think we all benefitted from that decision.'

'I'm glad,' mumbled Nate. 'It's not something I ever thought I'd do. But now I'm wondering if maybe I can, one day. With the right support, you know.'

'You deserve it,' said Lucy happily.

'Thanks,' said Nate. 'You've made this adventure really special. And in the immortal words of George Michael, I think you're amazing.'

Lucy turned to look at him, now entirely confused about whether this was a genuine moment of connection between them, or just her wanting it to be something it wasn't.

'Ah, you're just drunk-flirting with me now,' she laughed, trying to take the tension out of the situation.

'I can't deny it,' said Nate with a soft smile, shaking his head as he drained his drink.

'Shower's free,' said Willem, sticking his head through the door of the bar. 'You might want to get in quick before Andrea drags Felix in there by his remaining hair.'

'I'm on my way,' said Lucy, dumping her glass on the table. Lovely as this moment with Nate was, she wasn't turning down an opportunity to wash. She ran up the stairs and grabbed her towel from the attic room, then stripped down in the bathroom and sighed as the hot water sluiced away the sweat and grime of the past two days. She washed her hair and body whilst using her feet to trample her clothes underfoot like she was treading grapes, then rinsed everything off before her three minutes was up. The hardest bit was trying not to fall sideways and hit her head on the glass door in a haze of wine and impure thoughts about Nate.

When she came out, wrapped in a towel and clutching her wet clothes, Nate was waiting in the corridor.

'You OK?' asked Lucy.

'Mmm,' said Nate. 'I smell of bar.'

'Me too. Well, not any more.'

Nate tilted his head and raised an eyebrow. 'What do you smell of now?'

Lucy laughed and rolled her eyes. 'See, now you're definitely drunk-flirting with me. Which isn't fair when you're so much more dressed than I am.'

Nate nodded thoughtfully. 'Does that mean I can drunk-flirt with you when I'm wearing fewer clothes?'

'I'll see you upstairs,' said Lucy, rolling her eyes and no longer sure if the feeling of unsteadiness was due to wine or Nate. Either way *I'll see you upstairs* definitely sounded like some kind of invitation, and she couldn't be sure if she'd done that on purpose. She hurried up to the attic and wondered how she could make it feel less like a spooky cave, which wasn't quite the vibe she was going for right now. In the end she draped her purple bra over the torch to create a softer, more dissipated light. Still not exactly romantic, but better.

Lucy pulled on Monica's pyjamas and hastily re-inflated both their beds, hoping Nate didn't arrive in time to see her pumping madly in ugly polyester florals. Should she keep them on, or get into bed naked, just in case? Nate had definitely been giving off flirty energy just now, and she hadn't exactly sent him packing. But where did Sasha fit into all this? Much as she definitely wasn't averse to pushing their two airbeds together, it wasn't worth getting fired or punched over.

Lucy wriggled into bed, deciding to ditch the pyjama bottoms but keep the top on. *Am I too drunk for this?* she asked herself. Wine was definitely coursing through her veins, but the ache between her legs implied both body and brain were in a state of full consent.

She waited in anticipation of Nate's footsteps on the stairs, pushing the idea of having sex with him around in her brain. *Do I actually fancy him, or has the intensity of this whole mountain hostage situation addled my brain?* Maybe it was like being trapped in a lift with someone for so long that you decide you might as well fuck them just to pass the time.

No, thought Lucy. Before this trip she'd dismissed him as dull, but now she'd got to know him a bit, she liked him. And she also definitely fancied him. He was funny and talented and complicated and undeniably hot.

Nate appeared at the top of the stairs, wearing nothing but a dark grey towel around his waist. He sat on the edge of Lucy's bed, and there was a purpose and urgency to his movements, like he'd been thinking about it all through his shower and decided not to beat around the bush. Lucy took in his naked chest and shoulders and narrow waist – he was less lean than Marco, but not as muscular as Anthony. He reached out to take her hand, gently running his thumb across her palm, and for a second Lucy stopped breathing again.

'Just before this gets entirely out of hand,' she whispered, 'I need to ask a question.'

'I have condoms,' said Nate, kissing the palm of Lucy's hand and making her shiver. 'I put the ones Kristoff supplied at dinner in my coat pocket. We can live the brand experience.' Wine and bourbon and the dark privacy of the attic had made him more confident, and it was undeniably sexy.

'That wasn't the question,' said Lucy, extracting her hand and sitting up to hug her knees. Under different circumstances she might have taken umbrage at the assumption that she was obviously up for sex, but the knowledge that they were both on the same wavelength was actually kind of thrilling.

'OK,' said Nate. 'What's your question?'

'I thought you were seeing someone.'

'That's not a question.'

Lucy laughed and rolled her eyes. 'Pedantry is NOT sexy, just so you know.'

'I disagree,' said Nate, shaking his head. 'I've sat in lots of meetings where you're being a massive pedant, and I find it incredibly sexy.'

Lucy's mind boggled at the idea of Nate even looking at her in meetings, never mind thinking she was sexy. 'OK, fine,' she said. 'I'll be more specific. Do you have a girlfriend or not?'

'No,' said Nate. 'Not . . . currently. I'm working on it.'

'OK, that's a weird answer.'

'It's true. I don't officially have a girlfriend. Nobody is going to turn up at your door with a shotgun.'

What about unofficially? thought Lucy. She considered telling him that she'd seen him with Sasha at the hotel, but him questioning why she was lurking in corridors and peering around corners was guaranteed to kill what was left of the mood. 'I just . . . I just want to be sure we both understand what this is. And that I'm not treading on anyone's toes.'

Nate smiled and took her hand again. 'You're definitely not. Do you want me to sign some release forms?'

Lucy pulled a face. 'No, of course not.'

'Then please let me kiss you,' whispered Nate, leaning closer. 'It's something I've wanted to do for a really, really long time.'

'Really?' asked Lucy, the word catching in her throat.

'Yes,' said Nate, leaning in a little further. 'I was too scared to tell you. But now I'm not.' His lips touched hers, and it felt like a wave of electricity from the tips of Lucy's toes to the roots of her hair. She locked into the moment, feeling every inch of Nate's desire moving into her space, but determined to take it slowly and savour every second. He kissed her harder, his hands trailing down her back and under the hem of her pyjama top.

'Oh God,' whispered Lucy as Nate's warm fingers on her skin set off a whole box of fireworks in her chest. She yanked off the pyjama top and pulled him back onto the bed, frantically trying to loosen the towel from around his waist so she could feel all of him against her. There was a small *pop* from the plug on the airbed, then a hiss as the mattress slowly started to deflate. They both stared at each other as the bed gently lowered them to the floor like the world's slowest lift.

'This is . . . not ideal,' said Nate, turning onto his back as the mattress continued to hiss and fart out the remaining air.

'Shall we relocate to yours?' suggested Lucy, as her backside slowly sank into the wooden floor.

'No,' said Nate, turning back to kiss her neck and trail his hands across her stomach. 'Then we'll have to pump them both up later, which I absolutely can't be arsed to do.'

Lucy laughed, then gasped as his hands trailed lower. It didn't matter if this seduction scene wasn't movie-perfect; it was absolutely in keeping with the drunk, chaotic madness of the day. Being here with Nate felt like a blissful release from the stress and uncertainty of their situation, and the only thing she was absolutely certain of right now was that she wanted to be with him in this useless shitshow of a bed. Not as a boyfriend, not for deep and meaningful conversations over nightcaps at 3 a.m., but just for them to be naked and alone together in this moment.

Nate drew away and paused for a moment, pulling back the duvet and drinking in her naked body. 'Jesus,' he muttered, the words catching in his throat. The heat of his desire could have melted the entire mountain, and Lucy couldn't wait any longer. The towel disappeared, and now it was just her hands in his hair and his fingers carving a trail on her spine and his raw, urgent breathing and the taste of his lips, like wine and smoke and pure lust. When they finally came together it was nothing like the romantic seduction she imagined Nate favoured; it was a sweaty, potent coupling in a frantic and urgent tangle of limbs. Lucy tried not to cry out as Nate's tongue and fingers ravaged her all at once, but it was so intense, so incredibly fucking incredible, that she had to clamp her lips together so as not to let the entire house know that, right now, she and Nate had found each other and nothing else mattered.

CHAPTER EIGHTEEN

When Lucy woke up the next morning, both beds had deflated, and Nate wasn't in either of them. She lay in the dark stillness of the attic for a moment, taking an inventory of the state of her compound hangovers, and all the bruises she'd incurred from hours of rolling around on a wooden floor. Her head felt pretty OK, all things considered, but her knees felt like they might never recover.

It was definitely worth it, she mused, wondering if it would be considered bad form to grab another three-minute shower. Surely they'd be getting off this mountain today? She took a moment to work out what day it was, and eventually came to the conclusion that it was Sunday. Her flight back to Bristol was booked for this afternoon, and presumably if they were rescued this morning that would still go ahead. She could be in her bathtub back in her flat by the end of the day, then relaxing in her lavish superking bed. She even remembered to change the sheets before she left, just in case she fancied putting a call in to Marco or Anthony on the way back. Occasionally she went to one of their places, but she preferred it if they came to her. Neither of them lived like pigs, but her flat was guaranteed to be spotlessly tidy and she could vouch for the sheets being clean.

Talking of being clean, where were her clothes? She

remembered washing them, but then what? The realisation dawned that she'd come straight upstairs after her shower in a state of sexual anticipation, and forgotten to go down and hang them up in front of the fire before she fell asleep. She reached over and clicked on the torch, and sure enough, there was a mound of damp clothes by the wall, probably permanently staining the wooden floor. She sighed, wondering if Chantal had some things she could borrow, then she could take her wet stuff home in a plastic bag. Or actually just throw them in the nearest bin.

How will last night change things between Nate and I? she wondered. She'd definitely be leaving Switzerland with a very different impression of Nate to the one she'd had when she arrived. Was that going to make office encounters awkward? Probably, but they were both adults, and if he could hide a relationship with a member of senior management, he could definitely hide a one-night stand with Lucy. He'd go back to whatever his thing was with Sasha, she'd go back to Anthony and Marco, and this would become a memory of a thing that happened in a crazy and surreal situation.

Why hadn't he told her he had a girlfriend? The most obvious answer was that his relationship with Sasha was just a casual one, like she had with Anthony and Marco. So he wasn't answerable to her, and could do what he wanted. The alternative was that they were a couple but it was an open relationship, the rules of which might compel him to tell Sasha that he and Lucy had slept together. This idea was less palatable, but that wasn't her decision to make.

She wondered what time it was, and whether Nate might be interested in another roll around on this hard floor before breakfast. What were a few more bruises between friends? He'd been something of a revelation, in the end – not as much of a virtuoso as Anthony, or as romantic as Marco, but something else entirely. Parts of it had been tender and intimate; the kind of sex you have with someone you know inside and out and feel entirely at ease with. Other parts had been unexpected and fearless and had taken her breath away, quite literally. The idea of doing it again, but sober this time, was actually very appealing.

Nate reappeared up the stairs, and Lucy could see in the murky light that he was carrying two cups of coffee. He sat cross-legged on the edge of her deflated mattress and put the two mugs on the floor next to her, taking the opportunity to drop a kiss on her forehead as he leaned over. It felt like such a familiar, domestic gesture, like there was no awkwardness or regret on his part. There was none on Lucy's, obviously, but she'd half-expected Nate to be spinning out about the impulsive, terrible thing they'd done.

'You've had another shower,' said Lucy, noting that his hair was wet and he smelled of citrus and toothpaste.

'I have,' said Nate. 'Monica was hovering outside, so I made it quick. Didn't want her to think I was . . . you know.'

'You know . . . what?' asked Lucy, entirely confused.

'Like, having a wank.'

'Why would you be having a wank?' she laughed.

Nate pulled back the duvet and snuggled in beside

her, draping his arm over her naked waist. He was far too close, considering Lucy's morning breath, but there was nothing she could do about that other than clamp her lips together and breathe through her nose.

'I wouldn't,' said Nate. 'I don't need to, obviously. But I thought that if I took too long, she might think I was.'

'Wouldn't she think you were just diligently washing?'

'I don't know. I wasn't prepared to risk it.'

'Right,' said Lucy, noting that Nate's anxiety clearly wasn't just restricted to flying and avalanches. They were both quiet for a moment, enjoying the luxury of being together, with nowhere else to be.

'Incidentally,' said Lucy. 'If wanking is on your agenda, I'd be happy to help.'

'It's definitely on my agenda,' said Nate. 'In fact, it's my entire agenda for the rest of the morning.'

Lucy shivered as his hand trailed down her ribcage to her hip, bringing her out in goosebumps as he pressed himself against her.

'We might be rescued this morning,' she said, weaving her fingers into his to prevent further activity until she'd at least cleaned her teeth.

'That would be very disappointing,' said Nate, kissing her shoulder. Lucy noted that he didn't suggest moving his agenda to Bristol, presumably because Sasha would be there. It felt weird not knowing what was happening outside this tiny bubble, and feeling so disconnected from everything.

'Oh wait,' said Nate, sitting up suddenly. 'That reminds me. I have news.'

'What?' said Lucy.

'Apparently Gunther got the generator going for a bit earlier. But then something else went bang.'

'Really?'

'Yeah. I saw Willem in the kitchen when I was getting coffee. He was awake, so he went out with Gunther and tried to help.'

'So there was electricity and Wi-Fi and everything?'

'Yeah,' said Nate. 'For about half an hour.'

'Shit,' said Lucy. 'That's annoying. I could have checked in with Jonno and charged my phone.'

'We were both asleep, but Alex was all over it, apparently. He uploaded their engagement video and let his TikTok followers know he's not dead.'

'Did any of them think he was dead?'

'Apparently there was some kind of panic about him being missing, because he hadn't been online for thirty-six hours. Somebody had started a crowdfunder for a helicopter rescue.'

'Why am I not surprised?' Lucy breathed a sigh of relief, knowing that Jonno would have definitely followed Alex on TikTok or Instagram by now, in case he posted any updates from the Guntherhütte.

'Did Gunther or Monica manage to get any information about our rescue?' she asked.

'Yeah. Gunther spoke to a couple of people in the village, the signs are good for rescue today. Monica's going to brief us all in the bar in an hour.'

'OK, great.' Lucy thought about the list of people who would be wondering if she was all right, and it was very short. Jonno, obviously, and the others from LUNA and Titan who were probably enjoying being on the fringe of all the drama. Presumably her mother had messaged, and was either in deep denial or permanently on hold to the Swiss Embassy. But other than that, she was pretty sure nobody was crowdfunding for a helicopter rescue for *her*.

'So what do we do for the next hour?' said Nate, detaching his fingers from hers and restarting manoeuvres down her left hip.

Lucy laughed, sitting up and leaning over him to grab her coffee. She took a gulp, feeling inexplicably, ridiculously happy, then immediately having a panic response to such an unfamiliar emotion.

'You know this is just an extreme holiday romance, right?' she said, trying to keep her tone light.

'Yes,' said Nate, raising his eyebrows. 'And even if it wasn't, you don't do proper relationships.'

'I do not. But hey, we'll always have Zermatt.' She said it breathlessly, like the star of a drippy romcom movie, making Nate laugh.

'But just on the off-chance there's a rescue vehicle coming,' he said, his voice muffling as he dipped his head under the covers, 'I'd quite like to make the most of your naked body.'

'I haven't had a shower,' shrieked Lucy. 'Let me out!'

'No,' said Nate. 'I'm half French, washing is strictly optional. You smell filthy in the best possible way.'

'Yes, but I'm NOT half French.' Lucy laughed as she reluctantly batted him away. 'I need to wash.'

'Fine. But I need you to come straight back to bed and not get dragged into one of Gunther's schemes to fix things.'

'I promise,' said Lucy, extracting herself from his grip and crawling onto all fours as she looked for Monica's discarded pyjamas. 'While I'm gone, can you pump one of these beds up? I'm going to have bruises for days.'

'I will kiss every one of them better.'

'You're too good to be true,' laughed Lucy, draining the rest of her coffee. 'You know that, right?'

Nate shrugged. 'Maybe you bring out my best side.'

'Hmm. Maybe it's the altitude.'

'Does it matter? I'm still going to be here waiting when you get back.'

Lucy rolled her eyes and padded downstairs, feeling a little lightheaded and giddy. Was that a hangover, or Nate? The bathroom door was firmly locked, so presumably Willem was still in there. She waited impatiently, desperately needing the loo and taking an inventory of all her bruises. Her neck felt like she'd scratched it, and her inner thighs ached too, possibly from spending too much time with her legs open.

The door opened in a billow of steam, but it wasn't Willem, it was Chantal.

'Oh, hi,' said Lucy. With no make-up and her wet hair hanging down her back, Chantal looked about twenty, making Lucy feel ancient and haggard in comparison.

'Hi,' said Chantal, her eyes widening at the sight of Lucy.

'Just going to grab a quick shower. My clothes from yesterday are wet, is there any chance I could borrow some of yours?'

'Sure,' said Chantal, her eyes drifting from Lucy's dishevelled hair to the scratch on her neck. Her eyes hovered there for a moment, and it occurred to Lucy that the scratch was possibly a love bite. She blushed, mortified that she was a thirty-two-year-old woman who'd spent the night making out like a teenager at a school disco. And even worse, Chantal knew it too, and presumably within ten minutes everyone in the Guntherhütte would also know it.

'I'll leave some clothes on the stairs for you,' said Chantal, looking like her world had ended.

'Thanks,' said Lucy, edging past Chantal and quickly closing the door behind her. The shower was tepid at best, but it still felt blissful on her tender skin and within moments, she was restored to her usual self.

She wrapped herself in a towel that was still damp from last night, and hurried back upstairs to the attic, the cool air on her skin making her shiver. She imagined Nate waiting, warm and naked and ready, and pushed aside the thousand reservations she had about making this more than a one-night stand. What else were they going to do while they waited for mountain rescue? Take up knitting?

'I've pumped up the beds,' said Nate as she closed the door and picked her way back across the floor. Nate had turned the torch on again, but hidden it under his towel so it gave off a soft glow that made him look ghostly pale.

'Hmm,' said Lucy, ditching her towel and sliding under the duvet next to him. 'Not a line you ever hear in sexy movies, is it?'

'No. What would we call the movie version of this adventure?'

'What, the story of the Guntherhütte crew?' asked

Lucy, rubbing her cold feet on the mattress. Nate wrapped his arms around her and spooned her cold body into his warm chest.

'No,' said Nate, his voice low and seductive as he softly stroked her arm. 'This story. You and me.'

'Oh,' said Lucy, feeling slightly off-balance. 'Well, that would probably be one of those cheesy Netflix rom-coms, wouldn't it?'

'Almost certainly, but it needs a name. That's your speciality.'

'Hmm . . .' Lucy felt like she was at one of those crossroads in a conversation where she could keep things light and fun, or head down a path signposted *deep and meaningful*. Right now, light and fun felt like the safer option. 'How about *Things Snowballed*?'

'I love it,' laughed Nate. 'It sounds ridiculous, but romantic.'

'My bruises aren't very romantic,' said Lucy, reaching down to poke the cluster of purple blotches on her knee.

'Let me take a look,' said Nate, easing her onto her back and leaning over her. He gave her another long, smouldering look, then ducked under the duvet and gently kissed her knee before marking out a trail up the inside of her thigh. His warm breath and the featherlight touches of his lips on her cold, damp skin set her nerve endings alight, and she wondered how she could have worked in an office with this man for over a year and never sensed how spectacularly good in bed he would be.

Lucy had one final, inexplicable thought before Nate's tongue disappeared between her legs and she entirely lost her mind. *Maybe we don't need mountain rescue. Maybe*

Nate and I are rescuing each other. But by the time they'd decoupled in a panting heap of sweaty limbs half an hour later, the thought had entirely left her head.

'Could you check on the stairs and see if there are any clean clothes for me?' asked Lucy, sitting up on the bed with the duvet tucked under her arms as Nate got dressed. 'I asked Chantal earlier, but I reeked of sex and somebody had left a love bite on my neck. So I'm pretty sure she will have forgotten on purpose.'

'Sorry about that,' said Nate, hopping on one leg as he pulled his jeans on. 'It's your fault for being so entirely delicious.'

Lucy shook her head as Nate popped out of the room, reappearing seconds later with a pile of clothes and a huge grin on his face. 'These are quite something,' he smirked, dropping them on the bed. Lucy inspected what were clearly Monica's aubergine purple polyester leggings with stirrups to go over her feet, which Chantal had paired with a violently floral blouse with a frilly collar. Actually they were too frumpy and unfashionable even for Monica, so perhaps they belonged to Chantal's grandmother.

'Wow, Chantal really hates me,' said Lucy, holding up a pair of giant, greying granny knickers and some pink socks with yellow pom-poms on the heels.

'She really does. Are you actually going to wear those?'

'Yep,' said Lucy, hauling herself off the floor. 'And do you know why? Because if I make a fuss I'll look like an ungrateful twat, and Chantal knows it. So I'm going to style it out.'

Nate shook his head. 'Lucy, you are one of the most

beautiful women I've ever met, but I'm honestly not sure even you can style out . . . whatever these are.' He took the leggings and turned them around so she could see the sagging in the bottom where the elastic had gone.

'Watch me,' said Lucy with a grin. She pulled on the knickers, which came up to her ribcage but were undeniably comfy, then wrestled her feet into the leggings. The fabric was heavy and unexpectedly lined with some kind of fleece, and because her legs were longer than Monica's she stretched out the baggy sections.

'Can you lend me your jumper?' asked Lucy, tossing the floral blouse to one side. Even she couldn't make that look half decent.

'What am I going to wear?'

'Can you ask Willem? Or Alex? I bet you any money he's got some spare cashmere in his bag.'

'Fine,' said Nate, handing over his navy sweatshirt. Lucy pulled it over her head; it was far too big, so she let it fall off one shoulder and show a peek of bra strap. She bundled her hair into a messy bun on the top of her head, then anchored it with a hairband and gently tugged on a few strands to give it some volume. The whole effect was artfully sexy, and the last thing anyone was looking at were the yellow pom-poms on her socks.

'Holy shit,' said Nate, his eyes wide with wonder. 'You've actually gone and done it.'

'Say what you like about these leggings,' said Lucy breezily. 'But they're actually really warm. Shall we go down and find out what today's plan is?'

'Do we have to?' said Nate weakly. 'Can't we go back to bed?'

'No,' laughed Lucy. 'I need food and fresh air and an update from Alex on what's happening in the world.'

'Fine,' said Nate. 'But I might drag you back up here later.'

'There's a possibility I might allow that,' said Lucy, wondering if the tingly feeling between her thighs was going to be a permanent feature of today. *God, listen to me*, she thought. *One night with Nate, and I'm a pile of smush. A walking romcom cliché.*

Nate smiled at her, and for a moment Lucy felt like she was back at the window yesterday morning, taking in the snow-laden trees. Dazzled, speechless, and with only the vaguest idea of what day it was.

Get a grip, she told herself. *Before Nate gets the wrong idea, and this snowball turns into something too big for you to handle.*

CHAPTER NINETEEN

'We have good news,' said Monica, beaming around at the group. Lucy glanced at Chantal, who was glaring at her from behind the bar, no doubt furious that she'd failed to make her look frumpy. Andrea and Felix were both on their usual stools in the corner, and Willem and Alex were in the booth next to Lucy and Nate. It occurred to her that this was exactly how things had been at lunchtime on Friday before everything got out of hand.

'Gunther spoke to the team in the village,' continued Monica. 'They have started blasting to be sure of no more avalanches, and then later this morning they will be using a snowplough to clear the piste for the bus. They are coming to collect you all today.'

'So when will they be here?' asked Alex excitedly.

'Sometime this afternoon,' said Gunther. 'The road to the village should be opening today, and they are expecting some of the pistes to be open again tomorrow. You will be able to leave Zermatt today if you want to, and things will get back to normal.'

Lucy smiled at Nate, who reached over to take her hand. She instinctively snatched it away, more forcefully than she had intended, but it was too late. Nate looked crestfallen, and Chantal and Andrea had obviously noticed. She glanced over at Alex, who was giving Willem a nudge and a nod in their direction.

Shit, thought Lucy, feeling exposed and annoyed with herself. Now everyone would think this was a big romance, which it clearly wasn't. But then she reminded herself that she was never going to see any of them again, so it hardly mattered. Though actually, she could imagine a boozy weekend in Amsterdam with Willem and Alex, but it was impossible to imagine Nate being there. In Lucy's head they would go back to being colleagues, with fond memories of this crazy experience, and never mention it to each other or anyone else. That was how it was supposed to be, right? Her brain felt foggy, like things were moving too fast and in several directions at once.

She tried to catch Nate's eye, but he kept his gaze firmly fixed on Monica as she answered Felix's irrelevantly detailed questions about the rescue plans. Clearly she and Nate were going to need to have a conversation at some point, set some clear boundaries for when they got back to Bristol. She mentally kicked herself for letting her guard down; it was always easier when you kept things simple and transparent.

'So there are guests back in the village again?' asked Andrea.

'Yes,' said Gunther. 'They are already arriving, and the machines will be clearing pistes all day. By this afternoon all the hotels will be full.'

'This is good news,' said Felix. 'Andrea and I have a hotel gig tonight, so maybe that will still go ahead.'

'You should change your name,' said Lucy, absently

picking at some crumbs on the table. 'Instead of Night Fever, you can be the Refubeegees.'

Felix paused for a second as he processed what Lucy had said, then roared with laughter. 'This is fantastic. You are very funny!' Everyone else joined in, looking at Lucy like she was some kind of comedy genius. Even Nate's mouth twitched into a smile.

'Refubeegees!' exclaimed Gunther. 'How did you think of that?'

'Lucy is a writer,' said Nate. 'She channels all her emotions into clever words.'

Ouch, thought Lucy, feeling the temperature of the air between them drop by a couple of degrees. If this is how upset Nate got because she wasn't up for a public display of affection, they definitely needed to have a chat.

'Alex and I only arrived for our holiday on Friday,' said Willem. 'We dropped our bags at the hotel and came up here for lunch before we checked in. So maybe we can ski tomorrow and enjoy the rest of our holiday.'

'No,' said Alex firmly. 'We have to go home.'

'Why?' asked Willem, looking even more upset than Nate.

'Because when I had Wi-Fi earlier I checked my emails. I have many requests for TV interviews about this experience. I need to get back as soon as possible.'

'Why can't you do interviews from Zermatt?' asked Willem. Lucy imagined how good Alex would look on camera, the Matterhorn in the background as he happily embellished their perilous adventure for every Dutch news outlet.

'Because some of them are requests to be in the studio, or on a talk show. I need to be in Amsterdam.'

'But this is the holiday I organised for our engagement,' said Willem. 'I had the whole thing planned out.'

'I'm sorry,' said Alex with a shrug, not sounding very sorry at all. 'But this is my job, and I am literally the only person with any profile who can talk about what we've been through.'

'You say that like it's been some kind of ordeal.' Lucy tried not to roll her eyes. 'We've hardly suffered.'

'You may have had a great time,' said Alex, giving her and Nate a significant look. 'But I'm not used to this kind of food and sleeping on a sofa bed and not having electricity or Wi-Fi. It's, like, medieval.'

Lucy gave him a hard stare back. 'Can I give you some advice, Alex?' she said, leaning forward and resting her hands on the table. 'As someone who works in advertising and spends a lot of time thinking about brand reputation?'

'No,' said Alex sulkily.

'How many people in the Netherlands are homeless?'

He shrugged. 'I have no idea.'

'Neither do I, but I suspect it's tens of thousands. And if you go on TikTok and talk about your ORDEAL being stuck in a Swiss ski hut with food and heat and wine and music and nice people, you're going to sound like a massive arsehole.'

Alex looked at Willem, then Nate, who shrugged and muttered, 'She's right.'

'And what's more,' continued Lucy, 'I will be all up in your comments, telling people what it was really like.'

'Me too,' said Andrea quietly. 'And I don't really know what TikTok is.'

'Right,' said Alex. 'So I should be humble and grateful, then.'

'I think that would be wise.'

'Good,' said Willem, clapping his hands to break the tension. 'I'm glad we've got that cleared up. Monica, what can we do today, while we wait for rescue to arrive?'

'It is nearly eleven, so I will make brunch now,' said Monica. 'While I do that, maybe you could all help us clean this place up. Bag up all the spoiled food, bring in more logs, make it our home again. So we are ready for guests tomorrow.' She turned and glared at Gunther. 'Ulrich is bringing a new generator, so we will have power again.'

'We'd be delighted,' said Lucy, looking at Alex. 'Wouldn't we?'

'I am humble and grateful,' said Alex, pushing his phone across the table to Willem. 'Make sure you video me cleaning up.'

Nate cornered Lucy a few hours later, as she was sitting at the bar drawing a flyer for Chantal to hand out to customers with the usual lunch menu. Words were Lucy's forte, but she could also draw some nice pictures if required, which Jonno sometimes requested as he realised that Lucy could scamp up some visual ideas in less time than it would take him to brief a designer. She'd also learned calligraphy as part of her post-Leo art therapy, so she could do fancy lettering. Proper pens would be nice, but coloured Sharpies would do.

'What's this for?' asked Nate, taking in the headline that said *AvaLUNCH special – any pizza and 0.5L beer only €10.* Underneath, Lucy had drawn one of the Guntherhütte booths laden with pizzas and tall glasses of beer, with snow-capped mountains and trees visible through the window behind.

'I've convinced Gunther and Monica that they should capitalise on their fifteen minutes of fame,' said Lucy. 'Apparently Alex gave the name of the bar on the TikTok post he uploaded this morning, so they're bound to be famous by now. Monica has a photocopier out the back, so I only need to do this once.'

'Wow,' said Nate, inspecting Lucy's artwork. 'This is really good. Look, can we talk?'

'Sure,' said Lucy, putting the cap back on her black pen and trying to quell the butterflies in her stomach. She hated confrontation and avoided big, emotional conversations at all costs. But this one clearly needed to be had.

'Can we go upstairs? Just for a minute?'

It definitely didn't sound like much of an invitation, but Lucy nodded and followed Nate through the door and up the stairs to their attic. The air mattresses and bedding were all gone, and the only sign of their occupation was a dark patch on the wood floor where Lucy had left the pile of wet clothes overnight. Monica had re-washed them and hung them by the fire earlier, brushing off Lucy's apologies for damaging the floor. Monica had pointed out that caring about the floor in the attic would be a whole other level of Swiss.

'What are your plans?' said Nate, turning to face her.

'When we get back?' He looked pale and nervous, much like he had when they'd met in the airport three days ago. How was it possible that it was only three days? It felt like they'd travelled a lifetime since then.

'What, to the village?' replied Lucy. 'We'll be too late for our booked flight, so I guess I'll sort out another one for later tonight. Or tomorrow.'

'No, I meant when we get back to Bristol. Can we hang out? Grab dinner or something?'

Lucy laughed, trying to buy herself time while she worked out a way to navigate through this conversation. 'Aren't you sick of me? Don't you have family you need to spend time with?' *Like Sasha, for example?*

'No, Lucy,' said Nate, his expression a little lost, but determined to have his say. 'I'm not sick of you at all. Last night was . . . I mean, it wasn't just me who thought that was incredible, right?'

'No,' said Lucy with a soft smile. 'It wasn't just you.'

'Right. So . . . what happens now?'

Lucy gave him a penetrating look, wondering exactly what he was asking, but knowing that the answer was simple.

'Nothing happens now,' she said, trying to keep her voice steady. 'You go back to your life, I go back to mine. We both go back to working together, and nobody needs to know what happened here.'

'OK,' said Nate, rubbing has hand across his face. 'I'm glad we've got that cleared up.'

Lucy swallowed hard, wanting to tell him that last night had felt special; that Nate was the first man she'd actually woken up next to in over a decade, that he'd made her feel something beyond desire for the first time pretty much ever. But the implications of those feelings were too foreign and terrifying to think about, let alone say out loud. This was how it had to be.

'It's been an amazing escapist mountain encounter,' she said, trying to sound casual even though the words felt like sand in her mouth. 'But nothing more than that.'

'Right,' said Nate. 'You can chalk me up as one of your — what do you call them? Booty calls? Fuck buddies?'

There was an unmistakeable edge to his voice, and Lucy immediately bridled. 'That's how I do things,' she said. 'You always knew that, and I'm not going to apologise to you or anyone else.'

Nate's shoulders slumped, his sails all out of wind. 'I'm sorry. I'm not judging you,' he said quietly. 'It just seems a waste, that's all.'

Lucy shook her head, wondering how the energy between them could have shifted so quickly. 'With respect, how is it any of your business?'

'It's not,' said Nate quickly. 'Obviously I'm not pitching to be your boyfriend or anything.'

Obviously, thought Lucy. *You've already filled that role with someone else. If there were any more elephants in this room it would be a circus.* But she also rationalised that they'd been through a lot together over the past two days, and she probably owed it to him to at least try to explain.

'Look, I'm honestly happier on my own,' she said. 'I don't need someone to validate me, or, or . . . to make me feel good about myself. Invariably men just leave in the end, anyway.'

'Or die.'

Lucy gave him a sharp look. 'What's that supposed to mean?'

'Nothing,' said Nate with a shrug.

'No, you can't say *nothing*. What does that mean?'

Nate sighed and backed away a little, holding the palms of his hands up. 'Look, I just assumed that this is actually all about your brother.'

Lucy said nothing, her mouth hanging open as she stared at Nate and tried to make sense of what he had just said. 'Leo? You think the situation between you and me is about Leo?'

'No, not just you and me. I mean . . . your unwillingness to commit to a relationship. Or let anyone get close, or give up any kind of control, or whatever.' His voice tailed off, and he looked away, unable to maintain eye contact.

'I have no idea what you're talking about,' said Lucy, a sick feeling rising in her throat.

Nate blew out his cheeks and put his hands on his hips. 'I'm just saying that Leo was the most significant partnership of your life, and then he died. So maybe now . . . you subconsciously can't form meaningful relationships.'

He tried to make the words sound casual and throwaway, but they hit Lucy like a punch in the gut, leaving her feeling like she'd been winded.

'It's just a thought,' he added when Lucy didn't reply. 'I guess it seemed pretty obvious to me.'

'Fucking hell, Nate,' said Lucy, once she'd got her breath back. 'Who made you Poundland's answer to Sigmund Freud?'

Nate backed away a little further, like he was worried Lucy was going to hit him. 'I'm sorry, I didn't mean to offend. It's just an observation.'

'Yeah, well, if I'm in the market for some unsolicited therapy, I'll ask for it.' She looked away, feeling confused and exposed and nauseous. Like Nate had peeled open her chest and found a malignant growth that she'd never even known was there, and definitely didn't want to dissect further.

'But if you asked for it, it wouldn't be unsolicited,' said Nate with a helpless smile, trying to take the heat out of the conversation. 'Aren't you the copywriter?'

'Fuck off, Nate,' snapped Lucy, folding her arms tightly around her body. 'I really don't appreciate this conversation. We barely know each other.'

'You didn't say that last night,' said Nate, clearly knowing he was beaten and playing the only card he had left. 'Or this morning.'

Lucy shook her head, the angry, metallic taste in her mouth turning bitter. 'Don't you dare throw that at me. You knew the score, we both did.'

'I'm sorry,' said Nate, hanging his head. 'That was a low blow.'

Lucy was about to answer, but was interrupted by footsteps on the stairs and a gentle knock on the door. Willem's head appeared, his face pink and animated. 'The rescue people are nearly here,' he said excitedly. 'We can hear the tractor thing. It's really close.'

'OK,' said Lucy. 'We'll be down in a minute.' Willem took in the scene, clearly reluctant to leave without getting the gossip for Alex, then left again.

'I'm really sorry,' repeated Nate, after Willem's footsteps had retreated down the stairs. 'I shouldn't have said anything. Please, can we not leave things like this?'

'Fine,' said Lucy, taking a deep breath and forcing a weak smile even though she felt like she might be sick. 'But at some point in the next few days we'll both be back at work, and I think it's reasonable to assume that neither of us wants people gossiping about us.' She tilted her head and gave him a significant look, hoping he would join the dots without her having to actually say what she knew about Sasha. His brow furrowed for a few seconds, then softened into realisation as the penny dropped.

'Ah,' he said. 'Right.'

'So let's put this down to an incredible and extraordinary experience,' she continued, 'and leave it there.'

'OK, I accept that,' said Nate earnestly. 'But that doesn't mean I want to forget.'

Neither do I, thought Lucy, but telling Nate that wouldn't be helpful, and the alternative was too terrifying. She looked down at her hand, which was still clutching the black marker pen. 'Fine,' she said. 'I'll give you a reminder that will last a few days, before you go cold turkey.' She took his wrist and turned it over, then carefully wrote WAHZ in a swirly calligraphy script just below the crook of his elbow.

'There,' she said with a smile. 'We'll Always Have Zermatt.'

Nate laughed, and for a moment Lucy wobbled, wondering what would happen if she leaned in to kiss him. Even when she was angry and upset, there was this strange connection that drew her to him. She thought about last night, and what it might be like if their bodies came together in a haze of fumbling zips for a sweaty, urgent coupling against the cardboard boxes in the corner, all finished in a passionate few minutes before Ulrich's bus arrived. The look in Nate's eyes suggested he was thinking the same thing, but it was way too complicated for a hundred different reasons.

'So that's it, for me and you,' he said quietly.

'Yes,' said Lucy, keeping her voice strong and confident so Nate couldn't hear her lack of resolve. 'There is no me and you, there can't be. We both know that.'

'Yeah,' he said, swallowing hard. 'So just work friends, then?'

Lucy forced a smile and nodded emphatically, determined not to let him see her wavering. It felt like her heart was already starting to unravel at the edges, like Nate had tugged on its strings and set something in motion that she couldn't stop. Clearly the sooner she got off this mountain and back to the safety and familiarity of her flat in Bristol, the better.

And yet somehow, the thought of that made her feel more lost and stranded than ever.

CHAPTER TWENTY

When Lucy and Nate returned downstairs, the front door to the Guntherhütte was open and everyone was already gathered in the space they'd dug out yesterday. The throbbing diesel engine of the snowplough sounded like it was just on the other side of the first row of trees, so Lucy grabbed her clothes from the drying rack and darted into the bathroom to change. It felt wrong to re-enter civilisation in giant knickers and purple stirrup pants, so she left Monica's clothes in the washing machine and found a plastic grocery bag hanging on the back of the door for her jumper, deciding to keep Nate's sweatshirt on. He was wearing a spare sweater of Alex's, so they could all swap back to their original clothes later.

By the time she joined the others outside, the approaching snowplough was shaking the snow from nearby treetops. She looked for Nate, who was chatting to Andrea and Felix on the other side of the terrace, determinedly looking the other way. Willem and Alex were eyeing them both with interest, so Lucy resolved to keep her distance from Nate for the time being – they'd have to travel back to Bristol together, but there was no need to make this parting any harder than it needed to be. Instead she watched with Willem and Alex as the cab of the snowplough appeared through the trees, then the wall of snow at the end of the terrace cracked and crumbled. The huge yellow shovel pushed all the snow to the sides with a deafening roar that echoed through the mountains, then dug a further path over to one side so that Ulrich's bus could drive in alongside him. Both drivers killed the engines, and everything was silent again.

'And now you can go home,' said Monica, putting her arm around Lucy's shoulders. It felt like a bittersweet relief – Lucy was happy that they were all safe and going somewhere where she could have a bath and change her clothes, but she was sad to leave Gunther and Monica behind. Even Chantal had been tolerable on occasions.

'Thank you,' she said. 'You've all been amazing.'

'It has been an adventure,' said Gunther, pulling Lucy into an unnecessarily full-contact hug. 'Come and visit us; you will always be welcome here. Free glühwein for life!' In contrast, Chantal gave Lucy a zero-contact hug and a watery smile that lived somewhere between *I want to be your friend* but also *I hate you with the force of a thousand suns*.

Lucy looked up as Monica said her goodbyes to Nate. 'You have such talent,' she said, her hand on his shoulder. 'Be sure to follow your dreams.'

There was a flurry of activity and shouting in German as Ulrich and the snowplough driver helped Gunther unload a generator from the back of the bus and carry it to the shed. Then another few minutes of ferrying bags of provisions, and Ulrich updating his family on everything that was happening down in the village. Alex videoed everything, turning his camera on Lucy and the others so they could wave and look excited. She took in the beautiful vista of mountains for a final time, wondering if she'd ever come back here, before picking up her plastic bag and getting ready to board the bus.

'We should all have a photo together before we leave,' said Alex. 'The Guntherhütte crew. Can you take it?' He thrust his phone at Ulrich, then waved his arms to organise everyone into a group under the Guntherhütte sign. Nate fell in beside Lucy, and put his arm loosely around her shoulders. He felt warm and solid and safe, and for a moment Lucy really didn't want him to let go. What he'd said about Leo had been a punch in the gut, but it was too huge and painful to think about now. Maybe they could go and get a drink down in Zermatt, just the two of them? There was no harm in that, and she absolutely, definitely wouldn't sleep with him again. Just friends from now on.

'One more,' said Ulrich. 'Everyone say "Guntherhütte!"'

They all shouted in response, like a ramshackle crew of intrepid explorers who had conquered the mountains and lived to tell the tale. A final round of goodbyes to the family, and within minutes they were all bundling onto Ulrich's bus.

Lucy got on first and sat at the back, followed by Willem and Alex, who took the seats in front of her, Alex staring at his phone like he was willing it to be back within range of some phone signal. Nate was outside helping Andrea and Felix load their instruments into the luggage compartment at the back, then he followed them onto the bus and took the seat at the front.

Lucy felt a flash of disappointment, then reminded herself that she was the one who had insisted on the distance between them, and he was probably already glad to be getting back to Sasha. There was a minute or two of ploughing and turning so both vehicles could get back on the piste in the other direction, and then they were on their way.

In the end the journey back was considerably less perilous than the trip up – the snowplough had created a deep channel through the powdery snow so it felt like driving down a toboggan run. Also Ulrich could only drive at the speed of the plough in front of him, which really wasn't very fast at all. Presumably by tomorrow this would all have been properly cleared and he would be able to come and go like a maniac again, but right now Lucy was grateful for the sedate and careful drive down. She kept one eye on Nate, who was in his own little world, looking out of the steamy window, but didn't seem to be struggling. Her thoughts drifted to his hands on her body this morning, and her thighs clenched with desire. There was a lot she needed to unpick about this weekend – what had happened, what had been said, how she felt – and Nate seemed to be at the heart of most of it.

'Who are all those people?' asked Willem, using his hand to clear the condensation from the window as they reached the bottom of the piste and the village. It was already starting to get dark, but there was a crowd of twenty or thirty people bundled in coats and hats waiting by the bus stop. Some of them were holding cameras and microphones with huge foam covers.

'Holy shit,' said Alex, tapping frantically on his phone. 'Oh my fucking JESUS.'

'What's happened?' asked Lucy, not sure she could cope with any more drama today. Nate, Andrea and Felix all turned to look at Alex.

'We've gone viral,' he said.

'Who has?' asked Willem.

'I have. I put a load of videos on my TikTok and Insta first thing this morning, when the Wi-Fi came back, and now everyone's talking about them. Like, hundreds of thousands of shares.' He kept swiping and tapping, his screen a flickering blur of videos and comments.

'So all these people, they're here for us?' asked Felix, waving through the window at a man holding a camera. 'Are we famous? Is now the time to change our name to the Refubeegees? Come on.' Ulrich opened the door to a blast of cold air and a cacophony of excited shouting, and Felix grabbed Andrea's hand and dragged her off the bus behind him. They were quickly swallowed up by the crowd, as Ulrich opened the luggage compartment to retrieve their instruments.

'If they're here for anyone, it's Alex,' said Willem, looking somewhere between bored and exhausted. Lucy tried to imagine what living in the shadow of a famous influencer must be like, and decided it was probably kind of tiresome.

'No,' said Alex. 'Oh shit.'

'What is it?' asked Lucy.

He looked up, pressing one hand over his mouth as the other continued to tap and swipe. 'I think they're here for Nate.'

'Wait, what do you mean?' asked Nate, shaking his head as everyone turned to look at him. He stood up and made his way down the bus, sitting down on the seat in front of Lucy, fixing Alex with a narrow-eyed glare.

'I uploaded a video of you singing,' said Alex, glued to his screen excitedly and oblivious to Nate bearing down on him. 'I'd done a really nice edit, because I was bored. So it had Ed Sheeran from Friday, then a bit of Elton and George Michael and the other guy from yesterday.'

'Craig David,' said Lucy, not taking her eyes off Nate.

'Yeah,' said Alex breathlessly. 'Shit, these numbers are insane. It's been on my TikTok since first thing this morning, and now everybody is talking about it.'

'Everybody who? Where?' demanded Nate.

'Everywhere,' said Alex, his face breaking out into a smile as he waved his phone at Nate. 'You've gone mega-viral, my friend.'

'Who gave you permission to put my singing online?' said Nate, pressing his fingers into his forehead as he tried to breathe.

'Hey,' said Lucy, pushing down the aisle and sitting in the seat that Andrea had just vacated. 'It's OK.'

'It's NOT OK,' said Nate, burying his fingers in his hair. 'I didn't ask for a welcome committee.'

'I'm sorry,' said Alex. 'Actually I'm not sorry. This is going to make you a superstar.'

'I don't want to be a superstar.'

'Everyone wants to be a superstar. This could be your big chance.'

'He's right,' said Lucy quietly. This was exactly what Nate had said he wanted yesterday morning, but it was all moving too fast for him. 'Look, you don't have to do anything right this minute. Just smile and wave and look surprised and confused, which you are. Then we'll go back to the hotel and work out what's going on.'

'I'll answer any questions for you,' said Alex. 'You don't have to say anything. I know what I'm doing.'

'What's the alternative?' asked Nate breathlessly, looking at the group outside the bus, then back at Lucy.

'Living on this bus with Ulrich?' said Lucy gently, wishing she could take the burden of the stress for him so he could somehow enjoy this moment. 'One way or another, we need to get off.'

'Shit,' said Nate, letting out a long, slow breath, then closing his eyes and taking a few more, his hand on Lucy's arm to steady him. 'OK. Let's do it.'

Alex hurried down the bus and spoke to Ulrich about helping him create some space, then took Nate's arm and guided him through the noisy crowd who were calling his name and asking questions. The noise retreated as they moved away, leaving Lucy and Willem watching from the steps of the bus.

'Come on,' she said, already worried about Nate's state of mind after being in a crowd like that. She climbed down from the bus and bowed her head against a biting wind, then followed the mass of people moving towards the hotel.

'This is wild,' said Willem. 'I've seen Alex pull some shit before, but this is next level.'

'Did he know?' asked Lucy quickly. 'Was he expecting this reception for Nate?'

Willem shook his head quickly and laughed. 'Lucy,

you've spent the last few days in Alex's company. Do you really think he'd have engineered a welcome that wasn't all about him?'

'No,' said Lucy. 'He must be gutted.'

'Are you kidding?' laughed Willem. 'He'll appoint himself as Nate's manager and be forever known as the person who made him a star.'

'Hmm,' said Lucy, wondering if that was a good or a bad thing. 'Is there money in that?'

Willem shrugged. 'Yes, but Alex doesn't need money; his family are very wealthy. He just needs a profile and a spotlight.'

'OK, but will he look after Nate?'

Willem stopped on the path outside the hotel and looked intently at Lucy. 'He will be taken care of, Lucy. Alex is a good guy. I'm marrying him, remember?'

They pushed through the waiting crowd of . . . *who are these people?* thought Lucy. *Press? Fans?* She tried to take the measure of them, but they were all bundled up in coats and scarves. Men and women, young and old, talking in a mix of French and German and English. Handy, since Nate spoke all three. The only thing Lucy knew for sure was that they had seen Alex's videos barely eight hours ago and immediately made their way to Zermatt to wait for him to get off the mountain, which seemed entirely deranged. Without seeing the online discourse, it was hard to imagine how that had happened. They barely gave her and Willem a passing glance, so clearly Nate was why they were here.

Willem flashed his room key card to the doorman to gain access, then led Lucy into the foyer of a very fancy

Alpine hotel. Nate and Alex were by reception, talking intently to a woman in a long green coat. Lucy did a double-take, then realised it was Sasha, holding the handle of Nate's luggage. *She's already packed his bag, then*, thought Lucy, realising how entirely surplus to requirements she was right now.

Alex hurried over to them, holding his phone to his ear and talking at a million miles an hour. 'Hold on,' he said to the person on the other end, then turned to Lucy and Willem. 'There's a car waiting to take Nate to the airport,' he said importantly. 'Sasha has asked me to go with them, give her a debrief and put together a plan. They're expecting a crowd at Geneva and Heathrow.'

Heathrow? thought Lucy. *What happened to flying back to Bristol?*

'Who's Sasha?' asked Willem.

'Nate introduced her as a friend,' said Alex with a shrug. 'She knew we were staying here and has been waiting for us to get back. She seems to be very much in control of things.'

'She works with me and Nate,' said Lucy. She tried to catch Nate's eye, but he was deep in what appeared to be an intense conversation, Sasha holding his hand. 'Am I booked on the same flight?'

'No,' said Alex bluntly. 'Nate asked the same question. There weren't enough seats, so Sasha said you could fly back tomorrow.' He turned to Willem before Lucy could say anything. 'Can you take my stuff back to Amsterdam? I'll buy whatever I need in London.'

'Sure, no problem,' said Willem, his tone weary and resigned.

'It was great to meet you, Lucy,' said Alex, already turning his attention back to whoever was on the phone. Lucy could see that he was in influencer mode now, thinking of all the ways he could milk this for every content opportunity. A little make-up in the car to hide the shadows under Nate's eyes, maybe videos of him walking through the airport, a short interview on the plane where he'd humbly say how shocked he was by the welcome party. Alex would ask him to sing a verse or two, and Nate would say an embarrassed no. And because it was Nate, it would all feel totally authentic and charming.

'*Ik houd van je*,' said Alex, kissing Willem on the lips and hurrying off, holding out his arms to herd Sasha and Nate out to the car. Nate was hidden from view, so there was no way of knowing if he had looked back, or hesitated and said he wanted say goodbye to Lucy but was told there was no time. Within moments he was gone.

'What did Alex say?' asked Lucy.

'He said "I love you",' said Willem with a hollow laugh.

Lucy tried to remember the last time anyone had ever said that to her, other than Jonno or her parents. *Nope, not once*, she thought, blinking away tears of exhaustion and grief and loss and a whole bunch of other emotions she didn't have a name for right now.

'You really liked Nate, didn't you?' said Willem, putting his arm around Lucy's shoulders.

'We hardly knew each other,' said Lucy, tempted to shrug him off but instead leaning into his sturdiness. 'But then . . . things snowballed. It's complicated.'

'Love always is,' said Willem wearily. 'Where are you staying?'

'A hotel down the road,' said Lucy. 'I need to get back there and charge my phone.'

'Same,' said Willem. 'And I need a shower and some sleep. You want to meet up later, get some dinner?'

'Sure,' said Lucy, already not relishing the idea of being in the Titan hotel on her own. 'Are you going back to Amsterdam?'

Willem shrugged. 'I'm booked here until Friday, so I'll probably stay and do some skiing. There's nothing to rush home for now, Alex could be in London for a while.'

'Shit,' said Lucy. 'This has really fucked your holiday. And your engagement announcement. I'm so sorry.'

'It's fine,' said Willem with a resigned smile. 'When you date a man like Alex, you get used to the rollercoaster. I might start planning our wedding for the autumn; it will give me something to focus on. Will you come?'

'Of course,' said Lucy, reminded that she'd agreed to go to a wedding with Anthony next weekend, and she really needed to let him and Marco know she wasn't dead.

'Go back to your hotel, Lucy,' said Willem, putting his hand on her arm. 'You look exhausted.'

'OK,' she said, feeling suddenly overwhelmed by tiredness and an aching, hollow feeling she hadn't felt since the months after Leo had died. She grabbed a pen and piece of paper from reception and scribbled her number on it. 'When you've charged your phone, drop me a message so I have your number, and we can meet up later.'

'Sure,' said Willem, pulling her into a hug. 'Keep me updated.'

Lucy blew him a kiss and headed back out into the snow, slipping and sliding her way back to the Alpina. It was almost dark, but the front door was open and the key to her room still worked. Everything was just as she'd left it, apart from the note from the owner on her bed that read *It is fine for you to stay tonight but we have new guests arriving tomorrow. Please vacate by 10 a.m.*

She sighed and plugged in her phone and her watch, unable to decide if she needed food or sleep more. A trip to the bathroom necessitated a glance in the mirror while she washed her hands, and she was forced to acknowledge that she looked like someone had drawn a pair of eyes on a crumpled paper bag. Maybe she'd have a snack, then a shower and a nap, then meet Willem for dinner later.

She padded down to the breakfast room in her socks, filling a bowl with some kind of muesli, then sat by the window to eat while she watched the gentle flurries of snow. Nate would be well on his way to Geneva airport by now, Sasha and Alex already working together on a strategy. Lucy wondered how Nate was feeling, and whether there was a tiny part of him that was still thinking about her, or if that had been left behind on the mountain to melt into nothing.

CHAPTER TWENTY-ONE

When Lucy trudged back upstairs and turned on her phone, she found a message from Willem so she had his number, along with dozens of messages from, in order of volume, Jonno, her mum, Sasha, Anthony and Marco, then a handful of colleagues and a couple of old friends she hadn't heard from in years, the ghouls. All expressed varying levels of concern and disbelief about her predicament, and urged her to get in touch. Lucy smiled at Anthony's message, which just said *Heard you were stuck on a mountain. Need me to rescue you?* and included a picture of him holding a chunky rubber torch instead of his penis. How far had Alex's videos spread for him to realise that Lucy was part of the drama? Or had hers and Nate's predicament been on the local news? Her mind boggled at the thought of what had been going on while she and Nate had been obliviously having sex this morning.

Lucy cut and pasted the same *I'm fine, back in hotel and home tomorrow* to everyone, then left her phone charging and lay on the bed. She wondered for the twentieth time in the past hour what Nate was doing now, but all thoughts eventually drifted to memories of him naked and horizontal and driving her wild with those beautiful hands that might not be able to play the piano, but had composed a symphony that had spanned the length of her body. The confusion she felt manifested as a dull ache that was definitely not going to dissipate in this lonely hotel room.

She shivered, even though the room didn't feel cold, and pulled the cuffs of her sweatshirt down over her fists. Except it was Nate's sweatshirt, not hers – she hadn't had a chance to give it back in the rush of his departure. She held the sleeve up to her face and breathed in the smell of him, wishing she could time-travel back to last night and the peace and contentment she'd felt falling asleep in his arms. Thoughts of what he'd said earlier about Leo kept creeping in, casting a dark shadow over the memories.

I need to get out of this place, she thought, focusing her mind on how to make that happen. Jonno would be on a plane, Sasha was on her way to the airport with Nate and Alex, and there were no more flights back to Bristol today. But there was three hours of Switzerland between her and the airport, and absolutely no reason why she needed to spend the evening in this oppressive room.

Kristoff, thought Lucy, grabbing her laptop from the desk by the window and finding a work email from him that included his mobile number. She copied it into her phone before she changed her mind, then pressed the call button.

'Kristoff Berg,' he said. She could hear classical music playing in the background, and the clatter of a spoon. She imagined him in an enormous kitchen, all glossy cabinets and chrome fittings, like a Swiss operating theatre.

'Hey, it's Lucy. From LUNA. Sorry to bother you.'

'Lucy!' he exclaimed. 'So great to hear from you. How are you?'

'I'm fine. Back in the village.'

'Sasha told me you were on your way. One hell of an adventure, right?'

Lucy gave a hollow laugh. 'It was definitely an experience.'

'And all that shit today with Nate and the viral videos, that's been totally wild.'

'Mmm,' she said vaguely. Definitely not a conversation she wanted to get into right now.

'You looking for Jonno and Sasha? They both left Geneva earlier. I'm here for a couple more days, then heading to New York.'

'Yeah, I know they've gone. I can't get a flight back until tomorrow.'

'OK,' said Kristoff. 'What's your plan?'

'Actually, I was ringing to ask for your help. I kind of need to . . . not be in Zermatt right now.'

'Totally get that,' he said, and Lucy heard the air hiss of a fridge being opened. 'PTSD is real.'

'No, I'm fine,' said Lucy, not wanting Kristoff thinking he needed to stage an intervention. 'I'm just on my own here, and it's . . .'

'Yup, yup, got it,' he said. 'I'm going to organise a car now to bring you to Geneva.'

'Please don't go to any trouble,' said Lucy quickly. 'I can sort out transport myself, I just wanted to get your recommendation for a hotel.'

'Totally, totally. Let me get my people onto it. There's a local transfer firm we use, if you get the shuttle bus to Täsch now there'll be a car waiting for you.'

Lucy paused, wondering if it was cheeky to ask for an extra half an hour so she could have a shower, then decided it could wait a bit longer. 'OK, thank you,' she said. 'Any hotel is fine, please don't go to any trouble. I really appreciate it.'

'Get going,' said Kristoff. 'You'll get a message with the details of the car. See you soon, Lucy.'

'OK, thanks,' said Lucy, as Kristoff ended the call. She dropped Willem a message to say that she was leaving Zermatt but would stay in touch, then started sweeping all her belongings into her weekend bag. A worry nagged at the corner of her brain, that maybe Kristoff was going to have her delivered to his house and she'd have to spend the evening being serious and professional, rather than falling asleep in a heap of bones and skin and swirling emotions. But she rationalised that she could politely refuse his hospitality and find a hotel for herself – he was hardly going to take her hostage.

True to his word, when Lucy got to Täsch there was a car waiting for her; a glossy black Range Rover driven by a swarthy man with a beard, who took her bag and opened the door with nothing more than a nod. That was fine with Lucy; the last thing she needed was three hours of inane conversation. She briefly wondered how much Kristoff was paying to have her taken to Geneva in this executive drug dealer wagon, but decided he could probably afford it.

'Where are you taking me?' she asked as they pulled onto the main road down the mountain. She asked first in English, and then when he shrugged helplessly, she took a moment to work out a version in French. '*Où allons-nous?*' Probably terrible grammar, but he'd get the gist. German was entirely beyond her.

'*Genève,*' he said gruffly.

'*Où à Genève?*' she asked, crossing her fingers that his response wouldn't be *Chez Kristoff*.

'*Les Armures,*' said the driver. '*Un bel hôtel.*'

Thank you, Kristoff, thought Lucy, frantically tapping Les Armures into her phone. It looked like a gorgeous boutique hotel in Geneva's Old Town, housed in a seventeenth-century building with bags of charm. Google Maps said the journey time was three hours and the car was toasty warm, so she pulled off her coat, folded it into a pillow, and fell asleep.

'Mr Berg has left a message for you,' said the receptionist, handing Lucy a small envelope and her room key, along with a look that suggested she was questioning why a man like Kristoff Berg was leaving messages for a woman who looked like she'd slept in a bin. 'Can I get someone to take your bag?' Lucy shook her head and muttered a thank you, then hurried up the plushly carpeted stairs to her room. She couldn't help but gasp as she opened the door – it was a stunning haven of wood panelling and exposed brickwork and a huge bed with a rolltop bath at the end of it. It smelled of expensive room spray and luxury bedding; exactly the kind of place that she'd book for a luxury night away.

She looked down at the envelope still in her hand, then kicked off her boots and sat on the end of the bed to read Kristoff's note, which had clearly been pasted from an email and printed by the receptionist. *Dear Lucy*, he'd written. *I hope you like Les Armures, it's my favourite hotel in Genèva. The room service is great, so order whatever you want – it's on Titan. If you'd like to meet for a drink in the bar later, I'm still in town, but totally understand if you need some time out. I've also taken the liberty of organising a car to take you to the airport tomorrow – it will pick you up at 1 p.m., you don't need to check out before then. Best wishes, KB.*

Lucy flopped back on the bed, feeling like she might cry with relief. She'd order room service, have a bath, get up to date on everything that was going on in the world – including what was happening with Nate; there was no point pretending she wasn't interested – then sleep for at least ten hours in this incredible cloud of a bed.

She could already feel herself drifting, so she pulled her phone out and tapped out a message to Kristoff. *Am at Les Armures, it's beautiful – thank you so much. Am going to crash this evening, but really appreciate all you've done.*

He replied immediately with *It's my pleasure, safe travels tomorrow.*

Right, down to business, thought Lucy, picking up the room service menu. She called reception and ordered a goat's cheese salad and a glass of wine for an hour's time, then ran the bath with hot, foamy water. It felt blissful to finally ditch the clothes she'd been wearing since Friday; even though they'd been handwashed twice in that time, they didn't feel clean enough. Just before she sank into the bath up to her chin, she called Jonno and put her phone on speaker on the side of the bath.

'Lucy?' he asked.

'Hey, you,' she replied with a smile, relieved as ever to hear his voice.

'Ah, there you are. You still alive?'

'I am. My mountain adventure is over.'

'Where are you now?'

'I'm in a fancy hotel in Geneva, in the bath, with Kristoff picking up the tab.'

Jonno laughed. 'Wait, are you naked?'

Lucy rolled her eyes. 'Very.'

'Is Kristoff also in the bath?'

'You're so incredibly funny.'

'Is he on his way over for pre-seduction martinis?'

'No. He offered to meet me for a drink, but made it clear it wasn't mandatory if I needed time out.'

'Good man,' said Jonno. 'Where's French Exit?'

'Heading back to London,' said Lucy. 'Accompanied by a minor Dutch royal who's going to make him a superstar.' She didn't mention Sasha; that would only prompt further questions that she really didn't want to answer.

'Shitting hell,' said Jonno. 'I haven't even started to get my head around what happened with all the singing stuff.'

'I think it's what the kids call "going viral".'

'Yeah, so I'm told. They were discussing him on Radio 2 earlier. He's fucking everywhere. My kids haven't stopped talking about him, and I've seen that clip of him singing George Michael about fifty times.'

'I need to catch up on all that,' said Lucy, shivering despite the hot water. 'But I'm one of only eight people who heard it live.'

'Was it as good as it comes across on the video?'

'Yeah,' mused Lucy. 'He's pretty amazing. Like, proper talent.'

'Shame he's such a personality vacuum.'

'He actually grew on me,' said Lucy vaguely. She tried to keep her voice light, knowing that Jonno would pounce on any suggestion that Lucy and Nate had inched closer to each other.

'Oh really? Tell me more.' *Like that*, thought Lucy.

'No, not like that,' she said quickly. 'He's just a lot more personable once you get to know him a bit.'

'Christ. Being "personable" is really going to get the groupies flocking his way.'

'Not everyone has your charisma,' said Lucy with a smile. 'He's definitely not a natural megastar. I just hope he's being looked after.'

'I think Sasha has got involved,' said Jonno. 'No doubt protecting LUNA's interests.'

'Yeah, I saw her in Zermatt,' said Lucy, gratified that Jonno wasn't entirely in the dark. 'She and Alex whisked him off through a crowd of waiting press.'

'Who's Alex?'

'The minor Dutch royal. He's now the mastermind of Nate's superstardom. You need to follow him on TikTok.'

'I'm too old for TikTok,' grumbled Jonno. 'I've been all over it for a few days, keeping an eye out for you, and it's full of weirdos dancing or people mowing the lawn in a mindful way. You back in the office tomorrow?'

'No, my flight's not until half three. I'll be back on Tuesday.'

'Pint in the Brunel after work?'

'Yeah, that would be great.' The idea of getting back to some kind of Bristol normality felt appealing, but then also left Lucy feeling oddly hollow. Only the thought of seeing Nate again made her heart skip.

'You're OK though, right?' Jonno sounded worried, which she couldn't help but love him for.

'I'm fine. The whole experience feels a bit surreal now. Like, I'm not sure if it actually happened.'

'We'll get you and French Exit to do an agency talk. I'm guessing it will be more interesting than that time when Derek talked about data protection.'

'Ha, sure,' said Lucy. 'How was the Geneva Convention? Maya and Olly OK?'

'Yeah,' said Jonno. 'A bit gutted to leave Zermatt, but the place Kristoff booked by the lake had a fancy spa, so they were pretty happy after that. We've done some planning for next year, and squeezed a bit more budget out of them.'

'Good work,' said Lucy. She tried to care about the work element of the weekend, but right now it was hard to muster much enthusiasm. 'Right, I need to go,' she said. 'I've got food coming, and my water's getting cold.'

'I can't believe you're calling me naked. How am I supposed to get anything done?'

Lucy laughed. 'Is your beautiful wife home?'

'Yes. She's watching TV while I cook her dinner.'

'Then go and worship her. She deserves it.'

'Fine. But I want you to know that it gets confusing sometimes.'

'No, it doesn't, you just like me to think it does.'

'Yeah, you're right. Who's getting wanked off on WhatsApp this evening? Iron Manuel or Tentpole Tony?'

'Neither,' said Lucy emphatically. Under different circumstances, she'd definitely be putting in a video call to one of them, but today she didn't feel like it. Tiredness, partly, but also that strange feeling of emptiness that remote video masturbation definitely wasn't going to fix. Had it been there before Nate, or was it a new thing? Everything felt too confusing right now.

'How boring,' said Jonno. 'See you Tuesday, mate.'

Lucy said goodbye and ended the call, then scrubbed herself down with a tiny bottle of luxury body wash and wrapped herself in an obscenely fluffy bathrobe. She applied a layer of fancy moisturiser from the hotel bathroom to her parched face, then curled up on the bed and opened TikTok. A search for #natelambert yielded hundreds of videos – sharing Alex's footage, reaction videos, analysis from people in the music industry, girls swooning about how he was the new Harry Styles. The sheer volume of it made Lucy's mind boggle, so instead she searched for @BaronAlexJansen and scrolled through Alex's videos from the weekend.

By the time her food arrived she'd watched them all up to this morning, from Friday's live video of Alex introducing everyone at the Gunterhütte, followed by another of him trying to wrestle with a sofa bed. Then the edit of Nate's singing, which was two full minutes of one goosebump moment after another. There was the video of them eating her birthday ice cream, then an edit of highlights from Saturday's snow digging. Willem's proposal was artfully edited with music and captions, then a few more videos showed Alex talking about the various challenges he'd faced during this ordeal, like he was a victim of a mountainside plane crash and would shortly be forced to eat his fellow passengers. He'd just about managed humble and grateful, although Lucy could see how much he wanted to rage about the hardship and indignity of it all.

She sipped her wine and picked at her goat's cheese

salad as she ventured into the unknown of videos from today. First there was Alex pushing through the crowds outside the hotel with Nate, providing a running commentary, then a short interview in the back of the car where Nate looked genuinely shellshocked about what had just happened. Then their arrival at Geneva airport, where another gaggle of cameras and phones and microphones surged towards them. Nate gave a short statement, saying he'd been blown away by all the attention and so grateful for all the messages he'd received, but his priority right now was getting home to his family. He'd apparently started his own TikTok channel, so please follow @NateLambertMusic. Lucy clicked on the link, but there were no videos yet.

Sasha didn't appear in any of the videos, other than a glimpse of her dark hair in the front seat of the taxi to the airport. Clearly she'd ordered Alex to leave her out of it, which was hardly surprising. But Lucy knew she wouldn't be far away, and was momentarily grateful that Nate was in the care of someone who knew and understood him. Alex may be masterminding Operation Superstar, but Sasha's priority would be looking out for Nate. She paused on a shot of Nate smiling for a selfie with a girl in the airport, his hair flopping over one eye. He was laughing at something, his eyes sparkling.

Shit, thought Lucy, putting her fork down on the barely touched salad and downing the rest of the wine. *I really miss him, and it feels like I've totally messed this up.*

CHAPTER TWENTY-TWO

Lucy's return to the LUNA office on Tuesday heralded a barrage of excited squawking and questions about her mountain adventure, mostly as a way in to interrogate her about Nate. Had she heard from him? Had she seen the latest video on his TikTok? How was he coping with being the UK's next big thing? She fielded every question as quickly as she could, then took her coffee straight upstairs to the Headspace – a windowless room on the mezzanine above the main open-plan area that was filled with brightly coloured sofas and beanbags. It was a room designated for creative thinking, and there was an unwritten rule at LUNA that if someone was working in the Headspace, you didn't interrupt.

Lucy closed the door and shrugged off her coat, taking a moment to breathe in the muffled quiet of the room. She kicked off her trainers and sat cross-legged on the biggest of the three sofas, opening her laptop so she looked busy. There was a new campaign brief from Titan that she needed to get working on, but it wasn't due until early next week, so she could just sit here and read it while she drank her coffee, letting the noise in her head subside. Her stomach was fluttering at the prospect of seeing Nate again; no doubt someone would tell him she was up here when he arrived, and they'd have a chance to talk. Things between them hadn't exactly been clear the last time they'd seen each other, but they could work that out.

'Hello, Lucy,' said Sasha, bursting into the room with Olly in tow. 'We need to talk.'

Lucy looked at them both, alarm bells going off in her head. Sasha was all business, a woman with things on her mind. Had Nate told her what happened between them? Lucy mentally cleared her desk and did an audit of what was on her laptop that shouldn't be. A few sad poems, a best man's speech she wrote for Jonno a couple of years ago, an abandoned young adult novel about a pair of crime-busting twins. Nothing that would get her into trouble if they took it away and put her on extended leave.

Her work phone, however, was a whole other matter. She'd never bothered having a personal one, and her iCloud photo storage was a festival of explicit pictures that she and Anthony had swapped. Nothing with her face in, obviously, but that didn't mean she wanted the agency IT department swapping close-ups of her labia. It was in her coat pocket, so she'd have to pretend she'd left it at home and give it a clean-up before she gave it back.

'How are you?' said Sasha, sitting sideways on the sofa next to Lucy so their knees were almost touching. Olly dragged a beanbag over and fell backwards into it with a huff of compacting polystyrene.

'I'm fine,' said Lucy warily. 'Happy to be back.'

'We're happy to have you back,' said Sasha with the briefest of smiles. In that moment it felt genuine, but maybe that was just something you said to soften the blow of *Look, I think it's best for everyone if you leave quietly*. Lucy said nothing, waiting for Sasha to make her next move. If there was about to be an awkward conversation, there was no reason for Lucy to make it easy for her.

'Look,' Sasha began, wiping her hands on her designer jeans in a way that suggested they were potentially sweaty. 'You're probably wondering why I turned up on Sunday, and left with Nate.' It was the first time Lucy had ever seen Sasha look mildly uncomfortable and out of her depth, and Lucy debated how much to let her suffer. On balance and in the interests of getting this conversation over and done with, maybe not very much.

'No,' said Lucy, holding her gaze. 'I'm not wondering. It made perfect sense, actually.'

'Right,' said Sasha, colour flushing her cheeks. 'So . . .?'

'Look, let's make this easier,' said Lucy. 'I know about—' She glanced at Olly, unsure whether saying the words out loud would be a huge bombshell.

'It's fine,' said Sasha quietly. 'There's nothing Olly doesn't know.'

Poor Olly, thought Lucy. *Who needs to shoulder that emotional baggage?*

'Fine. I know about the . . . relationship. Between you and Nate.' In reality she didn't know anything much at all, but Sasha was nodding and taking deep breaths, so she'd clearly hit the mark.

'Right,' said Sasha, her eyes darting in all directions, so Lucy could practically see her brain whirring at one hundred miles an hour. 'Does Nate know that you know?'

'No,' Lucy replied, almost too quickly.

'Can I ask how you found out?' She glanced at Olly, like maybe he was the culprit. He raised his eyebrows and shook his head vehemently.

'By accident,' said Lucy. 'It doesn't matter.'

'Does anyone else—?'

Lucy shook her head. 'Not from me.'

'Not even Jonno?'

'No,' said Lucy emphatically, remembering how close she'd come to messaging him the gossip whilst on the toilet in a Zermatt hotel room.

'Well,' said Sasha, looking relieved. 'Let's—'

'But I just want to say that it's unethical. To be part of a close-knit team like ours and have someone in the team with a hotline to the boss.'

'We never talk about work stuff,' said Sasha defensively. 'And Nate didn't ask to be on the Titan team, it was Fran who poached him from Pukka Paws.'

Lucy rolled her eyes. 'He could have said no.'

'It was a brilliant opportunity,' said Sasha, as Olly followed the discussion intently. 'A chance for him to work with really good people. And a promotion too, obviously. Nate earned it in his own right; I had nothing to do with it.'

'I'm not saying you did,' said Lucy coolly.

'And at that point I already knew I was in line for the Exec team, so there was hardly any crossover. Nate kept his head down, which he was used to anyway. He'd been doing it for years.'

Lucy realised what Sasha was saying – that her relationship with Nate had been going on since before he started working in London, so presumably going back to his time in Paris. Or before that, even. Somehow it felt worse that she'd smoothed a career path for her toyboy, rather than a whirlwind romance after he started, maybe off the back of a late night in the office and a shared taxi home. That kind of thing happened all the time in their industry, but the longevity of Sasha and Nate's relationship felt more underhand, somehow.

'Is that why he didn't make a pitch to come on the Zermatt trip? Let Fran take all the credit for his work?'

'Of course,' said Sasha with a shrug. 'It felt too risky. Obviously it's better for both of us if nobody knows.'

Lucy realised that the bitter taste in her mouth was nothing more than jealousy, and she was angry at herself. She'd let Nate get under her skin, despite knowing that he had something going on with Sasha. She'd convinced herself that it must be a casual thing between them, because that made it permissible for her to take what she wanted from him in that moment. But there'd been something else that she couldn't quite put a name to – a kind of connection between her and Nate, a tiny breach in the fortress she'd built for herself. Even though they'd used each other as a port in a snowstorm, it still hurt, somehow. She couldn't explain it, but it did.

'It's fine,' said Lucy, holding up her hands. 'I'm not planning to tell anyone. It's none of my business.'

'Right. Thank you.' Sasha looked mightily relieved. 'Is there, you know, anything—?' Lucy realised that Sasha was offering to repay her silence and loyalty, and she could ask for pretty much whatever she wanted right now. A promotion, a pay rise, a job in the Paris office with a view of the Eiffel Tower. But in her world those things were earned, not acquired through blackmail.

'No,' she said quickly. 'Let's move on.'

Both Sasha and Olly gave her a look of absolute respect, and Lucy knew that this wouldn't be forgotten. It was a moment of female solidarity; understanding that they would back each other. Lucy had just banked the mother of all favours, and everyone in the room knew it.

'Fine,' said Sasha, all business again. 'I actually came down here to make an announcement to the team. But I wanted to tell you first.'

'What announcement?' asked Lucy.

'Nate isn't coming back.'

Lucy felt like the air had been pushed out of her lungs as she looked up at Sasha in question. 'Really?'

'Really. He's in London with Alex, who it turns out is extremely well connected. There are all kind of discussions going on – TV appearances, record deals, festivals.'

'Wow,' said Lucy, her genuine happiness for him mingling with her own disappointment, creating a murky soup of feelings in her stomach that tasted like sick. 'Good for Nate.'

'It's now or never for him,' said Sasha briskly. 'Right now there's a window for him to launch himself as a singer/songwriter, but that window won't stay open forever.'

'A songwriter too?'

'Yes. He's got all kinds of stuff filed away.'

'I know,' said Lucy, her mind drifting back to their conversation on Saturday morning, over coffee and a stale pastry. What was the song he'd told her about? Something in French that meant *dream big*.

'. . . lots of conversations about the best route for him,' continued Sasha, snapping Lucy back into the room. 'But it all needs to happen quickly, while he's hot property. Him being here is just going to hold him back.'

'Yeah, I get that,' said Lucy, still wrestling with how inexplicably gutted she was that he wasn't coming back. Would she ever see him again? 'Where's he living right now?'

'At my place in Chiswick, at least for now. But obviously, nobody outside of this room can know that.'

'No. Of course not.'

'I'm about to announce his departure to the team,' said Sasha, gathering herself and standing up.

'Have you told Fran already?'

'No. She can find out at the same time as everyone else. I don't have time to brief everyone individually.'

'Well,' said Lucy, wiping her damp palms on the upholstery. 'I appreciate you giving me a heads up.'

'Hmm,' said Sasha, already thinking about what was next. 'You're going to get a lot of questions.'

'Yeah, I already have. I'll just say I haven't spoken to him and I don't know anything, which is true. I was going to message him later, actually.'

Sasha paused, then sat down again. 'This is an incredible opportunity for him, Lucy,' she said. 'But he's not the most confident, as you know. There's a lot of work to do to make him ready for this, and he's going to need all kinds of support. But it's what he's always wanted, and we need to help him look forward, not back. Make sure he doesn't lose his focus and get distracted.'

'Right,' said Lucy, noting the unspoken *leave him alone*. Maybe Sasha knew more than she thought, or maybe she'd just guessed. You didn't make it as far as Sasha had in advertising without a certain amount of gut instinct. 'Understood.'

'Good,' said Sasha. 'I'll leave you to it, then. Agency briefing in twenty minutes.' She picked up her bag and left the room, Olly giving Lucy a wave as he closely followed behind her.

The room was quiet again, and Lucy sat in silence for a minute, thinking about what had just happened and what it all meant, until her phone buzzed in her pocket. She fished it out to see a message from Marco, asking if she was free later.

Lucy thought about it for a moment, weighing up her options. The tension release would be welcome, but the questions wouldn't. She still felt mentally and physically exhausted, and even tidying up her bikini line felt like too much effort.

Can I come back to you on that? she replied. *Loads of work stuff to catch up on. Will let you know.*

It was dismissive, she knew, but Marco wouldn't take it personally. It was the thing she valued most about their relationship – the lack of effort required to meet each other's needs. What had Monica called it, back in the Guntherhütte? *Sterile.* Maybe that was a bit much, but it was certainly clean. And wasn't clean a good thing, in the end?

★

'So,' said Jonno, dumping their drinks on the table. 'What happened in Zermatt?'

Lucy took a sip of her cider, unable to meet his gaze. 'There was this avalanche. I got caught in a mountain hut and it was all quite dramatic.'

'No,' said Jonno patiently. 'I mean between you and French Exit.'

'Don't call him that,' said Lucy quietly.

'Why not?'

'Because I found out why he's uncommunicative and leaves the party early. He has an anxiety disorder.' It wasn't the only thing she'd found out about Nate, but Jonno didn't need those details.

'Shit, really?'

Lucy nodded.

'OK, well now I feel like a total prick,' said Jonno, blowing out his cheeks.

'Yeah,' said Lucy. 'So did I.'

'But don't think I haven't noticed how you've changed the subject.'

'In what respect?'

'Fine,' said Jonno, putting down his pint and folding his arms. 'Let's do this the hard way. How many years have we known each other?'

'I don't know,' said Lucy. 'Nine?'

'It's well over ten, as you know. And in that time, how many conversations have we had about your sex life?'

'Christ,' said Lucy with a hollow laugh. 'I have no idea. Hundreds, I should think.' Lucy noted how Jonno called it her *sex life* and not her *love life* and pushed that under the mental rug labelled *things I can't deal with right now*. If that rug covered much more stuff, it would qualify as a mountain.

'So we know each other pretty well, right?'

'Yeah. Course.' She twitched with discomfort, knowing Jonno was getting closer to the big question. Could she outright lie to him? Probably not.

'When Sasha told the team Nate wasn't coming back this morning, you looked like you might puke,' he continued. 'And you've been mooning around all day. You look, in short, like a woman who's lost something she actually cared about.'

'What are you asking, exactly?' said Lucy, deciding she might as well pull the plaster off sooner rather than later.

'Did you sleep with him?'

'No,' said Lucy emphatically. 'Absolutely no sleeping was involved.' She shrugged and half-smiled as Jonno beamed triumphantly.

'YES,' he said, punching the air. 'I KNEW it. I bet Olly one hundred euros that you two had totally banged.'

'You can't tell Olly,' said Lucy quickly. Jonno raised his eyebrows and she batted him away. 'Look, it wasn't a big deal. An outlet for the stress of the situation, nothing more.' The words had a distant echo in Lucy's head, like she was talking about someone else. But clearly Jonno wasn't buying it.

'I don't believe you,' he said.

'On what basis?'

'Because I think you like him more than you're letting on.'

'And since when were you the expert on women's feelings?'

'Since my amazing wife decided I needed to read some Caitlin Moran books so I can better help our daughters navigate the road to womanhood.'

'Jesus,' said Lucy, choking on her cider. 'That sounds horrific.'

'I've finished *How to Build a Girl*, and I'm now on to *How to Be a Woman*. They're going to help me be more attuned to women's needs, apparently.'

'Christ, I've heard it all now. You're wrong, obviously, but even if I did have some kind of . . . feelings for him, what difference would it make? He's gone, and I'm still here.' She could feel the anger building, but it wasn't directed at Jonno, or Nate. She was angry at herself, for opening up to Nate in a way she hadn't for a long time. She'd told him things she'd never told anyone, not even Jonno. And now that wound had been opened, conversations about Nate just felt like salt being rubbed in.

Jonno's response was interrupted by Lucy's phone buzzing with a message from Anthony. *Hey babe, call me about wedding on Sat. Assume you have something drop dead to wear?*

'Oh, shit,' muttered Lucy.

'What is it?'

'I've agreed to go a wedding on Saturday.'

'Whose wedding?'

'Anthony's cousin.'

'What, like an actual date? With Tentpole Tony?'

'It's not a date,' said Lucy, pulling a face. 'Something to do with his family expecting him to turn up with a woman.'

'OK, this is incredible. You're actually going on a date.'

'I am NOT,' insisted Lucy. 'It's a favour for a . . . friend.'

Jonno grinned and held up his hands. 'You're going to meet all his friends and family, and they're all going to make a big fuss of you, and that is, by any standards, the definition of a date. He's stealthed you into the girlfriend zone.'

Lucy shook her head and picked up her phone. *My mate says you've stealthed me into the girlfriend zone*, she typed. *Confirm or deny?*

Deny, replied Anthony immediately. *You're too cool for that kind of game.*

She showed the message to Jonno and pulled a smug face. 'See? You're wrong.'

'You know he doesn't mean cool in a good way, right? He means cold. Emotionally unavailable.'

Lucy raised her eyebrows. 'Well, thanks for making me feel really great about myself, J. I'm having a fabulous first day back.'

'Oh, don't be like that,' said Jonno, wafting his hand at her. 'Since when do you care what I think?'

'Since forever, Jonno,' said Lucy. 'In fact, you're at the top of a very short list of people whose honesty I value. But that doesn't mean it's always easy to hear.'

'Shit, I'm sorry,' he said, looking like he genuinely meant it. 'You want to get dinner? Marcia's been asking after you, we can pick something up for all of us.'

'No,' said Lucy, draining her glass. 'I'm going to go home and drink wine in the bath.'

'How dramatic,' laughed Jonno. 'But you know where I am if you change your mind.'

'I really do,' said Lucy affectionately, putting on her coat and dropping a kiss on his cheek. She hurried out of the pub towards the bus stop, pulling up the hood on her coat against the rain. Both Anthony and Marco would probably be available tonight, but right now she didn't want to see anyone but Nate.

She stood under the shelter of the bus stop and pulled out her phone, then scrolled to his details to write him a WhatsApp message. But Sasha's words earlier loomed big in her mind – Nate had other things to focus on right now, and Lucy wasn't on the list. And anyway, what would be the point? He was living with Sasha, with all his hopes and dreams laid out in front of him, ready for the taking. Whereas she, Lucy Glover, thirty-two years old, was still in Bristol, her hopes and dreams locked in a box for so long that the lid had rusted shut and she'd forgotten what was in there.

She put her phone back in her bag as the bus swished to a stop in front of her, considering for one tantalising moment that maybe it was time for things to change.

CHAPTER TWENTY-THREE

'This is my girlfriend, Lucy,' said Anthony for the fifteenth time that day. Lucy gritted her teeth and smiled, shaking the hand of yet another one of Anthony's mates whose name she'd already forgotten. He and his cousin Lee had grown up together, raised by their mutual grandmother and extended family, so they had a common circle of friends and still boxed at the same club. Hence Lucy and Anthony had been invited on countless double-dates, including holiday to Tenerife with one of Anthony's old school friends and his girlfriend, who were a lawyer and an art teacher from Portishead. They seemed lovely and under different circumstances Lucy might have considered it, but Anthony wasn't her boyfriend and she was in no position to accept holiday offers.

'Where you been hiding this one then?' leered a friend from the boxing club, who was clearly plastered. 'She's the first knockout you've had in a while.'

'Away from you,' muttered Anthony, steering Lucy towards a standing table by the bar, the friend's jeers following them. 'You're punching, mate. She's too good for you.'

'Sorry about that,' said Anthony.

'Can you please stop introducing me as your girlfriend?' said Lucy, trying to keep her tone light and friendly. 'I don't mind being your date, but your Auntie Diane has invited me to Sunday lunch.'

'Shit, really?' said Anthony. 'When?'

'Tomorrow.'

'What did you say? Can you make it? She's a friend of my nan's and not actually my auntie, but she's an incredible cook.'

'I'm sure she is, but obviously it's a no. I'm not your girlfriend, remember?'

'Yeah, I know, sorry,' said Anthony, holding up the palms of his hands. 'It's just easier to say girlfriend. Date makes it look like I've dragged you along for the optics.'

'You HAVE dragged me along for the optics,' laughed Lucy.

'And can I just say that you look incredible.' He gave Lucy an appreciative gaze from top to toe, from her emerald green wrap dress that showed a very demure amount of cleavage, to her nude heels that were nearly new Louboutins bought from Vinted for £100, and the only reason Lucy had woken up looking forward to this event.

'You don't look so bad yourself,' smiled Lucy. She'd never seen Anthony dressed up; in fact she'd never seen Anthony wearing much of anything. There were few men who didn't scrub up nicely in a well-tailored three-piece suit, and Anthony was no exception. He also smelled glorious, but she still hadn't decided if she was up for getting naked with him later. She'd kept both him and Marco away all week, and still didn't feel very in the mood.

'You're having a good time, right?' She smiled and

nodded; it was impossible not to be a tiny bit charmed by how much it obviously mattered to him.

'Yes,' said Lucy, holding out her hand so he could take it. 'You have a lovely family.'

'See, told you. You want to stay at mine later?'

'Maybe,' said Lucy with a shrug. 'I've got my eye on at least two of your cousins, including the groom.'

'You're hilarious,' said Anthony. 'Seriously though, don't cross Zoe, the bride – she's a chef and owns a lot of really sharp knives. Stay there, and I'll get us a couple of drinks.' He gave her a kiss on the cheek, then plunged into the crowd at the bar and disappeared.

Lucy pulled a compact out of her clutch bag and touched up her red lipstick, half-watching Zoe chatting with three of her bridesmaids at the next table. Lucy had always assumed she'd never get married – you needed to do long-term relationships, for a start – but looking at the bride and groom obviously having the best day of their lives, it was hard not to wonder if she was missing out on something. Yesterday she'd seen a therapist for the first time in nearly eight years, and spent an hour trying to explain how she was feeling right now. Like the things she hung on to as safe and familiar – the places, the rituals, the routines – had grown horns and teeth and were closing in on her, laughing at her. She'd booked another appointment for next Friday, in the slot normally reserved for going to the pub with Jonno. She'd decided that wine therapy could probably go on hold for a while, and persuaded him to come to the gym with her instead.

'Yeah, Nate Lambert,' said Zoe, just as Lucy had moved on to nervously imagining what her dream wedding dress might look like. A 1930s-style diaphanous, bias-cut satin condom with a train and a cowl neck, she'd decided. Maybe she could get Titan to sponsor it. 'You know? The TikTok guy who did that Ed Sheeran mountain thing.'

'Really?' said one of the bridesmaids. Lucy smiled, wondering if Nate's ears were burning. Everyone was talking about him these days; they must be on fire 24/7.

'Yep,' said Zoe. 'I went to school with him in Clevedon. He couldn't make the ceremony cos he had a TV thing this morning, but he said he'd try his best.'

Lucy's heart started to pound as she looked around, piecing together the implications of what Zoe had just said. Before she could even regroup, Anthony reappeared with two glasses of champagne and . . . Nate.

'Look who I found loitering by the door,' said Anthony. 'You guys know each other, right? From your Swiss adventure?'

'Nate!' exclaimed Zoe, hobbling over in her mermaid dress to give him a hug. 'So glad you could make it, babes. Oh my God, look at you.' Lucy took in Nate's very obvious TV glow-up – a haircut, a subtle tan that was definitely not the norm for January, and a dark blue velvet suit that was very un-Nate and extremely sexy. She looked away self-consciously, suddenly aware of how this must look, and how much Nate knew about her compared to everyone else in this room. The thought made her feel naked.

'Congratulations,' muttered Nate, hugging Zoe but barely taking his eyes off Lucy. 'You look amazing.'

'Do you know Anthony's girlfriend too?' asked Zoe,

looking a tiny bit put out that Nate seemed to be transfixed by Lucy and entirely ignoring her.

'Yeah,' said Nate, glancing at Anthony with a look that was both confused and . . . something else. Angry, maybe? As self-conscious and regret-filled as Lucy? She felt a powerful urge to explain, to tell him that this was all just for show and she was doing Anthony a favour, but clearly she couldn't say any of that stuff out loud. And what difference would it make, anyway? It didn't change the facts of their respective situations.

'I reckon you guys will be next,' said Zoe, beaming at Anthony and Lucy. 'You've been so loved up all day.'

'Yeah, well. You set a great example,' said Anthony, giving Lucy's hand an apologetic squeeze.

'Will you sing for us later?' said Zoe, turning her attention to Nate.

Nate visibly paled under his tan. 'Oh,' he said with an awkward laugh. 'No, I don't think so.'

'Please?' said Zoe. 'It would totally make my wedding.'

'No, I really can't,' said Nate, looking slightly panicked. 'It's a contract thing. I can't sing in public without . . . you know . . . I'm really sorry.'

'Oh,' said Zoe, looking devastated. 'Well, never mind.' She tossed her head, her hair rigid with hairspray, and Lucy could tell that she actually minded a great deal. How many people had she told that Nate Lambert was going to sing at her wedding?

'I just need to . . . I'll be back in a minute,' said Nate, giving Lucy a final glance and hurrying towards the door to the hotel reception.

'Give me a minute,' muttered Lucy, extracting herself from Anthony's grasp and hurrying after him, ignoring the swooping, sick feeling in her stomach. 'Nate,' she called as she spotted him in the corridor. He ignored her and pushed through the front door into the car park, so Lucy shouted his name again, but with feeling. 'NATE.'

'What?' said Nate, turning to face her. It was freezing out here, and the word was accompanied by a cloud of vapour in the frigid air.

'Is that true?' she asked. 'The singing contract thing? Or do you just not want to?'

'What does it matter?' snapped Nate. 'Lying seems to be all the rage these days.'

'What does that mean?' demanded Lucy, feeling suddenly wobbly in her heels. Christ, it was cold.

'Forget it,' said Nate. 'It's none of my business.'

Lucy opened her mouth to explain about Anthony, to justify herself, but couldn't find the words. Nothing she could say would make the smallest amount of difference, other than to make her situation look even more messed-up and pathetic. A broken, lonely, freezing-cold woman in a green dress, pretending to be someone's girlfriend.

'For fuck's sake,' said Nate. 'Take my jacket.'

'No,' said Lucy, reaching out to stop him before he'd wrestled one arm out. 'Why didn't you tell me about Sasha?' It struck her that she might never see Nate again, and she felt a powerful need to hear him say it.

There was a pause of maybe three seconds, but it felt like forever to Lucy. 'Shit,' breathed Nate, visibly paling under his unseasonal tan. 'How did you find out?'

'I guessed,' said Lucy. 'But Sasha already knows that. Why didn't she tell you?'

'I haven't seen her all week,' said Nate, looking desperate. 'I've been all over the place, with Alex and his team. We're catching up tomorrow, she's got a list of things to talk to me about.'

Lucy swallowed the sick feeling in her throat at the thought of Nate and Sasha chatting in bed on a Sunday morning, the way she and Nate had last Sunday.

'So why are you upset with me?' she asked. 'Switzerland was a surreal experience, but we're back now. What do you want from me, exactly?'

'I don't know,' said Nate helplessly, burying his hands in his pockets as he shuffled awkwardly in the cold. 'You feel like some kind of . . . anchor, I guess.'

'An anchor?'

'Yeah. Like, everything is mad and moving too fast right now. But thinking about you makes me feel . . . I don't know. Calmer. More on top of things.'

Lucy took a deep breath, feeling a mix of humiliation and disappointment that Nate's connection to her was one of stability and safety, and not the same burning, aching desire she felt for him.

'I can't be your anchor, Nate,' she said gently. 'I can barely anchor myself half the time.' *And I have feelings for you*, thought Lucy, properly admitting it to herself for the first time. *I didn't see it coming, but it's there. And that's a mess I definitely can't get into.*

'I know,' said Nate. 'I'm sorry. Things are a bit crazy. I just—'

'It's fine,' said Lucy. 'Sasha is amazing, and Alex

clearly knows what he's doing. You're in good hands, Nate. It's a once-in-a-lifetime opportunity.'

'Yeah,' said Nate, looking a little lost. 'I guess it is.'

'You should go back in,' said Lucy. 'There are two hundred people in there waiting for a selfie.'

'Yeah, might give that a miss,' said Nate. 'You look great, by the way.' He glanced over her shoulder, and Lucy turned to see Anthony heading their way.

'Thanks,' said Lucy, wishing they were back in the mountains, just the two of them. 'So do you.'

'See you around,' said Nate, giving her a half-smile before hurrying off through the car park. Within seconds he'd ducked round the side of the building and disappeared.

I'm not sure I will see you around, thought Lucy, and the cold, hollow void in her chest was a kind of pain deeper than any she'd felt in eleven years.

'You OK?' asked Anthony, appearing by her shoulder. He was carrying her coat, and the simple kindness of the gesture made her want to cry.

'Yeah,' she said, sliding her arms in and leaning over to kiss him on the cheek. 'Can you give me a minute?'

'Sure,' said Anthony softly, resting his hands on her shoulders for a moment. 'See you back in there in a bit.'

Lucy wrapped her arms around herself and took deep breaths, the vapour making white plumes in the frigid air. *What am I doing?* she asked herself. She was at a beautiful wedding with a man she knew intimately, and yet didn't know at all. In a city that used to feel like a refuge, and now was beginning to feel like a prison. Shutting down any opportunity to seize the day or spread her wings or open her heart, other than to a man whose heart was already taken.

You are self-sabotaging, she told herself. *You've been doing it for years.* Not the way Leo did – he'd lost himself in drugs and booze and party people, whereas Lucy had chosen expensive sheets and organic surface cleaners and the safety of familiar, well-trodden paths that rarely led to anywhere outside her comfort zone.

This needs to stop, she told herself. *Nate isn't the one, but he can be the spark that becomes a flame and changes everything.* She swallowed hard, feeling the resolve warm her blood and quell the sick feeling in her stomach. She turned on her heel and headed back inside, wondering idly if Anthony could dance.

CHAPTER TWENTY-FOUR

'Hola,' said Marco, taking off his coat and sliding into the booth opposite Lucy. He looked nervous, which was no great surprise considering a) Lucy had been turning down his offers to hook up for several weeks, and b) they had never eaten a meal together beyond occasional re-fuelling snacks in bed. Early on in their relationship Lucy had declared she was starving and he'd unearthed a mini Soreen bar from a pouch on the back of his bike. She'd devoured it in two bites, and since then he'd invariably bring her one every time he came over. *Post-sex Soreen*, thought Lucy. *The ad campaign they never knew they needed.*

'You OK?' he asked, looking around the restaurant. It was Japanese, one of her favourite places that served great food and good wine with lots of quiet corners with overstuffed chairs in green and mustard and red.

'Yeah,' said Lucy. 'I'm fine. Sorry for all the intrigue; we're just waiting for someone else, and then I'll tell you what this is all about.'

'Who?' asked Marco, with a playful smile. He probably thought this was a precursor to a threesome, which they'd done once before. A female yoga teacher friend of his, who was undeniably hot and bendy and extremely open to getting naked in Lucy's flat. It had been fun as a change of scenery, and not the first time Lucy had been with a woman, but the whole experience had felt a bit like rearranging furniture into different configurations. To his credit, Marco had never suggested they do it again, but presumably Lucy wasn't his only sexual partner so maybe he didn't need to.

'A friend,' said Lucy enigmatically, as the door opened to admit Anthony in a gust of cold air. He handed his coat to the waitress and smiled broadly at Lucy, clocking Marco and raising his eyebrows. He and Lucy had never had a threesome, but if they did, this scenario would be very much his bisexual jam.

'Hey,' he said, sliding into the booth next to Marco. He turned and shamelessly checked out Marco, clearly liking what he saw.

'Thanks for coming,' said Lucy to both of them.

'Is this a proposition, or something?' asked Marco. 'Because I really—'

'No,' said Lucy. 'It definitely isn't. Let's get some food, and I'll tell you both everything.'

'Fair enough,' said Anthony. They all perused the menu, Lucy making her usual choice of sushi rolls with a side order of edamame beans and a glass of Picpoul. It was only a few minutes' walk from the LUNA office, but since it was Saturday she didn't expect to see any of her colleagues here. Clifton village was a great part of Bristol to work in, but nobody on a LUNA salary could afford to live there.

'Are you going to tell us what this is about?' asked Anthony, once the waiter had taken their orders and topped up their water glasses.

'Sure,' said Lucy, clearing her throat. 'I've been seeing both of you for the past eighteen months or so,' she said, folding her arms on the table. 'You knew about each other, but obviously you've never met.'

'Ah, OK,' said Marco, the penny dropping. 'You never told me what he looked like.'

'Same,' said Anthony, holding out his hand. 'I'm Anthony. Nice to meet you, mate.'

'Marco.' They shook hands like they'd just met in a bar, presumably feeling an instant bond over screwing the same woman on different nights of the week. Lucy had been worried that this would turn out to be some kind of alpha-male stand-off, but perhaps she was flattering herself. They both looked pretty relaxed in each other's company right now.

'Spanish, right?' asked Anthony, and Marco nodded. 'Which part?'

'Pamplona,' said Marco. 'But I lived in Barcelona for a long time. And I have been in Bristol now for—'

'Sorry, can we do this later?' Lucy interrupted.

'Yeah, sorry,' said Anthony. 'Are you after a threesome?' He looked Marco up and down and grinned. 'Because I would be totally up for that, just to be clear.'

'That is very kind, but sadly I am very much women only,' said Marco. He looked genuinely apologetic, which Lucy thought was rather sweet.

'Then what's this all about?' asked Anthony.

'I'm breaking up with both of you,' said Lucy.

'At once?' asked Marco, his eyes wide.

'Yes,' said Lucy.

'And you decided to buy us lunch to break the news?'

said Anthony teasingly. 'Gutted as I am, babe, this meeting could have been an email.'

'No, this is nice,' said Marco with a grin. 'Respectful, you know?' This was Lucy's other worry, that they'd gang up on her and take the piss. Honestly, men were so predictable.

'This isn't me being dramatic,' said Lucy. 'I wanted to ask you both something, and I need you to be honest.'

'OK,' said Anthony, looking less confident now. They hadn't seen each other in the two weeks since Lee and Zoe's wedding, and what Anthony didn't know was that she hadn't seen Marco either. The past few weeks since she'd got back from Zermatt had been a sexual wasteland while she worked her thoughts and feelings through, and she needed the help of these men to get her to the next stage.

'I've never had a proper relationship,' said Lucy. 'I mean, I had boyfriends at school, obviously, but not as an adult.'

'What, never?' asked Marco. 'Aren't you, like, thirty-three?'

'In June,' said Lucy. *Or already, if you count my fake birthday.*

'You went to uni, though, right?' asked Anthony. 'You must have dated some posh boys.'

'No,' said Lucy, a sick feeling rising in her throat. University had been about finding her feet, reinventing herself as an edgy metropolitan millennial who would one day be a celebrated and badass feminist writer. The question 'Where are you from?' was answered with 'South London' or occasionally 'Surrey', but never

'Croydon'. Casual sex had felt like a declaration of independence and a source of power, but proper boyfriends were for losers.

After Leo died she'd been a barely visible wisp, a half-person, a subject of pitying head-tilts and gentle pats, like an abandoned dog who'd lost a leg. She'd buried herself in the library for months, studying for her finals and trying to patch her broken heart with the timeless words of strangers, so she didn't have to face up to her own story. Having fun would have been stealing unwritten chapters from Leo; a betrayal of the only person who'd loved her unconditionally.

'So what is this all about?' asked Marco.

'I want you to tell me what you think of me,' said Lucy, holding her head up. 'What kind of person I am, from your perspective.'

'Why?' asked Anthony, looking confused. 'With respect, what does it matter what we think?'

'Because sometimes I feel like I come across as cold,' said Lucy. 'And I've decided I want to have normal relationships and fall in love, at some point in the future. But I'm not sure I'm very loveable.'

'Babe, I fell in love with you ages ago,' said Anthony with a soft smile, as Marco nodded. 'You're, like, ridiculously hot, obviously. But you're also funny and smart and really cool to hang out with. If I thought I'd have even the smallest chance of being worthy, I'd have totally suggested we date like normal people.'

'The same,' said Marco. 'You are my dream woman – after Jennifer Lopez.'

'Isn't Jennifer Lopez, like, fifty-five?' asked Anthony.

'Yes,' said Marco. 'But she is timeless, like a Picasso.'

'Can we focus?' laughed Lucy.

'Sure,' said Anthony, fixing his eyes firmly on her. 'Sorry.'

'So if both of you had feelings for me, why didn't either of you ever suggest a proper relationship?' she asked, her eyes wide. Whatever she'd expected them both to say, it wasn't this.

'You go,' said Anthony, nodding at Marco.

'Because you are very hard to reach,' he said with a shrug. 'And you made it totally clear from the start that all you wanted was sex. So I took what you were offering, which has been amazing, by the way.'

'Fucking incredible,' said Anthony.

'You're not cold,' said Marco kindly. 'You're just your own woman. Strong, independent. You take what you want from life. That is sexy in itself, no?'

Anthony nodded furiously. 'Totally. And it's not like I haven't tried, babe. Why do you think I took you to Lee's wedding? I thought you might start to think of me as more than just some guy you fuck.'

'Wait,' said Marco, sitting up. 'You went to a wedding with this guy, but you wouldn't go to Paris with me?'

Lucy started to laugh. 'Please don't fight. It was a favour.' The heartfelt respect of these two warmed her fragile heart – even if it was just sex, she'd chosen two genuinely good men.

'So what are you saying?' asked Anthony. 'That you're ready to, like, date properly?'

'I think so,' said Lucy, pushing aside the inevitable thoughts of Nate. 'I'm ready to give it a try, anyway.'

'Are either of us on the list?' asked Marco. 'Because I would like to apply for this position.'

'How would she choose, though?' asked Anthony, his brow furrowed.

'Hmm,' said Marco thoughtfully. 'Some kind of competition? I am very good at chess.'

'I'm a boxer, mate,' said Anthony. 'But I'd love to learn to play chess.'

'When you're both finished,' Lucy cut in, feeling like a weight had lifted already. 'Neither of you is on the list, I'm afraid. I need to start again. A fresh page, no history.' Again she thought of Nate, and whether she'd apply the same rules if he were sitting on the other side of the table, asking her to love him. Almost certainly not.

'Fair enough,' said Anthony. 'As long as you promise to call if you change your mind.'

'Same,' said Marco with a grin. 'And I will miss being naked with you.'

'Yeah, me too,' said Lucy. 'Thanks for coming today, both of you. I really appreciate it.'

'What do we do now?' said Anthony. 'You've dumped us both before the food has even arrived.'

'Chat? Enjoy each other's company?' said Lucy. 'We can still do that, for today at least.'

'Yeah, I s'pose,' said Anthony, turning to Marco. 'What do you do for a living, then?'

Lucy smiled as Marco launched into a monologue about the importance of insurance for heritage buildings. The next part of her plan started this afternoon, when she planned to sign up for some dating apps. She waved at the waiter and pointed to her empty glass, working on the basis that some things should never, ever be done sober.

'I need your help,' said Lucy, pushing in her earbuds as she rummaged in the fridge for snacks and more wine. 'What do you know about dating apps?'

'Why are you asking me?' said Jonno. 'I'm in Wagamama for a birthday lunch with sixteen fourteen-year-old girls. I've been married to the same woman for over twenty years, and she would cut off my balls if I so much as looked at a dating app.'

'OK, but you probably have lots of friends who do this kind of thing,' said Lucy. 'I need one that's going to filter out the fuckboys and ghosters. I want all members screened for emotional intelligence and basic human decency.'

'And dashing good looks, obviously.'

'Well, obviously,' said Lucy.

'How much are you prepared to pay?'

'I'm not sure. Quite a bit, probably.'

'There are definitely member-only sites, for sure,' said Jonno. 'Like, exclusive dating clubs where all the members are vetted and you have to meet certain criteria, or something. But it means you don't have to wade through all the dross.'

'I want that,' said Lucy, despite having no idea if she would meet the criteria.

'Hold fire then,' said Jonno. 'I'm going to message a woman called Tamsyn. She's a friend of Marcia's, very high up in tech. Met a guy through one of these sites, they're getting married in July.'

'Excellent,' said Lucy. 'Can you ask her to call me?'

'Yeah,' said Jonno. 'Leave it with me.'

'You're a babe,' said Lucy. 'Good luck with Wagamama.'

'I'll definitely need it. Good luck with finding Mr Emotionally Intelligent.'

Lucy smiled and ended the call, then poured herself another glass of wine, deciding that was probably enough if she was going to write herself a bio that was vaguely coherent. She'd earmarked today as Day One of her plan to start eating properly, sleeping alone and being open to relationships like a normal person. But she hadn't expected to find the online dating landscape quite so overwhelming – she'd found both Anthony and Marco on Tinder, but that definitely wasn't the kind of relationship she was looking for any more.

Since she had no idea when Tamsyn might call her, she clicked on TikTok to kill time. A week ago she'd watched a video of a woman trying on a wedding dress that looked just like the one she'd imagined she might wear one day, then fell down a rabbit hole of episodes of *Say Yes to the Dress* on YouTube. Now the algorithmic social media goblins had decided she was definitely getting married, so her feed was awash with suggested videos featuring wedding dresses and weight loss tips. Presumably the two went hand in hand, which was depressing in itself.

She casually scrolled to Nate's page, and found two new videos – one of Nate travelling to Amsterdam for an LGBTQ+ charity gala, chatting on the Eurostar about how excited he was. Then a video of the event itself, where he performed a brilliant version of Elton and Kiki's 'Don't Go Breaking My Heart' with Sophie Ellis-Bextor. *Too late*, thought Lucy. *But I'm getting there.* She reminded herself that the experience with Nate had been a good thing — it had shown her that she could experience deeper feelings for someone than just a sexual connection. And now she was about to embark on a journey to find someone else who made her feel the way he had. It couldn't only happen once in a lifetime, surely?

Her phone rang, making her jump. She glanced at the screen to see it was an unknown number, then took a deep breath before pushing her earbuds back in and answering it.

'Hello?'

'Hi,' said a brusque, no-nonsense voice. 'I'm Tamsyn, friend of Jonno's. He asked me to call you?'

'Yeah,' said Lucy. 'Thanks for getting back to me.'

'No problem,' said Tamsyn. 'You're looking for an executive dating club?'

'Definitely. But I'm not sure I'd meet the criteria to join. I just work in advertising, I'm not special or anything.'

'That's not what Jonno tells me; he talks about you like you're royalty,' said Tamsyn, and Lucy could hear the smile in her voice. 'And anyway, it's not about being rich or famous or anything. The one I used decides if you're an interesting addition to their membership.'

'Based on what?'

'Your job, your lifestyle, your interests. They have members all over the world, mostly busy professionals who want to avoid time-wasters. And they don't tolerate any kind of shitty behaviour.'

'It sounds expensive,' said Lucy, mentally cancelling her gym membership in favour of spending her evenings wading through time-poor executives in search of love.

'It is. But definitely worth it.'

'OK,' said Lucy. 'Can you send me some information? Is there a website?'

'Not that you can access until you're a member. I can refer you, I'll do it now.'

'Really? That's so kind.'

'You come highly recommended, it's fine.'

'I really appreciate this, Tamsyn. It sounds great.'

'It is. You'll meet some extraordinary people. Keep an eye out for an email from EMNA.'

'Emma?' asked Lucy. 'Who's Emma?'

'No, EMNA,' laughed Tamsyn. 'Elite Matches, No Arseholes.'

'Ha,' replied Lucy. 'Sounds perfect.'

She ended the call with a fizz of anticipation in her belly, wondering whether this would be her first ever summer of falling in love. It was now February, and she was due to turn thirty-three in June. Four months to find someone special to share her birthday with. How hard could it be, really? People did it all the time.

New beginnings, thought Lucy, feeling excited for the future for the first time in years. *Time to dream big.*

PART TWO

CHAPTER TWENTY-FIVE

Four months later

'So what time is Ken picking us up?' said Jonno, tearing down the side of a bag of crisps and putting it on the pub table between them.

Lucy rolled her eyes. 'Please don't call him Ken.'

'Why not?'

'Because if he's Ken, that makes me Barbie.'

'Yeah, but not all Barbies are dumb blondes,' said Jonno, looking very pleased with himself. 'You're one of the smart ones, smashing the patriarchy.'

'Oh God, you've seen the trailer for the new Barbie movie, haven't you?'

Jonno nodded. 'It's out in a couple of weeks, Marcia's got tickets. It's all part of her mission to improve me.'

'How's that going?'

'I've finished all the Caitlin Morans,' he said gloomily. 'Now we're on to the feminist movies. She's adamant that a father of two girls should be able to see the world from their point of view.'

'Shitting hell,' laughed Lucy, eyeing the crisps but not wanting cheese and onion breath. 'You might want to buckle in for a bumpy ride.'

'Anyway, you've changed the subject. We're off to

Glastonbury today, but where's Ken taking you tomorrow? Paris? Rome? Stockholm?'

Lucy scowled and gave him the finger. 'Croydon. Kristoff is taking me to see my parents.'

'Shit, that's a downgrade. Is this their first encounter with Jet Set Ken?'

'No,' said Lucy patiently. 'He's met them once before, as you well know. My mum got all breathless and my dad dribbled over his car on the driveway.'

'What a beautiful image. Which one of his wankpanzers was it?'

'Actually, it was the Aston Martin,' said Lucy, trying not to blush at the indecency of it all. 'But I believe he's picking us up in the Range Rover today. More practical for Somerset roads.'

'Jesus,' muttered Jonno. He drained his pint and shook his head. 'I still can't believe you're dating fucking *Kristoff*, of all people.'

Lucy laughed. 'It's been over three months, Jonno. You can't STILL be in denial.'

Jonno shrugged. 'I miss you on Titan and that's definitely his fault.'

'Bullshit. I moved off Titan before he and I started going out. You're just reinventing history because it gives you something to moan about.'

'Writing about booze, though. How tedious for you.' In March, LUNA had won the Shine Spirits account, which was owned by a collective of A-list Hollywood actors who were making a fortune selling premium gin and vodka in highly collectable glittery bottles. Lucy had been promoted to the job of creative lead on the account, which meant she oversaw a team of LUNA designers and copywriters in London, Paris and New York. She still had her flat in Bristol and worked out of the local office occasionally, but now most of her time was spent travelling.

'It's fun. I get to use words like *artisanal* and *botanicals* and hang out with Ryan Gosling.'

'Who's going to be a better Ken than Kristoff, I might add. Remind me how you even landed that job?'

'Through sheer talent and hard work,' said Lucy, pulling a snarky face. She squirmed a little, because even though she'd put everything into the interview process and had already proved she could do the job, she also knew that Sasha had originally floated her name and got her on the shortlist. A huge favour repaid with a gentle nudge, and the rest was up to Lucy.

'Yeah, well. You're hardly ever here these days – if you're not swanking around the Met Gala, you're doing birthday holidays in Lake Como with Ken, drinking Nespresso with George Clooney.'

'I've never met George Clooney, don't exaggerate. And Kristoff will be here soon, so be nice.'

'I'm always nice. He's my fucking client, remember? As opposed to a client you're fucking.'

'Oh, get over it,' sighed Lucy. 'You're just jealous – five months ago you were in a bar in Switzerland calling him *K-Dog*.'

'Shit, was that really five months ago?'

'Yeah.' Lucy's thoughts drifted to Nate, as they invariably did about three hundred times a day. It was hard not to think about him, because he was everywhere. TV, radio, online . . . the whole country seemed to be madly in love with Nate Lambert.

'I wish I'd got stuck on that mountain too,' grumbled Jonno. 'You end up shagging a multimillionaire, and Nate Lambert ends up playing Glastonbury.'

'It's been quite a year for both of us,' said Lucy casually. 'We should definitely try to watch his set.' She knew Nate was playing the Woodsies stage at six, and was hoping that Kristoff and Jonno would be pissed enough that she could sneak off and watch from a distance. Even though she and Nate hadn't spoken since their freezing encounter at Lee and Zoe's wedding in January, it was nice to think that they were going to be in the same field, for a little while at least. The past few months had been a journey of self-rediscovery, and she felt ready for it.

'Is today the last of your birthday presents from Ken, or are there more to come?' asked Jonno, taking a swig of his pint.

'One more to come,' said Lucy. 'He's got Centre Court tickets for Wimbledon in a couple of weeks.'

'Fucksake,' hissed Jonno. 'A dirty weekend in Lake Como, VIP Glasto tickets, and then Wimbledon. Thirty-three isn't even a milestone birthday. What's he going to do when you hit forty?'

'Steady on,' said Lucy quickly. 'It's not like I'm going to marry him.'

It was a throwaway comment, but Jonno paused, giving her an intense look that made her realise how well they knew each other. 'Interesting,' he said. 'I thought this whole dating thing was about finding *the one*?'

'It was,' said Lucy, suddenly feeling a bit warm.

'But that's not Kristoff?' Lucy noted that the references to *Ken* were gone, because now this was a serious conversation and Jonno's fun was over.

'No,' said Lucy, a nervous, jittery feeling in her stomach. 'I'm not sure it is.'

'Shit,' said Jonno, sucking through his teeth. 'What's he done?'

'Nothing,' said Lucy. 'I'm just not sure it's, you know, a *forever* thing.'

'OK . . . Does Kristoff know that?'

Lucy shook her head, trying to look breezy. 'We haven't discussed it. We're still in the "living in the moment" stage of our relationship.' She used her fingers to form quotes around the words, hoping she didn't sound too ungrateful.

'Right. And that's not what you want for the long term.' It was a statement, not a question. *Isn't that what it all comes down to, in the end?* thought Lucy. *Whether Kristoff is what I want, for the long term?*

The door to the pub opened with a blast of street noise and warm air. Kristoff appeared, looking entirely delicious in a linen shirt, cargo shorts and white trainers – the perfect casual millionaire festival outfit. The forecast for today was warm and sunny, so she'd gone for a mini-skirt/vest combo that showed off her hastily fake-tanned legs, paired with white leather trainers and various beads and bangles. Kristoff had suggested her leopard print all-in-one playsuit, which clearly demonstrated his lack of knowledge about toilets at festivals.

'Hey, beautiful,' he said, dropping a kiss on Lucy's

lips. He smelled musky and expensive, like someone had just lit a Diptyque candle in the Brunel Arms.

'Hi, gorgeous,' smirked Jonno. 'I thought we agreed not to call each other the bedroom names while Lucy is around?'

'You're cute,' said Kristoff, resting his hands on Lucy's shoulders and clearly not planning to sit down anytime soon.

'You want a drink?' said Jonno. 'The Limping Bishop is nice.'

'We need to go,' said Kristoff. 'Andy is on double yellows, and Sasha's waiting in the car.'

'Sasha's coming?' asked Lucy, alarm bells ringing furiously.

'Yeah,' said Kristoff. 'She asked if she could join us, so I got her a ticket.'

'And you can magic up an extra ticket to Glastonbury, just like that?' asked Jonno, clearly impressed. Presumably if Kristoff hadn't been able to deliver, Nate would have. By any standards, Sasha was pretty well connected.

'Titan's a sponsor,' shrugged Kristoff. 'We're handing out a hundred thousand free condoms this weekend, probably saving the UK from a wave of chlamydia and unwanted pregnancies. I have a number of VIP wristbands I can give to my guests.'

'We are honoured to make the list,' said Jonno, grabbing his jacket. 'Let's go.' Kristoff turned to open the door, as Jonno gave Lucy a significant look that clearly communicated *we're not done with this conversation*. Lucy found Kristoff's black Range Rover parked right outside, the rear door being held open by Andy, his driver.

She climbed into the back, where Sasha was waiting with a nervous smile. They saw more of each other than they used to, now that Lucy was spending more time in the London office. But whilst Sasha was always available to give advice or support with any issues Lucy was encountering on Shine, there was a wary distance between them that was presumably about Nate. Lucy had been too busy to worry about it, but the knowledge that Sasha was coming today definitely took the edge off her excitement.

'Hey,' said Sasha stiffly.

'Hi,' said Lucy. Sasha shuffled into the middle so Jonno could climb into the other side, which at least meant Lucy wasn't trapped between them.

'Are we ready?' said Kristoff, climbing into the front. 'I've got a couple of calls to take on the way, but Andy will have us there in no time. Let's go.'

They pulled into traffic, Lucy relaxing into the buttery leather seats as they navigated through Bristol. Within minutes, Kristoff had plugged in his AirPods to take a call from his New York team, which mostly involved him listening and making occasional 'mmm' noises so they knew he was still there. Jonno and Sasha both kept their voices low, discussing a meeting Sasha had had with a potential new client yesterday morning.

How did I end up here? thought Lucy, looking out the window as the south Bristol suburbs flew by. By coincidence and happenstance, as it turned out – Kristoff had been signed up to the same dating site as Lucy, and had spotted her profile and sent a friendly message to say hello and *What are the chances?* Nothing more than that, but it had instigated a friendship where occasionally he'd send a photo of whatever glamorous setting he was currently enjoying a glass of wine in. Then Lucy had responded by messaging him reports on her dates, which were largely disastrous and seemed to make him laugh. After a few weeks of increasingly depressing encounters with men whose egos far outweighed their ability to communicate with a woman, the post-match WhatsApp exchange with Kristoff became the thing she looked forward to more than the date.

In late March it was announced that Lucy was leaving the Titan team to head up Shine, and Kristoff invited her for dinner in London as a farewell. They both knew it was anything but, and it turned out to be one of those heady evenings of eating and drinking and laughing in the corner of a cosy bistro that she hoped would never end. He'd kissed her on the doorstep of her hotel like a romantic hero, then left her wanting more, just as she'd known he would.

The following day a plant had been delivered to her new desk at LUNA's London office in a wooden box – a tiny succulent with a single heart-shaped leaf. The note read, *I could have sent flowers, but I thought you might like something that sticks around for a while. Free this weekend?* She'd sent him a message saying yes, and on the Friday he'd picked her up from Bristol in a silver Aston Martin and taken her to a beautiful boutique hotel in the Cotswolds. It was, without exception, one of the most special weekends of Lucy's life. Apart from . . . the other one, which she tried not to think about more than fifteen times a day.

Lucy told Sasha about Kristoff a week or two later, and she'd taken it well – but then Sasha was hardly in a position to lecture Lucy about inappropriate workplace relationships, so that was no surprise. There'd been some grumbling from the Exec about conflict of interest, professional integrity, blah blah blah, but they also knew that Titan would drop LUNA in a heartbeat if they punished Lucy for dating their CEO. So they agreed that everyone would pretend it wasn't happening, which suited Lucy just fine. She caught some looks and whispers in corridors occasionally, but that was nothing new either.

'You OK, babe?' asked Kristoff, unplugging his AirPods and twisting round in his seat so he could take her hand.

'Yeah, I'm good,' said Lucy with a smile. In truth, the conversation with Jonno was still playing on her mind. She'd been brushing how she felt about Kristoff under the rug for weeks, which was easy to do when you were being whisked off to a house on the banks of Lake Como for your birthday weekend. Obviously it had made her think about her other birthday weekend, back in January, but for the most part she'd been able to file that under *ancient history* and have a wonderful time.

So what's your problem? Lucy asked herself, as Kristoff casually kissed the back of her hand, prompting Jonno to duck down behind the seat and mime being sick. There was no denying that, on paper at least, Kristoff was a dream boyfriend – attentive and handsome and emotionally intelligent. He took her to beautiful places, but was also happy to hang out in her flat in Bristol and eat M&S

picnics on the Downs. He didn't drink too much, take drugs, or have one of those extreme fitness regimes that meant he had to get up at 4 a.m. to ride his Peloton. He didn't flaunt his wealth with extravagant gifts or grand, overblown gestures. He was respectful of her career and her time, great in bed, and gave a lot of his money away to charity without telling anyone. He was, by any standards, an absolute catch. Lucy's parents definitely thought so; her mother was already dropping wedding hints even though they'd only been seeing each other for three months.

I don't love him, thought Lucy. *I love his company and I'm having a great time, but it's a superficial connection. I'm living in the moment, but this relationship doesn't have a future. I don't long for him when he's not around, I don't want to live with him, and I don't want to grow old with him. And I think he feels the same way.*

'Hey, J-Dog, can you join this call too?' said Kristoff. Jonno tried to look enthusiastic about working on a Saturday, pulling out his phone and plugging in his headphones so he could dial in.

'How are you?' whispered Sasha stiffly.

'I'm good,' said Lucy. 'Looking forward to today.'

'Are you planning to watch Nate?' It was a perfectly normal question to ask one of his former colleagues, but Lucy glanced at Kristoff and Jonno anyway. Both were absorbed in their call and paying them no attention.

'Yeah, of course,' said Lucy. 'How is he?'

'Fine, I think,' said Sasha, then paused for a moment. 'I haven't seen him in a while.'

Lucy looked up at her, blood suddenly pulsing through her veins. 'I thought he was living with you?' She barely mouthed the last few words, just in case Jonno had one ear tuned in.

'No,' said Sasha breezily. 'He moved out a while ago. He's got his own place in London now.'

Shit, thought Lucy. *Have Nate and Sasha split up? How do I ask that without . . . asking that?* 'Is . . . everything OK? Between the two of you?' she whispered, like she was a concerned friend.

'Of course,' said Sasha briskly, brushing non-existent dirt off her white jeans. 'We still talk all the time. It was just time for him to move on.'

'Right,' said Lucy, her brain going at a hundred miles an hour. Kristoff reached out to take her hand again, like he could sense that she'd mentally just bolted into someone else's arms. The car stopped at some traffic lights, then took the right-hand turning towards Backwell.

'Where are we going?' said Lucy, leaning forward to talk to Andy. 'This isn't the way to Glastonbury. You need the Wells road.'

'It's the way to Urchinwood Manor,' said Andy, not taking his eyes off the road.

'What's at Urchinwood Manor?' asked Lucy, thoroughly confused.

'A helicopter,' said Andy, like this was the most normal thing in the world.

Lucy sighed and flumped back into her seat, revisiting her assessment of Kristoff not being into grand, overblown gestures. *Oh God, this isn't me*, she thought, wishing she could get out of the car and thumb a lift with a camper van full of normal people. She'd been to Glastonbury once before – in 2007, when she and Leo were seventeen. Arctic Monkeys headlined, it poured with rain, and they'd dragged their trolley of cider through a river of mud.

Lucy's main memories of that year were her and Leo drinking themselves stupid in the Dance Village, and both trying Ecstasy for the first time. It was also the last time for Lucy, but for Leo it was just the beginning of his relationship with a new type of mood-altering chemicals. They'd come home exhausted and filthy and euphorically happy, having made a sibling vow to go every year for the rest of their lives. But by 2008, Lucy was getting ready for uni and Leo's life was taking a different path, and she'd never been back.

I'm in a chauffeur-driven Range Rover, about to get into a sodding helicopter, thought Lucy. In the last few years of his life, Leo had been a regular on anti-capitalist marches, raging against economic inequality and the ravages of climate change. The clouds broke and the sun came out just as they turned off the road signposted for Urchinwood Manor, a shaft of sunlight pointing at Kristoff's car like an accusatory finger. *I'm sorry*, whispered Lucy to Leo, acknowledging that this wasn't quite the scale of life-change she'd imagined back in February.

CHAPTER TWENTY-SIX

'I feel like Freddie Mercury,' said Jonno, as the chauffeur-driven minibus pulled up to the pedestrian entrance gate closest to the Pyramid Stage. The helicopter flight had taken barely ten minutes, and Lucy had to admit that seeing the size and scale of the festival from the sky had been pretty breathtaking. Kristoff had held her hand the whole way, and provided a live commentary of the whole journey for his TikTok. Lucy had resisted the urge to ask him not to feature her, on the basis she didn't want to seem ungrateful.

She'd been in Kristoff's videos before, of course – first as a girlfriend soft launch back in April, when he'd occasionally featured her hand on a table or the back of her head. When the speculation from his fans had reached fever pitch, he'd shared a video of them walking through blossom-laden cherry trees in Central Park, and they were officially a couple. The disappointment from his fans that she wasn't anyone remotely noteworthy or famous had been palpable, but she'd learned that nothing good ever came from reading the comments.

'You feel like Freddie Mercury, and yet you look like Brian May,' muttered Sasha, flashing her gold wristband at the man on the gate. There was a moment of confusion about whether they could have access without tickets or

ID, which Kristoff quickly cleared up by showing the man some paperwork, and they were inside. Lucy grinned, already feeling the buzz of the crowd and the shimmering heat on the parched grass. There was a unique smell and energy to Glastonbury, of sweaty bodies and baking toilets and scorched earth and spicy food and anticipation. The rain in 2007 had drowned it for a few days, but she remembered this feeling from the Sunday, and couldn't wait to throw herself into the fray.

'Where are we going now?' asked Jonno, looking as excited as Lucy. 'What's the plan?'

'That wristband is VIP hospitality,' said Kristoff. 'It means you can hang out backstage. There's no need to go out front.'

'Why wouldn't we want to go out front?' laughed Lucy. 'Out front is where the festival happens.'

Kristoff shrugged. 'Most of the people here haven't washed in three days. The backstage area has some lovely bars and hangout areas. And proper bathrooms.'

'Right,' said Lucy, pressing her lips together. *Kristoff has arranged all this*, she reminded herself. *It's your birthday present. Don't get annoyed.*

'Titan has a private cabana with hammocks and a champagne bar,' said Kristoff. 'Between the Pyramid Stage and the Other Stage. You can watch the TV feed from there. That's where I hung out all day yesterday, it was really cool.'

'No,' said Lucy, shaking her head emphatically and trying to keep her voice even. 'I don't care if people haven't washed; I'll breathe through my mouth. I don't want to come to Glastonbury and drink champagne in a hammock. I want to actually go to the festival.' She looked at Jonno, who shrugged helplessly.

'I've been here loads of times,' he said. 'But never backstage. I kind of want the VIP experience, mate. Sorry. We'll definitely go over to Woodsies to see Nate at six, though.'

'I've never been here,' said Sasha, looking slightly overawed by the heat and the noise and the sea of people as far as the eye could see. 'And the only way I'm staying for the day is if I don't have to mix with the great unwashed. Although I'll watch Nate, obviously.'

Obviously, thought Lucy, feeling increasingly tetchy. 'What time are we leaving?' she asked Kristoff.

'Andy's picking us up from here at ten,' he said. 'It's too late to helicopter out, so we'll be in the car, I'm afraid.'

'I'm sure we'll cope,' said Lucy waspishly. 'I'll meet you back here at ten.' She turned on her heel and plunged into the crowd, muttering 'Fucksake' and 'Unbelievable' under her breath. Kristoff didn't follow her, but even if he'd been fast enough to keep up in this sea of moving bodies, it wasn't really his style. He'd feel a moment of uncertainty that Lucy was upset, then remember she was her own woman and head for whatever fully catered VIP experience he'd paid tens of thousands of pounds for. She imagined Leo giving her a heavenly round of applause, and looked for the nearest place that would sell her a pint of cider in a reusable cup.

The rest of the afternoon was one that Lucy was pretty sure she would remember as one of the best days of her life. She danced along to Rick Astley on the Pyramid Stage, then ate an amazing vegan curry as she meandered over to the Other Stage for Tom Grennan. It was impossible to watch two male singer/songwriters without wondering what the future held for Nate, and whether one day he'd be playing to a crowd of tens of thousands, all screaming his name. *What's the deal with him and Sasha?* wondered Lucy, itching at the thought of him seeing someone else. Probably a fellow musician, or some supermodel socialite. But then she reminded herself that she was dating a millionaire condom entrepreneur, so she was hardly in a position to judge.

By the time Tom Grennan's set was finished, it was gone three o'clock and Lucy was keen to see Nate, even if it was just from a distance. She slowly made her way towards Woodsies, stopping for an hour or so in the dance area at Silver Hayes to drink some more cider and do some mad dancing in Leo's honour. It was much bigger than it had been in 2007, but it still had the same high-octane buzz that they'd fallen in love with that weekend. She purposely avoided the interstage VIP hospitality area, knowing she was being petty but not wanting to feel an obligation to hang out in Kristoff's cabana with his celebrity friends.

It was a beautiful day, warm and sunny with a light breeze, with the kind of summer-festival vibe she and Leo had imagined and hoped for all those years ago, but never experienced. Even though he wasn't there, Leo was such a huge part of her memories of this place, and she didn't feel alone. How could you, in a crowd of two hundred thousand people singing and smiling and dancing and being generally off their head?

She made it to the Woodsies circus tent just after 5.30

p.m., but it was unexpectedly packed to overflowing with Nate Lambert fans, and there was no hope of her getting inside. She acknowledged to herself how much she wanted to see him perform, swallowing her pride with a silent apology to Leo as she walked round to the back of the tent where there was a gate for backstage access. She showed the security guard her wristband and was waved straight through.

It was busy back here too, and not very glamorous, but this was a satellite stage that wasn't for the headline acts, and the backstage area of the Pyramid Stage was probably a whole other world. There were trucks and cables and caravans and little in-between areas with deckchairs or benches where people could hang out in the sunshine.

She bought a falafel wrap and another pint of cider and mooched around for a while longer, wondering if Jonno and Kristoff and Sasha were somewhere nearby. Sasha had implied earlier that she and Nate were no longer seeing each other, but that things weren't bad between them, but Lucy had never really known how intense their romance was in the first place. It was ten minutes until Nate's set was due to start, which meant he was probably in one of the caravans. She glanced at the closed door of the nearest one, half-expecting him to pop out.

'Hey,' said Jonno, appearing through a flap in the back of the striped tent. 'I've been calling you.'

'I turned my phone off,' said Lucy. 'There are a million more interesting things to look at.'

'Very wise,' said Jonno. 'I think Kristoff is worried he's pissed you off.'

'I'm absolutely fine,' said Lucy. 'I've had a lovely day. How was VIP backstage?'

'Ridiculous,' he replied, swaying a little on his feet.

'Are you pissed, or high, or both?' laughed Lucy.

'Pissed. I've drunk a great deal of breathtakingly expensive champagne, paid for by your insanely rich boyfriend. But he doesn't do drugs of any kind. Did you know that?'

'I did,' said Lucy. 'He lost a friend to an overdose while he was at college.'

'Shit,' said Jonno. 'I assumed all millionaires were coke fiends.'

'Hoped, more like.' Lucy rolled her eyes. Like pretty much everyone who worked in advertising, Jonno enjoyed the occasional line if someone else was offering it. Lucy had never gone there – Leo had been a big fan, and somehow she'd always connected any kind of party drugs with his mental health issues, even though he'd been clean when he'd died.

'AND I had the least disgusting poo I've ever had at Glastonbury.'

'I'm happy for you,' said Lucy. 'Seen any celebs?'

'I think I saw Kate Moss hanging out by the Other Stage, but it was hard to tell from the back.'

'Goodness, that's one to tell the grandchildren,' said Lucy with a smirk.

'You want to watch Nate?' said Jonno, gesturing to the flap in the tent where he'd just come from. 'Kristoff and Sasha are at the side of the stage, she got us all permission. We could join them?'

'Did Kristoff send you to find me?' asked Lucy, narrowing her eyes.

'Not exactly,' said Jonno, shuffling awkwardly. 'I volunteered to come out and see if you were here, but didn't really expect to spot you. Come on; it's the only way you're going to get a view.'

'Fine,' said Lucy, figuring she should throw Kristoff a bone since he'd organised the tickets for today, and she really did want to see Nate perform. She followed Jonno through the flap and up some metal stairs to the side of the stage, flashing their wristbands at another security guard who nodded them through and told them to be careful of all the cables.

Lucy gasped as the announcer boomed, 'Please welcome to the Woodsies stage . . . NATE LAMBERT.' The crowd roared, and goosebumps broke out all over Lucy's arms. She could see Nate, all alone at the front of stage with just his guitar. Behind him was his band – a woman on keyboards, two guitarists, and a guy on drums. Having previously only seen him perform live in the Guntherhütte, it was mind-boggling to see.

'Hello, Glastonbury,' breathed Nate. 'I can't quite believe I'm here.' He glanced to the left as the crowd roared, and Lucy craned her neck to see Sasha, hidden just behind the wings at the front of the stage. She beamed at him and gave him a double thumbs up.

'Hey, baby,' said Kristoff, putting his arm around her shoulders. 'You had a nice day?'

'Yeah, amazing,' said Lucy, not taking her eyes off Nate. He started with a George Michael medley, then segued into some Ed Sheeran crowd-pleasers that everyone sang along to. The three of them picked their way down to the front to join Sasha, so they could see Nate properly and feel more like they were part of the crowd. Lucy lost herself in the music, swaying along with Kristoff and grinning from ear to ear with every song. It was like being back in the Guntherhütte again, a little bit drunk and euphoric, living in the moment and hoping it would never end.

'I don't know if I've mentioned it, but I've got an album coming out,' said Nate, as the crowd roared. 'Would anyone mind if I sang the first single from it?' Another roar, so Nate said 'Thank you. This is called "Can't Be Mine".'

He cleared his throat and started to strum, then closed his eyes and began a haunting ballad.

'Don't say it's for the best
Don't tell me I'll be fine
You tore my heart to pieces
Telling me you can't be mine.'

Lucy glanced at Sasha, wondering if this was their break-up song. Sasha's lips were pressed together and tears were flowing freely down her cheeks, and it occurred to Lucy that it was Sasha who had ended things with Nate, not the other way round. His voice cracked in the final chorus, and Lucy could feel the depth of his pain. *God, poor Nate*, she thought. *He has the opposite problem to me. He's in love with Sasha, who doesn't want to be with him, and I'm with Kristoff, who I don't love.* It was the closest she'd felt to Nate since Switzerland, and she wished it was something they could talk about.

Nate wrapped up his set with a couple of Craig David hits, bringing the roof down on Woodsies in style. Then a video message from Elton John – *actual Elton John!* – and

'Your Song' as the encore. Then the crowd started to pour out of the tent, and it was all over.

'Come on,' said Kristoff, as Nate exited from the other side of the stage. 'Let's go and say hello.' They headed back outside, where the heat of the day was drifting into a gloriously warm and sultry evening. Lucy had planned to rush back to the Pyramid Stage for Lizzo at 7.30, but right now her only priority was seeing Nate.

'Lucy!' shouted a voice, as Alex ran across the grass to pull her into a tight hug. 'Did you see the show?'

'Yeah,' said Lucy, fixing her eyes on Alex even though Nate was just behind him. 'We watched from the side of the stage.'

Alex turned to Kristoff and held out his hand. 'I'm Alex, Nate's manager,' he said. 'Big fan of your condoms. I use them all the time.'

'Lucky you,' laughed Kristoff.

Lucy turned to Nate, feeling like she might wet herself if she didn't look at him soon. 'Hey,' she said quietly, awkwardly opening her arms in the hope he might let her hug him. He obliged, and the brief moment of contact between them felt like taking off the backpack of tension she'd been carrying around all day. He smelled of sweat and adrenaline and something else that was unmistakeably, distinctively Nate, and Lucy had to force herself to let go.

'Thanks for coming,' said Nate, turning to shake Kristoff and Jonno's hands. Everyone started prattling about how amazing Nate's set was, but Nate's eyes kept drifting back to Lucy. She tried to look away, hoping Kristoff wouldn't notice, because that would make for a very awkward car ride home, but he was too busy chatting intently with Alex.

'Come and have a drink,' said Alex, hooking his arm through Sasha's and leading them all in the direction of the backstage bar. The tables were cable reels stood on their end, surrounded by stools made from recycled metal milk churns. Nate hung back to walk with Lucy, and even though Kristoff gave them a curious glance and Sasha was breaking her neck to look at them, they didn't intrude.

'I heard you were with Kristoff now,' said Nate quietly.

'Mmm,' said Lucy. 'For a few months now.'

'He's a nice guy,' said Nate. 'I'm happy for you.'

'It's just a casual thing,' said Lucy quickly.

'Right,' said Nate, not looking remotely convinced. 'Look, I'm sorry about Zoe's wedding back in January. I was out of order.'

'It's fine,' said Lucy.

'No, it isn't, but I've been wanting to explain. That week had been crazy, with everything that happened after we got back from Zermatt. I'd barely slept, and I wasn't expecting to see you there.'

'I wasn't expecting to see you either,' said Lucy. They walked side-by-side, close enough that Lucy could feel the heat of his body.

'Anyway, I—' he continued.

'It's OK, Nate,' said Lucy, reaching out to touch his arm. The crackle of electricity made them both gasp and jump back.

'We've still got some chemistry, I see,' laughed Nate, blushing.

More than I've ever had with Kristoff, thought Lucy, feeling simultaneously guilty and more alive than she'd felt in months. This *feeling* – this hum in her veins, this tingle of anticipation on her skin – was what she'd been trying to find since she'd finished with Marco and Anthony. She'd forgotten what it felt like, until now.

Lucy looked away, feeling a bit flustered and needing to get a handle on the conversation. 'It's nice that Sasha is here,' she said. 'She told me you'd moved out.'

'Yeah,' said Nate. 'It wasn't really working. And look, I really appreciate you keeping quiet about her being . . . you know. It was a lot to ask.'

'It's fine,' said Lucy again, feeling like there were still a million things to say apart from *It's fine*, and time was running out. 'You seeing anyone else?'

'Er . . .' muttered Nate, looking away. Lucy's heart sank, furious with herself for asking the question. What purpose did it serve? They'd both travelled a thousand lifetimes since Zermatt, but in entirely different directions.

'You guys want anything?' shouted Kristoff, waving a bottle of champagne.

What do I want? thought Lucy. *I want to feel absolutely sure that I'm in the right relationship with the right man. That I'm not still holding out for something I can't have.* She looked at Nate, who smiled bleakly.

'Do they have any Jägermeister?' said Nate, and Lucy started to laugh.

CHAPTER TWENTY-SEVEN

'Done,' said Kristoff, pulling out his AirPods and throwing them in the tray on the dashboard. 'Sorry about that, I hate doing meetings on Sundays. You want some music?'

'Sure,' said Lucy, glad that it was just the two of them and he'd given Andy the day off. She was feeling tired and restless after yesterday, her head still reeling from an incredible day that had ended with Lizzo on the Pyramid Stage and a final round of champagne in Titan's admittedly lovely backstage cabana. The videos Kristoff had posted on TikTok had captured the buzz and frenzy of it all, and she'd had to drag herself away at 10 p.m. Today the whole thing felt like a dream, and being chauffeured to Croydon would just be another reminder that this thing with Kristoff wasn't real life. *Nate's not real life either*, she told herself, trying to shove thoughts of Nate aside. He'd joined them for Lizzo, wearing a fedora and a pair of sunglasses so he didn't get mobbed by fans, which had mostly worked in the gathering dark. But now he'd gone back to his celebrity life, and it wasn't fair on Kristoff that she was still thinking about him.

Kristoff pressed some buttons on the steering wheel until Radio 1 started playing, then reached over and took Lucy's hand.

'What's the plan for this evening?' he asked.

'My mother's cooking. I think she's attempting something from an Ottolenghi cookbook that's been collecting dust for a decade.'

'Not on my account, I hope,' he said, pulling a face. He hated people going to any trouble, and would much rather have taken everyone out for dinner. But Shirley had been insistent.

'I think that's reasonable to assume. They've both got work tomorrow, so we can head back after breakfast.'

'I need to head straight back to New York,' said Kristoff. 'Sorry.'

'It's fine,' shrugged Lucy. 'I'll come with you to the airport and get the train back to Bristol.' Short notice changes of direction weren't unusual in Kristoff's world, which was another reason why they rarely made plans beyond the next week. Titan was flying high right now, and there was a lot of talk about whether the next step was a merger or a buyout or an IPO.

'Why don't you come with me?' he asked. 'You can work out of LUNA's New York office and stay at mine.'

Lucy swallowed down an anxious flutter in her belly; this was something new. They'd never spent more than three consecutive nights together, and she'd never stayed at his place in New York. London, yes – he had a riverside apartment in Chelsea that had a lot of glass walls and very little furniture. But when she'd been to New York for work, she'd always stayed in a hotel.

'I don't have any clothes,' said Lucy feebly. Her overnight bag contained the bare minimum, and there was an unsettling amount of laundry waiting for her back in Bristol.

'We'll go shopping in Manhattan tomorrow afternoon,' said Kristoff happily. 'Get you a New York capsule wardrobe. You can leave it at mine for next time.'

'My God, can you imagine?' laughed Lucy, who had never owned a capsule anything. There was a long moment of heavy silence, and Lucy realised he wasn't joking. She could actually feel the temperature in the car dropping.

'Well, maybe another time,' said Kristoff, then turned the radio up.

'And here's our record of the week,' said the DJ, unnecessarily cheerful for a Sunday afternoon. 'It's the brand-new single from a guy who's had an incredible few months, going from total unknown to British music's next big thing, about to start his first UK and European tour. With his new single, "Can't Be Mine" – it's Nate Lambert.'

Lucy held her breath as the raw, heartfelt vocals played out through Kristoff's top-of-the-range car stereo. She tuned in to every word, feeling like Nate's pain was her pain. Somehow his situation with Sasha felt inexplicably tangled up in her situation with Kristoff, and she wasn't sure how much longer she could hold it in. She'd stayed as far away from Nate as she could after Lee and Zoe's wedding, partly not wanting him to think she was one of a thousand people sniffing round him because he was famous now. Yesterday had been a gut-punching reminder that the thing she'd felt in Zermatt – that powerful, indefinable human connection – hadn't gone away.

But she'd kept track of his career, and felt quietly proud of him when she heard him on the radio or watched a live performance on YouTube. She'd read some of the interviews he'd given to the press about his music and his mental health issues, feeling pathetic for hoping he might say something about the Zermatt avalanche story that only she would understand.

'This guy,' said Kristoff with a shake of his head. 'He was great yesterday, sure. But it doesn't seem to matter which radio station I listen to, I never seem to be more than five minutes away from a Nate Lambert song. It's like rats in New York.'

'You're just angry he's not at LUNA any more,' said Lucy, forcing a laugh.

'I definitely liked him better when he was getting shit done for Titan,' he grumbled. 'What is it with all the sappy love songs, anyway?'

'Maybe he's singing from experience,' said Lucy thoughtfully. 'Maybe he actually knows what love is.' She hadn't meant to say it out loud, but the words were hanging in the car before she could stop them.

Kristoff's head swivelled to look at her, his eyes wide. 'What does that mean?'

Lucy held her breath for a second, then hung her head, knowing the time had come to have a very big conversation. The exit sign for Junction 5 of the M4 loomed large in her window – they were barely a mile or two from Heathrow, which would save a lot of time in the long run. 'Can you pull off here?' she asked.

'Really?' said Kristoff. She looked at him intently and nodded, so Kristoff veered left across two lanes of traffic to make the exit, earning himself an outraged honk from a Megabus.

'What's this all about, Lucy?' he asked, his beautiful hands jittery on the steering wheel.

'Just find somewhere to stop,' said Lucy. 'We need to talk.'

Kristoff said nothing as he navigated the traffic lights, his lips pressed firmly together, his eyes on the road and the silence lying like a heavy fog in the car as he turned onto the A4. A mile further on, he pulled into a BP garage on the Colnbrook bypass and parked. He killed the engine and took off his seatbelt, then turned to face Lucy.

'So. What's up?'

'We need to break up,' said Lucy, figuring she might as well not mince her words. Kristoff wouldn't appreciate it, and it wasn't really her style.

He was silent for a moment as he took deep breaths through his nose. 'Can I ask why?'

'Because when I joined that dating site, back in February, it was because I was looking for the person I was going to spend the rest of my life with.'

Kristoff said nothing, so Lucy ploughed on.

'And I've had the best time, Kristoff, I really have. You're amazing.'

'But?' said Kristoff. 'I definitely feel like there's a huge BUT incoming.'

'But . . . I don't love you. I love spending time with you, but I don't feel . . . that thing you feel when you're in love.'

'Wow,' said Kristoff, raking his hand through his hair. 'That's . . . quite the announcement.' He looked genuinely confused, and for a moment Lucy wavered. Was this actually the stupidest thing she'd ever done?

'But it's not a shock, right?' said Lucy, hoping she hadn't read this all wrong. 'I've always assumed you felt the same way.'

Kristoff's brow furrowed. 'What do you mean?'

'I mean, we've been living in the moment and having a great time, but I've never got the impression it's been anything more than just a fling.'

'What, you don't think I'm in love with you?'

'No,' said Lucy, a sick feeling rising in her throat. 'It's never even crossed my mind. It's not . . . I guess I figured I'm not the kind of woman men like you fall in love with.'

'Wrong,' said Kristoff, looking at Lucy like she was mad. 'Shit, Lucy. I'm totally crazy about you.'

Lucy stared at him, her mouth hanging open. 'I don't . . . oh God.' She pressed her hands to the sides of her face, feeling like the ground under the car was crumbling. 'Why didn't you say?'

'Because . . . because I didn't want to overwhelm you with some big declaration. I thought we could start to spend more time together, maybe in New York, and then at the end of the year I'd ask you to move in with me.'

'Move in with you? As in, live together? Are you serious?'

'Of course I'm serious,' said Kristoff, as the heat rushed to Lucy's cheeks. 'And I thought that if that was all going well a bit further down the line, I'd take you back to Zermatt to propose.'

'You were planning to propose? Ask me to MARRY you? In Zermatt?'

'Yeah,' said Kristoff. 'How could you think I didn't love you?'

Lucy took a long, uneven breath, until it felt like there was no air left in her lungs. 'Kristoff, we've been dating for *three months.*'

'I know. The proposal was planned for—' he stopped and did some mental arithmetic, 'nineteen months' time, on the two-year anniversary of the day we first met.'

'Shitting hell, Kristoff,' said Lucy, unable to stop herself laughing. 'Have you got all this on a spreadsheet?'

'Only the one in my head,' he replied with a half-smile.

'Fuck,' gasped Lucy. 'I had no idea.'

'Clearly. Does any of this make a difference, or are you still breaking up with me?'

Lucy looked at him, considering the question. Would it have made any difference, if she'd known how he felt about her? In her heart she knew that it wouldn't, and if anything it might have prompted her to make this decision sooner.

'God, Kristoff, I'm so sorry,' she said, reaching out to take his hand. 'I honestly thought you were in the same place as me.'

'You didn't answer my question,' said Kristoff, but he didn't take his hand away.

'I know,' said Lucy, mentally crossing her fingers that she wasn't entirely insane and wouldn't totally regret this later. 'But it hasn't changed anything. I'm still breaking up with you.'

'OK,' he said, rubbing his hand across his face. 'OK. But can I ask you something?'

'Sure,' said Lucy, quelling the jittery feeling in her stomach. Whatever it was he wanted to know, he'd earned the right to an honest answer.

'What is it you're looking for? What do you want that we don't have? Because it seems to me that we have a pretty great time.'

'We do,' said Lucy. 'We absolutely do. And for most women, this would be more than enough.'

'But it's not enough for you.' It was a statement, not a question, and Lucy thought she detected a note of respect rather than irritation. Of all people, Kristoff understood the concept of not settling for second best. He'd been chasing his dreams all his life.

'No,' said Lucy. 'It's amazing, but I need something more, something deeper. A proper soulmate connection, I guess.'

'How do you know that even exists?' asked Kristoff. Lucy said nothing, and after a few seconds, realisation dawned on Kristoff's face. 'Right,' he said quietly. 'You've felt it before.'

'I . . .' said Lucy, feeling like the conversation was running away from her. 'I don't know.'

'Come on, Luce,' said Kristoff softly. 'We've come this far. Be honest with me.'

'Yes,' said Lucy quickly, before she bottled out completely. 'I had a connection with someone once, and it was a different feeling from how I feel about you. I don't know exactly what it was, but it felt . . . special. And I don't want to settle for less than that.'

Kristoff nodded slowly, a resigned smile on his lips. 'Nate Lambert, right?'

Colour rushed to Lucy's cheeks, and she swallowed down another rising wave of nausea. There was no point denying it; Kristoff deserved better than that. 'Yes,' she said, unable to look at him.

'You and he got together in Zermatt.'

Lucy nodded. 'Yes, but it was a one-off. We haven't seen or spoken to each other since . . . you and I got together.'

'Until yesterday.'

'Yes.'

'So the timing of this announcement isn't a coincidence.'

'Actually, yes,' said Lucy, looking up at him and keeping her voice strong. 'I'd already realised that you and I weren't the real deal before yesterday. But I will concede that seeing him again clarified things.'

'You're in love with him?'

Lucy paused and considered the question. It felt so ridiculous, to say she was in love with someone she'd spent one weekend with. And a pop star, for goodness' sake. They barely knew each other, and right now the whole thing felt like an embarrassing cliché.

'I think so. I don't know. All I know is that one weekend with Nate felt more powerful than—'

'—three months with me.'

'It sounds brutal, when you put it like that,' said Lucy, feeling suddenly cold and empty. Was she a bad person? Had she led Kristoff on, made him think she felt more than she did? Or had she just read him completely wrong? It all felt so confusing right now.

'It's fine,' said Kristoff. 'I can take it. And I appreciate your honesty.'

They sat in silence for a minute, Lucy not knowing what to do next. Car after car drove past them onto the petrol forecourt, and a man comforted a screaming child who'd dropped her ice lolly. Flights took off and came in to land overhead with a whoosh and a roar.

'What are you going to do?' asked Kristoff. 'About Nate?'

'I have no idea,' shrugged Lucy. 'He and I are in really different places, and it's unlikely things will ever work out between us.'

'His loss,' muttered Kristoff, trying to force a smile. It hurt Lucy's heart that even now, Kristoff was trying to make her feel better. He really was the best of men.

'But that isn't the point,' she said. 'I want to feel the way he made me feel, even if I have to stay single for a really long time to find that.'

Kristoff gave a hollow laugh. 'Despite feeling like shit right now, I have to admire your uncompromising commitment to your own happiness.'

'It's all I have,' said Lucy. 'If I don't commit to that, who will?'

'I would have tried,' said Kristoff, his voice cracking a little. 'You know that, right? I'd have spent my whole life trying to make you happy.'

'I know,' said Lucy, tears starting to pour down her face. 'But you deserve someone who feels the same way about you as you feel about them. It's what both of us deserve.'

'Yeah, I guess,' said Kristoff, pulling a pack of tissues from a slot in the dashboard and handing her one. 'And it's not like I need to settle for second best. I'm a super-hot millionaire.'

'Yes, you are,' laughed Lucy through her tears. 'And you're an incredible person. You definitely don't need to settle.'

Kristoff nodded, then took a deep breath. 'What do we do now? Much as I adore you, I'm not sure I can cope with dinner with your parents.'

'I wouldn't ask you to,' said Lucy. 'Park at Heathrow, get a flight to New York, and I'll get a train back to Croydon.'

'You sure? I can drop you there, then fly from Gatwick.'

'I'm sure.'

'OK.' He leaned over to kiss her cheek, then pulled her into a tight hug. 'You are the most incredible woman, Lucy Glover,' he whispered. 'Don't settle for anything less than the love of your life.'

'Thank you,' said Lucy, blinking back more tears. 'But only if you promise me the same.'

'I promise,' said Kristoff. 'Let's check in a couple of times a year, see how we're doing.'

'I'd like that,' said Lucy, blowing her nose on the tissue. Kristoff pulled back onto the main road, taking the turning at the traffic lights through the tunnel towards Terminal 5. Her mind reeled with what had just happened, a mix of relief and fear and confusion and nausea. Kristoff's hands were steady on the wheel, and she reminded herself that he was the kind of man who would bounce back in no time, because Kristoff's life had no jagged edges. He'd walk her to the Terminal 5 Tube station, then call his Executive Assistant to ask her to book him on the first flight to New York. Andy would collect his car later, and a line would be drawn under Kristoff and Lucy with minimal mess and drama. By the weekend he'd already be open to dating offers, because in Kristoff's world you didn't waste time dwelling on the past. You looked up, and you looked forward.

What do I do now? thought Lucy. The short-term answer to that was easy, involving a series of trains to Purley before her mother's dinner was physically ruined, rather than just emotionally spoiled by the breaking news that Kristoff Berg was never going to be their millionaire son-in-law. Lucy would rather have her teeth pulled than face that conversation, but it had to be done.

The world beyond that, however, felt like an abyss of uncertainty; the kind of discomfort zone that Lucy had been avoiding for over a decade. She had no idea where it might end, or whether Nate was anywhere on that journey. But the decision had been made, and she had no choice but to face it. She swallowed hard and tilted her chin, trying to quell the butterflies in her stomach. *Look up, Lucy*, she told herself, taking strength from Kristoff before he was gone for good. *Look up, and look forward.*

CHAPTER TWENTY-EIGHT

'He's not coming,' said Lucy, as her mother peered out of the front door to see a taxi, not Kristoff in a Range Rover. 'We broke up.'

'WHAAAT?' screeched Shirley. 'Please tell me you're joking.'

'I'm not joking,' said Lucy, who had considered breaking this news by text message so her mother had time to mentally prepare, but had chickened out somewhere around Ealing Broadway. 'And to be honest, Mum, getting here by train from Heathrow has been an absolute nightmare, so please don't yell at me.'

'Elizabeth Line to the Thameslink? Or did you splash out on the Heathrow Express?' asked Lucy's father, poking his head through the door that led to the lounge.

'Oh, for goodness' sake, Richard, is that really important right now?' Shirley interrupted, rounding on him.

'Elizabeth Line,' said Lucy, rolling her eyes in her dad's direction. 'But there were signalling problems at Norwood Junction, so Thameslink was a mess. It probably would've been quicker to get the bus.'

'Mmm, I don't miss commuting at all,' muttered Richard. He'd worked as a research scientist for a hospital in London throughout Lucy and Leo's childhood, but a few years ago he'd been headhunted by a pharmaceutical company closer to home. He worked half the hours for twice the money, but was still battling with the guilt that he'd sold his soul for Big Pharma dollars.

'But I've done Ottolenghi,' wailed Shirley. 'Sweet potato shakshuka followed by sticky miso bananas.'

'It sounds delicious,' said Lucy, wondering why anyone in their right mind would miso a banana. 'But I'm afraid Kristoff is on a flight to New York, and we're no longer a couple. So it's just me, sorry.'

Lucy held her breath — now she'd said the words out loud, she was squarely faced with the magnitude of her decision and the realisation that she was back to the beginning, relationship-wise. 'Can you give me ten minutes?' she asked, feeling suddenly overwhelmed. She dropped her bag in the hall and hurried upstairs before she started to cry or scream or bang her head against a wall.

She gently closed the door to her childhood bedroom, which had in the intervening years been turned into an elegant guest room with a wrought-iron double bed and crisp white sheets. Shirley had wound fairy lights through the bedframe; they were already turned on to create a soft, romantic glow. There were pale pink roses in a vase on the chest of drawers, next to a lit Jo Malone candle that was making the room smell like a fancy hotel. No doubt this was all for Kristoff's benefit, but that was all over now.

It was the right thing to do, thought Lucy, taking deep, calming breaths. *I'm thirty-three, I need more from a relationship than just fun times. I made that decision in February, when I called it a day with Anthony and Marco. This is just the next step on that journey.*

'Darling, are you OK?' said her mother, poking her concerned face around the bedroom door.

'I'm fine,' said Lucy with a weak smile. 'It's just been quite a big day.'

'What happened?' asked Shirley, sitting down on the bed and wrapping her arm around Lucy's shoulders. 'Did Kristoff do something terrible?'

'No, Mum,' laughed Lucy. 'Quite the opposite, actually. Turns out he was madly in love with me.'

'Really?' said Shirley, with a tone that suggested she found this deeply unlikely. Lucy took more calming breaths and resisted the temptation to snap back; she was well used to her mother's withering comments by now, and most of the time they bounced off. 'I was going to show Kristoff all your baby photos. Did he know about Leo?'

'Yes,' said Lucy, wondering whether her mother was planning to check that before she told Kristoff about Lucy's dead twin brother over coffee and petit fours. 'Yes, I told him.'

'It's a hard thing for other people to understand,' said Shirley, her hand pressed against her locket.

'Maybe you and I could look at the photos together,' said Lucy, feeling like she should make a magnanimous gesture since her mother had gone to such a lot of trouble today.

'If you like,' said Shirley. 'Although when we go down memory lane together, it just makes me wish Leo was here . . . too.'

The pause was a fraction too long, and the word *instead* hung heavy in the fragranced warmth of the bedroom. Lucy tried to push the stab of pain aside and understand – her mother's heart had been ripped in two eleven years ago, and what remained belonged to Leo. It was her way of honouring his memory, and Lucy shouldered the rejection because she was still alive, and Leo wasn't. To be living and breathing AND expect to benefit from the remaining crumbs of her mother's capacity for love was probably too much to ask. Wasn't it?

'Are you going to ask me why we split up?' asked Lucy.

'Of course,' said Shirley, settling her hands in her lap. 'I'm all ears.'

Lucy relayed their conversation earlier this afternoon as her mother patiently listened, her eyes getting increasingly wide and incredulous.

'He wanted to marry you?' asked Shirley. Her tone wasn't exactly accusatory, but Lucy suspected a lecture about letting go of her one chance at happiness wasn't far away.

'Yes,' said Lucy. 'Eventually.'

'Are you absolutely sure about this?' said Shirley. 'You're closing the door on what could be the most wonderful life. You know that most women would bite his arm off?'

'I know that, Mum,' said Lucy testily. 'But I don't love him. I loved being with him, but that's not the same thing.'

'No,' said Shirley softly. 'It's not.'

'So you're not angry with me?'

'I'm angry I spent all bloody day making sweet potato shakshuka and miso bananas, obviously. And I'm disappointed, I suppose. He seemed like a decent man, and he could offer you a great deal of security. But if you really don't love him, then I understand. It's too important a thing to compromise on.'

'Thanks, Mum.' Lucy leaned her head into her mum's shoulder, wishing their relationship had always been this easy.

'And in many ways it's better that you finish with him now, rather than him dumping you when he finds someone better.'

Lucy closed her eyes, wondering how many more years she was expected to shoulder her mother's passive-aggressive jabs. Years of every kindness being offset by a decent chunk of awful.

'Why would he find someone better?' she asked, deciding that today was, in fact, the very last day.

'Oh,' said Shirley, physically recoiling. 'I just meant—'

'I know what you meant,' interrupted Lucy. 'It just wasn't very nice.'

'Are you hungry?' asked Shirley, moving to stand up. 'Let's get some dinner.'

'No, Mum, I'm not hungry,' insisted Lucy, grabbing her mother's arm and pulling her back down. 'I need this to stop.'

'Need what to stop?' Shirley clutched her locket nervously.

'You . . . punishing me for Leo's death. Reminding me that I'm the lesser twin.'

Shirley gasped, jerking away from her daughter in horror. 'I don't—' she spluttered. 'I would never—'

'Please, Mum,' said Lucy softly. 'You've been doing it for years. Don't make me list examples.'

Shirley crumpled, her chin dropping to her chest. 'I just want . . . I just wish . . .'

'You miss him,' said Lucy. 'I understand. I miss him too.'

'He was such a good boy,' said Shirley, shaking her head and forcing a weak smile. 'You were always more like your father, but Leo . . .'

Lucy nodded, understanding her mother's need to gloss over the shadier bits of her son's history. Over the years, Leo's shortcomings and spiky edges had been smoothed off by the idealism of grief, and Lucy had learned to accept it. Leo had been far from perfect, but elevating him to sainthood made his absence easier for her mum to bear. Her dad just avoided talking about him altogether, which was also fair enough.

'I know,' said Lucy. 'But he's gone, and there's nothing we can do to bring him back.'

Shirley said nothing, absently picking at the fibres of the duvet cover as a single tear rolled down her cheek.

'But I'm still here, Mum. Living and breathing, trying to make something of my life so you can be proud of me – not because I'm the girlfriend of someone like Kristoff, but because I'm Lucy.'

Shirley sniffed and sat upright, giving herself a little shake. 'Have you told your dad you feel like this?' she asked.

Lucy shook her head. 'No. I didn't even know I was going to tell you until just now.'

'He's told me off before,' she said, wiping her face with the back of her hand. 'For being hard on you, or not showing an interest in your job. I thought maybe you were both ganging up on me.'

'No,' said Lucy, her heart filling with love for her father, who never visibly took sides but always had her back.

'Well, you can't both be wrong,' said Shirley with a heavy sigh. 'I'm sorry, Lucy. It's been a terrible time, for all of us. And sometimes, when I should be grateful that you're here, it just makes me more angry that Leo is gone. I know that's not fair on you.'

'No,' said Lucy, taking her mother's cold, shaking hand in hers. 'And whilst I understand, it needs to stop. For all our sakes.'

'Yes,' whispered Shirley, her voice barely more than a husk.

'I've been seeing a therapist again,' said Lucy. 'It's been helpful, but she's suggested maybe we could have a family appointment. Me and you and Dad.'

Shirley looked up doubtfully. 'Really? I'm not sure that—'

'I've never asked you for anything, Mum,' said Lucy. 'But I'm asking you for this. For me. For US.'

Shirley nodded, sitting up straighter on the bed. 'OK,' she said. 'We'll talk about it with your dad over dinner.'

'Thank you,' said Lucy, feeling another tiny weight lifting from her shoulders. Maybe some good would come from today, after all.

'So what's next?' asked Shirley. 'What's your plan to find the man of your dreams?'

Nate's face floated into Lucy's mind – it had blurred over time, and was now a strange composite of the beautiful, anxious Nate she remembered from Zermatt, the hurt version from Lee and Zoe's wedding, and the glow-up version she'd seen at Glastonbury. Like an AI-generated Nate that was wispy and insubstantial and impossible to hold on to.

'I don't really know. I met someone a little while back, and that felt like something amazing. A connection, you know. Something I never felt with Kristoff. But it wasn't the right time.'

'If you have chemistry, the only other thing you need is timing, right?'

Lucy's brow furrowed as she looked up at her mum. 'Where does that come from?' she asked.

'It's a thing your father used to say, when we first starting going out. "Love is just a matter of chemistry and timing."'

'I'd forgotten that,' said Lucy. 'I remember him saying it to me when I got dumped by my first boyfriend. You remember Dan? His family moved to Reading, and my heart was broken.'

'I remember,' said Shirley. 'Leo didn't like him much, as I recall.'

'We were fifteen,' said Lucy. 'Leo didn't like anyone much.'

'He'd have liked Kristoff, I think.'

Lucy let out a barking laugh. 'Mum, come on. We wouldn't have made it through pre-dinner drinks without him kicking off about the CO_2 emissions rating on Kristoff's car. He'd have probably keyed it down the side.'

'Was he bringing the Aston Martin? Your father had told all the neighbours. They'll be terribly disappointed.'

'No, it was the Range Rover.'

'Well, I don't think Leo would have done anything

bad,' said Shirley indignantly, plucking another non-existent bit of fluff from Lucy's duvet cover. Lucy waited, until Shirley realised that their new, more honest mother–daughter relationship was expected to start now. 'Well, perhaps he might not have approved entirely. Anyway, what about this man you liked?'

'There was definitely chemistry,' said Lucy. 'But as I said, the timing wasn't right.'

'Well, you know the other thing your father would say. He'd tell you to reset the experiment and try again.'

'I haven't really seen this man in months,' said Lucy. 'A lot has changed since then, for both of us.'

'Chemistry is just another word for love, Lucy,' said Shirley earnestly. 'If the bond between you was strong enough, it will still be there. What's his name? The man you like?'

'Nate,' said Lucy.

'That's a nice name,' said Shirley breezily. 'I was listening to Nate Lambert earlier, while I was cooking dinner. He's got a lovely singing voice.'

'Mmm,' muttered Lucy, definitely not keen to let her know she'd dumped a millionaire and was now setting her sights on a pop star. They may have begun to build bridges, but this would definitely test Shirley's tolerance for Lucy's drama.

'Maybe we'll play some of his songs over dinner,' said Shirley.

'Isn't it all love songs, though?' said Lucy quickly. 'I'm not sure I can handle that right now.'

'All right, we'll find something else. Just don't ask your dad for his choice, he'll put on the Bee Gees.'

Lucy resisted the urge to laugh, wondering how life was for Andrea and Felix these days. She'd watched a bit of one of their sets on YouTube a couple of months ago, and they'd definitely diversified their repertoire a little.

'Come on, then,' she said, holding out her hand to help her mum up. 'Let's eat this bloody dinner, I'm starving.'

'Miso bananas,' said Shirley. 'Who'd have thought I'd cook something like that? Do you think Kristoff would have liked them?'

'I'm sure he'd have loved them, Mum,' said Lucy, feeling suddenly exhausted. 'But he's not here. It's just me.'

By 10 p.m. Lucy was back in her room, having eaten a meal that tasted like a science experiment conducted by someone who had sniffed too much glue, talked her dad into a family therapy session, and taken a two-hour photo journey through her childhood. Lucy's father had been a keen amateur photographer, and the first sixteen years of her and Leo's lives had been captured and printed and carefully catalogued in sixteen leather-bound photo albums, each one labelled with the year and lined up on the bookshelf like a set of encyclopaedias. School photos, birthday parties, holidays, school plays – every moment was there, and in every photo she and Leo were together.

The photos had dried up in the last five years of Leo's life, prompted partly by the advent of smartphones, and partly by Leo being less inclined to let his parents shove a camera in his face. He had a memorial Facebook page, which featured photos taken by friends at school and college, and a handful of him and Lucy together looking like moody adolescents.

Where are all my school friends? she thought, scrolling through the sparse collection of photos on her own Facebook page. She had acquaintances now, obviously – mates from university and the gym and people who lived in neighbouring flats. But nobody from when they were at school. Because when they were kids, it was just her and Leo. Twins with an unbreakable bond, always together, always a partnership. The two of them hadn't needed anyone else.

And now she was thirty-three years old, and could count her trusted, ride-or-die friends on one hand. Actually, on one finger, because Jonno was it, really. *I lost a brother, and that made a tiny space for Jonno, who I love and trust like a brother*, thought Lucy. *But I've never let anyone else get close.*

And the funny thing was that Nate had instantly seen what Lucy had been blind to, even though he'd only known her for a few days. *Leo was the most significant partnership of your life, and then he died. So maybe now you subconsciously can't form meaningful relationships.*

And in the end, it all came back to Nate, didn't it? Chemistry and timing.

She sat cross-legged on the bed and took a few deep breaths, acknowledging that today had been about being open and honest – with herself, with Kristoff, with her mother . . . and now it was time to be honest with Nate. She clicked on WhatsApp, but weirdly he wasn't listed in her connections any more, and their previous messages had disappeared. Perhaps he was getting besieged by everyone in his contact list and decided to delete the app, which seemed like a reasonable course of action. Instead she clicked on the speech bubble icon and composed an old-school text message.

Kristoff and I have split up, and I got the impression that maybe you and Sasha had too? Perhaps that's a sign that we should talk? I know you're busy right now, but I can't stop thinking about you. Lucy x

She read it through a few times until she was happy that it was short, to the point and unambiguous in its intent. She clicked send before she could change her mind, then immediately received a message back that said *Cannot send. Number unknown.*

Shit, thought Lucy, her heart sinking. *He's changed his number. What the hell am I supposed to do now?* She could WhatsApp Sasha and ask for his new number, but the prospect of that conversation made her feel itchy, so she opted to avoid taking that plunge by looking at Nate's TikTok instead. She scrolled back to January and lost herself in his extraordinary journey for a while, starting with the videos from that first week after they got back from Zermatt. Then snippets from live TV shows, walking the red carpet at the BRITs in February, meeting fans, studio sessions, some public appearances, and then Glastonbury. And most recently, a behind-the-scenes video in London, filmed just this afternoon. Nate was currently in rehearsals for his UK and European tour, and the video showed him performing with his band. He was wearing a white T-shirt that hugged his newly gym-honed chest, and there was a – *wait*, thought Lucy. *What IS that?*

She paused and rewound the video, then watched it again. There was something on his right arm that definitely hadn't been there in Zermatt. A bruise, maybe? Or a scar? But however many times she watched, the video scanned across him too fast for her to see what it was.

She opened her laptop and put his name into Google Images, then started scrolling through the thousands of pictures that had been posted online in the past four months. Lots of him in suits and shirts or his standard uniform of plaid shirts, but the sleeves were never rolled up far enough. A couple of him papped by the *Daily Mail* wearing swimming shorts in Ibiza, looking tanned and fit, but none of the pictures showed the right angle of his arm, or maybe the mark hadn't been there then. A few pictures of him with various female celebrities, which Lucy glossed over because she definitely didn't need to go down that pit of despair. She kept scrolling, becoming increasingly frustrated that she couldn't find one decent picture of his right arm.

Lucy opened YouTube and started with the most recent video. It was the same studio as the one featured on TikTok earlier, with Nate wearing the same white T-shirt, but the video was a longer version that featured a quickfire Q&A where Nate dropped a few hints about the upcoming tour.

There! thought Lucy, pausing the video and winding it back a couple of frames. The mark was intimately familiar, and entirely unmistakeable. Four letters tattooed in black ink on the inside of his forearm, just below the elbow.

WAHZ. Exactly as she'd written them in marker pen in January, with the same oversized Z and calligraphy typeface, but now permanently tattooed on his arm.

We'll always have Zermatt.

CHAPTER TWENTY-NINE

Lucy woke up on Monday morning after a restless night, mostly spent reliving every moment she'd spent with Nate, and trying to work out what the tattoo on his arm signified about his feelings for her. He'd clearly preserved the letters she'd written in marker pen, but why? And when? It had to be in the few days afterwards, otherwise the pen would have faded too much for the tattoo artist to get an exact match. But he'd also been actively trying to hide it for the five months since, so maybe he was already having tattoo regret. It all felt quite confusing, but Lucy's instinct told her that it *had* to be a good thing.

By the time she'd eaten toast with her parents and waved them off to work, she'd come to the inevitable conclusion that the only person who was going to help her get in touch with Nate was Sasha. She'd grudgingly discounted Alex, on the basis she have to go via Willem, who she'd exchanged a handful of messages with since Zermatt but definitely wasn't a close enough friend for awkward favours. So, whilst she was packing up her stuff to head home to Bristol, she bit the bullet and messaged her.

Hey Sasha, can we meet? If Lucy was going to beg for Sasha's help to win the love of a man they'd both slept with, she'd much rather do it over coffee in London or Bristol. Woman to woman, no messing about.

Yes, of course, came the reply. *Message Olly and he'll put some time in for later this week.*

Ouch, thought Lucy. She could feel the dismissal from however many miles away Sasha was right now, like a bug being swatted with a tea towel. She sighed and started to type another message, then deleted it and called her instead.

'Hello, Lucy,' said Sasha's voice. 'I thought you had a day off today.'

'I do,' said Lucy, trying to keep her voice light and breezy. 'I was actually hoping you could give me Nate's new number?'

There was silence for a few seconds, then the sound of a door being closed. 'I can't do that without his permission, obviously,' said Sasha coolly. 'The best I can do is tell him you asked, and then he can message you.'

'Right,' said Lucy.

'I don't think it will be anytime soon, though. He's in the studio right now. Rehearsing for the tour.'

The implication from Sasha was clear – *I'm still an influence in Nate's life, and you're not.* Lucy swallowed down her disappointment and kept her voice strong. 'I know,' she said. 'If you could let him know I called, I'd appreciate it. I need to speak to him pretty urgently.'

'I'll do my best,' said Sasha, giving the impression that Lucy probably shouldn't hold her breath. 'Give Kristoff my love.' Sasha hung up before Lucy could answer, leaving her feeling like she'd made zero progress. *What now?* she thought, itching to do something that would help her feel like she was getting closer to her goal, somehow. The exact nature of that goal was less clear, but she would worry about that later.

She clicked back to Nate's TikTok from yesterday, and sure enough, there was footage of him walking through a door next to a sign for Fountain Road Studios. She googled it, and found the address in Dalston in East London. Before she had a chance to change her mind, she was closing her parents' front door and hurrying up the hill to Purley train station, and an appointment with . . . destiny? Madness? More frustration? Something that didn't feel like lead boots, anyway.

When she arrived at the studio there was a crowd of fans outside, eyeing her beadily as she elbowed her way to the door, and clearly wondering if she was going to gain access where they had not. She pressed the doorbell and waited, trying to look nonchalant when her heart was pounding out of her chest.

'Fountain Studios,' said a woman's voice.

'Hi,' said Lucy into the intercom, aware that every single person was listening. 'I'm here to see Nate Lambert?'

'What's your name, please?'

'Lucy Glover. I'm a . . . friend.'

'Right,' said the woman, with a tone that suggested she'd heard all this before. 'Is he expecting you? You're not on the list.'

'Not exactly,' said Lucy.

'Mmm, right,' said the tinny voice of the woman. 'I can't let you in.'

'Can you give him a message? Tell him I'm here?'

'No, I can't do that either. Sorry.' The intercom line went dead.

Lucy pressed her lips together and took a deep breath, conscious that twenty people were hanging on every word of this conversation and willing her to fail. She pressed the bell again and waited longer this time.

'What now?' snapped the woman's voice.

'Is Alex Jansen there?'

'Yes,' said the voice sarkily. 'Is he a friend too?'

'Yes, he is,' said Lucy firmly. 'Can you please tell him that Lucy Glover is here. Say Lucy from Zermatt. He'll know what that means.'

'He's in a meeting,' said the voice.

'Then interrupt,' said Lucy, starting to lose patience. 'He won't mind. But he WILL mind if you've left me standing out here all day.'

The line went dead again, and Lucy waited, avoiding eye contact with the fans glaring her down from the pavement. After what seemed like an age, the door unlocked and a resentful-looking woman appeared.

'You Lucy?' she asked.

'Yeah,' said Lucy, as half a dozen other women leaned forward, looking like they might also declare themselves to be Lucy in an *I'm Spartacus* chorus.

'Come in,' said the woman, opening the door enough for Lucy to slide through, then firmly closing it again. 'Sorry about making you wait, I had to check with Alex. People try all kinds, no offence.'

'None taken,' said Lucy. 'I guess you've seen it all.'

'Yep,' said the woman, who had a slightly world-weary

air despite probably not being a day over twenty-five. 'The TikTok stars definitely have the craziest fans. There were loads more of them earlier, when Nate arrived. They'll all be back later, but there's always a hardcore group who hang around all day. It's mad.'

She led Lucy to a reception area with a sofa and a couple of plastic chairs, then left her with a vague, 'Wait here, Alex will come down.' There was no coffee, so Lucy filled a plastic cup from the water dispenser and hoped her hands would stop shaking.

'Lucy!' said Alex, bursting into the room and pulling her into a hug. She closed her eyes and leaned in to him, then opened them to see that he was being trailed down the stairs by . . . Sasha. *Shit*.

'Hello, Lucy.' Sasha's expression suggested she'd stepped in something unpleasant. 'What are you doing here?'

'I was hoping to see Nate,' Lucy replied, giving Sasha a challenging look.

'I thought we agreed that I'd give him your message,' said Sasha coolly.

'And have you done that?' asked Lucy, raising her eyebrows. Alex followed the conversation warily, and Lucy wondered what he would do if a catfight started. Video it, probably.

'No, Lucy, I haven't,' said Sasha through gritted teeth. 'Nate has been in tour rehearsals all morning, and me saying, "Hey, can you give Lucy a call?" isn't going to help him stay focused.'

'He's in a good place, Lucy,' added Alex. 'We need to keep him there.' The two of them had a tag-team vibe, like they'd just held an emergency meeting and agreed how to get rid of Lucy as quickly as possible.

Lucy narrowed her eyes at him. 'What does that mean?'

'It means no drama, no distractions. The UK tour starts in three days. Now isn't the time for surprise visits from old friends.' Lucy registered the 'old friends', even though Alex knew what had happened between Lucy and Nate in Zermatt. It was clearly for Sasha's benefit.

'He's emotionally fragile,' said Sasha. 'Small things, changes of direction, unexpected surprises – they can all make him spiral. But you already know that. He's going through a lot right now.'

'Yes, but he's also a grown man. If he doesn't want to talk to me, that's fine. But can we at least give him the option?'

'Yes, but not now,' said Alex pleadingly. 'Please. It's not personal, I'm keeping everyone away right now. Three weeks of touring UK venues, then some time out for him to write some new stuff before he goes to Europe in October. Right now, the UK tour is the only thing he needs to think about.'

'Ask yourself if whatever you want to talk about is going to simplify his life right now,' said Sasha, and Lucy's heart sank.

'No,' she admitted. 'Probably not.' She wondered what Nate had told Sasha when he got the tattoo. Had he made something up, or had that been the first crack in their relationship?

'Why are you even here, Sasha?' she asked. 'I thought Nate had moved out of your place?' *She's having just as much trouble letting go as I am,* thought Lucy. *But if I have to go into battle for Nate, I'd rather know exactly where things stand between him and Sasha.*

'He might have moved out, Lucy,' said Sasha, tossing her hair. 'But I'm still his mother.'

There were a couple of seconds where Lucy's mind went entirely blank, then Sasha's words flashed through her brain in technicolour neon.

'His what?'

CHAPTER THIRTY

'So when I saw him coming out your room in Zermatt, and you hugged him and blew him a kiss, and then you said you were living together, I just assumed you and he were . . . you know. Sleeping together.'

'That's disgusting,' said Sasha, sipping her coffee and shaking her head. They'd decamped to the nearest cafe within minutes of Sasha's revelation, both realising that they needed to have the kind of conversation that Alex really didn't need to hear.

'And you were crying at Glasto on Saturday when he was singing "Can't Be Mine",' continued Lucy. 'I took that as confirmation that you had split up.'

'Of course I was crying,' snapped Sasha. 'I was watching my only son on stage at Glastonbury, singing a song he'd written in front of a crowd of screaming fans. Wouldn't YOU cry?'

'Well, it's obvious NOW,' said Lucy, rolling her eyes. 'And please take it as a compliment when I tell you that it genuinely never occurred to me that you were old enough to be his mother.'

'I had him when I was sixteen,' said Sasha. 'It's a very long story, that only a handful of people know about.'

'Why is it such a secret?' asked Lucy.

Sasha shrugged. 'For the same reason it would have

been a secret if I was actually having sex with a member of the account team.' She pulled a face and shuddered. 'Because people would have called him Nepo Nate, and I wanted him to succeed on his own merit.'

'But what does it matter now? He's left LUNA. And you can't keep it a secret forever. The more famous he gets, the more people are going to be digging into his background.'

'You're right, it doesn't matter, but I've got a new venture I'm getting off the ground at LUNA, and I'd rather everyone focused on that for as long as possible.'

'What new venture?' asked Lucy.

'I'm starting a spin-off division of the agency called LUNA Gold, specialising in advertising for luxury brands. A team of our top talent, charging a premium price tag. Olly is coming with me, along with a couple of others.'

'Like who?' asked Lucy, already anticipating the answer and feeling her stomach start to ache.

'You, if you're interested,' said Sasha, arching an eyebrow. 'I was planning to talk to you about it later in the week.'

'Why me?' asked Lucy, playing for time.

'Because you're the best we have, and Shine Spirits is a perfect fit for us.'

Lucy thought about it, feeling flattered but also a little empty inside. If she worked for Sasha, she'd be closer to Nate. But she'd also be under the eye of his *mother*, which was still blowing her mind in fifteen different ways. Sasha had already shown that she had very strong opinions about Lucy dating her son, and even though it might never happen – *could* never happen, in the real world – it felt like she'd be firmly closing that door.

'I'll think about it,' she said. 'It's a big step.'

'I'm planning to set up the office out of Paris,' Sasha said. 'I hold a French passport; my parents were French but we moved to the UK when I was young.'

'I'm sure Nate told me it was his father who was French, not you.'

'I'm sure he did,' said Sasha with a small smile. 'I'm also sure he quickly moved the conversation on.'

'Yeah,' said Lucy, remembering how reluctant Nate was to talk about his family. *No wonder.*

'Anyway, Paris,' said Sasha. 'LUNA Gold, launching at the end of the year. I'd love to take you with me.'

Take me away from Nate, thought Lucy, wondering if that was part of Sasha's agenda and figuring there was no better time to ask than now. 'Is this actually about keeping me close, so I can't get near Nate? You've clearly worked out that I have feelings for him.'

'And yet you're dating Kristoff,' said Sasha testily. 'You can see why I might think you're not entirely reliable.'

'Kristoff and I split up. Yesterday, actually.'

'Goodness. You DO move fast.'

Lucy took a deep breath, determined not to lose her temper. 'Not that it's any of your concern, but I ended things because I don't feel the same way about him as I do about Nate.'

'Hmm,' said Sasha, taking a sip from her drink. 'It must be hard, juggling the incredibly successful and high-profile men in your life. Tell me, what happened to the two guys you kept on speed dial for sex? Or was it more than two?'

Lucy raised her eyebrows, realising that Sasha was only just getting started. 'How did you know about that?'

'Everyone knew about that,' said Sasha dismissively. 'You can understand why I might think you're not entirely up to scratch when it comes to my son.'

'Yes, I can see how it might look that way,' said Lucy through gritted teeth. 'But he's also a man in his thirties who can make his own choices, and also it's none of your fucking business.'

Sasha stared her down, taking a moment to decide which way to play it. 'Your reputation is on a knife-edge, Lucy. I built you up at LUNA, don't think I won't take you down in exactly the same way.'

Lucy shook her head, the sick, nervous feeling in her stomach being washed away by a renewed feeling of strength and determination. What had Nate said in Zermatt? *You're the most talented copywriter I've ever worked with.* She'd stayed in Bristol for Leo, worked at LUNA because it was safe and familiar, but there was a whole world of opportunity waiting for her. And if she was honest, she'd been working towards this moment for months.

'I'm leaving LUNA,' said Lucy quietly.

'I'm sorry?' said Sasha.

'I'm leaving LUNA,' she repeated, more confidently this time. 'I'm done, I quit.'

Sasha stared at her, a tiny flash of panic in her eyes. 'You can't just quit.'

'I just did,' smiled Lucy, feeling a surge of adrenaline pump through her veins for the first time since the earth had moved several times in Zermatt. 'And just so we're clear, if you even think about dumping my shit on the table, I'll dump yours right next to it.'

All the colour drained from Sasha's face. 'Are you serious?'

'Yes,' said Lucy, standing up and grabbing her bag. 'And don't ask me to work three months' notice. I'll stay for a few weeks to hand over, then I'm out.'

'Well,' said Sasha after a shocked pause, smiling at Lucy with an expression that looked a little bit like admiration. 'I certainly underestimated you.'

'Yes, you did.' Lucy tossed her hair. 'I'll confirm my notice by email later today. Are we done?'

'One thing,' said Sasha, her face softening. 'A favour. A huge one, but it's important.'

'What is it?' Lucy wasn't inclined to give Sasha the time of day right now, but they'd come this far.

'Stay away from Nate, just until the end of the UK tour. Please. After that, you can do whatever you like. But just wait a few weeks.'

Lucy paused for a moment, processing Sasha's request. Her instinct was to tell Sasha to do one, but this wasn't about her and Sasha. It was about Nate, and what he needed right now.

'Fine,' said Lucy. 'I can do that.'

'Thank you,' said Sasha, looking relieved.

'But I need to know that you aren't going to get in my way. I know I don't seem ideal, on paper. But I know him, and I really care about him. I'm not going to mess him around.'

Sasha stared at her, like she was taking the measure of

Lucy and deciding whether she was worth going into battle with over Nate.

'OK,' said Sasha. 'I won't get in your way. He's a grown man who can make his own mistakes.'

'Good,' said Lucy. 'Can I tell Jonno that you're Nate's mum?'

Sasha pulled a face. 'Why would you want to do that?'

'Because I want to video his reaction, it's going to be epic.'

Sasha thought about it for a moment, then gave a heavy sigh. 'He's going to find out eventually, obviously. Can you give that a few weeks too? And persuade him not to tell anyone?'

'Sure,' said Lucy.

'Fine,' said Sasha, wafting her away. 'It will save me the horror of that conversation. Send me the video, though. God knows I need a laugh.'

They stared at each other for a moment, as Lucy weighed up the decision she'd just made. Yesterday Kristoff, today LUNA. It was turning out to be a fairly momentous few days.

'I've always respected you, Lucy,' said Sasha. 'I think we're very alike, in lots of ways. Are we going to be able to come back from this, do you think?'

'I don't know,' said Lucy. 'If I'm wrong about how Nate feels about me, it won't matter.'

'But if you're right?' asked Sasha, raising her eyebrows.

'Then we'll work it out, for his sake. It's what adults do.'

'Yes, it is,' said Sasha, seemingly satisfied for now. 'Just give him three weeks.'

CHAPTER THIRTY-ONE

Three weeks later

'I can't believe I'm doing this,' said Jonno, tanking his car down the M4 at eighty-five miles an hour. 'It's your last day, we should be pissed at your leaving party right now.'

'There isn't a leaving party,' smirked Lucy. 'Unless somebody organised one without inviting me.'

'Oh my God, Fran would totally do that,' laughed Jonno. 'What are you going to do next?'

'I'm not entirely sure,' said Lucy. 'I've got a couple of interviews lined up, both really good agencies. But I've also told both of them that I'm not available until January, so it depends on how happy they are to wait.'

'What are you going to do between now and then?'

'Do some freelancing. Maybe take some time off.'

'And do what?'

'Well, that depends on how tonight goes.' The basket of snakes in Lucy's belly wriggled and squirmed, and she wondered if she was going to make it through this evening without throwing up. She'd had too long to think about this plan, and it already felt entirely stupid and destined to fail.

'Whether Nate goes for this ridiculous overblown gesture, you mean?' asked Jonno.

'Yes,' said Lucy, wishing that, just occasionally, Jonno could be a tiny bit less honest.

'What if he sacks you off?'

'I haven't got that far,' said Lucy. 'I might go travelling. Take ayahuasca on a beach in Mexico and find myself.'

'Sounds fun,' said Jonno. 'Can I come?'

'No,' said Lucy with the ghost of a smile. 'You and Marcia already found each other.'

'Yeah, I s'pose. Where are the jobs? The ones you've got interviews for?'

'One in London, and one in New York.' To be honest she'd only applied to go through the motions, and hadn't really expected to get an interview for either. Right now it felt difficult to think about anything beyond today.

'Wow,' said Jonno.

'If I end up in the States, you can come over to stay.'

'Do bars in New York serve Three-Eyed Goblin? No, I don't think they do.' He was using humour to deflect from his feelings, as Jonno always did, but Lucy could tell that the idea of her being on the other side of the Atlantic was causing him pain.

'Jonno, we both need to spread our wings. We've been drinking in the Brunel for over a decade. We always talk about why I'm still here, but never you. Why aren't YOU applying for jobs in London and New York?'

Jonno said nothing for a moment while he considered the question. 'I don't know,' he said. 'Marcia likes the countryside, Lottie and Ava are settled in school. Giving them everything they need is my number one priority, I guess.'

Lucy smiled, feeling a wave of love for her friend.

'See, this is why we're friends. You're an incredibly selfless human.'

'In four or five years they'll both be in university and Marcia and I can decide what's next. I might take early retirement, actually. That's definitely an option. Spend some time travelling. Maybe take ayahuasca in Mexico with my incredibly beautiful wife.'

'And in the meantime?'

He turned to glance at her, then fixed his eyes back on the road. 'I actually really love my job, Luce. I just love it more when you're there. It kind of hurts to realise you don't need me any more.'

Lucy laughed. 'Did I ever really NEED you?' She knew the answer to that, obviously, but it didn't make it any easier to admit.

'Yeah, you did,' said Jonno firmly. 'When you started at LUNA it was about eight months after Leo died, and I was living in a house with two girls under five. We were both shellshocked and looking for a lifeboat.'

'Those two metaphors don't really go together, just so you know.'

'Fuck off,' laughed Jonno. 'You do the words, I do the pictures. Remember?'

'Yeah, OK.' Lucy grinned.

'You'd been through a lot, and were a vulnerable mess. I liked you, and I wanted to protect you. I still do.'

'Thank you,' said Lucy, blinking away tears. 'You are, without question, the love of my life.'

'That's a lovely thing to say,' said Jonno. 'But I think we both know that it's time for you to . . . I don't know.'

'Transfer that love to someone else?' suggested Lucy.

'Yeah,' said Jonno sadly. 'Leo had it for the first twenty-one years, I've had it for the past eleven, in a different way. And now it's Nate's turn.'

Lucy looked at him hopefully. 'You really think? You don't think I'm insane?'

'Oh, I absolutely think you're insane,' laughed Jonno. 'You've quit your job, dumped your millionaire boyfriend, and now we're on the way to London so you can declare your undying love to a pop star, even though I have to be up at six tomorrow to drive Lottie and her friends to Alton Towers. We're both absolutely mental.'

'I'm technically supposed to wait until tonight's show is over,' said Lucy. 'Sasha made me promise.'

Jonno's brow furrowed. 'What the fuck has it got to do with Sasha?'

Lucy smiled, then pulled out her phone and swiped to her camera.

'What you doing?' asked Jonno.

'Taking a video. Are you buckled in?'

'Yeah, of course,' he said, pinging his seatbelt. 'What's this about?'

'It's about Nate,' said Lucy with a grin. 'And Sasha.'

'The fuck?' said Jonno, almost driving into the back of a minibus.

'Please tell me why we have to watch this gig,' grumbled Jonno, nursing an alcohol-free beer at the bar as people flooded through the doors. The London venue for Nate's UK tour was a live event space in a basement on Tottenham Court Road; it could take about fifteen hundred people, and by the looks of this crowd, it was going to be packed. Annoyingly he'd played a venue in Bristol the previous week, which she'd been to watch to help her formulate the plan. But she'd made no attempt to let him know she was there, because she'd promised Sasha to wait until the end of the tour. And now it was the final night, and the time had come.

'Why wouldn't we watch the gig?' asked Lucy.

'Because this place is full of fourteen-year-old girls and their mums, and I look like a pervert. And also because I sat through a Nate Lambert gig at Glastonbury a few weeks ago. If I go to any more, I'm going to have to register at the police station as a fan.'

'I believe we stood at the side of the stage at Glasto, technically,' laughed Lucy. 'And you were buzzing on free champagne and a helicopter ride.'

'Shit, I miss Kristoff,' muttered Jonno wistfully. 'Why can't you get back with him?'

'Because I wasn't in love with him,' said Lucy. 'And even if I was, he's now dating a twenty-five-year-old Swiss chocolate heiress called Sophia.'

'Can I keep calling her Lindt Linda?' grinned Jonno.

'Depends if you want to keep your job,' said Lucy. She'd forced herself to look at Kristoff's social posts over the past few weeks, mostly featuring him and Sophia looking blissfully happy and beautiful. She took the absence of any pain as a sign that she definitely hadn't loved him, and genuinely hoped things worked out for him. Sophia looked like the kind of woman who was no stranger to a helicopter and a Manhattan capsule wardrobe, so that felt like a good start.

'But just so I'm clear,' asked Jonno, looking serious

for a moment. 'You ARE in love with actual Nate Lambert?'

'Yes,' said Lucy patiently. 'That's why we're here, and also why I've shit myself empty over the past three weeks from stress.'

'And you're not bothered that pretty much every other woman in this room would also say they're in love with Nate Lambert, plus about half the men?'

'No,' said Lucy, trying to calm the nervous twitch in her hands. 'Because I think he loves me too.'

'Based on what?'

'I'm not sure,' said Lucy. 'Just . . . vibes, I guess.'

'Right,' said Jonno, nodding thoughtfully. 'We're here to make total twats of ourselves based on "just vibes".'

'Why are you being such a bitch?' asked Lucy, pulling a face. 'You offered to help.'

'I'm having a crisis of confidence. Why can't you just get his number from Sasha, who is also his fucking MUM, and call him tomorrow?'

'Because I want him to know how I feel, and I thought that warranted a grand gesture.'

'OK,' shrugged Jonno. 'But I beg you, please don't make me sit through this whole gig. Let's go out for dinner, and then you can storm the stage naked during the encore or something.'

'Can't be done,' said Lucy. 'I have a plan, and I can't do it without you. We only need to be here for the first half, and we can stand right at the back.'

'Well, that's something,' said Jonno. 'At least I don't have to get in the mosh pit with a load of teenagers. What if I accidentally touched one of them?'

'Keep your hands in your pockets,' said Lucy. 'Actually, that looks weirder.'

'If I have my hands in my pockets, I can't hold up the other end of your stupid banner,' he said, nodding to the bundle of poles and fabric in Lucy's hands. She'd snuck it into the venue wrapped in a coat, but the security staff had been more interested in inspecting the contents of her bag, and even that had been a token gesture.

'He's on stage in five minutes,' said Lucy, checking her watch. 'We should go in.'

'You sure you don't want a drink?' said Jonno.

Lucy wiped her clammy hands on Nate's navy sweatshirt, feeling jittery with nerves. Tonight felt like it was going to be either an ending or a beginning of something, and she really didn't want to mess it up.

'No,' she said. This might be a big gesture, but the least she could do was deliver it sober.

'I'm going to take a short break after this song,' said Nate, adjusting his microphone and raking his hands through his hair. 'Leave you in the very capable hands of Cara Louise, who's an incredible up-and-coming singer that you're going to love. But before that, I want to play my new single.'

The crowd roared, and Jonno feigned pain for about the twentieth time. Lucy had loved the show as much as she had last week in Bristol – a mix of Nate's music and a few covers and some special guests who'd joined him on stage. The whole set was full of joy and optimism – just a guy living his best life and still not entirely able to believe it was all happening.

'Jesus, what's wrong with these people?' said Jonno, covering his ears.

'Did you never scream at a gig when you were a teenager?' laughed Lucy.

'No,' said Jonno, not entirely convincingly. 'OK, maybe once, at a Pixies gig. But that was actual music.'

'OK, it's time,' said Lucy, her heart pounding as the opening bars to 'Can't Be Mine' filled the venue. She started to unfurl the banner, until she was ten feet from Jonno and the fabric was taut enough to hold it up. She checked behind, to make sure nobody's view was going to be blocked, but they were so far back they were practically leaning up against the doors.

'I am dying inside,' said Jonno as they both held the banner high above their heads and people nearby turned to see what was written on it.

'What did you say?' asked Lucy, steadfastly ignoring the stares and pitying looks from nearby fans. She focused on Nate, who was singing a song that Lucy was now pretty sure had been written about her.

'Don't say it's for the best
Don't tell me I'll be fine
You tore my heart to pieces
Telling me you can't be mine.'

'I AM DYING INSIDE,' yelled Jonno.

Lucy ignored him as she held the banner steady, her head high. She'd made it from two white sheets, folded lengthways, stitched together along the short end and properly hemmed at the edges so it didn't look tatty. She'd stapled it to two wooden poles, then used blue fabric paint to decorate the edges with snowflakes, and in the middle she'd written nine words in huge letters.

Nate – I CAN be yours. But if not, WAHZ

'You need to put that down,' said a burly security guard in a high-vis jacket, elbowing his way through the crowd towards them.

'Please, just to the end of the song,' said Lucy pleadingly. They'd held it up for less than two minutes, and Nate might not have registered it in the sea of swaying bodies. Maybe she should have added fairy lights.

'No,' said the man firmly. 'Take it down NOW, or I'm throwing you both out.'

Lucy sighed and dropped the banner, glaring at the guard as she moved towards Jonno and bundled it all up. He nodded and gave them both a final glare, then disappeared.

'You proper embarrassed yourself there,' said a teenage girl, witheringly. 'Aren't you a bit old for Nate Lambert?'

Lucy pulled a snarky face. 'Aren't you a bit young?'

The girl gave her the finger, then turned back to watch Nate.

'My arms were killing me anyway,' said Jonno, handing her the other end. 'Don't you have any lighter-weight sheets?'

'Egyptian cotton,' said Lucy with a tired smile. 'A throwback to when my bed experienced higher traffic flow.'

'Well, if that didn't work, you can always switch to Plan B and call him tomorrow,' said Jonno. 'It's a good story to tell him either way.'

'Yeah,' said Lucy, feeling stupid and embarrassed and deflated.

'Shall we head off now?' said Jonno.

Lucy shook her head as the song came to an end and the crowd cheered and whooped. Nate waved and left the stage, and his place was taken by a young woman in a yellow dress. She had a husky, soulful voice that reminded Lucy a bit of Andrea. 'I just need to stay here for a few minutes, but you can go to the bar if you like.'

'Stay here for what?' asked Jonno, looking confused.

'I'm not sure,' said Lucy, her face burning hot. 'I'll join you in a bit.'

'I'm not leaving you here on your own, you look like a twat,' said Jonno, leaning up against the back wall next to her.

After a few minutes the security guard reappeared, his face grim. 'Still here, then,' he said, raising his voice over the sound of the singing.

'I took the banner down,' said Lucy. 'Please don't throw us out.'

'What's your name?' he asked.

'Lucy,' she said.

'Come on then.' He gestured towards the exit door.

'Where are we going?'

The security guard gave her a conspiratorial smile. 'I've been told by one of Nate's team to find out who was holding the banner. And if it's a woman called Lucy with blonde hair, I'm supposed to take you backstage.'

Lucy grinned, then passed Jonno the bundle of sheets and poles. If her hands had been clammy before, they were sweating freely now.

'I'll just wait around here, shall I?' said Jonno lightly.

'Go to the bar,' said Lucy breathlessly. 'I won't be long.'

Jonno threw an arm around her and kissed her hair. 'Go get 'im, babe.'

'Come on,' said the security guard. 'We need to get a move on.'

Lucy half-jogged behind him as they slipped out into the vestibule and headed down a corridor, then through a door with a keypad and along another series of dimly lit passages full of cables and equipment. Lucy hoped the security guard was going to hang around long enough to take her back, otherwise she could be lost in this back-stage labyrinth for days.

'Here,' said the security guard, knocking on a door with a laminated sign saying *Nate Lambert*. Lucy barely had time to remember to breathe before the door opened, and a woman holding a pouch of make-up brushes appeared.

'Come in,' said Nate's voice.

'I'm just leaving,' said the woman, edging past Lucy. She disappeared with the security guard, leaving Lucy all alone in the doorway, staring at Nate over by a rack of clothes and suddenly entirely lost for words.

'Come in,' said Nate again, waving her forward until she was inside enough to close the door behind her. She looked around for Alex, but it was just the two of them. The smile on Nate's face told her how happy he was to see her, so she did the only thing that felt right in that moment and took three huge strides across the room to kiss him. He gathered her into his arms with a fervour that felt like passion, relief, desire and joy all at once, and for a heady minute there was nothing in Lucy's head other than love for this extraordinary man.

'How do you feel?' whispered Nate, pulling away and giving her a searching look, the flickering anxiety in his eyes betraying that even now, he needed to be sure of her feelings.

'Like I've reached the end of a really long journey,' said Lucy, holding his gaze. 'I'm sorry it took me so long.'

'It doesn't matter,' said Nate, pulling her tightly into his body and letting out a long, slow breath. 'You're here now.'

CHAPTER THIRTY-TWO

'I've only got five more minutes,' said Nate, glancing at his watch as they lounged on the sofa in his dressing room, his arm thrown casually around her shoulder. 'I told Alex I needed some time alone, but he'll be along in a bit to check I'm OK. He'll go apeshit if he finds you here.'

'I'll go in a minute,' said Lucy, tilting her head up to kiss him. It felt like the latest of a thousand kisses she'd been storing up for him, and it was hard not to pepper him with all of them at once.

'I thought you were dating Kristoff, anyway?' said Nate with a grin.

'We broke up a few weeks ago,' shrugged Lucy. 'But you already knew that.'

'Yeah, I did,' muttered Nate. 'But if you're still secretly dating, you should know that he's cheating on you with a really hot Swiss woman.'

'Condoms and chocolate,' said Lucy. 'They're the ultimate match.'

'I don't know,' said Nate, burying his face in her hair and breathing her in. 'A singer and a writer seems like a pretty good combination to me.'

'And obviously I thought Sasha was your girlfriend,' said Lucy, colour rushing to her cheeks. 'It turns out that wasn't remotely correct.'

'I heard about that,' laughed Nate. 'I'm sorry I wasn't honest with you, but I didn't want you to judge me, or Sasha. And I never imagined you'd come to the conclusion I was banging my mum.'

'I don't think she thinks I'm good enough for you,' said Lucy.

'I think she's just wary of me getting hurt,' said Nate. 'She told me you'd promised not to get in touch until after tonight. And Alex made me promise to do the same.'

'I almost made it,' said Lucy. 'You've only got half a show to go.'

'I was going to give you until tomorrow lunchtime, then send out a search party.'

'You have more patience than me,' laughed Lucy, feeling so ridiculously happy she thought she might cry. But there was still one question she needed to ask. 'When we were in Zermatt, you said there was somebody you liked, but it was complicated.'

'Yeah,' said Nate, picking awkwardly at some fluff on his jeans. 'That was you.'

'Really?'

Nate nodded and blew out his cheeks. 'I'd had a ridiculous crush on you for ages. But you weren't the dating type, and I wasn't exactly Mr Confident, so I never told you. Apart from "Can't Be Mine", which is very much about you.'

'Wow,' said Lucy, not sure what else to say. It was what she'd suspected and hoped for when she was devising this mad plan, but it still felt unbelievable to hear it from Nate.

Nate nodded. 'I wrote it after Zoe's wedding, back at my mum's place in Bath. I don't think I'd even taken my suit off.'

'I thought that was about Sasha too.'

Nate gave a barking laugh, his thumb stroking the back of her hand in a way that gave her goosebumps. 'Yeah, that's all kinds of disgusting.'

'I'm sorry about shutting you out,' said Lucy, looking up at him. 'In Zermatt, and at the wedding. You were right about Leo, and I was scared about how you made me feel, and at the time I didn't know what to do with that.'

'And now?' asked Nate, holding her gaze.

'It feels a lot clearer,' said Lucy with a shy smile. 'And I'm in a much better place, generally.'

'So am I,' said Nate. 'Who was holding the other end of your incredible banner?'

'That was Jonno, obviously.'

'Outstanding,' said Nate. 'That man really loves you.'

'Yeah, he does, the idiot,' said Lucy. She stroked her finger up his forearm, nudging it under the rolled-up cuff of his shirt to reveal the Z of his tattoo. 'I saw this, on YouTube,' she said. 'That's what made me realise that maybe you hadn't entirely left me behind.'

'I've been trying to hide it,' said Nate, pulling the sleeve loose so she could see the whole thing. 'It's been causing quite a stir in the fan forums; they're all trying to work out what secret message it holds.'

'I love that you had it tattooed,' said Lucy, tracing the letters with her finger. 'When did that happen?'

'A couple of days after we got back, before the marker pen completely faded. Everything was mad, all endless meetings and social stuff and getting sucked into Alex's crazy vortex. I just asked for a couple of hours on my own and found the nearest tattoo parlour in London that could do me a walk-in.'

'It's beautiful,' she said, feeling Nate's breath catch as she pressed her finger against it, their bodies arching towards each other.

'I just wanted a reminder of where it all started,' he whispered, weaving his fingers into hers. 'The crossing point from the old Nate to the new one. And the person who was with me when it happened.' He leaned down to kiss her, and for a long moment Lucy couldn't feel her toes.

'So what happens now?' she asked when they broke apart, conscious the clock was ticking on their time together.

'Now, I have to go back on stage,' said Nate, checking his watch again. 'Like, right now. But I'm going on a European tour in a few weeks. Just bars and clubs in France and Germany and the Netherlands, nothing massive. I could definitely do with some PR help.'

'I don't know anything about music PR,' said Lucy, realising what he was asking. 'Or PR, for that matter.'

'Fine, then you can do all my social. Write all the funny little captions for my TikTok.'

Lucy laughed and shook her head. 'That's not a real job.'

'You're right, it's not.' He shrugged. 'Maybe you can just have an adventure with me for a few weeks?'

'What about my job?'

'You've quit your job. Sasha told me.'

'Shit,' said Lucy, rolling her eyes. 'I forgot you have family spies.'

'Do you have something new lined up yet?'

'Not quite, but I'm working on it. I've been thinking about taking the rest of this year off, actually. Doing some freelance stuff and starting something new in January.'

'Well, then,' said Nate. 'Maybe it's perfect timing.'

'Maybe,' said Lucy, knowing that she'd go to the ends of the earth for this man right now, but not wanting to make all the decisions at once. *Chemistry and timing.*

'Look, I'd just love for us to spend some time together. Just think about it, OK?'

'I will,' said Lucy, giving him a final kiss and extracting herself from his arms so they could both stand up.

'I need to get back on stage. You can watch from the mezzanine with Alex and Willem. They're both here. And some other people you know too.'

Eek, Sasha's here, thought Lucy, wondering if she already knew that Lucy had broken her promise and was in the building. Maybe she would steer clear for now.

'I should get back to Jonno. He's in the bar with a bunch of teenage girls. He's giving me a lift back to Bristol.'

'Take him up too, I'll get one of my people to show you the way. You're staying for the second half, right?'

'I hadn't planned to,' said Lucy awkwardly. 'For Jonno's sake, really. He's gone above and beyond today, and he's got a really early start tomorrow. Is that bad?'

'I'd like you to stay, if you can,' said Nate. 'I added a couple of new songs to the set tonight, just for you.'

Lucy looked confused. 'How did you know I'd be here?'

'I didn't,' said Nate. 'I asked Alex to film your songs for YouTube, they're being uploaded tomorrow. So I knew you'd see them; I just wasn't expecting you to be here in person.'

'Well, I'll stay, then. How will I know which songs?'

Nate smiled. 'You'll know.'

'It's just for another hour,' said Lucy, following a harried woman in a radio headset up the stairs to the mezzanine that overlooked the main floor and the stage. 'I'm really sorry.'

'It's fine,' said Jonno, emerging onto a balcony with a neon-lit private bar and tables laden with buffet food. They were directly above where they'd stood with their banner, and it afforded a stunning view of the stage. 'This is much more like it.'

'Lucy!' said a familiar voice, and before she could look up she was yanked into a hug by Willem. Lucy looked over her shoulder to see Sasha's head whip round in her direction.

'Lovely to see you,' said Lucy to Willem. 'This is my friend Jonno, can you both give me a moment?' She extracted herself from Willem's grasp and headed in the direction of Sasha's steely glare.

'You couldn't wait until the end of the show, then?' said Sasha coolly.

'No, not really,' said Lucy. 'But I did manage to hold out for this long, so hopefully that counts for something.'

'It does,' said Sasha. 'Have you seen Nate?'

'Yes.'

'I'm sure he's thrilled you're here.' There was a genuine note of kindness in Sasha's voice, like she had resigned herself to the inevitable, so Lucy softened a little.

'So, we're not mortal enemies, then,' said Lucy.

'Of course not,' replied Sasha. 'I'm his mother, I just want what's best for him. Doesn't every mother feel that way about her son?'

Lucy thought about her own mother, and how she and her dad never had the chance to see Leo find happiness. She'd spoken to them a lot over the past few weeks, explaining her decision to leave LUNA and scheduling their first family therapy session for the following week. They'd even agreed to come to Bristol and see Lucy's therapist, rather than finding a different one. It felt like a small step towards some kind of healing, and in that moment she knew that, the situation with Nate aside, a job in New York wasn't her future. She'd focus on London, rent out her place in Bristol, and find somewhere south of the river, not too far away from Croydon, that she could make feel like home.

'I'm not here for a day trip, Sasha,' said Lucy. 'I really want to make things work.'

'I know,' said Sasha, putting her arm around her as Cara Louise left the stage and the crowd roared for Nate's return. They leaned on the balcony railing together as the music started and Nate opened the second half with a George Michael song. '*I think you're amazing,*' he sang, and Lucy wondered if she'd ever stop smiling.

'I've got two songs now that are for someone really special,' said Nate, as the applause died down. 'She's in the house tonight, actually, so I'm going to try not to mess it up.' He launched into a ballad called 'Things Snowballed', and Lucy wondered if her heart might burst.

'*Things snowballed, they snowballed,*' sang Nate, smiling

up at the balcony as he got to the chorus, '*and the further we both roll . . . the more I know I love you and the more you make me whole.*'

'Look at your face,' said Jonno, elbowing in beside her as the song came to a close. 'He actually wrote a song about you.'

'Yeah,' said Lucy. 'He actually did.'

'I mean, how is any other man supposed to compete with that?'

Lucy turned and looked at him. 'When did you last tell Marcia you loved her, Jonno?'

Jonno thought about it. 'I don't know. About an hour ago? I messaged to tell her I'd been sucked into your stupid scheme for a bit longer, and she told me to stop whining and focus on being the best friend I could be. So I told her I loved her.'

'You don't ever need to compete,' said Lucy. 'Honestly, Jonno. You've already won the biggest jackpot there is.'

'So, you'll know this song,' said Nate. 'I hope you'll sing along. And because I'm absolutely not worthy of singing Adele, I've got some help from my friend Andrea.' The crowd cheered politely as Andrea emerged from the wings with her guitar, waving nervously.

'Oh my God,' said Lucy, realising what was about to happen.

'Who the hell is that?' asked Jonno.

'It's Andrea. She's a singer who was in the bar in Switzerland with us.' She looked around for Willem, who was on the other side of Sasha with Alex. 'Where's Felix?'

'Who's Felix?' asked Jonno.

'He's down in the crowd,' said Alex happily. 'He

wanted to be somewhere where he could tell everyone that Andrea was his wife.'

'He's got over her not singing the Bee Gees, then?' laughed Lucy.

Alex shook his head. 'He begged Nate to sing "How Deep Is Your Love" instead, but he wasn't having any of it.'

'Nate should have invited Gunther, Monica and Chantal too,' said Lucy as Jonno looked even more confused.

'He did,' said Willem, clapping furiously as the music started. 'But it's peak summer hiking season in Zermatt. He's doing a show in Zurich in a few weeks, they're coming to that.'

Lucy had a second to wonder what Adele song they were going to sing, before she realised that this was another song for her. Andrea and Nate performed 'When We Were Young' as a haunting duet, with stunning harmonies that told Lucy how hard they'd rehearsed. Tears flowed freely down her cheeks – for Leo, for the years not lived, for everyone in this room who was as helplessly in love with Nate as she was, and for a future she couldn't even imagine right now, but couldn't wait to begin.

'Here,' said Jonno, handing her a tissue.

'Thanks,' said Lucy, dabbing her blotchy face. The five of them stood in a row – Jonno, Lucy, Sasha, Willem and Alex – entirely absorbed in Nate's show until the encore was over and the lights in the hall finally came up.

'That was amazing,' said Lucy, blowing her nose. 'Best night of my life.'

'Yeah,' said Jonno. 'That was pretty special.' In the stark lights of the hall she could see how shattered he looked, and felt a wave of guilt for how much she'd asked of him this evening.

'Come on,' she said. 'Let's get home.'

'Don't you want to wait for Nate?' asked Jonno.

'No,' said Lucy. 'I look like a crying bag of shit, and I can talk to him tomorrow.' She gave Willem and Alex a hug, and took a minute to say her hellos and congratulations to Andrea and Felix as they appeared up the stairs. Alex had told her that Andrea was going to be singing with Nate on his European tour, so maybe she'd see them again soon. Maybe.

'Sasha, I need to go,' said Lucy, as she reappeared from the bathroom. 'Will you give Nate a message for me?'

'Sure,' said Sasha.

'Tell him I had to go back to Bristol, but I'll be waiting for his call tomorrow.'

Sasha smiled and pulled out her phone. 'Why don't I give you his new number, so you can tell him yourself?'

'No, I trust you,' said Lucy. 'And he knows where to find me.'

'Yes, he does.'

'Thank you,' said Lucy, giving her a hug.

'Safe travels, Lucy,' said Sasha, which made her think of her final conversation with Kristoff, and what a turning point that was. 'We'll miss you at LUNA.'

'Well, I'm sure you'll see me around.'

'I'm sure I will,' said Sasha. 'Take care of her, Jonno.'

'Always,' said Jonno, taking Lucy's hand and leading her back down the stairs.

CHAPTER THIRTY-THREE

'Well, that was quite a night,' said Jonno, relaxing for the first time in an hour as they pulled off the slip road onto the M4 in Hammersmith. The exit from the breathtakingly expensive underground car park near the concert venue had taken forever, followed by a slow crawl through west London to the motorway. It was now nearly midnight, and Lucy was already planning to suggest a quick stop at Heston services to get Jonno jacked up on coffee.

'Yeah,' said Lucy, squirming in her seat at the memory of the ten minutes she'd spent making out on the sofa in Nate's dressing room. Her face actually hurt from grinning.

'I really hadn't expected your stupid idea to go to plan in quite such style.'

'You and me both. We actually excelled ourselves.'

'Hey, don't give me any credit,' laughed Jonno, wafting her away. 'I just held one end of your stupid banner.'

'It was a very important job,' said Lucy.

'I feel bad that you have to leave. Felt like it was turning into quite the reunion party.'

'It doesn't matter,' shrugged Lucy. 'You've done enough for one day, and I'm going to talk to Nate tomorrow.'

'So, where did you leave things? What's the next chapter of the Nate and Lucy love story?'

'I don't know,' said Lucy. 'I mean, I'm pretty sure it's going to be OK, but I'm not sure exactly how the story goes yet.'

'Is Nate Lambert about to enhance his superstar swoon narrative by falling in love with the beautiful woman who shared the avalanche adventure where it all began?' said Jonno, in his movie-trailer-guy voice.

Lucy laughed. 'When you put it like that, it's a pretty good story.'

'I mean, him ending up banging Taylor Swift would also have been a pretty good story. But I like your version better.'

'Yeah, me too.' She paused, trying to process everything that had happened in the past few hours. 'I think I'm going to be away a lot, over the next few months.'

Jonno nodded. 'I assumed as much.'

'But I'm going to try for the job in London, rather than New York. I'm not ready to be that far away. From Nate, or my family. Or you, for that matter.'

'Well, I'm delighted to be third on that list.'

Lucy punched him playfully on the arm. 'I just want you to know that, whatever happens, you will always be my best friend.'

'Honestly, Lucy, you really don't need to do this.'

'Yes, I do,' said Lucy, putting her hand on his arm. 'I've been thinking about what you said on the drive up, and I've never thanked you for saving me over the past eleven years. I lost my brother, and found a friend. You've never let me down.'

'It has been my pleasure,' he said, glancing at her with a watery smile. 'Genuinely.'

'But that doesn't change, if I move away or go travelling or whatever. Friends for life.'

'Stop it,' croaked Jonno. 'You're making me cry.'

'Yeah,' said Lucy, swiftly wiping the tears away with the back of her hand before the floodgates opened again. 'Me too.'

'You deserve this,' said Jonno firmly, placing his hand over hers. 'You deserve to be with someone who worships you the way I worship Marcia. You deserve to be happy and excited about the future.'

'I know,' said Lucy. 'It took me ages to realise it, but I know that now.'

'You want to crash in our spare room?' he asked, as Lucy yawned. 'Marcia won't mind.'

'No, drop me home,' said Lucy. 'I need a shower, a glass of wine and some quality masturbation. In that order.'

'You and me both, babe,' muttered Jonno.

'Well, as long as we're not thinking about the same thing, that's absolutely fine.'

'Go to sleep,' said Jonno softly, reaching over to pat her on the arm. 'I'll wake you up when we're back in Bristol.'

'You sure?' asked Lucy. 'You don't need me to keep you awake?'

'Nope,' said Jonno. 'I had two Red Bulls from that free bar, I'm absolutely caffeined off my tits.'

Lucy smiled and cranked her seat back, pulling Jonno's jacket over her to shield her from his icy air conditioning, which he'd set to 'hypothermic' to help him stay alert. She let her face relax as the highlights from today drifted through her mind like scenes from a silent movie. In the end it was just Nate singing, and smiling at her, and the heady feeling of being surrounded by friends who wished them nothing but happiness.

'Lucy, wake up,' said Jonno, pulling her out of a sleepy fug.

'Mmm?' she said blearily.

'We're home.'

'Shit, really?'

'Sort your face out, you've got a visitor.'

'Who?' said Lucy, cranking her seat back up.

'Take a look.'

She sat up and peered out of the window into the murky darkness of the street. It took her a moment to process that it was gone 2 a.m. on a Saturday in July and Nate was waiting on the steps to her flat.

'Oh God,' she gasped, her heart pounding. 'Can you buy me some time? And have you got any mints?'

'In the glove box,' said Jonno, driving slowly to the end of the road as Lucy hunted amongst the family detritus for a packet of Polos. She crunched down two and raked her fingers through her hair as Jonno performed a laborious three-point turn in the parking area.

'Lip balm,' said Lucy, rummaging in her pocket and unearthing a tube of Burt's Bees caked in lint. She wiped it off on her coat and hastily applied it. 'Will I do?'

'You look glorious, as ever,' said Jonno, as they pulled up next to Nate. 'Seems like you might get the live action version of your wank fantasy, after all.'

Lucy leaned in to hug him. 'Thank you for everything tonight, J. And for the lift. You're the best.'

'Yeah, I know,' he said. 'Just remember me when you're

a superstar WAG. Tell French Exit I want a family ticket to the BRITs.'

'I will move heaven and earth to make that happen, just to show how much I appreciate you.'

'Oh, let's not pretend any of this is about me. Bugger off and message me tomorrow.'

'I will,' she said, giving him a final squeeze. 'Love you.' She reluctantly let go, relishing how safe he made her feel. Everything outside this car was entirely unknown, and for a moment she was scared to leave.

'He's waiting,' said Jonno gently. 'Your whole future is waiting. Go and get it.'

'Yeah,' said Lucy taking a deep breath. She grabbed her bag and climbed out of the car, hoping Nate didn't notice how nervous she was.

'Hey,' said Nate, standing up to greet her. The air was warm and still, a sultry July night in the city. Rain was forecast for tomorrow, but Lucy wouldn't have cared if her flat had been washed away in her absence. She only had eyes for Nate.

'Hello,' she replied. 'How did you get here so quickly?'

'I've got a faster car than you,' said Nate with a shrug. 'With a driver who was waiting outside the venue.'

'Get you, Mr Bigshot Celebrity,' said Lucy playfully. 'What are you doing here?'

'Sasha told me you'd left the party.'

'Yeah, I'm sorry,' said Lucy. 'I really needed to let Jonno get back. Unlike me, he has family commitments.'

'It's fine,' said Nate softly. 'I understand.'

Lucy raised her eyebrows, waiting for him to say what he'd come here to say.

'I just couldn't wait until tomorrow. It felt too long.'

God, he's adorable, thought Lucy. 'Really?'

'And also I lost you for a long time, and I didn't want to risk losing you again. Is that cheesy?'

'Yes,' laughed Lucy. 'It's a giant fondue of a chat-up line, but I'll allow it.'

'Thank God for that,' said Nate. 'Can I come in? I don't actually have a flat in Bristol any more.'

'What would you have done if I wasn't here? Jonno offered me a sofa at his.'

'I've got his address from Sasha too.' He tapped his forehead with his finger. 'Covering all bases, see.'

'I need a shower,' said Lucy, very conscious that she'd been wearing the same clothes for eighteen hours and her face was tight and blotchy from all the crying earlier. 'And I've got no food in.'

'I also need a shower,' said Nate. 'And I'm not hungry.'

'Fine, then we'll both have a shower and not eat.'

'Is it three-minute-showers only?' asked Nate, giving her a challenging look. 'Or can we stay in there a bit longer?'

The intent behind 'we' made her shiver, and she fought the urge to drag him upstairs immediately and rip his clothes off. But there was no hurry, and there was a part of her that wanted to draw out the romance of this moment for as long as possible.

She dropped her bag on the step and sat down, waiting for him to join her. Their thighs were close enough to touch, and as he put his arm around her shoulders and she let her head fall on his shoulder, it felt like they were back in Zermatt. The feel and smell of him, the anticipation of his naked body against hers. They'd be having that moment again soon, but in the decadence of her bed rather than two deflating airbeds. Nate would be the first person who'd slipped between her luxury sheets since Kristoff, and hopefully the last. She shivered, then turned and held his piercing gaze for a moment.

'I can't give you a definite answer yet about coming on tour,' she whispered, the words feeling thick in her mouth. 'I'm pretty sure it's a yes, but everything is happening a bit fast.'

Nate smiled and took her hand, his long fingers weaving between hers. 'Things have snowballed again, sorry. I know it's a big decision to make when we've literally spent three days together in total.'

'But I'm definitely up for us spending more time together,' said Lucy, watching his thumb press the back of her hand and feeling a pool of warmth flooding the pit of her stomach.

'I've revised my plan,' said Nate, brushing the hair from her shoulder so he could lean in and gently kiss her neck. 'I've decided it might be better to spend the next couple of weeks persuading you to fall in love with me, THEN ask you to come on tour.'

Lucy gasped and closed her eyes as his grip tightened and his lips carved a trail to her shoulder. 'Nate,' she whispered helplessly. 'I've been in love with you since you sang Ed Sheeran to an audience of eight drunk people.'

'I always assumed it was when I hit you in the head with a snowball,' he whispered, gently moving her shirt to one side so he could kiss her collarbone.

'No, it was Ed,' said Lucy, the words catching in her throat. 'But the snowball definitely sealed the deal.'

'I wrote a song about that,' said Nate, his hand now stroking her back in a way that made her want to sit astride him and ravage him right there on the hard, cold steps.

'I know,' breathed Lucy. 'You just sang it to me in front of a thousand people. There's video evidence and everything.'

Nate kissed her gently on her lips, one hand buried in her hair as the other continued to make featherlight trails around her waist in a way that made her arch her body towards his. 'Kind of cute though, right?'

'Mortifying. Please don't do it again. When do you have to be back at work?'

He pulled away and clasped her hands in his. 'I'm supposed to be in the studio tomorrow, but Alex has just given me three days off. Turns out that as well as being a hard-nosed taskmaster, he's also a hopeless romantic.'

'Well, I have no plans at all.' *Until January*, thought Lucy, feeling breathless with excitement at the prospect of what lay ahead.

'Can we hang out for a few days? Like we did in Zermatt?'

Lucy laughed. 'Will I need to be rescued at the end of it?'

'No. I was kind of hoping we might rescue each other.' Nate leaned in to kiss her again, deeper this time. He tasted vaguely of mint, and Lucy wondered if he'd done some strategic teeth-cleaning in the car on the way down.

She stood up and held out her hand, waiting for him

to stand up too so she could slide her hands around his waist and press herself into his body. 'You want to stay here?' she asked, glancing at the sports bag on the step. 'Until you have to go back to work?'

'If that's OK.'

Lucy nodded and kissed him again, wishing she could freeze this moment for as long as it took to remember every detail. It felt like the whole night was laid out in front of them, full of promise and opportunity. And then tomorrow, and the day after that, and then the weeks and months ahead where they would each build their own careers, but also a life together.

'The only place I want to be right now is wherever you are,' he said, pressing his forehead against hers.

Lucy sighed and closed her eyes for a second. Being this in love, and being loved in return, was like being warmed by the sun from both sides. And Nate was here, on her doorstep at two in the morning, because he knew, and because he felt it too.

She fished her keys from her pocket and led him towards the door, feeling like she'd been given back a piece of her soul that she'd never realised was missing. *The more you make me whole*, thought Lucy, as the butterflies in her stomach danced to a song that hadn't even been written yet.

Acknowledgements

The idea for this book came in late November 2021, when two things happened in the same week. Firstly, my boss announced that if we hit our targets for the following year, we'd all go on a company ski trip. We never hit the target or went on the trip, but thank you Bamf for the inspiration anyway. The characters in this story are entirely fictional, but feel free to assume you are Kristoff if that means you actually read beyond chapter two. There is no sex in this one until . . . oh, chapter two. Oops.

Secondly, there was a story in the news about a bunch of people who got stranded in a pub in the Yorkshire Dales with an Oasis tribute band. So somehow my brain smushed these things together, threw in a lyric from a song by The Saturdays (if you know, you know), and *Snowed In With You* was born. I hope you enjoyed reading it as much as I loved writing it.

This was also an opportunity to pay tribute to my brother Jon, who I'd like to thank for always being there for me, even though we don't see as much of each other as I'd like. Your pride in my writing career means a lot.

Thanks also to my incredible publishing team – particularly my editor Bea Grabowska, who has been by my side for all six books and knows my stories inside and out. I'm also grateful for my support crew at Headline Accent who once again have made this process a joy.

To my agent for these six books, Caroline Sheldon, I say thank you for everything – I couldn't have done this without you and you have earned the longest and happiest of retirements. I'm excited about embarking on a new adventure with Safae El-Ouahabi at RCW, and can't wait to see what the future holds.

To my family, thanks for reading and turning out in droves for everything I do. I've now dedicated a book to each and every one of you, so may go rogue from now on. To the booksellers, bloggers and fans who continue to champion my writing, it is appreciated more than I can say without getting gushy and emotional. But you know who you are.

And finally, thanks to Pip for your unending love and support. Here's to a lifetime of snow days.

**Discover more utterly irresistible
novels from Heidi Stephens . . .**

HEIDI STEPHENS

Two sisters. One crumbling house. Where will they be

SAME TIME NEXT YEAR

Sisters Bel and Marie are poles apart. Whilst Marie is a free spirit who spurns alcohol, casual sex and material possessions, Bel needs all of those things just to make it through to lunchtime.

When their mother dies suddenly, leaving them a rundown house on the Norfolk coast, they are unexpectedly thrown together. Because there's a condition: before they can inherit it, they have to live in it for one year – together.

Marie invites some old friends to Orchard House to form a working party, and Bel is drawn to the devastatingly handsome, yet silent and brooding, Nick. The only problem is, they want entirely different things . . .

If Bel can make it through the year unscathed, she'll consider it a success. But that means dealing with everything she's been sweeping under the rug for decades. Could it be time to leave the past behind and embrace the future? And in doing so, will the sisters finally find their way back to each other?

Available to order

H

ACCENT

HEIDI STEPHENS

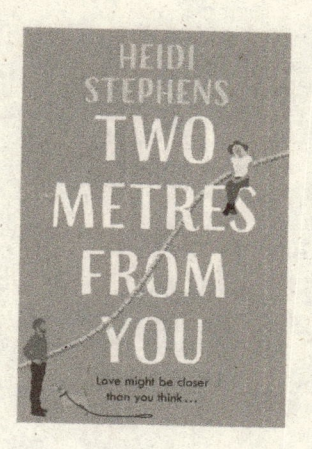

TWO METRES FROM YOU

Love might be closer than you think...

Gemma isn't sure what upsets her more.
The fact she just caught her boyfriend cheating,
or that he did it on her *brand-new* Heal's cushions.

All she knows is she needs to put as many miles between
her and Fraser as humanly possible. So, when her
best friend suggests a restorative few days in the
West Country, it seems like the perfect solution.

That is, until the country enters a national lockdown
that leaves her stranded. All she has for company is her dog,
Mabel. And the mysterious (and handsome!)
stranger living at the bottom of her garden . . .

Available to order

ACCENT

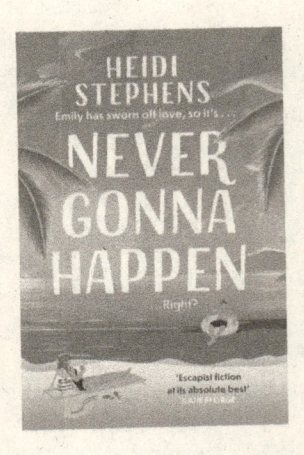

Emily Wilkinson has lost everything. Literally. In a hair-straightener fire. Oh, and her boyfriend (and boss) has announced he's going back to his wife. So, she needs a new job, a new plan, and somewhere to live that isn't her childhood bedroom.

Charles Hunter is looking for a live-in PA to help run Bowford Manor and Emily thinks she's the perfect fit. Well, she's spent ten years propping up demanding men, so she can definitely handle some tricky characters – like Charles's eldest son and heir, who's got plans for the estate that might raise a few eyebrows.

No one's mentioned Jamie though. The stable hand – and youngest Hunter. Dashing, of course, but totally unsuitable. And Emily's not about to make that mistake again.

Definitely not. No, really.

Available to order

H
ACCENT

THE ONLY WAY IS UP

HEIDI STEPHENS

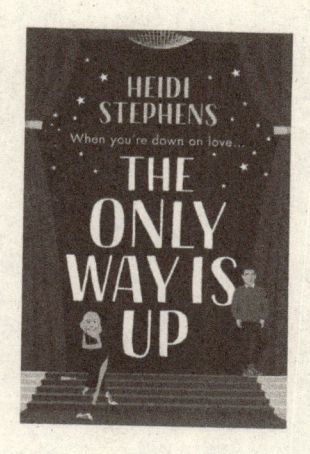

When you're down on love...

Twenty-five years in showbiz is a good run, right? Because after tonight, when her small (read: huge) wardrobe malfunction was broadcast to the nation's living rooms, Daisy's time in the spotlight might be over.

It's all about damage control now, and Daisy needs an escape route. Fast. Especially when her sporting hero boyfriend publicly announces their engagement – the one she hasn't actually agreed to tell the world about.

All she needs is space from prying eyes and time for the press to get bored and move on. But the only place she can run to at such short notice is the Cotswolds cottage she used to own with her ex-husband. Not ideal, but at least it's in the middle of nowhere and close to her teenage daughter.

Seems like a perfect plan, apart from the person selling stories to the tabloids about her and Tom, the local headmaster.

But that's just a rumour, right?

Available to order

H
ACCENT

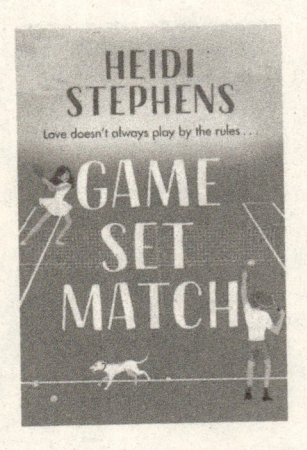

HEIDI STEPHENS

Love doesn't always play by the rules...

GAME SET MATCH

Hannah has been married to Graham since they were eighteen – a union of desperation to escape their strict families. He's the only man she's ever kissed and honestly, she's not sure he's any good at it. But fourteen years of washing his underwear is more than enough to kill the romance.

Well, that and the fact that he's got a work colleague pregnant.

Hannah's new-found freedom is an opportunity to finally put herself first, and a trip to Spain sounds like the perfect start. Yes, it might be with three near strangers, but it's also a chance to play tennis every day under the Spanish sun, before heading off on a solo road trip and starting the next phase of her life.

Then Hannah meets Rob, who has kissed ALL the women and is 100% not her type. And besides, she's *really* not looking for love right now. But if there's one thing Hannah knows about tennis, it's that sometimes taking a risk can pay off – and when you fault on your first serve, you get a second chance.

Available to order

H
ACCENT

HEIDI STEPHENS

Discover more
 @heidistephens
 @heidistephens
www.heidistephens.co.uk